Broken Places

Broken Places

Wendy Perriam

ROBERT HALE · LONDON

© Wendy Perriam 2010
First published in Great Britain 2010

ISBN 978-0-7090-9098-4

Robert Hale Limited
Clerkenwell House
Clerkenwell Green
London EC1R 0HT

www.halebooks.com

2 4 6 8 10 9 7 5 3

Typeset in 10/14.25pt Sabon
Printed in Great Britain by the MPG Books Group,
Bodmin and King,s Lynn

For Debra Baldwin

In celebration of her brilliant mind,
her brave heart
and her buoyant spirit

'The world breaks everyone and afterward many are strong at the broken places.'

A Farewell To Arms
Ernest Hemingway

For Librarians

Librarians know where wisdom's stored.
They catalogue the countless forms
of silence and tell people what they
didn't know they wanted to know.
They treat the mentally fractured
as if they're whole, the dull as if they're
sharp, Winter as if it's Summer.

At a table in a library, a circle of light
lies on a book. The hand not writing turns
the page, and something important happens.

Hans Ostrom

chapter one

Eric chained his bike to the railings and struggled out of his waterproofs, indignant that the weather should have let him down so flagrantly on this all-important date. Having stuffed the soggy rainwear into his saddle-bag, he dived into McDonald's – the only visible refuge from the downpour. Skulking past the counter, with its enticing smell of grilling meat, he headed for the gents, yet a brief glance in the mirror was enough to make him want to bolt for home. The wind had tousled his hair into the untidiest of birds' nests, flushed his face an unattractive pink and, to cap it all, sneaky drops of water were trickling down his neck.

Switching on the hand-drier, he moved his head into the current of hot air, before beginning the usual tussle with the comb. His curly crop was obstinate; preferred to go its own wild way, rather than submit to any form of restraint. Red hair on men was very rarely flattering and his particular shade was, to say the least, unfortunate. But, short of shaving it off or investing in a hair-transplant, he was stuck with it until senescence, when, he hoped, it would fade to merciful grey. For the moment, though, if he wished to impress Olivia, he would have to rely on conversational skills. Fat chance! He was so nervous about meeting her, he would be lucky to string two words together.

He checked his watch. Still only 7.15. He was always early, for everything, but to turn up late required a degree of casual confidence he simply didn't possess. If only confidence was sold in shops, he could buy a pound or two, along with milk and bread. Although a pound would hardly suffice tonight. He'd need a ton and more.

But he must concentrate on his good points, not give way to negativity. At least he *had* hair, unlike the naked-pated fellow who'd just barged into the gents. And at least he was slim and fit – no sign of any beer-gut yet, to rival the baldie's paunch.

Heartened, he completed his wash-and-brush up; crunched three extra-strong peppermints, to ensure his breath was triple-fresh, then decided to brave the elements once more. He did his best to shelter under shop-fronts as he zigzagged the fifty yards to *Chez Guillaume*, having deliberately left his bike a safe distance from its vicinity, in case Olivia expected him to roar up in a Porsche. Bikes weren't cool, especially not his third-hand Raleigh Shopper. But, early or no, he would wait for her in the restaurant, otherwise he would make a bad impression, with damp splodges on his suit. In any case, she might appreciate punctuality – and even the fact he'd worn a suit at all.

Thank God he *was* dressed up, he thought, as he came face-to-face with a liveried doorman, complete with a top hat – a figure as daunting as the place itself, which, rigged out in stylish green and grey, was flanked by two pretentious bay trees in important-looking tubs. Olivia had suggested the restaurant, as conveniently close to her Chelsea flat, as well as being recommended as a gourmet's paradise. Any gourmet's paradise was probably way beyond his means, but then a search for love was bound to involve some degree of financial sacrifice.

Racheting up his courage, he nodded to the doorman, who ushered him in with a sycophantic smile. His experience of doormen was sketchy in the extreme, so he had no idea whether to tip the guy or not. Fumbling in his pocket, he withdrew a cache of coins, only to realize they were mostly paltry 2ps. He quickly put them back again, trying to assume the air of someone so superior he never bothered with small change.

As he ventured in with an air of false bravado, the maître d' approached, greeting him with such deference, he might have been Montgomery returning from El Alamein. He was escorted to his table with further bowing and scraping; his chair pulled out; the wine-list proffered – the latter bound in gold-tooled leather, not unlike a Bible. The table, he noticed to his chagrin, was opposite an elaborate gilt-framed mirror. The last thing he wanted was to study his reflection again.

'May I get you a drink, sir?' A waiter had swooped over and was also dancing attendance on him; kowtowing and salaaming in a manner that mixed swagger with servility.

'I, er, think I'll wait for my friend.'

'Friend' wasn't strictly correct. As yet, he hadn't set eyes on Olivia; seen nothing but a small photo of her face. And all he knew about her was the details on her profile in the *Guardian* Soulmates site (some of which she had deliberately left blank). The few texts they'd exchanged said nothing really meaningful and when, at last, he'd plucked up the courage to phone, he'd been so relieved to hear her voice – not estuary or shrill or pleb, but well-modulated and feminine – he had barely taken in a single word she said.

'As you wish, sir.'

The waiter was dark and dashing, with an enviable thatch of straight, black, glossy hair. The lucky guy probably had women flocking round him in shoals and swarms and squads, and certainly wouldn't be reduced to searching for females on the Internet. Even his eyebrows were emphatically dark and authoritative. Should he have dyed his own wishy-washy brows before embarking on a new love-life, he wondered anxiously – although why stop at eyebrow-dye, when a full-scale makeover might be more to the point?

A quick glance at the wine-list made him fear that this one dinner would swallow up a whole week's salary. But it was worth it, wasn't it? For an attractive woman, nine years younger, who, according to her profile, was 'keenly interested in art and literature'? Even her name was a bonus – an elegant, Shakespearian name, which made his own 'Eric' seem definitely plebeian.

There was bound to be a catch, though. The photo showed her neck-up only, so she might be hugely fat, or missing some vital body-part, like an arm or leg or kidney. Or she could be a dating addict – the sort of woman who went through twenty men a month, just for the thrill of the chase, rejecting every one of them for some trifling reason like eye-colour.

Despite himself, he checked the mirror opposite. Blue eyes should be deep, dramatic and definite; not, like his, the colour of over-washed and faded denim jeans. Indeed, he could barely make them out at all in the stylish gloom of the restaurant, just the pale blur of his face, topped by his insolent hair.

He tried to distract himself by studying the other diners; most of them well-heeled, judging by their outfits and general air of sophistication. Would Olivia take one look at him and immediately make an excuse to leave? Well, he'd find out soon enough, since she was due in precisely eleven minutes.

No eleven minutes had ever seemed so long – except the *following* eleven, which appeared to take an hour to dawdle by. He mustn't panic, though. She had mentioned in passing that her journey from work was complicated and, what with traffic snarl-ups and closures on the tube, delays were more or less inevitable. Indeed, he himself had only chosen to cycle because his own tube-line was suspended.

He kept his gaze fixed on the door, checking every new arrival. As yet, he had seen no solo females, but, at this very moment, one was actually venturing in. Could that be Olivia? She was nothing like her picture: older and more lined, with a mousy bob, instead of honey-coloured tresses. But she might have airbrushed her photo; eradicated the wrinkles, lightened and lengthened her hair. Deception was rife on dating sites.

He studied her every movement, coiled like a spring in case she approached, but, having proceeded to the far end of the restaurant, she joined a slender, fair-haired chap, who sprang up to embrace her. Now, he was the only person sitting on his own; couples all around him; the pair at the adjoining table parading their togetherness by clasping hands, inter-locking fingers and gazing raptly into each other's eyes. He was also the only one with neither food nor drink – everybody else tucking in, with relish, and downing fancy wine. The buzz of conversation underlined his own tense circle of silence; the whiff of garlic butter and sizzling steak reminding him how empty he was. He'd been too uptight to eat much lunch, and breakfast had been one quick slice of toast.

Suppose she *didn't* come? Red-haired men with freckles weren't exactly sexy, nor, for that matter, were librarians. She had probably met a hunky City banker and was already in bed with the lout; all thought of dinner forgotten as they climaxed in mutual bliss. But if she had stood him up, what then? Did he brazen it out and eat here on his own, risking bank-ruptcy for no reason or reward, or sneak out of the restaurant to the sniggers of the staff?

He was overreacting – as usual. It was still only 8.04. Nineteen minutes late didn't mean she had called it off. He must stop studying his watch and switch his mind to something more absorbing – for instance, his idea of using the music library for some sort of music therapy, as an extension of his existing poetry group. Trevor might dismiss it, of course, as a waste of time and resources, or issue gloomy warnings about the risk of anti-social behaviour from some of those attending, or claim it inter-fered with the core business of the service to provide books and information. Well, he'd simply have to stand his ground and stress his scheme's advantages; emphasize its social value and the partnerships that might be formed with other community groups, bound to win approval from the council.

Soon, he had developed a creditable case. Indeed, Trevor had not only acquiesced, he was actually supportive and they were working on the project together, in (unusual) harmony. Unfortunately, however, there was still no sign of Olivia, nor any text or message on his mobile, which he'd been checking since he first arrived. Since she was more than half an hour late now, surely she should have got in touch – unless she'd been mugged at knifepoint, or blown up by a terrorist.

Images of bloody, mangled flesh tornadoed through his stomach. He needed a drink – a strong one. The waiter had glided back a couple of times, to see if he had changed his mind, but he'd repeated the same mantra about waiting for his friend. No point, however, in waiting for a woman who was a body on a mortuary slab.

'A vodka and Coke, please,' he blurted out, as the fellow approached for the third time. What the hell was he saying? Vodka and Coke was *Stella's* tipple – he had never actually drunk it in his life. But Stella was on his mind, of course, since she it was who'd encouraged him to sign up for several dating-sites.

'D'you realize, Eric, it's ages since your divorce, and you haven't so much as looked at another woman. It's time you fixed yourself up with someone else.'

Fixed himself up. The phrase offended his romantic sense, but then the whole dating scene was a meat market. He should have put his foot down, right from the (unpromising) start. Only two of the women he'd emailed had bothered to respond. The first, still married, had spent an hour on the phone to him, slagging off her spouse. The second was seeking a companion to join her on a white-water-rafting excursion in deepest Ecuador. White-water-rafting, for heaven's sake, when he couldn't even swim.

All at once, his stomach rumbled – so loudly, so flamboyantly, the whole restaurant must have heard. Thank heavens for the waiter, who was just sauntering up with his drink. He gulped it quickly, in gratitude, although drinking spirits on an empty stomach was bound to end in disaster. He would probably start gabbling inanely, or even lose his balance and trip over his own feet when he rose to greet Olivia. Except she wasn't coming, was she? Thirty-six minutes late now.

His age might be the problem. Stella had pressed him to say he was thirty-nine, instead of forty-four.

'Even thirty-nine is *old*, Eric, when it comes to women's preferences. Many fifty-something females still prefer a man of twenty-two or -three. I suppose it's a question of testosterone. Once a guy hits thirty, it's downhill all the way.'

Despite her views (outrageous), he had stuck to the depressing truth; refusing to lie on principle. Figures were on his mind tonight. Not just his age, but the four-and-a-half and five-and-a-half inches respectively of his limp penis and his stiff one. Measuring both or either had never crossed his mind before, until Stella put him right.

'You have to remember, Eric, all some women care about is ILBs.'

'"Interesting Librarian Blokes", you mean?'

'No, you dolt. "Incredibly Large Bits".'

Not much point in fretting about his bits when he'd be lucky to swallow a mouthful of dinner before the restaurant closed, let alone embark on an erotic encounter. Besides, where on earth could they *go* for the encounter? Bike-sheds were for teens – and not exactly common in Chelsea – yet he could hardly take her to his shabby basement flat. In his fantasies last night, the problem had solved itself, since she had invited him back to her riverside penthouse and, before they were barely inside, had changed into a skimpy négligé. Having whipped it off in a trice, he'd plunged with her on to the king-size bed, where they had remained the entire weekend, only emerging on Monday morning, exhausted but blissed-out; all thought of work or—

Oh my God, she'd come! Yes, she was really, truly here – just bursting through the door; every bit as gorgeous as her photo: not overweight, not missing arms or legs, not even lined or mousy, but radiant, fresh-faced and as near to blonde as dammit.

He leapt to his feet and swooped exuberantly towards her, barely able to believe his luck.

She, too, was smiling; displaying not a hint of disappointment. 'Eric, I know it's you – it *must* be! You simply couldn't hide that fabulous auburn hair!'

He all but kissed her feet, just for the joy of the word 'auburn'. Already, his four-and-a-half inches were stirring into majestic masthood.

'Sorry I'm so late. This fearful crisis blew up at work and I just couldn't get away. And, to top it all, my mobile's on the blink. You must have thought I wasn't coming.'

'Not at all,' he lied. 'It's wonderful to see you.' He couldn't tear his eyes away from the girlish waist, voluptuous breasts, long, curvy legs, displayed now to perfection as a waiter took her coat. 'But are you all right?' he asked with genuine concern. 'I mean, you must have got soaked to the skin. I've never known a November like this – rain every day, so far. Although I have to say you don't look very wet.'

'No, I took a taxi in the end – couldn't face sloshing through the puddles.'

If she could afford a taxi all the way from her office, they weren't exactly evenly matched when it came to basic income. Never mind. When searching for a soulmate, higher things than money were involved.

A second waiter came bustling up and proffered her the wine list. 'A drink for you, madam?'

Eric watched the fellow jealously. This exquisite woman's lips were made for kissing, but kissing *him*, not some natty Frenchman with fatal Gallic charm.

'Oh, brilliant!' she exclaimed, as her eyes flicked down the page. 'They do Billecart-Salmon Rosé by the glass, and it's my absolute top favourite.'

Eric had never heard of it, although a quick glance at the wine list revealed it to be a vintage champagne – at £20 a glass.

'I hope you'll join me,' she enthused. 'It really is quite fabulous.'

'Y ... yes, of course.' He tried to sound less grudging: £40 for just two pre-dinner drinks was exorbitant by any standards, but this dazzling creature's company surely justified all manner of expense.

The waiter returned with two stylishly slender champagne flutes, orgasming with bubbles and preening on a silver tray.

'To us!' she purred, clinking her glass to his.

'To us!' he echoed, elated by the fact that she had already turned them into an item – and after a mere five minutes. His mind leapt ahead to the future: marriage, babies, Silver Wedding....

She cocked her head to one side, swilling a little champagne round her mouth. 'It tastes like apples, don't you think? Sweet, ripe English apples, smothered in double cream.'

Nervously he nodded. Wine appreciation wasn't his strong point. Besides, he was still finishing his first drink, so he could taste only Coke, not apples. He quickly switched the glasses over, but the frisky bubbles tickled in his nose, resulting in a mortifying hiccough. 'Oh, I do beg your pardon!' he spluttered, cheeks flaming with embarrassment. He should have stuck to beer.

'You're not allergic, are you?' Olivia asked. 'Allergies are really common nowadays, so my GP says. You can even be allergic to yourself, would you believe?'

Yes, he *would* believe and, yes, he *was* allergic, although he quickly changed the subject, recalling Stella's advice not to mention boring things like health; to avoid all risky topics such as death, divorce or dentistry, and, above all, to be original.

'So what really makes you tick?' he asked, emboldened by his vodka-and-champagne cocktail, and desperate to distract her from the hiccough.

'Oh, books!' she gushed. 'No question. Which was why I was so enchanted to hear you were a librarian.'

Enchanted? Was he dreaming? For the average punter, librarians were irredeemably downbeat: menopausal females in cardigans and granny-specs; sad blokes, past their prime, with dandruff and no prospects.

'It must be so exhilarating,' she continued, fluttering her long, dark lashes in a disarmingly coquettish way, 'being surrounded by all that knowl-edge.'

His spirits soared still higher. She truly *was* a soulmate; not following the common view that books were dead and librarians were dinosaurs, but grasping the true appeal of scholarship, the open-sesame of learning. The only thing that worried him was the speed with which she was drinking; gulping down champagne as if she'd just run a marathon and was seriously dehydrated.

'Let's have another, shall we? It's such a brilliant vintage, it just floats across your mouth.'

Suddenly decisive, he opened the menu and set it down in front of her, in the hope of diverting her attention from the wine list. Apart from the cost, if he drank a third glass of anything without some food as ballast, he might lose his grip entirely and start babbling on about death, divorce and dentistry in one long, shaming spiel.

'Yes, do let's eat! Food's another passion of mine. In fact, I eat out almost every night.'

He refrained from comment. The last time *he* had eaten out had been the day his ancient cooker blew up, singeing off his eyebrows (which had grown back paler still). And it had been egg and chips at the local caff, not gourmet, five-star fare.

'Another two glasses of this, please.' She gestured to her glass, flashing a smile at the waiter. The wretched man was still hovering obsequiously, probably sizing up Olivia's breasts, which were, in truth, gratifyingly prominent.

'What do you suggest as a starter?' she asked, fixing her eyes on the menu – captivating dark-chocolate eyes. 'The ballotine of chicken sounds nice. Or how about the *Piedmont Bresaola, tête de moine?'*

He quickly scanned the starters for something he could pronounce – not to mention something cheaper. 'The soup for me,' he said, wishing it were homely oxtail, rather than coconut and lemongrass.

'But that's frightfully unadventurous! Why not have the game and *foie gras* terrine?'

Fatally weakened by her cleavage, he heard himself agreeing. Her top was so low-cut, he could all but see her nipples – in his mind was kissing them in an ecstasy of bliss.

'Actually, I think I'll have that too. *And* the ballotine of chicken.'

What the hell was Ballotine? 'The chicken as a main course, you mean?'

'Oh, no – as *well* as. I often have two starters. I have this weird metabolism, you see. However much I eat, I'm never full.'

He would have to pawn his bike at this rate, or even ring the bank and arrange an instant overdraft, but he kept his focus strictly on her breasts. He would gladly lose his bike – lose everything, in fact – for the chance to see them naked. 'And what to follow?'

She pursed her darling mouth. 'Well, I adore Beef Wellington, but it says they only do it for two. Would you fancy sharing it?'

At £45 the double portion, *no*! Best to pretend he was vegetarian, but the lie stuck in his throat. 'I'm not actually a great meat-eater.' That was true, at least. Since the divorce, his usual fare was beans on toast. 'I think I'll go for the' – his eye fell on a pasta dish, at a merciful £12.90 – 'the crab linguine.' Seafood brought him up in a rash, but so would a bill in three figures.

'In that case, I'll have the Beef Wellington all to myself. I'm ravenous tonight, so it'll suit me rather well. And I'll have the sautéed spinach to go with it, and the lemon-crushed Charlotte potatoes.'

Vegetables were extra, of course. Another reason he had opted for pasta, which could be eaten on its own. He wasn't mean – far from it. He would gladly buy a woman dinner – indeed, treat her every week, if things went well – but his wallet and this restaurant just didn't marry up. Even the basket of bread, just set down by the waiter, who had come to take their order, cost a flagrant £5.50. Admittedly, it was stone-ground, seed-encrusted and organic, but what was wrong with Sainsbury's 'basic'-range white – a mere 50p for a whole family-sized loaf?

Olivia grabbed the largest piece, spread it liberally with butter and began devouring it at frantic speed. 'Mm, yummy!' she enthused, spraying him with half-masticated morsels. 'I adore this bread, don't you?'

Since she hadn't thought to pass him any, he couldn't give his verdict. Bemused, he watched her seize a second chunk and down it at the same dizzy rate.

'So, tell me all about yourself,' she mumbled, between manic gobbles. 'Do you work at the British Library?'

'Er, no. I'm afraid I'm not quite in that league.' He gave a self-deprecating laugh. 'I'm in public libraries,' he explained, 'and my special interest is community engagement – you know, bringing in new readers amongst the socially excluded, particularly those with mental-health problems ...' The sentence petered out. Not only was he using jargon, but his line of work didn't sound exactly glamorous. Indeed, Olivia's expression was already one of mild distaste. Just as well he hadn't mentioned ex-prisoners or asylum-seekers as amongst those he burned to help.

'I've never met a librarian,' she commented, dismissively, still chewing hard and speaking with her mouth full. 'I prefer to buy my books. I mean, if you borrow them from some public source, you never know where they've *been*. You could pick up awful diseases – things like AIDS or—'

He dodged the shower of saliva-coated crumbs spraying from her mouth. She was now on piece number three, and clearly viewed the whole large basket as her own private property.

'Actually, I wouldn't be surprised if all libraries were made to close down – I mean, once the powers-that-be get wind of the real health risks. It's a bit like doctors not washing their hands in the early days of surgery. It took a while for society to grasp that patients were dying because of the surgeons' lack of hygiene, not on account of the operations. Oh, great – our starters! Which shall I eat first, Eric?'

Without waiting for an answer, she dug an eager fork into the terrine, swallowed a large mouthful, then repeated the exercise with the ballotine of chicken, which resembled a fat brown bolster floating on a lake of creamy sauce. He jumped as she cut into it, sauce spattering over the clean white-linen tablecloth, and leaving a yellow stain. She hardly seemed to notice, so intent was she on eating; alternating forkfuls of each starter, and washing them down with her second glass of champagne.

He was so astounded by her messy eating, all conversation died; the ensuing silence filled solely with the sound of rampant chomping. He thought back to the Soulmates site, which did include questions about one's eating and drinking habits. For drinking, she had answered 'rarely'; for eating, 'sparely but healthily'. 'Sparely' was an outright lie, and was it really healthy to eat so extraordinarily fast? At this very moment, she was emitting a succession of strangulated gasps, as her speed increased still further and a recalcitrant piece of chicken lodged itself in her gullet.

'Are you OK, Olivia?'

'Mm. Just starving! Eating actually makes me hungrier. My mother said I was like that even as a baby. My first word was "More!", apparently.'

As she talked – and chewed – he could see directly into her open mouth; had no choice but to watch the slimy brown gobbets slithering down her throat. She had mentioned her mother, but that mother had been seriously remiss in failing to teach her table-manners.

She paused, at last, although only for a second. 'Why aren't you eating, Eric?'

'I'm … just finishing my drink.' In fact, confronted by her greed, he was beginning to lose his appetite – even more so, as a gob of food-and-spittle landed on his face. He moved his chair back, in an attempt to dodge the firing line, but he was still stomach-churningly close.

'That reminds me, we ought to order our wine – red for my Beef Wellington, of course, but a Chardonnay right now. I'd like some with the rest of my chicken, and it'll go nicely with your linguine.'

Maybe *she* was paying, he thought, with a surge of relief. Surely no woman would take the initiative like this, then leave him to settle the bill. He couldn't count on it, however, and even if they agreed to go Dutch, it would still more or less clean him out. He didn't even want more wine – was in need of some plain tonic water to settle his queasy stomach.

Then, suddenly, she leaned towards him, mouth open, eyes ablaze, and for one dizzying moment, he assumed she was going to kiss him – an advanced French kiss, all darting, pulsing tongue. But all she did was help herself to his as yet untouched terrine. She had already devoured the whole of her own, yet now was cramming in a huge chunk of his.

'You don't mind, do you, Eric? I can see you're not a serious eater.'

Yes, he thought, with rising indignation – I *do* mind. He watched in revulsion as she continued to gobble his starter, only pausing to butter more bread and stuff that into her mouth, as well. Then, turning back to the ballotine, she sloshed another puddle of sauce on the cloth, in her feverish haste to scoop it up. Even her once-pristine top was now patterned with yellow splodges, and sauce had splashed the sleeve of his best suit. He could hardly bear to look at her as she bolted down her food – and his. A frond of parsley was stuck between her teeth; her mouth was moustachioed with grease, and her champagne glass all smeary from those unappetizing lips.

Literature and art? He all but hooted. Her sole concern was eating for Great Britain, so how could they discuss the things he longed to talk about: the role of fiction in fostering empathy and tolerance; his firm belief that illiteracy must be banished, root and branch; his passion for using books and libraries to help minority groups, underachievers, and indeed anyone in search of knowledge, or that satisfying sense of lives beyond one's own?

She had barely listened to a single word he'd said, nor had the simple courtesy even to offer him the bread or salt. Even her looks were fast losing their appeal. However blonde her hair or sensational her breasts, how could he be soulmate to someone who thought libraries were a source of plague and pestilence? The whole concept of a soulmate was desperately important to him – had been since his boyhood, when the notion, although impossible in fact, had still been a cherished dream and a future aspiration. Looks were less important than believing in some cause, sharing the same ideals, viewing the world through roughly the same eyes. But this woman *had* no ideals – only a serious eating disorder, combined with a drinking problem. Even if she offered to pay the whole exorbitant bill – even if she was a millionaire – she was still, at base, a slob and, frankly, his overwhelming instinct was to bolt out of the restaurant and keep running, running, running, until he'd put fifty miles between them.

In fact, he had come to a decision: he would rather spend his days alone – for ever, till he died – than settle for a female as gross and gluttonous as this.

chapter two

'Who the hell do you think you *are*, mate? I booked this sodding computer for ten o'clock and now you're saying it's not free.'

Eric deliberately adopted a calm and pleasant tone. The guy was leaning across the counter, one fist clenched aggressively. If he didn't defuse the situation, and defuse it pretty fast, that fist might well make contact with his face. 'I'm sorry, sir, but it's now ten-fifteen and we only hold the computers for ten minutes.'

'Listen, chum, I booked the bloody thing for half an hour, so it's mine by rights till half-past ten.'

'I'm sorry,' Eric repeated, in the same conciliatory manner. 'If you're late, we have to release the slot to someone else. It's library policy. But, look, why don't I make you another booking, for later on today?'

'Because I don't happen to have all fucking day to swan around doing damn-all. I told you – I want it now.'

'I'm afraid that isn't possible. In fact, the earliest slot I can give you, sir, is – let's see – half-past three.'

The fist veered towards his jaw. 999, he thought, glancing frantically around for Trevor, who at six-foot-two and built like a bull, might disarm the man at a stroke. But before he could call for help, the man – miraculously – backed off, pushing his way past the queue of people behind him with a torrent of abuse.

Eric realized he was sweating – and with reason. On two occasions he *had* been hit, once seriously enough to land him in A & E. Well, he thought, composing himself, at least he didn't work in Iraq. There, the National Library was subject to constant bomb-blasts, and staff-kidnappings were the order of the day. He suddenly saw himself cowering in a stinking cell, bound and gagged and blindfolded – and about to die of fear.

'I'm looking for this book....'

The next person in the queue was, he realized with relief, not a hulking prison-guard, come to march him to the torture-chamber, but an elderly woman too frail to hurt a flea.

'Yes?' he said, encouragingly. 'Could you give me the name of it?'

She shook her head. 'That's the trouble. I can't remember names.'

'Well, do you know who wrote it?'

'I think it began with a ...' Her voice tailed off and her eyes took on a glazed look.

He waited patiently. Who knew what she was suffering – loneliness, confusion, dementia, bereavement?

'It was red,' she said, in a sudden rush of words. 'A big red book, with a yellow bird on the cover.'

He ran through his mental repertoire. Although familiar with most of the stock, he couldn't recall such a volume. 'Was it fiction or non-fiction?'

It was obvious from her baffled frown that she didn't know the difference.

'Well,' he tried to explain, 'more of a story, with characters, or a book that told you how to identify birds?'

'A story – for my grandchildren.'

'Ah, I think you need the children's library. I'm just going up there myself.' However busy he might be, he had to have a word with Stella, to beg her help at lunchtime.

Once Harriet had relieved him at the desk, he took the stairs at a snail's pace, so the old lady could keep up with him, then left her in Kath's hands. Despite her youth, Kath was proving a real asset, although Harriet had complained, of course, about employing kids who should be still at playschool. But he, too, had started as a library assistant, at the age of just sixteen, so he felt a bond with Kath; still recalled the sense of being confused and overawed by all one had to learn.

The colourful shelves and frieze of children's drawings pinned in rows above them reminded him of being younger still; the pride he'd felt when his own pictures were displayed. The library had been his childhood refuge – in fact, almost a sort of prep school – and he'd continued to use it through his teens, not just as crammer and college, but as an escape from noise and bullying and the whole round of petty punishments. Without it, he'd be nothing now, or maybe – worse – a criminal or dope-head. Admittedly, reaching his favourite haven had often been a problem, since he'd had to rely on busy, non-bookish adults, with a thousand more important things to do. But, once there, he felt secure and – more important still – could be instantly transported to other, better worlds, simply by opening the pages of a book.

Stella's voice returned him to the present. She was just finishing her 'Rhyme-Time' session – clearly one with a marine theme, since she had set up a stretch of ocean (a blue tarpaulin), a beach (a yellow rug), and brought in various 'fishy' toys, including a green-plush crocodile, with a cavernous scarlet mouth.

'Now, our last song is "Row Your Boat". We learned that one last week, so shall we all join in?'

Eric found himself singing along with toddlers, mothers, nannies; even managing a creditable shriek when they reached the verse, 'If you see a crocodile, don't forget to scream.' The contrast with the church-like silence of libraries in the old regime never failed to strike him, in these days of exuberant sing-songs and boisterous events. He continued watching with a twinge of envy as the mothers prepared to take their children home; buttoning coats; retrieving hats and gloves; each mother or each nanny leaving hand-in-hand with a child. Incredible to have someone all to yourself, someone you didn't have to share, someone linked to you by blood-ties.

Once everyone had gone, Stella tidied away the rugs and books and toys. 'I'm off for my tea-break now, Eric. Any chance you can join me?'

'Well, only for five minutes. We're up to our eyes down there.'

Having left Kath to do some shelving, Stella followed him to the staffroom, where he remained standing by the door, too pressured to bother with tea.

'Stella, could you do me a favour?'

'Depends. If you want me to dress up in a rah-rah skirt and perform the cancan on top of the returns-desk, then—'

'No, nothing so exciting. I just wondered if you could heat the lunchtime soup.'

'I thought Helen usually did it?'

'She does, but she called in sick first thing. It won't take long, I promise. The stuff's all ready, right there on the worktop.'

'OK.' Stella flung a teabag into a mug. 'But I think I ought to warn you that Harriet's still pissed off about the whole idea of soup.'

'I know. But then she dislikes the group, full-stop. It just happens to be working, though, whatever she might think. The numbers are up every week, and hot soup helps to bring the punters in.'

'Yes, but she's worried that books will get nicked by what she calls "undesirables".'

He bristled in annoyance. 'What Harriet fails to understand is that there's only a thin line between so-called normal people and those who end up sectioned, or in prison, or on crack-cocaine or whatever. All it needs is enough bad luck, or some unhappy twist of fate. Just because she's been cushioned all her life, she—'

'We've no evidence for that, Eric. She never gives a thing away. And, actually, I suspect it's more a fear thing. People with mental-health problems probably make her feel vulnerable or threatened.'

'I'm sorry, that won't wash. It's her job to do away with stigma, not contribute to it.'

'She's not likely to change, at her age. Anyway, just bear in mind she's been complaining to Trevor – she told me so herself.'

'Well, she would do, wouldn't she? As the boss, he's bound to back her up.' Thank God, he thought, *he* was no longer a manager. He'd detested the whole headache of financial planning, cost-benefit analysis, performance indicators, health and safety issues, dictates from the council – all that endless stuff that kept him away from actual books and readers. And, as for sorting out spats between staff, it invariably left him both guilty and embarrassed. OK, he'd had to accept demotion *and* a cut in salary, but being free to do the work he wanted was well worth the disadvantages.

'The trouble with Harriet' – he lowered his voice to a whisper, although, in fact, they had the staffroom to themselves – 'is that she's so set in her ways, she opposes any innovation, on principle. Everything's been a threat to her – videos, DVDs, computers, Baby Rhyme-Time, whatever – and you can bet your bottom dollar she'll be agin the *next* thing, regardless of what it is. And, anyway, she's so close to retirement, I suspect she simply wants an easy life. She'd probably prefer it we didn't open the doors at all – kept the books in and the public out!'

'She does have a point, though, about use of council funds.'

'The soup's sponsored – I *told* her. Waitrose foot the bill. And if she has any more complaints about the shopping or the washing-up, it's me that does both those, as she damned well knows, in fact.'

'It's not the soup as such. She says you're using up resources on lame ducks, who do little for the issue figures, when you should be—'

'Stella, I don't need Harriet to tell me what I should or shouldn't be doing. And they're *not* lame ducks. We're attracting people we've never reached before.'

'That's the trouble, though, as far as she's concerned. She says we're meant to be librarians, not social workers or psychiatrists.'

'The two things go together – reading as therapy. Hell, she must know that by now – with all those "Books on Prescription" schemes and a load of other groups nationally. One of my little lot has actually decided to come off Prozac, and just because of the sessions. And she called them "a shaft of light in a dark cavern", which I thought was rather poetic.'

Stella dunked a biscuit into her tea. 'Eric, I'm on your side – you know that. But let's forget libraries for a sec. We need to talk about the dating thing.'

He hid his face in his hands. 'Haven't time,' he groaned.

'How about a quick drink after work, then? Are you free this evening?'

'Yes, unfortunately. No queue of leggy blondes fighting for the privilege of taking me to bed!'

'Well, all the more reason to put that right. See you in the Dog and Duck at six, OK?'

'OK, and thanks a million for doing the soup. Just heat it in the microwave, in batches, and bring it in at quarter to one.'

As he left, he glanced back at the staffroom: tatty lino, shabby chairs, no proper storage space. Toilet-rolls were heaped up in one corner; a pile of battered box-files in another. It all came back to lack of funds, of course. With more resources, he could work minor miracles; not with carpeting and cupboards – they were inessentials – but with every 'undesirable' and 'lame duck' in the borough.

> 'My own heart let me have more pity on; let
> Me live to my sad self hereafter kind,
> Charitable; not live this tormented mind....'

He glanced around the circle of faces, trying to judge their reaction. It was definitely a risk engaging with a poet as difficult as Hopkins, when some of the group hadn't opened a book since leaving school. But his own experience as an undereducated lad had taught him that, even if you didn't grasp the meaning of the words, the spirit of a poem could still seep into your soul. He refused to accept that great literature should be the preserve of a small cultured elite, instead of open to all and sundry.

'Well,' he asked, once Alice had read the second verse, stumbling over the challenging last lines. Incredible that she was reading it at all, when, a month ago, she had sat in silence throughout the sessions, literally shaking with nerves. 'What did you all think of that?'

'Couldn't understand a word!' Graham protested, shaking his bald head.

'Too downbeat for me,' Marjorie put in. 'We need cheering up, not made to feel worse still.'

'You've missed the whole point,' Barry countered. 'The bloke who wrote that is trying to cheer himself up, deciding to be kinder to himself. There's a lesson there for all of us.'

'I agree,' said Rita. 'He's saying we should have pity on ourselves, and I, for one, approve of that.'

'But I don't get the bit about thirst. What he's on about?'

Eric took the words apart and tried to fit them back together in a simpler, more immediate way. 'The language is difficult – for me as much as you. I'm not always sure what it means myself, but that's OK. We're learning as we go along. Hopkins has been called "obscure", so we shouldn't expect to grasp it all immediately.'

'So why choose an obscure poet?' Graham demanded, rocking back on his chair.

Eric took his time replying. He'd deliberately avoided self-help books, despite the fact that many of the members were suffering from depression and the like. So-called 'prescription literature' only told sufferers more about their pain, whereas poetry could transcend it; endow it with depth and meaning. He had proved that in his own case – although he could hardly explain in this particular setting that Gerard Manley Hopkins had helped him through his divorce. During those grim months, he had often lain sleepless, repeating, 'O, what black hours we have spent this night … I am gall, I am heartburn', and all the other desolate stuff he'd soon come to know by heart. To read of someone else's anguish, depicted in astounding words, had been weirdly comforting; made him feel less isolated; less alone with grief.

'Because Hopkins is deeply passionate,' he replied, at last, to Graham, 'and cares about the important things in life. And he's a true original. His style is so strange, it shakes you up. And if you want to know why poetry rather than prose, well, sometimes just the rhyme and rhythm can induce a sense of calmness.'

'Yes, I find poems helpful,' Warren declared. 'And I like the way they mean something they're not saying.'

An astute comment, Eric thought, from a guy who claimed never to have read anything except the backs of sauce bottles.

'The first poem was easier, though,' Marjorie observed. 'The one that Graham read.'

'*Pied Beauty*?'

'Yes, the words were really beautiful. In fact, I'd like to hear it again.'

'Well, we do have time, before we break for our soup, if the rest of you don't mind?'

Several people nodded their agreement, although anorexic Lee looked highly nervous, as usual, at the mention of the soup. She especially hated the buttered rolls and, while the others were eating, sometimes felt compelled to leave the room.

'Hannah, would you like to read it for us this time?' Another risk, since Hannah had a speech-impediment, as part of her cerebral palsy. But it gave her enormous pleasure to read aloud and have people actually listen – something unknown in her daily life. And, anyway, since everyone had copies of the poem, they could follow it for themselves, even if they couldn't quite decipher her distorted words.

In the brief silence after she'd finished, Sue cleared her throat, shuffled her feet, and suddenly said in an embarrassed tone, 'I wish I'd known about that poem all the time I was in Springfield. I'm sure it would have been a comfort.'

All eyes turned to her. Sue had not contributed a word, as yet, to any conversation or discussion, nor revealed a single fact about herself, yet here she was admitting to a stay in the local psychiatric hospital.

'And the other poem even more so. I mean, just to realize it's OK to feel such huge despair. You say Hopkins was a priest, yet he still comes very close to losing hope.'

All at once, several people started talking – Rita chipping in about her own spell in a mental ward; Graham remarking that religion couldn't always help and sometimes made things worse; Barry letting out that his shrink had been worse than useless and they had almost come to blows.

Eric watched as Warren, with his ear-stud and tattoos, leaned across to comfort Rita, in her tweeds and sensible shoes. It gave him a sense of achievement that this disparate group were confiding in each other; beginning to forge bonds. On paper, it shouldn't work – too big a difference in background, age and social class, yet they were actually sharing secrets, opening up, finding confidence to express opinions, when, at the start, they'd been tongue-tied, wary, highly nervous and mutually suspicious. Meeting in this small upstairs room, away from the main library, was definitely a plus-point, in that it afforded privacy to speak one's mind, and encouraged a certain intimacy, since they were all sitting round the table, like one big family – not a happy family, perhaps, but at least communicating.

He could do with some help, of course; needed to recruit a volunteer, to assist him once the project took off. And he was determined that it should succeed. He was aiming for higher numbers altogether; wanted more men in the group and more from ethnic minorities. And he planned to invite a poet along, to talk to them about producing their own poetry, and maybe set up a separate Creative Writing group, as well as develop his new idea of music therapy.

It would all take more funds, of course – funds they didn't have – demand energy on *his* part, but just give him time and he'd damned well make it work.

chapter three

'I thought we said six,' Stella tapped her watch in disapproval. 'I was just about to give you up.'

Eric plonked himself down on the faded red-plush banquette. 'Sorry, really sorry. Trevor kept me – I just couldn't get away.'

'What did he want?'

'Well, to tell the truth, he gave me a bit of a bollocking – you know, how I mustn't let my ideals run away with me. And how my attitude to Harriet leaves a lot to be desired. Well, what about her attitude to *me*?'

'Poor Eric! Let me buy you a drink.'

'No, I'll buy you one. It's the least I can do, after keeping you waiting.'

He fought his way to the bar, annoyed that all his earlier elation should have been punctured like a balloon. This afternoon he'd been flying high, ready to let go of any controlling string, so that he could soar up to the stratosphere, yet now he'd been reduced to a few shrivelled scraps of rubber. And the season didn't help. Just eighteen days to go till the Big Day of hype and hypocrisy, and every shop and restaurant and public place was trumpeting the fact full-force; this pub no exception. Normally, he loved the Dog and Duck; a cosy refuge within minutes of the library; what he *didn't* like was its ersatz Christmas overlay. The oak beams were wreathed in tinsel, sprigs of plastic holly blighted every table, and the bewhiskered barman (a Father-Christmas lookalike) sported a Santa cap. Even at home he couldn't escape; the dreaded C-word cropping up with depressing regularity every time he turned on the TV. Last Christmas had been bad enough, but at least his wife and child had been around.

'Cheers!' said Stella, raising her glass of vodka and Coke.

'Cheers,' he muttered morosely, feeling anything but cheerful amidst the aggravation of canned carols tinkling from the sound-system.

'Now, listen, Eric, we're here to talk about your love-life, not – I repeat not – about work. So will you please switch off and give me your full attention.'

He did his best to comply, although he was still smarting from Trevor's strictures and not exactly overjoyed to have to confront the desert of his love-life. Still, he thought, at least he wasn't condemned to a life of permanent celibacy, like poor Gerard Manley Hopkins, who had once described himself as a eunuch.

'You won't get anywhere, you know, unless you rewrite your profile. The existing one isn't working.'

'You're telling me!' Perhaps a vow of chastity might actually make things easier. From what he had read about eunuchs, they led quite a cushy life, with nothing to do in the harem except look after gorgeous girls.

'Mainly because you insist on sticking to the truth. Most people big themselves up, so you're putting yourself at an instant disadvantage.'

The word 'truth' induced the usual surge of guilt. How duplicitous he was, posing as a truth-teller, yet concealing so much from Stella – indeed, from all his friends. Yet the few times in the past he'd come clean about his background had not been a huge success. Those he'd told had viewed him very differently thereafter – with pity, with suspicion.

'I mean, you've put "average" for appearance, but that doesn't do you any favours. Can't you say "*above* average"?'

'No, because then they'll be disappointed. In fact, I reckon lots of people must get quite a shock when they compare the descriptions with the reality. Actually, I'm thinking of writing a guide to all the terms in current use, if only as a warning. "Lively and outgoing" means a noisy, manic, show-off. "Articulate": never stops talking. "Independent": bossy. "Honest": tactless. "Creative": out of work.'

Stella fiddled with a strand of her fairish, wavy hair. 'Mm, I suppose you have a point. I met this guy who described himself as sensitive, and he turned out downright moody. And another said he was thoughtful, but "dull and utterly boring" was a damned sight nearer the mark.'

'Yes,' said Eric, warming to his theme. '"Caring": soppy; "scrumptious": vain; "free-spirited": unruly; "home-loving" agoraphobic".'

With a sudden laugh, Stella began joining in herself. '"Spontaneous": tactless; "entrepreneur": crook; "fun-loving": vacuous; "no baggage": stony-broke.'

'"Family-oriented": mother of six; "down-to-earth": uncouth; "curvaceous": hugely fat.'

'Come off it, Eric, I used "curvaceous" myself.'

'Sorry! I forgot. You *are* curvaceous, Stella – in the true meaning of the word.'

'You can lay off the flattery, thank you very much! Anyway, it got me quite a few replies.'

'Yes, but neither of us have met anyone remotely suitable.'

'What d'you mean, "neither of us"? You've only had one date so far; *I've* had seventeen.'

He reached for his packet of crisps; crunched a couple despondently. 'Frankly, I've lost heart, Stella, after the fiasco with Olivia.'

'That was your own fault. I told you – twice – on no account to invite anyone to dinner.'

'She invited herself.' He was forced to raise his voice above 'Silent Night'. Hardly silent. The large party in the corner – office revellers, by the looks of them – were whooping and guffawing, and had just started pulling crackers, shrieking with excitement at every little bang.

'Well, you should have made some excuse, just settled for a quick drink after work.'

If only. The final bill, paid by him in total, and including service and three desserts for Olivia, had come to £325. Which meant none of his friends or colleagues would be getting much for Christmas beyond a card or calendar.

'If you go to a restaurant, you can get stuck with someone for hours, even if it's obvious you're not going to hit it off. So, best to meet in a bar, order one quick beer, then scat within the first ten minutes if you can see the vibes are wrong. Still, I admit you were unlucky with Olivia – you clearly met a weirdo.'

Another pang of guilt. Perhaps he'd been unfair – too critical, judgemental. There was a school of thought that believed greed was simply fear of scarcity, often associated with a lack of parental love. For all he knew, Olivia might have had a history not unlike his own.

'To be honest, I'm plain jealous of the woman. I mean, from what you say, she can stuff herself, yet not put on a single pound in weight.'

He glanced at Stella, who, despite her buxom breasts and ample thighs, seemed to exist on little more than cottage cheese, with the occasional bar of chocolate as a treat. As usual, she had refused to share his crisps; declined his offer of a sandwich or scotch egg. Of course, he had no idea what she ate in private, and he'd learned long ago that most people had a secret life, sometimes totally at variance with the façade presented to the world.

'Anyway, just because you drew a blank the first time, doesn't mean there aren't loads of decent women, panting for a date with you.'

'Oh, yeah?'

'But you won't attract them without a punchy headline. "A great catch!" – or something on those lines.'

'I'm not a great catch.'

'You *are*, Eric! If only you could see it. You're loyal, honest, generous and passionate about your job.'

'Try telling that to Trevor!'

'We're not talking about Trevor. I've told you – twice – forget about work and think about a headline. How about "Last of the Lost Romantics"?'

'No fear! They'll be expecting Byron.'

'OK, "Nothing ventured". Brief but enigmatic.'

He shook his head. The word 'venture' was risibly inappropriate for a coward on his scale.

'God, you're hard to please! I know – try a bit of humour. "Lowbrow Scrabble-Player Seeks"—'

'"Lowbrow" will only pull in all the air-heads.'

'Well, go the other way. "The Thinking Woman's Crumpet".'

'I'm no one's crumpet, Stella – more a stale old crust, fit only for the feathered kind of birds.'

'Stop putting yourself down. It's entirely self-defeating.'

'OK, I'm a paragon. But I also happen to be forty-four – which you said yourself was ancient. In fact, half my life is over – maybe more. Do you realize, according to life-insurers, every eight years we're twice as likely to die.' Tom Jones, he mused, was sixty-eight. On the radio last night, the singer had been boasting that, when he performed, women still flung their knickers on to the stage, along with their hotel-door-keys. Closing his eyes a moment, he imagined himself taking the applause, picking up the knickers, inserting keys into rows and rows of doors.

'Don't be so morbid, Eric. And, by the way, I hope you're updating your Facebook profile every couple of days. You have to try all avenues, you know.'

Facebook left him cold – all those people bragging about their thousands of friends, when the whole point about friends was that they *didn't* come in thousands. Friendship wasn't a matter of competitive acquisition, but required personal commitment, loyalty, unselfishness. 'I reckon most of them are pseuds – or "clicksters", as I like to call them.'

'"Clicksters"?'

'Yes, to rhyme with tricksters. One click and they bag a new friend – except it's *not* a friend, nothing like.'

'You need to be more adventurous in general,' Stella continued, ignoring his interruption, 'strike up conversations with women in the launderette or supermarket.'

'What, and get arrested for sexual harassment?' The woman in his local launderette was eighteen stone, with acne. He watched a group of girls troop in, all mouth-wateringly young and pretty. Having jostled their way to the bar, they stood giggling and chatting, waiting to be served. If he were a sheik and this was his harem, which one would he choose to pleasure him tonight? Easy – the redhead in the skin-tight jeans.

'D'you think I'm too old for jeans?' he asked Stella, with a worried glance at his own legs.

'No one's too old for jeans.'

Did Tom Jones still wear them, he wondered, although it was the *other* Tom Jones who had always been his hero – the eighteenth-century literary one. He kept the reason dark, of course, like so much else in his life.

Stella was looking at him critically. 'But perhaps you could do with some help with your wardrobe.'

'I don't have a wardrobe any more. There isn't room for one in my flat.'

She didn't appear to be listening; her gaze travelling from his sweater to his shoes. Was the sweater too bright; were the shoes uncool?

'Actually, you might really push the boat out and make an appointment with a dating coach.'

'A what?'

'Someone who helps you show yourself at your best.'

'Stella, *you're* my dating coach and, much as I appreciate your efforts, frankly one is more than enough. I mean, all that stuff you told me about body-posture. I practised it at home and got so hung up, I even embarrassed the cat! In fact, I used her for the eye-contact thing – gazed into her eyes, like you said to do with a woman – and she was out the window in one minute flat.'

'Cats don't count.'

'They're easier. At least, dear old Charlie loves me, whatever my body-posture.'

'Well, if you *want* to spend Christmas alone with your cat …'

'OK, you win! I'll update my profile tomorrow and you won't recognize me, Stella. I'll be vivacious, sparky, tactile, vibrant, athletic, classy, scrumptious and free-spirited.'

'Great! Only I'd play down the "athletic". You might attract a female jogger who expects you to run ten miles with her before you both start work. And, listen, talking of Christmas, you're more than welcome to join us in Ibiza. One of our party has just dropped out, so you'd be doing us a favour. I know you're short of cash, but it really is dirt-cheap.'

Eric played for time, spinning out his last few inches of beer. How could he reveal to Stella that he had never, ever, been on a plane, and didn't intend to start? Forget vibrant, sparky, free-spirited – a wimp and a coward would be closer to the truth. But dating sites avoided any mention of phobias or fears. OK to list your hobbies, your politics, your star-sign, but not the things that brought you out in a cold sweat. 'Er, can I let you know?'

''Course. But don't leave it too long.' Stella fumbled in her holdall and withdrew a Waterstone's bag. 'Listen, Eric, don't be offended, but I've bought you a little present.'

'Why should I be offended?' Opening the bag, he read the title aloud: 'Teach Yourself Flirting. Oh, I see,' he murmured, crestfallen.

'It's by this guy who calls himself a date-doctor and it's full of quite fantastic tips. I thought it might be useful, because it deals with things like the shrinking-violet syndrome and what he calls desperitis.'

'Oh,' he said again, feeling seriously deflated. Shy he might be, but hardly a shrinking violet – and hardly desperate, either. Besides, could you teach yourself flirting? He had once tried to learn to tango from a book containing diagrams of feet, but had failed to get as far as Lesson Two. 'Another drink?' he offered – a bid to make amends to Stella for his obvious lack of enthusiasm about her choice of gift.

'No, better not. Every one of these' – she pointed to her glass – 'is at least another hundred calories. Anyway, I must push off. There's a load of stuff I need to prepare for tomorrow.'

'OK,' he said, disappointed. Despite the seasonal excesses – a maddeningly jaunty Good King Wenceslas was now trilling out, full-volume – he much preferred this cosy pub and Stella's company to his lonely, chilly flat. On the other hand, he had homework, too: he had to teach himself to flirt in sixteen challenging chapters.

chapter four

'Excuse me,' Eric said. 'I wondered if you'd seen a ginger cat? It's gone missing, you see and …'

The small, black-haired woman standing in the doorway was gazing at him in total incomprehension. Indonesian, by the looks of her, or possibly Vietnamese. A pity he didn't speak a host of other languages – Bengali, Hindi, Cantonese, Arabic, Malay … Almost everybody he'd asked so far had been not just foreign but non-English-speaking, too.

'Never mind. It doesn't matter.' He backed away, sorry that he'd scared her. She'd looked seriously alarmed, as if he were a bailiff, come to cart off all the furniture.

Turning up his coat collar against the driving rain, he trudged on to the next doorway. He'd reached only the second storey of the huge council block opposite his flat, which meant five more floors to go. Although, on reflection, it was probably a complete waste of time. Most people were out, or perhaps had learned through bitter experience never to open their front doors in such a dodgy area, for fear of burglary or assault. The few who *had* appeared either failed to understand him or slammed the door in his face – apart from one pugnacious Asian who had launched into a tirade about filthy, germy cats that should never be allowed inside a human home, so the more that went missing, the better.

After four more fruitless calls, he decided to try his luck in the local shops, starting with the Indian corner-store.

'I've lost my cat,' he began.

'You lost your cash? Sorry, we don't cash cheques here, but Costcutters may be able to help you out.'

'No, not my cash – my *cat*.'

'Can't help,' the man said brusquely, cutting off the conversation as a customer walked in – a woman with three kids and a pushchair.

Well, Eric shrugged, he was obviously unwelcome here, but at least they knew him at the café. Having ventured in, he found Hanif and Abdullah sitting at a table playing draughts.

'No customers?' he asked.

Hanif grimaced. 'People stay at home in this weather.'

If only *Charlie* had, thought Eric, increasingly concerned about the cat. She had disappeared yesterday evening and, at twelve years old, was too decrepit to be out on such a stormy night. He had searched the entire area, in vain, returning only in the early hours. And, to make things worse, she was a cat from a rescue-centre and, before he and Christine had taken her on, they'd been questioned almost as closely as if about to adopt a child: did they have a garden, and prior experience of cats; how dangerous was their road; would they agree to fit a cat-flap? Eventually, they'd been given the all-clear, although, of course, the volunteer who came round to check the premises hadn't known that he and Charlie shared a bond, in the form of their early history.

Hanif handed him the menu. 'What can I get you? Coffee? Tea? A fry-up?'

'Sorry. I can't stay. I've lost my cat and wondered if you'd seen it?'

Both men shook their heads.

'Is it male or female?' Abdullah enquired.

'Female.'

'Pity,' Hanif said. 'Males come back. Females don't.'

Too right, Eric mused, his mind switching to his wife and daughter: 5000 miles away, and with no intention of returning.

'But we'll keep a look-out. What's its name?'

'Charlie.'

'Charlie's a *man's* name.'

'I know. My daughter christened her.'

The two men returned to their game, and who could blame them? A lost wife, lost daughter and now lost cat might be the stuff of tragedy for him, but not for the world in general.

Sighing, he mooched on to the launderette. The vast, pock-marked woman was there, as usual, guarding a row of empty machines. Today, this Vauxhall backwater resembled a Sunday in the fifties – at least from what he'd heard – a day of rest, stagnation, with everybody closeted indoors.

'I did see a black cat. It was hanging around outside all day yesterday.'

'No, mine's ginger.' Eric flushed, expecting the usual jibes about one copper-knob finding comfort with another. But the woman only shifted her huge bulk and stooped down (with difficulty) to inspect a broken machine.

'Why not ask at the farm?' she said. 'Your cat might have ended up there, for a bit of warmth and company.'

'Thanks. Great idea!' He'd never actually set foot in the Vauxhall City Farm, despite the fact it was just along the road.

He passed the boarded-up *George and Dragon*, and then a row of shops with iron grilles across the windows. The contrast with his previous home was marked. Kingston, although a mere ten miles away in distance, was a different world entirely. Most people in this area were shabby, scruffy, poor, and just didn't have the luxury of good schools, pretty gardens and relative peace and quiet. Sirens deafened the streets here, jolting one from sleep most nights. And the dreary, soulless council blocks did little to raise one's spirits. In fact, it was a relief to reach the farm and discover a green oasis, and even rustic smells of hay and straw.

As he picked his way between the muddy puddles, a small boy came up to greet him, wearing a sweatshirt blazoned 'VOLUNTEER'. 'Hi!' he said. 'Want me to show you round?'

'That's kind,' said Eric, 'but I'm looking for my cat. She ran off last night and—'

'Hold on a tick. I'll ask Bella.' The boy went dashing up to a black woman, busy sweeping the yard. A rather gorgeous female, Eric thought, looking surreptitiously at her big, bouncy breasts, prominently displayed in a skin-tight scarlet sweater.

'No, sorry,' the boy said, tearing back again. 'She hasn't seen any cats. But now you're here, why not stop and see the rabbits?'

Before Eric could decline, the boy reached down over the fence of an enclosure, picked up a plump grey rabbit and transferred it into Eric's arms. After the first ripple of surprise, Eric felt strangely comforted by the cuddly, flop-eared creature, which displayed no fear at all at being handled by a stranger, but settled contentedly against his chest.

'She's called Pebbles,' the boy informed him, clearly glad of company.

'And what are you called?'

'Zack. Short for Zachariah.'

Eric fought a sudden longing to grab Zack by the hand and take him and Pebbles back home to his flat. He had always wanted a son – wanted lots more kids; a whole tribe of them, like these rabbits.

'Rabbits have twenty-eight teeth, you know. That's one for almost every day of the month. See that rabbit there?' Zach pointed to the pen, where a huge brown and white creature was nibbling on a lettuce leaf. 'She's a rare breed – what's called an English Giant. We have rare chickens, too. Come and have a look.' Having grabbed the flop-eared rabbit, Zack replaced it in its enclosure and led Eric towards a life-size plastic cow, made of plastic or polystyrene, but looking surprisingly real. Beneath its black-and-white belly, a variety of unusual-looking hens were sheltering in a seething, clucking mass.

Eric was tempted to join them, if only to shelter from the rain, although in point of fact he was a lot less wet than Zack, who had neither coat nor anorak.

All at once, an exotic hen with a pompommed head was being thrust into his arms, the creature squawking in alarm and scrabbling with its scaly feet. But barely had he time to calm it, when Zack seized it back and moved him on, clearly determined to fulfil his role as guide.

'See those brown hens by the fence? They're Polish.'

'Really? All the way from Poland?'

'Not Poland – Italy. They come from near the River Po. And, by the way, you may not know that chickens are the closest living relative to Tyrannosaurus Rex.'

Zack would be useful in the library, Eric thought: a mine of information, to help with customers' enquiries.

'And those are our ponies,' Zack continued, pointing to a row of heads peering over the stable doors. 'You're not allowed in there, unless you've paid for riding, but if you cross the yard, you can see the calves and pigs and goats and things. Enjoy your visit!'

Eric found himself doing as he was told. Although little more than eight or nine, Zack had a persuasive manner and was quite the seasoned professional. Enjoy your visit, indeed!

His spirits fell, however, as he saw another man, with a small girl in tow, preceding him along the path. Fathers with their children always induced in him a pang of loss and longing. Even if the fellow was divorced, like him, he still had his daughter with him – maybe living close; not separated by the vast Atlantic Ocean and a cruel, uncaring landmass. Not that the guy seemed grateful for the privilege; rather distracted and impatient as he yanked the girl roughly by the hand, and told her off for splashing through the puddles.

'Dad, what are those?' she asked, as the pair stopped at a large outdoor pen, shared by various animals and birds.

'I told you – twice – they're goats.'

'What's goats?'

'Goats are goats, Jane. Don't be daft. And can't you hurry up? We should have stayed indoors in the dry, not come out on a shitty day like this.'

Go back indoors then, Eric all but said, and *I'll* look after your kid – although I'll change her name to Erica. It had always struck him as a miracle, not just to have a child, after a boyhood with no family at all, but a child named after him; bearing his own name, give or take an 'a'.

As the girl and her father moved on, a small female goat came lolloping over, put its feet up on the fence and shoved its nose into his hand. As he fondled its white head, it went into instant transports of pleasure, arching its back and trying to nuzzle against his chest. A pity, Eric speculated, I wasn't born a ram, then I'd have more success with females. The goat was even making eye-contact; its yellow eyes fixed adoringly on his.

Reluctantly parting from his new conquest, he inspected the next enclosure, where a large ruffled turkey suddenly stretched out its long neck and made a noise like water gurgling down a drain. Eric turned his back. There were enough reminders of Christmas without a turkey adding to the chorus. His last twelve Christmases had been built around Erica – food, presents, decorations, tree: all done in her honour. *This* Christmas was just eighteen days away. He'd better volunteer; help out at a shelter for the homeless, or a Salvation Army centre, if only to distract himself.

Lost in thought, he had completely failed to notice the large, spotted pig in front of him; a handsome beast, with bristly fur and a moist grey snout, munching enthusiastically; its mouth wide open and spraying bits of food all over the place. *Olivia*, he thought, leaning over the fence to watch the porcine glutton. Would he ever meet the right person (barring goats)? He'd read all 200 pages of Stella's *Flirting* book, but had done little more, so far, than diagnose himself with various so-called dating illnesses: 'Rejectaphobia', 'Stranger Danger' and 'Signal Failure' – the last nothing to do with trains. But, even if he worked through all the given cures, it didn't change the depressing fact that to find an intelligent, attractive woman, with compatible views on politics, religion and general philosophy of life, would be little short of a miracle.

Wandering on, he all but collided with the black girl, and racked his brains for something riveting to say beyond a flustered 'Sorry!' He must be more adventurous, strike up conversations, as Stella had advised, but there were other people in earshot – three teenaged girls, helping sweep the paths, and a young lad with a wheelbarrow. Did he really want the whole gang of them listening to his chat-up lines? They were all busy talking, anyway; exchanging jokes and banter; a little community in themselves, with a shared purpose and sense of belonging.

Far from astounding them with his conversational flair, he managed to get in the way of the wheelbarrow and was jabbed sharply in the leg. 'Sorry,' he gasped again, removing himself to the far end of the site – an area planted with flowers and vegetables, with allotment-plots beyond. The cabbages and carrots and cheerful marigolds brought a surge of regret for his much-missed Kingston garden. It had given him such satisfaction to keep it neat and tidy; grow dead-straight rows of lettuces and beans; pounce on any weed or other threat to its good order. Order was essential when one had grown up in a state of chaos.

'For fuck's sake!' he muttered under his breath. 'You're here to search for Charlie, not indulge in self-pity.' And since he hadn't seen a sign of the cat, he'd better push off home – although 'home' was hardly the word. It didn't feel like home – never had, never would. The bars on the windows seemed to turn it into a prison; he a lifer in solitary confinement.

'Come off it! You're lucky to have a place to live at all – *and* one so conveniently central.'

The black girl was looking at him curiously – and no wonder, when he was talking to himself. He'd better get the hell out of here, before he was locked up as a mental case.

As he retraced his steps and turned into the street, he spotted a child's red wool glove, waterlogged in a puddle in the gutter. On impulse, he retrieved it; shook and squeezed it dry. Erica had gloves like that, and he could almost feel her firm, woolly grip as she clasped her hand in his. Yet how limp and lonesome the glove looked. Things should be in pairs.

By the time he reached his flat, the rain was slackening off – although that didn't mean to say he wasn't drenched. He didn't bother to change, however, but just sat in his cramped kitchen with a consoling cup of tea. Dusk had already fallen, although basement flats were always pretty gloomy, even in the daytime. The big advantage, however, was that Charlie had access to the garden – access forbidden to *him*, since it belonged to the ground-floor tenants, whom, in fact, he very rarely saw. Those on the first and second floors were more in evidence: one couple prone to shouting-matches and the other engaged in non-stop DIY.

Still, now it was as quiet as the grave, which only underlined Charlie's absence. He missed her rumbling purr; her little mews of pleasure when he spooned food into her bowl; the way she scrabbled at the door when she wanted to go out. How could he tell Erica that Charlie had gone missing? – not that she was likely to ring. The divorce settlement had stipulated regular phone-calls, along with a raft of other measures to ensure they remained in contact, including a six-week stay in England every summer. This first year of her absence, though, the long-awaited visit had failed to come about, as she'd been stricken with glandular fever for most of her vacation. And, in the last few weeks, even the letters and the phone-calls appeared to be tailing off. He wrote, of course, every week; emailed almost daily, and rang whenever possible, but phone-calls were tricky to schedule when Seattle was eight hours behind, and Erica herself didn't seem that keen, of late, to return his frequent calls. He feared she might be suffering from depression, after her debilitating illness, although Christine had vehemently denied it.

But then how could he trust his ex-wife, when she'd been the one desperate to move to America, so as to join her loathsome lover in his home state? Naturally, when dealing with the lawyers, she had emphasized the advantages for Erica: better schooling; a higher standard of living; new hobbies and excitements, such as sailing on the fellow's ritzy yacht. Perhaps the girl was so enamoured of her new gratifying life – riding lessons, boat-trips, skiing on Crystal Mountain – she had forgotten all about her dad. The thought was so appalling, he removed the red glove from his pocket and pressed it against his face, remembering his loyal and loving Erica, who'd been content with simple pleasures and had never travelled further than Weston-Super-Mare.

He slouched into the living-room, to sit in front of her photo – his favourite one, in pride of place on his desk: taken when she was ten, with long pigtails and an easy, natural smile. And Charlie was with her, too, looking distinctly nervous, as if the flash had startled her. Perhaps fear was simply natural. Most animals and birds were scared – scared of noise and predators, unnerved by strange places or unknown situations. Yet cats and thrushes and squirrels didn't swallow Prozac or rush off to counsellors, but just accepted terror as a normal part of life. As a boy, he'd sometimes pretended to be an animal, crouching down in muddy ditches, or hiding in hollow trees; relishing the feeling of being secure and well concealed; the heady combination of safety and escape. Sadly, someone had always come and hauled him out; dragged him back to his more troubling human life.

If only he could haul *Charlie* out from wherever she was lurking. She might have tried to find her way back to Kingston and been hit by a car or become hopelessly lost *en route*. Or maybe she'd been stolen, or killed by some heartless yob. First thing tomorrow, he would phone the local vets and the cat-refuge; even the police – although they would hardly waste vital manpower on the whereabouts of an elderly cat when they had murder and mayhem on their plate.

He jumped as his mobile rang. Erica, with any luck. No – she always slept in on Sundays and it was only 9 a.m. in Seattle. Maybe someone from one of the dating-sites, in which case he must prepare his voice – a bright, engaging, fun voice, to give a good impression. He even switched on a smile. ('You can *hear* a smile,' the *Flirting* book advised.)

'Hi, Eric. Stella here.'

'Oh,' he said, reverting to his lost-cat, wet-jeans, alone-on-Sunday tone.

'What d'you mean, "Oh"?'

'Sorry. I've lost Charlie, so I'm feeling a bit down.'

'She's probably out on a date. I've just found this hilarious site – "Dates for Dogs" – so it can't be long before cats get in on the act. It's an absolute hoot – pampered pooches advertising for tummy-rubs and "yappy hours" and rolls in the hay and stuff.'

'Ha-ha. Very funny. Anyway, if you've rung about the Family History project, I'm afraid I haven't done a thing yet. I've been out all day and—'

'No, I've rung about this fantastic event we simply have to go to. It's called "Choc-a-Love" and it's just been set up by this group of *chocolatiers*, who—'

'Stella, I'm not *into* chocolate. I know it's your great passion, but—'

'Ssh! Be quiet – the chocolate bit's not actually the point. It's really a dating service and pretty classy, by the sounds of it. They make us all our own individual chocolates – you know, to express our personalities and quirks. Are we dark or milk, soft or hard, plain or fancy, bitter or sweet? Then they match the chocolates up – for example, Nutty Cluster meets Strawberry Cream, or Brandy Truffle fancies Nougat Parfait.'

'Stella,' Eric said, sinking down on to the sofa and stretching out his still sopping legs. 'I've read the book you gave me, faithfully from start to finish; I've signed up for three more dating-sites, and I've spent bloody hours on Facebook, but I'm sorry – I absolutely draw the line at "Choc-a-Love".'

chapter five

'Chocolate,' breathed Yvette, lowering her voice to a provocatively sexy purr, 'has been celebrated as an aphrodisiac for more than fifteen hundred years.'

Eric shifted in his seat. It wasn't an aphrodisiac he needed. Just the sight of all those women sitting in the audience was enough to turn him on. In fact, Yvette was pretty fanciable herself. His seat, just a few rows from the podium, was affording him a gratifying view of her truly voluptuous curves.

'The last of the Aztec emperors, Montezuma, drank fifty golden goblets of chocolate every single day, to enhance his sexual powers. And, from all accounts, those powers were pretty legendary.'

He couldn't have had a job, then, Eric thought. Today, the library had been so busy, he'd barely had time to snatch one cup of coffee, let alone devour fifty goblets of anything.

'And when chocolate spread to Europe,' Yvette continued, as a colour map displayed itself on the large PowerPoint screen behind her, 'it proved no less potent an aid to sex. The great lover, Casanova, called chocolate "the elixir of love" and always made sure he consumed it before bedding his many conquests.'

Eric closed his eyes a second; imagined himself servicing a whole string of willing conquests, pausing only to gulp yet another quart of chocolate.

'And do you know' – Yvette paused dramatically, her eyes roving round the room, to ensure everyone was listening – 'recent scientific research actually supports those claims. Chocolate contains highly complex substances that produce the same effects we associate with passion, high libido and being head-over-heels in love.'

Eric gazed at the succession of pictures now flashing up on-screen. Clearly he'd missed a trick or two living on baked beans, instead of chocolate bars. Although these chocolates were in a different league from any he had ever seen: each one a work of art; some patterned with scrolls or shells in shimmering gold leaf; others studded with pistachio nuts or tiny pieces of crystallized fruit. Some were even shaped like miniature coffee-cups, complete with chocolate handles, and filled with different coloured layers, although all the colours were subtle – nothing vulgar or over-bright. And most of the chocolate itself was determinedly, stylishly dark. On no account must he admit that he much preferred milk chocolate, let alone that he had a yen for Milky Bar. Apparently, white chocolate wasn't chocolate at all, or so he had learned this evening.

'Not only that – chocolate is good for our health. It lowers blood-pressure, reduces our risk of heart-attack, improves our brain power and is even effective as a cough medicine.'

Which, reflected Eric, made it all the more ironic that Stella wasn't here. Just this morning, she had gone down with bronchitis, and had rung to say she was coughing like a consumptive and couldn't come in to work, let alone join him for this evening's 'Choc-a-Love'. He had immediately tried to chicken out himself (having agreed to come solely for *her* sake, and only after endless persuasion), but again she'd overruled him; insisted that he go, so that he could give her a full account of the proceedings.

Now, he was actually relieved that he had let her twist his arm. Having done a speedy head-count (thirty-nine women to seventeen men) he had realized that, statistically, his chances were pretty good. Admittedly, the organizers had promised to balance the numbers for the chocolate dating proper, this coming Saturday, but there was no compulsion to sign up for it. With any luck, he would meet someone during this introductory evening. In fact, several women had already approached him in the pre-presentation drinks session; one of them, Penelope, now sitting right beside him. Definitely a turn-up for the books.

Yvette's husky cadences returned him to the matter in hand. 'Now, I want to tell you something about our fabulous range of chocolates, and how to choose the one that best expresses your personality. These chocolates are as unique and special as *you* are, and those of you who decide to come on Saturday will have your chocolates made for you by hand. They'll also be hand-decorated, with any kind of motif you choose, including your initials, if you want. And those chocolates will embody your individual nature; your very soul and essence; the sort of person you are – or maybe *want* to be.'

Eric fought a twinge of doubt – more than a twinge, a veritable tidal wave. How could a chocolate sum up one's soul and essence? He was determined to be positive, however, if only in the spirit of a new dating book he'd downloaded from the Internet, which had promised to rid him of 'negative inner demons', and to make females positively salivate the moment he showed up. Indeed, some of the chapter-headings bordered on the miraculous: '*How to make a woman believe you're rich, famous and hunky, even if you're poor, unknown and plain.*' '*Nine short words that will make a female feel totally at ease coming back to* your *place, even on your very first date.*'

OK, he could discount the hype, but he did undoubtedly feel more hopeful than of late. And if an elegant type like Penelope had chosen to sit next to him, something must be working. He turned to smile at her with what he hoped was genuine allure, and not only did she return the smile, she even leaned across to touch his arm a moment. A definite advance. Once the presentation was over, he would suggest they went for a drink in the stylish hotel bar and, if he played his cards right, who knew what might happen?

Yvette's voice was mesmerizing – indeed, fantasy-inducing. Yes, he thought, he and Penelope might even book a room here; spend the night together and …

'All of you who decide to sign up will have eight of your own personal chocolates waiting for you on Saturday, and these are the ones you'll swap. You'll get three or four minutes with each member of the opposite sex, to give you the taste of each other – if you'll forgive the pun! And you'll be issued with score-cards, so you can rate your approval, or other-wise.'

Eric suppressed a groan. This was simply speed-dating under another guise, and he'd avoided speed-dating on principle, so far. Stella had tried it, of course, only to suffer the humiliation of gaining only six ticks out of a roomful of thirty possibles. But since he didn't intend to sign up, why get into a state? His own particular goal was to gain Penelope's approval without the palaver of score-cards. He glanced in her direction again, keeping eye-contact for a provocative four seconds and, much to his delight, she didn't look away.

'I'm sorry,' said a woman in the audience, echoing his own former thoughts. 'I just don't see how you can judge someone by one small mouthful of chocolate.'

'Ah, but that chocolate will reveal a huge amount! You see, our preferences in chocolate go much deeper than you think. If you've chosen our
champagne range, for example, you'll probably be a thoroughbred,
someone with sophisticated tastes. Or if you've gone for Filipino Ylang
Ylang, you may well be highly sensual, with just a hint of Eastern mystery
to your character.'

As Yvette spoke, gigantic versions of the chocolates she was mentioning
flashed up on the screen in almost pornographic detail. 'Or suppose you've
selected our wild-strawberry-and-pink-pepper, then you're clearly a one-off,
a distinctive individual who never follows the crowd.'

'That's *crap*!' the woman exclaimed. 'A few minutes ago, you were
talking about science, but I've never heard anything so ludicrously unscien-
tific.'

Apparently unfazed, Yvette endeavoured to continue, only to be interrupted by someone else.

'What bothers me,' a slim, well-groomed woman remarked, 'is that I
couldn't eat eight chocolates without feeling distinctly sick.'

'Speak for yourself,' a younger female piped up. 'I could eat a hundred
without the slightest trouble.'

'I'm not sure the thing's workable at all.' The speaker was a man, this
time, with a top-drawer accent and a classy suit to match. 'I mean, we
sample each other's chocolates, but so what? I can't see it's any advance on
ordinary speed-dating – just a lot more pricey.'

'And, anyway,' another bloke put in, 'won't all the different tastes get
muddled up? – especially if we have only a few minutes to judge them on
our palate.'

Eric was tempted to chip in himself – he had objections by the score –
but he didn't want to run the risk of alienating Penelope, who, for all he
knew, might be passionately committed to the concept of chocolate-
dating. Besides, he was feeling slightly intimidated by the Sloaney types
who had spoken up so far: colour-supplement people, with the 'right'
watches, shoes, shirts, bags and hair-cuts. His own hair was cut by the
local Vauxhall barber – a friendly Pakistani, who charged a friendly fiver.
A further source of shame was the fact he hadn't understood some of the
words in use this evening – *feuilletine*, torrefied and *couverture*, to
mention but a few – unforgivable ignorance for an information professional.

'Ladies and gentlemen' –Yvette's tone had changed; its pillowy plush now tempered with a hint of steel – 'we'll have time for questions after-wards, OK? But first I'd like to finish, if you *don't* mind, so that we're all clear about the basics.'

Her laser-gaze – authoritative, compelling – quelled any last ripples of dissent. 'Now, as I was saying, whether you're sophisticated and smooth, or breezy and bohemian, zingy or laid-back, we can produce a chocolate to express your personality. Tunisian Bharat, for instance, might suit you if you're deep and complicated, with contradictory strands to your nature. When you first eat a Bharat, it's piquant and peppery on the tongue, then the warm sensation of cinnamon develops, followed by a gentle floral after-taste.'

Blimey, Eric thought, wondering if he had strayed into a wine-tasting, or a convention of *perfumiers*? But he mustn't let himself be cowed. Clearly, chocolate had its hierarchy, just as did wine and scent, but there was no reason why he shouldn't progress from Milky Bar to port-and-Cointreau truffles or geranium ganache – the two aristocrats now flashing up on-screen. After all, despite leaving school at sixteen, he had managed, through sheer willpower and a distance-learning course, to gain a degree in librari-anship, and actually achieved his dream of chartership, just three years ago. And, even if he missed out on the Saturday bash, he could still decide his chocolate personality. Was he a tough nut or melting cream? Unfortunately, the latter. Yet if he planned to interest Penelope, he must add a touch more class. How about cassis and hibiscus, or pomegranate and passionfruit? Yes, she was now running her exquisite tongue over his pomegranate protuber-ance, and expressing her approval with little moans of pleasure. His mind leapt ahead to Christmas – a horizontal Christmas. Why get out of bed, if she were lying naked beside him?

He stole another glance at her, wishing she wasn't quite so dauntingly chic. Aiming high in chocolate was one thing; aiming high in women more frightening altogether. Yet the new dating book kept stressing that simple self-belief could turn one's aspirations into fact. So be it. He'd left Milky Bar far, far behind and was now a connoisseur of extra-dark, exotic chocolate, grown from exclusive Criollo beans in—

All at once, he gave a monster sneeze, followed by another and another. Oh my God, he thought, some allergen must have set him off: a woman's scent, a cleaning product, dust-mites in the air. It happened very rarely, but, once he was in the throes of an attack, the sneezing rollicked on inexorably, as he knew from bitter experience.

'Are you OK?' Penelope whispered, although her expression suggested more alarm than sympathy – doubtless due to the fact he was clenching his teeth and screwing up his face in a supreme effort to control himself. And the woman on his other side – an older one he'd barely noticed up till now – was actually recoiling.

'People with bad colds,' she hissed, 'should stay indoors and keep their germs to themselves.'

'It's *not* a—' he tried to say; the words drowned by an explosive sneeze, which developed into a whole deafening series.

Yvette paused in mid-sentence – indeed, the whole shocked room seemed to be drawing in its breath as his sneezes hit the ceiling. Blundering to his feet, he grabbed his coat and bag, and had to suffer the humiliation of walking the length of the room – ten miles, or so it felt. He was desperate to apologize, but the sneezing made it impossible to say a word. At last, he reached the door and, closing it behind him, he scorched along the corridor, past banqueting suites and displays of exotic plants, towards the hotel entrance.

Only out in the cold December air did the sneezing finally shudder to a stop. He stood stock-still a moment, experiencing a wave of mingled relief and regret. No way could he go back. People would only stare; maybe mock him openly. Shaken, he put on his coat, glancing up at the imposing façade, with its colonnades and sculpted frieze; the pampered window-boxes full of hothouse flowers. He had been deluding himself all evening; building castles in the air – as usual. Penelope belonged in this swanky world; he ostensibly didn't. *She* might be an orange-blossom parfait or amaretto croquant – hand-made, gift-wrapped, exquisitely adorned – but he was just plain Eric and couldn't afford to date that sort of woman. His fuel and phone bills had increased substantially of late, and fifteen per cent of his income went on child support each week. Besides, the sooner he accepted that it was totally unreasonable to expect to find a mate by Christmas – let alone one so voguish and urbane – the better for his sanity.

Indeed, why accept the Christmas hype at all? It *wasn't* the most important date in the calendar, but just a day like any other. And, if he stopped dwelling on himself and spared a thought instead for those who'd spend the day in cancer wards or war-zones, in debt, despair or gaol – he might realize his own good fortune. Anyway, there were always little comforts to assuage his petty pains. In fact, the newsagent, still open, on the corner could provide the very thing he craved.

Having walked into the shop, he slapped 50p on the counter and picked out a Milky Bar: superior by far to any jasmine-scented, Cointreau-soaked, excessively dark – and frankly *bitter* – chocolate.

chapter six

Eric woke with a start. The phone was shrilling only inches from his ear. Testily, he reached to pick it up. Roseanne, again, no doubt. The wretched woman apparently existed without sleep, having rung him in the early hours on seven separate occasions. Each time, he'd been abrasive, yet here she was, still in hot pursuit. Just his luck to find an avid female, at last, but one who happened to be barking mad.

'Hello,' he growled. He had planned a lie-in this morning, to make the most of the peace, since both his sets of noisy neighbours were away for a merciful week. Some lie-in! It was still pitch-dark outside.

'Dad, it's me!'

'Erica!' He leapt out of bed. Who cared about lost sleep, when his daughter was on the phone?

'Sorry to ring you at the crack of dawn, but I wanted to say happy Christmas.'

'Oh Lord, yes! It's Christmas Day.'

'Had you forgotten?'

'Sort of.'

'Dad, how could you? No one forgets Christmas.'

'Well, now you've phoned, it *feels* like Christmas.'

'It's still Christmas Eve over here. We've all been to a party, that's why I'm up so late.'

The 'all' induced a surge of jealousy. 'All' included Dwight. Even the fellow's name was an irritant: comic and pretentious both at once.

'I love your present, Dad. It's great!'

'What, you've opened it already?'

'Yeah, we had presents round the tree, just before we went out.'

So what had Dwight given her? A diamond-studded mobile? A child-sized Cadillac? Something far superior to *his* gift – that was beyond all doubt. He wrung the fellow's neck, picked up the dead body and dumped it in the Puget Sound.

'Has mine arrived yet?' she asked.

'No. I reckon it must have got lost in the system.' This was the first Christmas he had received no gift from either his wife or his daughter.

'It's bound to turn up sooner or later. And listen, Dad – good news! I think I'll be able to come and visit during the Easter holidays, if that's OK with you. Actually, they don't call it Easter hols over here. It's known as the Spring Break – so as not to upset non-Christians – and it's only five mingy days and doesn't include Easter anyway, not this year, at least. But Mum says I can stay with you for longer – you know, to make up for not coming in the summer. And the school doesn't seem to mind, so long as I take the work I'll miss and get on with it in England. So they're probably going to allow me a whole three weeks, which means I'll be with you for Easter. And my birthday falls the Thursday of that week, so we can spend the day together, if you like.'

Like? Bells were ringing from every London church; red carpets unrolling across the length and breadth of England. 'I'd love it, darling. What a treat! We'll celebrate in style. Thirteen's a real landmark.'

'It's scary, too, though, being in your teens.'

He nodded. 'I remember.' Worse for a girl, though. Periods and breasts. Erica had neither yet, according to Christine, and that fact had made him stupidly relieved. Womanhood brought dangers, and he wasn't there to protect her. 'You've really made my day! I thought I wasn't going to see you till July, so I'm thrilled you've brought it forward by three months. But what would you like to do when you're here? I'll start organizing it right away.'

'It's a bit early, don't you think, Dad? But what I will need is some help with schoolwork and stuff. I'm still not used to the different syllabus. I mean, we never did Spanish at my old school, or things like Social Studies.'

'Don't worry, we'll crack it between us!' He'd do a crash-course, if necessary, in both Spanish and Social Studies – whatever the latter might be. Anything to help her.

'But I don't want to talk about school. Tell me what you're doing for Christmas.'

He hesitated, detesting the thought of her pity. In fact, he had deliberately chosen to spend the day alone, turning down several invitations. He just didn't have the strength to face other people's intact and happy fami-

lies, when the loss of his own was still so new, so raw. And, although he
had offered his services to a couple of different charities, both had told
him he'd left it too late to volunteer. 'I've … planned a bike ride to the
City.'

'What, on your own?'

'Er, no.' It wasn't quite a lie – he was going with Samuel Pepys. He had
dreamed up the idea as the basis for a library project, later in the year,
which he'd base on the *Diaries* and one or two biographies. Today, he
planned to get the flavour of the man by visiting the places connected with
his life and work, including his favourite pub, St Olave's Church, the Navy
Office, Trinity House and—

'But what about Christmas dinner?'

'Oh … that's all organized.' A cheese roll and a can of beer would do him
very nicely – although he was touched by her concern about his welfare.

'Isn't it a bit cold for cycling?'

He peered up through the bars of the windows. Dawn was breaking;
pale, milky light now banishing the gloom. 'No. The forecast's pretty good.
A risk of showers later on, but mostly bright and sunny.'

'It's been snowing here.'

'I know.' He always checked the Seattle forecast, although if the conditions were too different from those in the UK, it only underlined the aching
distance between them.

'Dwight helped me make a snowman.'

Eric committed a second murder. Infuriating, the cocky way the bloke
kept resurrecting, despite the fact he'd been done to death so often.
'Darling,' he asked, as he disposed of the corpse, 'I wondered if you've
changed your mind about Skype? I know you're not keen, but it's just that
I'd like to *see* you. I mean, phone-calls are great, but a bit disembodied,
don't you think?'

'Thank goodness! I've got these hideous zits, so—'

'Zits?'

'Spots.'

'You've never had spots.'

'Well, I have now.'

Puberty, most likely. Or was her diet to blame? Perhaps Christine was so
besotted with Dwight she had stopped bothering to cook and they all
existed now on burgers, fries and Coke. He had actually set up Skype on
the suggestion of the lawyers, as another means of contact, but, after the

first few months, Erica objected that it made her feel embarrassed. Embarrassed by her own dad, for heaven's sake!

'Did *you* have spots, Dad, when you were my age?'

'Not that I remember.'

'Lucky thing!'

Not so lucky, actually, but no need to mention that. 'So how's your new friend?'

'Kelly, you mean? She's great! And she has her own horse, you know.'

'Yes, you said.' He had contemplated robbing a bank, so he could buy a horse for Erica – before Dwight did, of course. But he was bound to get it wrong; go for some hulking cob, instead of a pure-bred Arab.

'Sorry, Dad, I've got to go. Mum says it's past my bedtime. D'you want to speak to her?'

'Er, later, maybe.'

Silence. Had he sounded hostile? It was imperative, for Erica's sake, to appear on good terms with his ex. 'I'll give you another ring when I'm back,' he added, 'and talk to her then, OK?'

'OK. Goodnight, then – I mean, good morning. And happy Christmas, Dad – again!'

It *was* happy now, with this unexpected gift. The divorce settlement had stipulated one long summer visit only, mainly in her interests – not that she shared his fear of flying, just disliked the idea of jetting back and forth during every school vacation. Yet here was a bonus out of the blue: an unscheduled springtime visit.

As he went into the bathroom to shave, he began planning it already: a day-trip to Brighton, tickets for *Billy Elliot*, London Zoo, *Madame Tussauds*, – everywhere and anywhere. To hell with the cost. He would find the money somehow. He'd also paint the whole flat in her honour; choose her favourite colours, however wild and wacky; make it worthy of a soon-to-be thirteen-year-old.

Once washed and dressed, he stood at the kitchen worktop, eating a bowlful of cornflakes and savouring the thought that, in just three months, he would be laying breakfast properly – for two – he and Erica sitting chatting over scrambled eggs and bacon. Maybe he'd invite her former friends for tea; even arrange a birthday party; change his solitary existence – if only for a short spell – to one of chatter, clutter, company: all the things he missed. He had always relished his role at her parties: organizing games, lighting the candles on the cake, taking endless photos, to ensure that proper records were kept (non-existent in his own child-hood).

Perhaps he thought, his mind still racing, he ought to buy a kitten, to soften the blow of losing Charlie, who still had not returned, despite his continued searches and enquiries. It would be *her* kitten, of course, waiting to greet her every time she visited. As yet, he hadn't found the courage to break the news of Charlie's loss; indeed, could barely believe that the cat had gone for ever and might actually be dead. Charlie was his family – the one and only part of it he'd kept – and also tied in with the whole history of his marriage.

He found himself making for the living-room – and the wedding photo he still kept on his desk. All other photos of Christine had been unceremo-niously dumped, but this one was too precious to destroy. His marriage had seemed momentous at the time: to have someone of his own, at last; someone there for him, committed to him, faithful unto death. And to be part of a real family, with intriguing new in-laws, when, up till then, he was unable to lay claim to a single relative. His younger self stared back at him from the elaborate silver frame: his carroty curls ablaze with sheer excite-ment; a triumphant grin stretching from ear to ear; one protective arm around his new, miraculous wife.

As his eyes moved to her face, he felt his usual sense of outrage at how that plump and homely girl had become the fashionably thin virago who had dragged him through the divorce courts. It was all down to Kroszner-Merriott, of course. Only an American-owned company would have dictated such long work-hours; insisted on assertiveness training for all higher-grade employees, and demanded exacting standards in personal grooming – tooth-whitening, manicures, slimming regimes, ultra-modish clothes. Gradually Christine had metamorphosed into a tough, go-getting materialist, instead of the simple girl he had met on a peace march, twenty years before. And then had come the blow.

'I've outgrown you, Eric. I'm sorry to be brutal, but that's the simple truth. And I can no longer live with a man who won't drive a car, get on a plane, or even go for a swim. That's grounds for a divorce, you know, so my lawyer says. He reckons your refusal to travel, along with all your other fears, have caused serious rifts in the marriage and left me isolated.'

Isolated! Whilst all the time, unknown to him, she was bedding odious Dwight; the pair of them plotting to destroy the marriage by classing his humiliating terrors as 'unreasonable behaviour', in order to deflect attention from their own repellent carryings-on. *He* could have cited adultery, had he decided to fight back, as equally valid grounds for a divorce. But he loathed the thought of a split-up; hated fighting, on principle and, anyway, had no weapons in his armoury. How could a mere librarian, who had never been abroad and was even scared of water, for Christ's sake, compare with a Harvard-educated CEO, who owned two houses and a boat, and used aeroplanes like buses? Besides, he was shamefully aware that most people would take Christine's part and regard his fears as totally unreasonable, since his terror of driving or of any sort of travel, had seriously restricted their married life.

And now that she and Dwight had triumphed, things were even worse. Whatever he, the loser, might lay on for Erica would only lead to invidious comparisons. A brief pony-ride at Vauxhall City Farm didn't have quite the cachet as private lessons in horsemanship at some swish equestrian centre in the foothills of the Cascade Mountains. And could a paddle-boat on the pond in Battersea Park really bear comparison with sailing on a fifty-foot ketch around the San Juan Islands?

Determinedly, he switched on the TV, to distract himself from Dwight. It was too early to leave for his bike trip – still bitter-cold outside, although the sun was doing its brave best to thaw the heavy frost. Flicking from channel to channel, he found only jolly kids' stuff, with Christmas, of course, the smug and cosy centrepiece of almost every programme. Did they have to underline it: the happy family gatherings, the compulsory good cheer? The word 'merry' particularly galled him, with its connotations of fun-filled frolics. 'Merry Christmas be buggered!' he retorted, out loud, to one of the bubbly young presenters, preposterously dolled up in a gold-and-ruby crown.

Look, you were merry yourself a moment ago, he reminded himself, but his thoughts refused to budge from Christmas in Seattle: the new family, new 'father', the pile of presents, gorgeous house.

Suddenly, on impulse, he grabbed his coat and cycling helmet, his wallet and his keys, and banged his way up the chipped stone steps that led out of the flat. Chilly toes and chilblained fingers would be far less detrimental than another disgusting wallow in self-pity.

Nice, he mused, as he cycled along Pepys Street, to have a street named in one's honour. Parkhill Street – he tried it out, although in point of fact he had never liked his surname, mainly because it had been chosen in so arbitrary a fashion. Well, Eric Street, maybe – except the same objection held good. Both his names were totally ad hoc; neither selected with any care or deliberation.

As he turned left into Seething Lane, he all but skidded across the road, as a sudden cloudburst erupted, lashing him with hailstones as fierce and furious as gunshot. Although he tried to cycle on, soon his eyes were blinded, his anorak was soaked and his face stinging from the assault. Showers, they'd forecast, not a Noah's Flood. Dismounting from his bike, he dashed towards a doorway, only to find his refuge already occupied.

'Mind if I join you?' he asked the bloke stretched out on a piece of matting, a fierce-looking dog beside him and a half-empty bottle of Scotch.

The only answer was a warning growl from the dog. In a toss-up between death by rabies and death by drowning, Eric opted for the former, purely on the grounds that having been on his bike – or feet – since seven in the morning, he was in sore need of a rest.

'Good boy!' he said encouragingly, reaching out a friendly hand, only to withdraw it pretty rapidly as the creature made to snap his fingers off. He edged warily away, cramping his wet limbs into the small space at his disposal. The dog was now barking hysterically, although its owner took no notice; apparently dead to the world. Well, thought Eric, one way of enduring Christmas was to get well and truly smashed. He had seen several homeless folk already, during his morning in the City, who had stirred in him both pity at their plight and an awareness of his own good fortune. *He* had solid walls; they only sheets of cardboard; he worked in a job with purpose, structure, colleagues and a salary, while they had only empty days and the uncertain hope of handouts. He had engaged in conversation with one, earlier, who hadn't even realized it was Christmas and appeared to have forgotten his own name.

Yet, despite his brighter prospects, he did actually feel lonely – not that he would admit it to a soul. Loneliness was a sort of mental halitosis that gave off fumes of failure and only made the problem worse, in that it kept people away. As a child, he'd felt encased in a dark, rigid shell, like a walnut or brazil, where no one could get in to join him, nor let him out to light and air. Marriage had been the nutcracker that split apart the shell and released his juicy kernel – which made its ending all the worse, of course. He had lost not just his precious family but the two Ds that came along with it: 'Dad' and 'Darling'; both, once, a source of triumph. Now his Ds were rather different: divorce, depression, disillusion.

'Cut it out, for Christ's sake!' he muttered to himself, as he crouched listening to the fanfare of the rain. It was thundering on the pavement, hissing along the gutters, drowning out the faint but insistent rumbles of his stomach. Having forgotten to bring his cheese roll, he had eaten nothing since the cornflakes, and it was now getting on for half-past one. The poor sod on the matting seemed equally provisionless – well, apart from his liquid lunch, of course: a bottle of cider lined up beside the Scotch.

Peering out at the waterlogged street, his mind moved from tramps to Pepys once more. This morning he'd been concentrating on the great man's great achievements, but his small vanities were equally intriguing – the way he'd paid the equivalent of £1500 for a fashionable new wig, then had the gall to deny his wife her equally fashionable face-patches. And, although he'd finally relented, that was probably only due to guilt, having betrayed poor Mrs Pepys with a whole succession of willing widows, wives and serving-wenches and even with her own maid.

No, he must keep away from the subject of betrayal and, in fact, he'd had enough of Pepys for one day, so, as soon as the rain slackened even slightly, he decided to push off home. He could eat his cheese roll there, in the dry, rather than risk a mauling by the still hostile and probably hungry dog, who might fancy a chunk of his flesh for Christmas dinner. Well, at least dogs didn't figure on his long, shaming list of fears, and nor did spiders, crowds, thunder or the dark. It gave him a weird satisfaction to know he wasn't prey to every fear imaginable. Although secretly he suspected that anyone of reasonable intelligence *should* be pretty scared. Forget flying, swimming, driving – just being alive in an unjust and random world was a terrifying prospect. And, apart from the huge global fears – climate change, terrorist attacks, biological warfare, nuclear apocalypse – the sense of being trapped in one's own skin and by one's own peculiar temperament, enduring things that no one else could share or comprehend, could bring on panic in itself. He had often longed for a Siamese twin: someone part of him and fused with him, to ward off his alarm at being separate, adrift and insufficient in himself.

He'd learned long ago, however, to put on a façade; to play the role of a brave and self-reliant chap, at least in any company beyond that of his wife – ex-wife. It also helped to keep extremely busy. In fact, even now, as he emerged into the less punitive rain, he changed his mind about cycling straight back home and opted for a final stop at All Hallows By The Tower – the vantage-point from where Pepys had watched the Great Fire. Having chained his bike to the railings, he pushed open the glass doors, stopping in his tracks as he saw, not an empty church, but a lively Christmas party in full swing. A long line of tables had been set up in the south aisle and a good forty or fifty people were sitting eating dinner; a buzz of conversation filling the normally hushed space.

As he made to back away, a matron in a pink silky dress came dashing in pursuit. Oh, Lord, he thought, the vicar's wife, or some pillar of the parish, about to reprimand him for trespassing on a private function.

'Do stay for lunch,' the woman beamed, clasping his arm, so as to steer him back inside.

'I … I'm afraid I haven't been invited. I just happened to be passing and—'

'Everyone's invited. We lay on Christmas lunch here not just for any parishioners who have nowhere else to go, but for visitors and tourists and all members of God's family.'

Eric swallowed, being neither visitor nor tourist, and certainly not a member of God's family. His early experiences in life had led him, long ago, to discount, any idea of a merciful God. 'I actually live in London and I'm afraid I've never been a church-goer.' Not true. Church had been compulsory in childhood – and had put him off for life.

'You're welcome just the same. Do come in and sit down.'

'But I'm not dressed for Christmas lunch.' His shabby jeans and battered, soggy trainers seemed all the more unkempt in contrast to the woman's bandbox appearance; her nails varnished pink to match her dress; her hair set in stiff, meringue-like curls and a row of expensive pearls around her neck.

'Doesn't matter,' she said breezily. 'It's the soul underneath that counts.'

He doubted if his soul was any less remiss than his attire, considering that he was guilty of anger, envy and homicide; the latter committed on a daily basis. 'But I don't even have much money on me and—'

'Lunch is free,' she declared. 'If you want to make a small donation, that would be very welcome, but there's no obligation whatsoever.'

Before he could raise any further objections, Lady Bountiful swept him towards the tables and seated him between an old woman in a wheelchair and a small, sallow girl with spots and spectacles. 'Now, what's your name, dear?' she enquired, still hovering behind his chair.

'Eric,' he said, uneasily aware that several dozen pairs of eyes had turned in his direction, examining this new arrival who had interrupted their lunch.

'Eric,' she repeated. 'My dear departed father's name. Now, let me do the introductions. This is Vera, on your right, one of our very loyal parishioners. That's Lily, on your left, Malcolm opposite, and Svetlana next to Malcolm. Svetlana comes from the Ukraine.'

He tried to remember all the names, whilst also thanking various people who came bustling up to pour him wine, bring his starter, offer him a roll and butter, or wreathe him in friendly smiles. There seemed almost as many servers as guests – all parish worthies, no doubt, although who was he to cavil when he was being offered a free lunch? OK, the decorations were over the top: four huge, separate Christmas trees – two by the altar and two further down the nave – and the table set with a Christmassy cloth and lavishly adorned with candles, fir-sprigs, glittery coloured baubles, expensive-looking gold-foil crackers and a cheerful-looking reindeer as festive centrepiece. The lunch itself, however, looked too good to refuse. The other guests were already on their main course, tucking in to turkey, stuffing, chipolatas and the rest of the traditional fare. And he certainly couldn't complain about his starter: a healthy assortment of fresh orange segments, melon balls, and maraschino cherries.

'So where are you from?' Vera asked, smiling from her wheelchair.

'I live in Vauxhall just at present.'

'What, in one of those ritzy new flats they've just built along the river?'

'Er, no,' he mumbled, surprised anyone should think that a bloke with a hole in his sweater would live in a 'ritzy' residence.

'*I* live in bloody Tower Hamlets,' groused the bespectacled girl, Lily. 'And it's a complete and utter nightmare.'

'I'm sorry to hear that,' Eric said, with genuine sympathy – a mistake, he realized pretty soon, since it opened up the floodgates.

'Yeah, a year ago, I had a decent place, but the landlord evicted me – the bastard! Not that I was surprised. Life keeps beating me up – always has, always will. I went to see this fortune-teller – just last week it was – and she said, "Lily, I'm very rarely downbeat with my clients, but I'm afraid Fate's got it in for you." Well, I knew that, didn't I? Might as well have saved my fucking cash. I mean, it all goes back to childhood, so I didn't stand a chance. My dad pissed off with some fancy bitch, and my mother went to pieces and started doing drugs and—'

At least you *had* a mum and dad, Eric didn't say – couldn't say, in fact, since Lily was still ranting on.

'And I never got no education. How could I, with no Mum to take me to school? And, even when I did go, the teachers were so fucking useless I never learnt a thing. So now I'm struggling to do my GCSEs at the age of thirty-five and with everything against me – saddled with huge debts and living in a tip. The other students don't know they're born, with rich mummies and daddies, and not having to earn a living, or keep the fucking bailiffs from the door.'

Eric noticed Vera twitch at every 'fucking'. His usual role was to crack down on bad language if it arose in any readers' group or school visit to the library, but he could hardly take a stand in this particular setting. It also seemed a little callous to guzzle his fruit cocktail while a tale of woe was in progress, so he politely put his spoon down, while Lily moved on to the iniquities of the government (both central and local), the Council Tax, the water rates and the state of London Transport. Only when she paused for breath did he take his first small bite of melon, but then Vera began cross-questioning him again.

'Are you in work?' she demanded.

'Yes,' he said warily. Perhaps this lunch was restricted to the unemployed, the disabled and the dispossessed. As well as Vera in her wheelchair and Lily with her bailiffs, he spotted an old guy in dark glasses, with a white stick by his chair, and a woman with her arm in a plaster cast, sitting further down. He wished he'd thought to don a bandage or an eye-patch before joining these good folk. 'I'm a librarian,' he admitted.

'Books are dead,' Malcolm declared, making a cut-throat gesture. 'Gone the way of the horse-drawn carriage, the gas-lamp and the typewriter.'

'Isn't that a slight exaggeration?' Eric said – or tried to, before Lily started up again.

'Don't talk to me about books!' Lily cut in again. 'They said we'd get our textbooks free, then they had the bloody cheek to charge us an arm and a leg for stuff we don't even need. I blame the—'

'Look, can't you stop belly-aching?' another man reproved her: a rough-looking customer, with a stubbly chin and tattoos on his arms. 'People make their *own* luck, mate. I was given all this bullshit when I was a kid: "Keep your nose to the grindstone, boy", but that's a load of crap. I worked things out for myself, took a load of chances, even survived attempts on my life. But then I had what it took – very quick reactions and a left fist like a sledgehammer.'

'So you're suggesting I bash the fuckers up?'

All this talk of violence seemed extremely disrespectful in a church – and such a grand, impressive church, with its soaring roof, its pillars, its monuments and tombs. Eric imagined the marble statues recoiling in revulsion; the figures in the memorial brasses flinching at the language.

'A show of force is useful sometimes, Lily, so as to let them know who's boss.'

Eric left them to it and turned to the Ukrainian sitting next to Malcolm. 'And are *you* studying, or over here to work?'

The woman's answer was completely indecipherable. He should have learned Ukrainian, he thought, along with all the other tongues he had vowed to master, sometime.

'She doesn't speak a word of English,' Malcolm said, with a shrug. 'I've tried hard myself, and got nowhere. Mind you, we poor natives are outnumbered by the immigrants.'

Eric tensed, expecting a tide of prejudice to follow, but Malcolm simply took refuge in his wine, downing the whole glass in one protracted gulp. Eric sipped more slowly, knowing if he overdid the drinking, he might fall off his bike and land up in the gutter.

'More turkey, Vera?' a server asked, proffering a large silver platter.

'Eric hasn't had his first lot yet,' Malcolm pointed out.

'Oh dear,' the woman twittered. 'That won't do, now, will it? Have you any special dietary requirements, Eric? We have fruit and nuts for vegans, rice and beans for vegetarians, and strawberry mousse instead of Christmas pudding for anyone who can't eat gluten.'

'I eat anything,' he said hastily, before they brought him sunflower seeds or suchlike. He had enough of rice and beans at home, and how could anaemic strawberry mousse compare with full-blooded Christmas pudding? Although, in truth, his appetite was waning, surrounded as he was by bigots, bruisers and moaners – not to mention the beheaded bodies of John Fisher, Thomas More *et al*, whom he knew were buried here. And the tattooed bloke was giving off an unmistakable whiff of sweat – again hardly conducive to eating. Presumably washing was as foreign to him as turning the other cheek. He was also missing two front teeth – the result, no doubt, of his pugilism. In fact, Eric's own confidence was steadily increasing, since several other people were lacking full dentition, and quite a number far worse dressed than he was.

Giving silent thanks for his dentist, he speared a melon chunk on his fork, but, before he could consume it, an extremely ancient bloke shouted in a booming voice from further down the table, 'I know you, Eric, don't I?'

Eric regarded the fellow blankly. Never in his life had he set eyes on this chap, with his swarthy face and sparse wisps of silver hair.

'Yes, we were together at Dunkirk. I was injured pretty badly and you helped me into the boat. We were both up to our necks in water, I remember, but you were a true hero.'

Dunkirk was twenty-odd years before his birth, but apart from that mere detail, it seemed unlikely in the extreme that he would be playing such a starring role – rather yelling, choking and spluttering as he tried to save himself from drowning. Fortunately, he was spared from having to answer by a tall, suave man in a smart grey suit, with a blue shirt and matching tie.

'Good to meet you, Eric. My name's Alistair and I, for one, am an enthusiast for books. Although music is my first love. I'm an opera singer – or *was*.'

'Gosh!' said Eric, goggling. He had been to the opera only once, with Christine, and had felt completely overwhelmed by the sheer passion of the thing. The arias had left him rapt and reeling, as the tenor poured out the depths of his soul for a love that knew no bounds; a love that would go through torture; confront death, disaster, exile, for the sake of the beloved. Yet, in the interval, Christine had said dismissively, 'It's lust, that's all. He just wants to get her knickers off!'

'Yes,' Alistair continued, 'I could sight-read at the age of five, although I'd never had a music lesson – not one in all my childhood. Yet, at eight, I had a greater grasp of technique than some singers have at *thirty*-eight. I've sung in all the major opera houses – Covent Garden, the Met, La Scala … By the way, La Scala pay much more than Covent Garden. My fee over there's a minimum of eighty grand a night. Although, actually, I retired in my forties, because now I prefer to conduct.'

But why on earth, thought Eric, would someone so rich and famous be sitting down to dinner here, rather than gulping champagne and caviar with fawning impresarios?

'Mind you, most contemporary opera singers are useless. Some can't even sing in tune. In fact, I've been known to read the riot act and refuse to conduct a second performance unless the understudy takes over the role.'

Was the guy deluded, Eric wondered, like the old Dunkirk survivor? Perhaps this lunch was for the disabled *and* deluded, in which case he wasn't keen to stay too long. In fact, he gladly handed over his more or less untouched starter in return for a plate of lukewarm turkey. The sooner he finished his food, the sooner he could find some excuse to leave.

Two hours later, he was still trapped, captive, in his seat.

'There's no such thing as a free lunch,' the deacon had announced, once coffee had been served, along with chocolates and *pannetone*. 'So now all you good folks have to sing for your supper!'

Eric's first instinct had been to bolt, but the vicar and various other clergy were standing by the piano, and the whole bevy of helpers had come trooping from the kitchen, virtually blocking any chance of escape. And the singing had been interminable, since the deacon's little plan was to work through every nationality in turn, asking, first, any Spaniards present to stand up, then any French, Italians, Portuguese, Greeks, Americans, Japanese – and so on, ad infinitum. In each case, only two or three had risen to their feet – sometimes none at all – yet each national song was still faithfully thumped out: *O, Tannenbaum, Frère Jacques, Bog Sie Rodzi, Kimi ga Yo*, and many more he could neither pronounce nor spell. A pair of young girls from Hong Kong had protracted things still further by making a succession of false starts on a dozen different Cantonese songs, breaking down in giggles between each aborted attempt.

After that, it was the turn of the English and the whole bunch of them, him included, had valiantly worked their way through 'Away in a Manger', 'We Three Kings', 'O, Come all ye Faithful', 'When Shepherds Watched' and 'Joy to the World'. This last had seemed singularly inappropriate, since the longer the proceedings lasted, the less joy there seemed to be, although he was in the minority when it came to sheer hilarity. Many of the other guests were in various stages of inebriation, and were clapping, cheering, heckling, or trying out weird descants of their own. The opera singer, he noticed, maintained a strict silence throughout, claiming he had to save his voice for a performance of Tristan at Bayreuth.

Next had come a seemingly endless vote of thanks, not just to the cooks and bottle-washers, but to the butcher who'd donated the turkey, the baker who'd supplied the bread, some foreign lady from Wapping who had made the special stuffing, a guy with an allotment who'd grown the (organic) potatoes, and countless other kindly souls. Each benefactor had been applauded separately and uproariously, thus spinning out the proceedings even more. Privately, Eric had begun to wish that some local worthy had donated a bottle of Airwick, to counter the increasingly unpleasant smell arising from the tattooed bloke. He ought to be more compassionate –

presumably the chap was homeless and thus without a bathroom – but his usual forbearance was sorely strained at present. Nor did his stupid head-gear help. Vera had insisted, once the crackers had been pulled, that they all don their paper hats, and he'd been landed with a puce-pink number that clashed deplorably with his hair.

'And now,' declared the deacon, raising his voice above the hubbub, 'a real treat for us all! Two of our parishioners, both keen members of the Tideswell Players, are going to perform some scenes from *Scrooge*, accompanied by Sydney on the guitar. For those of you new to England, *Scrooge* is a famous novel by one of our best-known writers, the great Charles Dickens....'

Eric shifted in his seat. The last thing he needed was a lecture on Charles Dickens. Besides, he was dying for a pee and increasingly worried about the safety of his bike. Some passer-by might vandalize it, simply out of spite. However, if he got up now, while the 'actors' were making their way to the piano, and before the performance began, he might be able to sneak out.

Fortunately, Lily, all grudges forgotten, was in a clinch with a drunken Brazilian, Vera was blissfully snoozing, and the opera singer engaged in a long argument with Malcolm. Edging his chair back as quietly as possible, he slipped unobtrusively from his seat, muttering something about needing to find the gents.

'The toilet's the opposite way!' some helpful person called, as he began sloping off across the nave.

'Er, need to check my bike first,' he gabbled, breaking into a sprint as he approached the glass doors that led to safety and the street. He was through them in a trice but, in his haste to get away, collided with someone coming in – a woman carrying a cake. Before he knew what was happening, the woman tripped and all but fell; the cake flying from her grasp and smashing into pieces, as it landed upside-down on the flagstones.

Dumb with horror and embarrassment, he lent her a supporting arm, steadying her against the wall. Although incredibly relieved to find she wasn't hurt, he was in agonies of shame about the cake. A large, elaborate creation, judging by the wreckage, it was now a shattered mass of crumbs and cream. Yet still he couldn't speak, although for quite another reason. This was his *mother* – yes, in the flesh and leaning on his arm – the mother he had pictured throughout his motherless childhood, and correct in every detail, except not older than him but young and wildly sexy. He stared in rapturous disbelief at the firm yet cuddly figure, just this side of chubby, the glorious auburn hair (not carroty, like his, but still decidedly red, to prove that he'd inherited it), the sweet face, rosy cheeks.

'Damn!' she exclaimed. 'My cake's a gonner! And it took me the whole morning to make.'

Never before had he felt such crushing mortification. His first all-important encounter with his 'mother', and he had made a total hash of it. But a mother who made cakes couldn't be more perfect – and was just as he'd imagined her: cosy, homely, nurturing, as she sieved flour and beat eggs, yet at the same time lushly sensual.

'I … I'm horrified,' he stuttered out, at last. 'I mean, to be such a clumsy oaf. I could have injured you quite badly, and look at your poor cake! I just don't know what to say.' He *did* know: hold me, kiss me, put your lovely arms around me, never let me go.

'Don't worry,' she smiled. 'It's not an arm or a leg, as my sister always says.'

He gazed at her in still deeper admiration. A natural philosopher, as well as a beauty and a cook; someone who didn't bear grudges or make the slightest fuss, even when she had every right to do so. Suddenly remembering his paper hat, he snatched it off in discomfiture. Just his luck to meet the love of his life when he looked half-tramp, half-clown. The woman, though, seemed hardly to have noticed, absorbed as she was in her dilemma.

'The only problem is, I made the cake for Freda's hundredth birthday, which happens to be today. I expect you know her, don't you?'

'Er, no.'

'So you're not a parishioner?'

'No,' he said again, although the word on his lips was '*Yes!*' – yes to taking her back with him, yes to keeping her for ever in his flat, his home, his heart.

'She went down with a cold last night, so she's not actually here for the lunch. But Sydney promised to deliver the cake later on today, as long as I brought it here to the church. Thing is, I can't make another – not at this late stage. I'm due at my sister's for Christmas lunch and she lives down in Guildford, which is a good forty minutes' drive. The whole gang will be ravenous by now – my parents, grandparents, aunties, uncles, my other sisters and their families – and you can bet your bottom dollar they'll all be saying "Trust Mandy to be late!"'

Exactly the sort of family he had wanted all his life: a whole big, loving tribe of them, who would come together faithfully for every Christmas, Easter, birthday, anniversary. 'Look, you get off,' he urged. 'I'll clear up this mess and tell them it was all my fault.' Thank God the pair of them were in the porch, he thought, which meant no one had actually witnessed the collision. Otherwise streams of well-meaning helpers would have come rushing to Mandy's aid and this miraculous one-to-one encounter would never have occurred.

'But *you* were leaving, too. And you seemed in a tearing rush.'

'Not at all. I ...' The sentence petered out, as frantically he began to rethink his plan. If she hared off down to Guildford, he would never set eyes on her again. Somehow, he had to accompany her, or at least try to spend more time with her than this inadequate few minutes. 'Well, actually, I *am* in a bit of a hurry. I'm desperate to get to ...' He paused – somewhere on the way to Guildford, where she could drop him off – and somewhere a fair bit further than his flat. 'Kingston,' he declared. OK, it would mean abandoning his bike and he would be stuck in Kingston with no public transport over Christmas to take him back to London, but he would just have to beg a refuge from his former neighbours, Annabel and Ted. Who cared what they might think? Nothing had ever seemed more crucial than to stick close to this woman. Even lying didn't matter. In fact, lies were now essential. 'Trouble is, my car's been nicked.'

'Oh, Lord!' she said. 'How awful! But look, I can give you a lift. Kingston's directly on my route.'

'Are you sure it's not a nuisance?'

'Not at all. I'd be glad of the company. Though I don't even know your name.'

'Eric,' he said reluctantly, tempted to change it to something more romantic or heroic: Apollo, Tristan, Romeo, Alexander, Galahad ... And if only he could change his clothes, as well; wear a laurel-wreath, a toga, a fig-leaf or a halo – anything to catch her eye; keep him in her memory. *She* was dressed in a fuzzy mohair sweater, which lusciously defined her just-waiting-to-be-fondled breasts, and was as blue as her blue-speedwell eyes. A coat was slung across her shoulders – again adorably soft and fluffy, and which made him want to hold her close and stroke her. And her short grey skirt displayed her lovely legs; legs clad in patterned tights, but naked now as he ran his hands along them.

'Great to meet you, Eric. But excuse me a moment, will you? I'd better go and find Sydney and explain what's going on, and also say hello to a couple of other people here. One of my sisters lives close by, so this is her local parish. That's how I got roped in – to make the cake, I mean.'

'Is she here?' he asked anxiously, refusing to have an inconvenient sister cramping his style on the journey down to Kingston.

'No. She went to Guildford last night – sensible girl! I always leave things to the last minute.'

Thank God, he thought – and yes, perhaps there *was* a God; a benevolent God who had arranged this miraculous meeting. Although the lunch itself had been a trifle disappointing – tasteless, tepid and overcooked – he no longer cared a jot, since he was now tucking into Mandy: nibbling on her succulent flesh, sucking up her juices, savouring each delicious crumb as he rolled her round his mouth.

'I mean, I should have made that cake last week, not on Christmas morning. And I rushed in here at a speed of knots, knowing I was frightfully late, so the whole thing's really my fault.'

'No, it's *my* fault. And I'll replace the cake, of course – that goes without saying. I'm afraid it won't be home-made, but I'll buy the nicest one I can find and deliver it in person to this Freda lady, if that would help at all.'

She laughed – the most wondrous sound he had ever heard.

'Don't worry. I make cakes for a living, so one more's not going to bother me.'

Already, he was biting into feather-light sponge and tooth-tinglingly sweet icing; a whoosh of jam and butter-cream ravishing his tongue. All those birthdays when no one had made him a cake were being gloriously rectified at this very moment, as she baked cake after cake after cake – yes, right there in the porch.

'Look, we'd better make a move, Eric. It's freezing out here and you don't seem to have a coat. Be an angel, could you, and see if you can find a shovel or a broom or something, and maybe a bucket of water. We don't want someone coming in and slipping on all this cream. And, while you're doing that, I'll put Sydney in the picture, and then we'll get off, OK?'

'OK,' he said – except he was singing it, declaiming it, with all the ardour and romantic fire of every impassioned tenor in Bayreuth, Covent Garden, La Scala and the Met.

chapter seven

'Right, Kath, we'll start here in Biography. What we need to do is weed out any stock that's tatty, dirty, or falling apart. For instance …' Eric checked through a few volumes, then withdrew a book from the shelf. 'This life of Mary Wollstonecraft.' He tensed at the author's first name: Amanda. Five whole days and still Mandy hadn't rung. Perhaps she was *dead*, he thought, with horror; mangled in a car-crash, once she'd dropped him off at Kingston and continued down the motorway.

'But that's not tatty or dirty.' Kath's voice was all but drowned by the shrilling siren of the ambulance as it sped towards the wreckage.

'It's not in prime condition, though.'

'Still, seems a shame to throw it out.'

He had felt the same at her age, reluctant to dispose of any book whatever. In his childhood, books had been precious passports to all the things he craved: happy, cosy families, seaside holidays, pet dogs and cats, visits to doting relatives. And, later, as an adult who avoided danger and had never been abroad, he valued books for their power to whisk him to every country in the world, or let him live vicariously as deep-sea diver, Arctic explorer, parachutist, mountaineer.

'Don't worry, Kath, many of the books we discard end up in good homes. Some are sent to other libraries and some to the prison book club. And the prisoners often pass them on to other men on their wing, or to visiting friends and family, who, in their turn, may give them to someone else, so they keep having a new lease of life.' He liked to think of all those readers bringing their own perspective to each book; gaining something unique from it; interpreting it in different ways. 'And we're planning a big book-sale in February or March, with all the other branches in the borough, which will take care of some of the weeded stock. Now, I'd like you to go along this shelf, Kath, examine the condition of each book and tell me whether you think it should go or stay.'

He was grateful that the library was uncharacteristically quiet, since he couldn't really concentrate – well, only on Mandy and why she hadn't phoned. Tomorrow was New Year's Eve: the day she was meant to be delivering his made-to-order cake. Yet he hadn't even given her the details: what sort of cake he wanted, its size and style and type of decoration. Had she *known* that he was lying; that the big bash at his flat was a total fabrication; the cake a mere device to ensure he stayed in touch with her?

'This one's slightly grubby, but the dirt's only on the cover, so should it go or stay?'

Reluctantly, he took the book from Kath, longing to be alone, at home, so that he could fix his entire attention on the only thing that mattered in his life. Except he'd been doing that the whole of yesterday; spent an exhausting Sunday veering from dizzy hope, every time the phone rang, to deep despair when it was some odd friend and not the woman he adored.

Was he raving mad? How could he adore a woman he'd met for precisely fifty-seven minutes? For all he knew, she might be gay or married. She hadn't worn a ring, though, nor made mention of a partner. But suppose she was a schemer or a cheat, or even a boozer or a druggie. 'No!' some voice inside him screamed. 'She's flawless, perfect, exemplary in every way.'

He forced himself to examine the book, although the picture on the jacket began changing before his very eyes to that of a gorgeous female with Titian hair and heavenly blue eyes. 'We'll keep it, Kath,' he stated, clinging on to it protectively.

If only he'd taken her phone-number, but he'd been so incredibly nervous in the car, they were fast approaching Kingston before he'd plucked up courage to trot out his string of lies: how New Year's Eve just happened to be the fortieth birthday of one of his close friends, so he'd decided to surprise him with a party and a cake. And, although she'd expressed immediate interest, she was in a tearing rush by then, and had simply jotted down his number, promised to phone him to discuss it, and accelerated off with barely a goodbye.

Kath was studying another tome, frowning in indecision. 'What about this Life of Wordsworth? I decided it should go, but I feel distinctly nervous chucking things that maybe ought to stay.'

'Don't worry, this is just a trial run. We won't rely on your judgement until you've had a bit more practice. Your first instinct was correct, though. It *is* distinctly tatty, so clearly you're getting the hang of it.'

He'd had to lie to Ted and Annabel, as well; forced to throw himself on the mercy of a pair of aged neighbours he hadn't seen for almost a year, and somehow explain the peculiarity of turning up on Christmas Day unannounced and uninvited. And, because no trains were running until December 27, he'd remained captive there, with them and their in-laws, enduring what seemed an eternity of tedium. And all for the sake of a woman who had broken her promise, or forgotten him entirely.

He made a supreme effort to return to his professional role, fearing Kath would notice his extraordinary state of mind. The way he felt at present, all books seemed dispensable. Indeed, he would gladly sacrifice the rarest writings in the world: the few existing (priceless) copies of Herodotus and Aristotle, Tacitus and Pliny, along with all the precious manuscripts in every leading library in the world – burn them to a cinder, without the slightest qualm, in return for one brief phone-call from his love.

'Right,' he said, trying to adopt an authoritative tone, 'let's start putting all the weeded books in a big pile on the floor here, and we'll pack them into boxes, once we've removed the labels and the bar-codes. I'll show you how to do that later on.'

Maybe she had *lost* his number. A small scrap of paper could easily be mislaid, or might have even blown away as she opened the car door at Guildford and dashed in to see her family.

'And another thing we need to check is how often the book's been taken out. If there are hardly any date-stamps on the label in the front, we get rid of it, OK?'

Perhaps she *had* rung – in just the last half-hour. The very thought filled him with such joy, he wanted to go down on his knees and worship her, adore her. Well, he'd wanted that from the first second they had met and, throughout the too-brief car journey, his mind had woven erotic fantasies: they were on honeymoon in a secluded little love-nest and he was slipping off her clothes; running a slow hand from her delicately white throat to her deliciously pink toes. Or making love on some exotic beach; the December sleet changed magically to tropical sun; her limbs enticingly warm as they threshed against his own. In point of fact, his spoilsport voice had been droning on in stilted fashion about the weather and the cost of housing; too shy to express the sentiments brimming in his heart.

'This one's been borrowed only twice since last December, so does that mean—?'

He was almost surprised to see Kath still standing there. Since Christmas Day, only Mandy existed. 'I'd suggest, as a rough rule of thumb, that if it's not been taken out for a year or more, then no point keeping it. So we'll give this one a reprieve for now and reassess it later. But can you carry on alone, Kath? There's something I need to check.'

His mobile, actually. Again he gave thanks that the library was near-empty, due partly to the appalling weather and partly to the date – many people still away for Christmas or New Year. It meant he could find a secluded corner and switch his mobile on, without being summoned by a customer, or sought out by some member of staff. However, his brief moment of elation gave way to deepest gloom when he discovered not a single text or message. Perhaps she'd picked up bad vibes from him – felt *he* was an alcoholic, a schemer and a cheat. Dead right. He would have had booze on his breath, after that bibulous Christmas lunch, and he *had* been lying through his teeth. He'd even told her his car had been stolen, when he'd never possessed a car in his life, and – worse – was too scared to drive. If she ever got to know that he'd gone to the church by bike (a bike he'd retrieved unscathed, thank God, after its long sojourn outside All Hallows), she would assume he was a pathological liar. She'd probably written him off already as seriously neurotic; detecting from his mere tone of voice that he was someone best avoided. But then why would she have agreed to make the cake at all – and agreed enthusiastically? 'I'd love to do it, Eric. And I'll really go to town and make something extra-special for your friend.'

He wandered over to the window and stared at his reflection in the pane. Today he was reasonably well dressed, but the day they met he must have looked a wreck, in his old cycling clothes and with his hair sticking up on end. Perhaps Mandy didn't quite believe that a scruff like him could afford a made-to-order cake. He'd had no idea what they cost, but quite a tidy sum, he'd guess. In fact, the more he reflected on their meeting, the more he realized that he'd obviously come over as a tongue-tied, clumsy oaf – the way he'd cannoned into her, destroying Freda's cake; then bored her rigid all the way to Kingston because he didn't dare reveal his genuine feelings. Could he really blame her if she decided she didn't want his custom? She was bound to have dozens of cake-orders from existing (reputable) clients, without taking on another from some bloke who seemed suspicious in the extreme? He wasn't a practised liar – that was the whole problem – so he'd tied himself in knots trying to invent a story that had clearly sounded bogus. She must have seen through him from the start, but, being kind, had simply played along, rather than call his bluff.

Angrily, he switched his mobile off again. She *wasn't* going to ring, so he might at least save the day by doing something positive. Today he had the chance, for once, to give Kath some extra training, so he would spend another hour with her, until it was time to relieve Helen at the desk. Then, at half-past five, he would lock up and go home; kill the evening watching something senseless on the box, which at least would keep his mind off Mandy. Because it was patently ridiculous to waste another second dreaming of a woman so far beyond his reach.

'Kath, I hope I'm not overloading you?'

'Not at all,' Kath replied. 'It's been very helpful, actually.'

'Well, I think that's it for now, unless there's anything you'd like to ask.'

'Yes – about the Dewey Decimal system. Harriet explained it quite some time ago, but I still haven't got it straight, and I wondered if I could have a list of all the different numbers and exactly what they relate to.'

'No problem. I'll sort that out immediately.'

He was reminded of his own delight, as a greenhorn library assistant, in discovering the Dewey system, in which every piece of information, from almanacs and astrophysics to zoology and Zoroastrianism could be slotted into its own specific category; the whole classification process securely based on step-by-step logic, and infinitely expandable. Even as far back as then, he was aware it had its critics – it was too Christian-centric, rigid and male-oriented – but he still found its regularity appealing, especially contrasted with his own chaotic childhood, where everything was random and haphazard. At a stroke, order had been established in at least one section of the world, and a consoling sense of harmony now surrounded him at work.

As he strode to the computer, to print out the list of categories, he stopped dead in his tracks. There, standing at the enquiry desk, was – no, he must be fantasizing, even hallucinating, for Christ's sake. She *couldn't* be here. She had dismissed him as a liar and no-hoper; vowed to keep her distance. Besides, he hadn't even told her where he worked.

'Eric!' she exclaimed, suddenly catching sight of him and racing over; her face wreathed in a gigantic smile. 'Thank heavens I've found you – and in the nick of time.'

chapter eight

Emerging into the murky night, Eric ran through the directions in his head: turn right out of the tube, walk on past the Gallery pub and a little Internet café, until you reach the church on the corner, then turn left into St George's Square. The church spire was already looming into view, a dark silhouette against the naked trees, and he fought a sudden longing to clamber to the very top and shout his news to the whole astounded world: 'She *did* phone – a dozen times – hadn't forgotten me at all; just jotted down my number wrong. And she even went to enormous trouble discovering where I worked.'

In fact, perhaps he ought to pop in to the church and pour out thanks to God – the God he didn't believe in. Yet, wasn't it little short of miraculous that he should actually be spending New Year's Eve with Mandy, and was now only minutes from her flat? Another minor miracle was the fact she lived so close: just one stop on the tube from him – although even if he'd had to travel to John O'Groats or Land's End, he would have gone there willingly; indeed, on his knees, or barefoot, like ardent pilgrims in the past, enduring any hardship for the sake of the beloved.

The wooden doors of the church stood open, as if urging him to enter. However, the inner glass door proved difficult to manoeuvre, encumbered as he was by a bottle of champagne, a bouquet of flowers and a huge box of Belgian chocolates. Had he gone overboard, he wondered, with sudden fierce anxiety? He didn't want to seem too keen, as if he were buying his way to her heart. Besides, she might be a teetotaller, or allergic to pollen, or on a slimming diet – or all three at once, if his recent run of good luck should give out.

He was suddenly aware of an officious looking woman, just inside the church, eying him suspiciously through the glass panel of the door.

'Can I help you?' she asked curtly, opening the door a crack. 'We're just about to close.'

On impulse, he stepped towards her and pushed the elaborate bouquet into her arms. It was definitely over-the-top – roses and Madonna lilies, set off with silvery foliage and clouds of white blossomy stuff, and tied with scarlet ribbon – and thus surely inappropriate when he and Mandy barely knew each other. 'Could you give these to the vicar?' he asked, blushing at his eccentric behaviour.

'With pleasure,' the woman purred – chastened now, even smarmy. 'What beautiful flowers! Who shall I say they're from?'

'Er, just … a grateful parishioner.'

Why did he keep lying? Far from being a parishioner, he had never seen this church in his life. Despite his lofty principles about not distorting the truth (except regarding his origins, of course), he now seemed mired in deception. He had even lied to Mandy again, spinning her a story about the birthday-boy having gone down with a stomach-bug, which meant cancelling the party and, unfortunately, the cake. Although lies, he'd found, could reap a precious harvest. She had seemed so genuinely sorry that his plans had been disrupted and that he'd been forced to put off all the guests at embarrassingly short notice, she'd invited him to spend New Year's Eve at *her* place.

'I'm at a loose end, too,' she'd said; a phrase which made him tingle with elation. A loose end, for heaven's sake! And he'd imagined swarms of lovers fighting for the privilege of being in her company.

'Well, many thanks, my dear. Father John will be delighted.'

Quickly he backed away from the church, feeling a total impostor, then stood in the light of a lamp-post, checking his watch for at least the twentieth time. Mandy had said eight o'clock and it was still only quarter to – although it would be wonderfully exciting to turn up early and find her stepping naked from the shower.

However, hardly had he proceeded fifty yards, when he began worrying about having ditched the flowers. A bouquet fit for a prima donna (which had all but cleaned him out) was now in the hands of some undeserving priest. Besides, looking mean was surely worse than seeming over-eager. Could he retrieve the flowers, by some means, fair or foul – maybe pretend he had dementia and had delivered them to the wrong location? Except if he were suffering memory-loss, how would he *know* it was wrong? No – best to simply regard the loss as spiritual insurance. The vicar was bound to pray for the 'grateful parishioner' and, since a successful outcome to his Mandy-mission was desperately important, he must be grateful for any source of help, celestial or otherwise.

Wandering on at a snail's pace, he was hit by a new anxiety as he peered across the railings at elegant St George's Square; a milieu distinctly more salubrious than his own shabby Vauxhall street. If she was used to such gentility, how could he invite her back, to slum it in his flat? Except there might never *be* a second date. Perhaps she had simply taken pity on him, or was alone on New Year's Eve only because her partner had to work. The wretched bloke was bound be an airline pilot, or celebrity chef, or distinguished surgeon – someone far more glamorous than him.

It was all he could do not to race back to the church and give the vicar the chocolates and champagne, as well, to ensure he prayed all night, all week. Or should he fall to his knees himself – here in the puddled street – and call on every Power Above to make Mandy fall in love with him – even better, to lure him to her bed?

No, he couldn't kneel. His new trousers were too pricey to spoil, as well as far too tight. He'd expended huge amounts of time trying to decide on his image: world-class athlete, City Banker, high fashion, arty Bohemian? Since the first three were impossible, he'd finally opted for smart casual, with just a hint of sexpot; spent a fortune on the trousers and even lashed out on some aftershave, purely on the strength of its name: 'Dark Temptation'. Which was patently ridiculous. How could a carrot-top be sexy, however tight his trews? He should have bought a wig, but, knowing his luck, it was bound to slip off at the crucial moment, maybe just as he was bending over to kiss her glorious pussy.

He shivered in the sharp December wind. It was crazy being out without a coat, but both his shabby mac and nerdy anorak would have ruined the stylish effect that had demanded so much effort. And style was on his mind at present, as he gazed up at the white-stuccoed façades, with their grandly columned porticos and elaborately carved balconies, and at the gracious plane trees preening in the square. The only vegetation in *his* street was the odd dandelion skulking by a fence, or blade of grass poking up between cracked paving stones. He would have to move – immediately! Although no pad within his price-range would be worthy of this woman. Even Buckingham Palace would fail to make the grade.

He took in a deep breath, trying to calm his nerves. If he continued in this vein, he'd be exhausted by 9.30 and never make it through the midnight celebrations. In truth, he was bushed already, having got up a 4 a.m., too overwrought to sleep. And he'd been rushing out all day on one errand or another – to suss out the best chocolates in South London, or track down hothouse flowers, or buy underpants and Durex. The latter two had caused further storms of indecision: did Mandy prefer boxer shorts or Y-fronts, and should he settle for plain condoms, or go for something flavoured, coloured or ribbed?

'Look, mate,' he told himself, 'she invited you for a friendly drink, not to run through the Karma Sutra and back, so lower your expectations, OK?'

However, as he approached number 102 and stood, finger poised to ring the bell of the top flat, his agitation crescendoed to an unbearable degree. This was the woman he had dreamed of all his life – an almost exact replica of the mother/mistress/goddess he had created in his fantasies since the age of nine or ten. Even Christine hadn't succeeding in matching that ideal. However thrilled he'd been to find a wife, discover love, establish a real family and so become a normal member of the human race, she hadn't possessed those mind-blowing qualities, which he'd presumed, till just this Christmas, lay only in the realm of fantasy.

Shifting from foot to foot, he ran through his opening lines. Since yesterday, he'd been practising what to say; determined not to sound a dullard, this time, but someone sparky, lively, deep. And perhaps he should lower his voice to a sexy growl; establish a seductive mood from the start. 'Mandy' – he tried it out, but merely sounded as if he were going down with a cold. '*Mandy*!' Worse still: angry now, rather than erotic.

Two minutes to eight. Perhaps he was still too early. Wouldn't a cool sort of bloke turn up casually late? Drifting away from the porch, he forced himself to walk up and down for what seemed like several aeons, becoming still more nervous, not to mention numb. If only there were more people about, to make him feel less isolated. Surely, on New Year's Eve, the streets should be packed with revellers – party-goers on their way to night-spots – yet the square seemed near-deserted. The only living thing in sight was a small black cat, slinking between the railings, but it brought back such sad memories of Charlie, he felt a lump rise to his throat. Charlie had always hated fireworks, so how would she manage without him there to calm her, and without the half a Valium he always used to slip her if the racket got too deafening?

He felt sorry for *all* creatures petrified by noises that must sound close to gunfire – pigeons, foxes, rabbits, rats, cowering in abject terror as their safe, dark world burst apart in bomb-blasts. Erica even used to worry about slugs and snails and worms, and had asked him once if they, too, should have Valium sprinkled on the soil. Imagining his beloved daughter so far away – and with her loathsome stepfather – caused him even more distress, but he made a valiant effort to fix his attention on his watch, rather than sail across the tempest-tossed Atlantic and murder Dwight again.

He peered closely at the second-hand until, at exactly quarter-past, he returned to number 102, and moved a chilblained finger towards the bell.

The hand faltered. He was *too* late now; might well seem rude, disorganized. Wouldn't it be better simply to go home? He could always rent a DVD and watch it with a takeaway – less stressful altogether than trying to play Casanova. In fact, the safety of his flat seemed increasingly appealing as he stood in the lonely street; his hair mussed by the bad-tempered wind, and his cheeks probably flushed (unflatteringly) from cold and terror mixed. 'Dark Temptation'. How pathetic! Orange Crush would be nearer the mark.

He turned on his heel and began walking back the way he'd come, having lost his nerve entirely. The whole thing meant so much that even partial failure would cast him into utter desolation. Suppose he fell down on the job: became all fingers and thumbs when he tried to unhook her bra, or failed to whip on a condom at precisely the right moment, or shot his bolt in five seconds flat, rather than holding on for seven hours, as Tantric Masters did. He'd just have to invent more lies: he'd caught his friend's bug; a colleague had broken her leg and he had to take her to hospital; *he* had broken his leg.

Half-convinced by his own falsehood, he hobbled along the shadowy street, with a pronounced and painful limp, although experiencing profound relief at being able to skulk at home, instead of having to dazzle and perform. However, he wouldn't scoff the chocolates or guzzle the champagne, but give them to the poor young fellow he'd seen huddled in a doorway near the tube. That would be his good deed for the day; his way of expressing gratitude for being spared humiliation in the sack. Then he'd watch his DVD, eat his Kentucky Fried, be in bed by midnight and let the whole razzmatazz of New Year's Eve rampage on without him.

'Eric! Eric! I'm so *sorry*.'

He stopped dead in his tracks, staring in disbelief. A woman was tearing towards him – a gorgeous creature, with auburn hair, a perfect figure and dressed in a cuddly coat. Mandy! In the flesh.

'You'd given me up. I don't blame you – I'm terribly late. I really do apologize. And you're limping, I saw. Have you hurt your leg?'

Wordlessly, he shook his head, unable to do anything but gaze at her in wonder.

'You should have come in the car if you're hurt. Oh, no, it was stolen, wasn't it? Gosh, poor you!'

His non-existent car – he'd forgotten it entirely. Guilt was now added to incredulity and joy.

'What *is* the time? I've lost my watch, though that's no excuse at all. You see, they needed me to help out in the café, but I'd no idea how long I'd have to be there. Still, never mind all that. I'm just so sorry you've been hanging around. I presume you tried my bell and got no answer, and so came to find shelter in the church?'

If he said 'yes', it would be another lie. In any case, he was experiencing such a turmoil of emotions, speech had temporarily deserted him.

'Except, of course, the church is shut, which means you're probably frozen stiff.'

Again, he shook his head; all the romantic, brilliant phrases he'd been practising for hours now reduced to silent gestures. And, far from being frozen stiff, he was boiling hot from sheer excitement. Coats were quite superfluous when Mandy was around. 'Th … These are for you,' he managed to stammer out, at last, handing over the chocolates and the wine.

'Oh, Eric, you *shouldn't*! Real champagne – how fab! And what's this?' she asked, fumbling in the gold and scarlet carrier. 'Wow! These are my absolute top favourite choccies. How on earth did you know?'

He gave a deprecating shrug, cursing his timidity. If only he were Shakespeare or John Donne; instant sonnets tripping off his tongue.

'Anyway, let's get out of the wind and open this champagne in my nice, warm, cosy flat. Here, you carry it for now, then I can take your arm.'

Oh, yes, he implored her soundlessly, take my arm, my heart, my love, my life, take everything I have.

chapter nine

'It's just five minutes to midnight, Eric. Let me give you a top-up, so we can drink a toast to each other.'

Could he be hearing right? She was drinking to him – already! With a beatific smile, he watched the bubbles sing into his glass. She, too, had bought champagne, so they were now on the second bottle. And the wine had unleashed his tongue, so that he had actually waxed lyrical all evening; even made her laugh; been something of a hit, in short.

'D'you mind if I turn on the telly?' she asked. 'I love watching the fire-works and hearing Big Ben boom out. It's so exciting, don't you think?'

Even more exciting was being in her pad – a flat every bit as colourful as she was. Christine had favoured plain white walls and a conventional style of furnishing, but Mandy's walls were wild: magenta here in the sitting-room; midnight blue in the bedroom; aubergine in her tiny, tingly kitchen. And, everywhere he looked, were rugs and cushions in striking shades; papier-mâché sculptures; silk and velvet flowers, and a wealth of unusual objects crowding every shelf and surface. Yet the overall effect was not one of clash or clutter, but of bold imagination, dazzling artistry.

'Right. All set.'

As she joined him on the sofa, he dared to put his arm around her, although prepared for her to edge away. Instead, she snuggled close; her milk-white mohair sweater soft against his chest; her fiery hair tickling on his neck; her musky scent inflaming him, so that he had physically to restrain himself. His hand yearned to trace the V-neck of her sweater; stray further down that enticing, teasing cleavage, until it cupped her luscious breasts. But all that would have to wait until the firework display was over. If she wanted to watch the box, who was he to stop her, when she'd cooked him an exquisite meal and waited on him hand and foot – treated him like a VIP, in fact? He'd had to keep pinching himself, to ensure he wasn't dreaming and about to wake up in his lonely bed, cold and disillusioned.

As the chimes of midnight began booming out on-screen, he contented himself with clasping her hand; his fingers pressing just a fraction tighter with each majestic b-o-n-g. The dizzy crowd in Trafalgar Square were joining in the countdown; Mandy, too, calling out each number, like an excited child, up way past its bedtime.

'Ten, nine, eight, seven ...'

He, too, was soon engulfed in all the on-screen drama. Staid, square-shouldered Big Ben stood unshaken, like a stern school prefect, as the tempestuous sky behind it went into madcap mode; rent apart with electric jolts of colour: emerald-blue, pink-purple, scarlet-gold. A whole brouhaha of rockets was whooshing up, up, up; exploding into bursts of shooting stars, and the entire river seemed alight, as another squall of fireworks erupted from a flotilla of boats; the inky water metamorphosing into a tidal wave of shimmering shot-silk. All the distinctions between up and down, liquid/solid, dark and light were blurring and dissolving as once-substantial buildings appeared to disintegrate into skittish showers of sparks, only to rebuild themselves in wild colour-combinations. Fire-trails blazed and faded in an eerie purple sky, whilst effervescent searchlights swooped in soaring arcs, and yet more pyrotechnics flung their whooping wizardry across the frenzied scene.

'Five, four, three ...' Mandy carolled, then, all at once, she sat up straighter, raised her glass, touched it to his and gazed deep into his eyes. He had never understood the genuine thrill of eye-contact until this actual moment, when the rapturous blue of *her* eyes seemed to laser into his. It was so magical, so mesmerizing, he barely heard the cries of 'Happy New Year!' shrilling from the screen; hardly saw her put her glass down and gently wrest his from his hand. The only thing in his consciousness was her sensuous, eager, parted lips, moving towards his own.

He held her close, surrendering to the most ardent kiss in the history of the world. And, as their tongues communicated, the whole of London began applauding, cheering, whooping; hosannas and hallelujahs rising on all sides, as a sensational New Year burst, brilliant, into life.

He opened his eyes, fazed by the deep-blue walls and by the fierce morning light streaming through the curtains. His gloomy flat was far less generous in its light-effects. Then, suddenly, he remembered where he was, and the utter shame of the previous night replayed itself in humiliating detail. He lay back again, with a groan of horror, pulling the sheet right across his head. Mandy was no longer there in bed with him. He had no idea when she'd got up, but he understood entirely her wish to remove herself from a bloke who couldn't perform – a damp squib, a faulty rocket, a burnt-out Catherine-wheel. He could blame it on the booze, of course, or on his stupid nerves, but what use were excuses? He'd better get the hell out, so as not to have to face her – tricky, when his clothes were in the sitting-room. His only option was to climb out of the window and shin down the front of the building, all five floors – stark naked.

Instead, he sat up on his elbow and listened through the wall. Not a sound. Maybe she'd gone out; arranged to see her celebrity chef, or her surgeon, or the pilot; each a handsome hunk, no doubt, who could remain stiff all day, all night.

Well, if she'd left the flat, at least the coast was clear. Hastily, he crept out of bed and cocked an ear at the door. Still total silence – thank God! Darting into the sitting-room, he grabbed his clothes, which were still lying in a pathetic heap where he had ripped them off last night in his haste to make endless love.

Endless – how ironical was that? Yesterday, he'd been scared he might come in five seconds flat, but worse by far not to come at all, and when Mandy was all but begging for it. He skulked back to the bedroom and began dragging on the tight, expensive trousers, which mocked him openly. 'So you planned to be a sexpot. What a hoot!'

Just as he was buckling his belt, he heard footsteps right outside and froze in guilty embarrassment. Perhaps she had brought her lover back with her: some great hulking stud, with equipment to match. He tried to conceal his own puny naked chest as the door burst open and in walked Mandy – alone, and in her coat.

'Eric, my love, why are you getting dressed? I thought we'd have breakfast in bed. I've just been out to buy some croissants. Nearly all the shops were shut, but – look – success!'

As she held out the package, he fought a sense of dizzy disbelief. She had called him 'my love' – or had he misheard? And she wanted breakfast in bed with him – a loser, a non-starter, a complete and utter dud!

'Would you like coffee or hot chocolate? My hot chocolate's rather special, though I sez it myself – made with cream and melted marshmallows.'

'Sounds wonderful.'

And she was still waiting on him, for heaven's sake! But *why*? True he had kissed her passionately last night, stroked every inch of her body, but it was clear she had wanted more. In fact, she'd made scarcely any effort to hide her disappointment and frustration. And that, of course, had only made things worse. The more *she* wanted it – *he* wanted it – the more feverishly limp he'd become: a melted marshmallow himself, in truth. Finally they had given up and gone to bed, to sleep. Not that he had slept – at least not until 4 a.m. – but had tossed and turned, endlessly rehearsing the fiasco, and horrified that he should be lying close to a luscious, naked female and still not have a hard-on.

'Won't be long!' she said, scooting towards the door. 'Why don't you get back into bed?'

So she planned a second act. The very thought made his former terror swoop back in a quivering rush. One failure might be overlooked; two would spell disaster. He saw his future stretching hopelessly ahead: Mandy-less and sexless; a eunuch like Gerard Manley Hopkins.

And he seemed incapable of making even the smallest decision: should he go or stay; undress or finish dressing; invent some reason why he had to bolt back home? He was so agitated he was perspiring from sheer nerves. God! Suppose he began to *smell*? Whatever else, he'd better have a shower. He dashed into the en-suite bathroom, removed the trousers he had just put on and started soaping himself vigorously, to try to scour away his mortification; scrub off his sense of shame. Useless. What he really needed was Viagra. Adverts for the stuff popped up daily on his computer-screen, but he had always airily dismissed it as something for *old* men. Why bother even to read the ads, when normally he could get it up just by seeing a flash of leg or walking past Anne Summers? Yet now he was ignominiously limp again – and when Mandy was about to join him in bed, in a matter of mere minutes.

In fact, he could hear her now: putting a tray down in the bedroom, by the sounds of it.

'Breakfast's ready!' she called. 'And I've heated up the croissants, so don't let them get cold!'

There was nothing for it – he'd have to jump out of the window. Leaping to a certain death was infinitely preferable to risking another failure. Except there *wasn't* a window – not here in the bathroom. And Mandy was waiting impatiently, not wanting things to 'get cold'.

He turned off the shower and stood paralysed, glancing down at his penis. Why had blokes been made so badly that mere thoughts and fears could kibosh an erection, however eager its owner might be to go full steam ahead?

He tensed. The bathroom door was opening; Mandy coming in; Mandy no longer in her coat but completely, wildly naked; Mandy stepping into the shower with him; Mandy kneeling at his feet; Mandy running her amazing hands across his buttocks, down his legs, then letting them glide up again until they were doing such exquisite things he was giving little strangled gasps of pleasure. And now she was taking him in her mouth; lips clamped tight; tongue flicking, swirling, busy. And the skulking blob had changed entirely into some great, headstrong thing that craved to thrust and thrust and explode like last night's rockets. But, no, he had to stop, control himself, hold back. He mustn't come, mustn't come, because this was *her* time and he intended to have her right there on the bathmat and make it really special for her – go on and on and on and on, till she was crying out in excitement, and *still* go on until, until, until …

'Hey, Eric …'

'What?'

'Were you ever a lion in another life?'

'Not that I remember. Why?'

'Because lions do it twenty times a day and you've almost beaten that record.'

'Come off it! We've only managed four, so far, and we've been in bed all day.'

'I know.' Mandy stretched and yawned. 'It's almost dark outside and I didn't even notice.'

'I don't want to get up – ever.' He twisted a strand of her hair round his finger, to yoke the pair of them together. 'If I let you go, you might disappear in a puff of smoke. Anyway, since you're obviously expecting me to perform another sixteen times, I can't afford to dissipate my energies!'

'I'm starving, though, aren't you?'

'Mm. Ravenous.'

'Well, suppose I cook us something really quick and bring it back here on a tray?'

'Fantastic! But let me help this time.'

'No. The kitchen's too small for both of us. You stay here and keep the bed warm. Though, actually,' she said, shivering as she reached for her blue dressing-gown, 'it's a bit chilly in this room.' She rummaged in a drawer and tossed him some long, hairy thing that looked more like a tunic. 'Put this on. The heating's not too brilliant.'

He sat up against the pillows and struggled into the garment, which did nothing for his image. That apart, everything else bordered on perfection: a woman who could cook and who fancied being pleasured twenty times a day! How different females were, he mused, in their attitude to sex. For Christine, it had been a solemn thing, with none of the crazy, giggly games Mandy seemed to like. Besides, the passion of their early married life had gradually cooled and dwindled, until making love became something of a duty for her; even a chore, he'd often suspected. And, once she'd joined Kroszner-Merriott, there was barely time for it at all – not with her high-powered business breakfasts, focus groups and the like. Mandy, on the other hand, made it clear that there was nothing more important than to try out new positions or enact erotic fantasies. Certainly, today had been a first for him, in that he had played the roles of Henry VIII as a young virgin-prince, along with an Arab sheikh and Mr Universe.

He slipped out of bed to glance at himself in the full-length wardrobe mirror. Perhaps he had actually changed; become a muscleman, a king, a sultry Eastern potentate. No, the same old Eric looked back at him – boring eyes, curls in disarray – although with a badge-of-honour love-bite on his neck. Inside, however, he was totally transformed. Mandy had told him she adored him, so now he was capable of anything. He could swim across the Channel; run up Everest and down again; beat Oscar de la Hoya in the boxing-ring – and all because of her. What a contrast to his state of mind at the time of the divorce, when he had shrunk to pygmy-scale; become so insignificant he could have drowned in a scant teaspoonful of water, or been felled by a falling leaf. It was as if he had taken on Mandy's own fearless-ness and confidence, and, indeed, while they'd been making love, he had experienced a sense of total union; become fused with her and part of her; their cries merging into one; even their bodies undifferentiated, so that he was no longer really sure where he ended and she began. For someone who had always felt incomplete and separate, that truly was incredible. And it was connected with New Year – his genuine new start.

He had even found the courage to own up about his string of lies, desperate to make her understand that the invented party, cake and car were simply proof of his desire not to let her slip away. If she had vanished from his life, he had dramatically declared, then that life would be rendered worthless at a stroke. And, far from rebuking him for falsehood, she had giggled in a delicious fashion and told him she was deeply flattered by such romantic sentiments. And, yes, he had to admit that, since his stuttering debut, he had definitely made progress in both the sexual department *and* the oratorical.

Knotting a towel around his waist, he went to find her in the kitchen, unable to be parted from her for more than fifty seconds.

'Too hungry to wait?'

'Hungry for *you*.'

'What, still?'

'Yes, still.'

'Won't be long. Why not park yourself on the sofa.'

Banished to the sitting-room, he examined all the photographs; envious of her parents and her sisters, who had known her so much longer. The sisters were all redheads; one of them a carrot-top, so he was beginning to feel a definite sense of belonging. He even knew their names now: Karen, Angela and Prue.

'Were you christened Mandy?' he called, 'or Amanda?'

'Amanda Sophia, actually – a bit of a mouthful, don't you think? It was shortened to Mandy pretty quick!'

How extraordinary, he thought, that she should share the name with the woman in *Tom Jones* – the entrancing, virtuous, well-born girl Tom had eventually married after a thousand dizzying vicissitudes. Perhaps it meant their relationship was blessed; that he, too, would win his Sophia; achieve his happy ending.

All at once, he knew, at some deep level, that he ought to tell her – *now* – about his origins; that it would constitute betrayal to conceal them any longer. Instantly, he panicked, remembering past occasions when coming clean had landed him in trouble. Even when he'd confided in his wife, she had been concerned about her family's reaction and what her friends might think. But since he and Mandy were one spirit and one flesh, he yearned to strip himself bare – as he had just done physically – so she could get to know the real Eric and not the man in the mask. Yet, there he was, cocooned in a woolly tunic (top half) and a luridly patterned purple towel (bottom half) – hardly the appropriate gear for broaching such a delicate subject. Too bad. If he didn't take the plunge now, he knew he'd lose his nerve.

Fastening the towel more securely, he went to join her in the kitchen. 'You know *Tom Jones*,' he said.

"Course I do. I can sing all those old favourites – "It's Not Unusual", "The Green, Green Grass of Home".'

'No, I mean the book.'

'I didn't know he'd written a book.'

'I'm not talking about the singer – the Tom Jones in Fielding's novel.'

She looked completely blank; seemed more concerned, in any case, with grating cheese into the omelette pan.

'It was written in 1749, by this famous—'

'Eric, it's all I can do to keep up with modern books, let alone dusty old historical things.'

It had been a struggle for him, too – 900 close-packed pages, when he was only seventeen. But the subject matter had kept him reading right until the gratifying end, when Tom had not only wed his true love but was proved to be of noble birth and thus heir to a great fortune. 'It's not the book itself. It's what it's about. You see …' The words faltered to a stop. He was going far too fast; should have waited till they knew each other better; introduced the subject more obliquely; seen how she reacted, then instantly backpedalled if she showed the slightest distaste. He could still do that, in fact. Best to move on to another topic – fast. 'It … it doesn't matter. Forget it.'

'Of course it matters if it's important to you. I want to know everything about you.'

'Everything?'

'Yes. I feel we belong together.'

'Oh, Mandy, that's just …' All the words were inadequate: wonderful, incredible, bordering on miraculous. 'Do you really mean it?'

'I wouldn't say it if I didn't. But, look, the omelette's almost ready now. Why don't we eat it in the sitting-room, then you can tell me all about this book. Though I have to confess I'm not the world's greatest reader, so you'll have to forgive my ignorance.'

Never mind her ignorance – what mattered was his 'confession'. If he waited till she served the meal, he knew he'd change his mind – again. 'Why it meant so much to me,' he blurted out, top-speed, 'is that it's the story of a foundling, and *I'm* a foundling, too.'

'What do you mean?' Mandy looked startled; all but dropped her spatula.

'What I said. My mother left me in a recreation ground. I presume she couldn't cope, so she had to simply dump me.'

'But, Eric, that's quite awful!'

Quickly he studied her face. 'Awful' in the sense of unacceptable, or a sympathetic 'awful'? The latter, thank the Lord.

And he was aware of the concern in her voice as she asked, 'What happened then?'

'I was discovered by the park-keeper, who called the police, and they, in turn, called an ambulance. Apparently, I was on the small side and pretty close to starving, so they rushed me straight to hospital.'

Mandy turned off the gas and came over to embrace him, stroking his hair, his cheek. It was all he could do not to blub. This was the mother he had imagined twenty-thousand times, reunited with him, at last – at last – and holding him with just such tenderness. He had always done his damnedest to make himself believe that she had abandoned him against her will and against her natural instincts; forced by some quite desperate plight beyond her own control. She was penniless and jobless; had strict, religious parents who had banished her from home; been seduced by her rough brute of a boss and was thus acting out of panic. The alternative was callous rejection – an act too cruel to countenance.

'Come and sit down.' Mandy led him to the sofa and sat holding both his hands. There was no trace of disgust on her face, only deep compassion. 'But who brought you up? Were you adopted or—?'

'I was meant to be, but it all fell through – and twice, would you believe? – despite the fact I was said to be the ideal candidate. You see, there's a huge demand for babies, rather than older children, especially babies who are white and not disabled. Sad as it may sound, people tend to shun kids with any sort of handicap, or those from ethnic minorities.'

'So why did it go wrong?'

'Well, it didn't until the very end of the process. All the checks were done – both times – and home visits and what-have-you, which take an age, in any case. But then my first adoptive mother fell pregnant with her own child, which apparently was quite a shock, since she'd been trying to conceive for years and had given up all hope. Eventually, she decided she didn't want two babies, so they had to start again from scratch, with another local couple. This time, it was the guy who lost his nerve, right at the last minute, and talked his wife out of it. I was in foster-care already, of course. Abandoned babies are always fostered for at least the first few months, to give the birth-mother a chance to change her mind and show up. Sadly, that didn't happen for me. So they moved me into long-term foster-care – except it wasn't very long-term. My foster-parents' marriage broke up, so I was sent on somewhere else, to—'

'But, Eric, this is absolutely outrageous! Three moves already and you were still a tiny scrap.'

'No, I was nearly a year old by then – although there were a lot more moves to come, I'm afraid.' He wouldn't tell her that, in the end, he'd stopped bothering to unpack his things; simply left them in black bin-liners, ready for the next upheaval. 'I suppose it was just unfortunate. It shouldn't really happen like that – and doesn't in most cases.'

'But how did you survive? I mean, you seem so normal, not screwed up or bitter or—'

He forced a laugh; had no intention of revealing all his insecurities – not yet, in any case. One thing at a time.

Mandy released his hands and sat back on the sofa, gazing at him wonderingly. 'I so admire you, Eric! Most people who'd endured all that would see themselves as victims and never stop going on about how unfair it was. Well, it *is* unfair – it's appalling. But I still think you're quite fantastic just to shrug it off.'

She didn't understand. It was impossible to shrug it off: the endless round of different 'mums' and 'dads'; different houses, different beds; followed by the children's home; then a second institution because the first was forced to close. It was proving quite a strain, in fact, reliving all this trauma, when his normal way of coping was to dam things up; pretend they'd never happened; escape through books and fantasies to a better, brighter world. He could feel the dreaded darkness choking through his mind; not helped by the fact that the room itself was dim; the curtains still undrawn; the black night pressing in; only one small lamp on, too weak to dispel the gloom. But it was imperative to adopt a cheery manner; otherwise he'd lose Mandy's admiration, and such admiration was precious beyond words. She had spoken almost disparagingly of 'victims', so no way would he become one.

'In some ways, I was lucky, you know,' he said, with determined optimism.

'Lucky?' Mandy looked aghast.

'Yes, some of the boys had such appalling parents, they'd have been better off as foundlings. I remember one kid, Jordan, who shared a room with me. His mum was an alcoholic and always threatening to kill herself – when she wasn't collapsing in a drunken stupor. She neglected him so badly, he'd been hospitalized a dozen times before the age of three. And she suffocated his baby brother when he was only four months old. She had seven kids in total – all illegitimate, all by different fathers, and all of whom landed up in care. Jordan was allowed home now and then, and he said it was a total nightmare, and he much preferred being in Grove End.'

'It makes my blood boil, Eric, that some poor innocent kid should be stuck with a mother like that.'

'Can you really blame her, though? She'd been abused and beaten up herself. The whole cycle just perpetuates itself.'

'But what about *your* mother? Did they ever trace her?'

He gave another casual laugh. 'Sadly, no. And they even went and lost my Precious Box, which was all that I had left of her.'

'Your what?'

'My first foster-parents made it for me, so I would have a record of everything that happened. They put in all the press-cuttings about my being found, and the old cardigan my mother wrapped me in. And there was a photo of the nurses at the hospital, and one of the guy who rescued me – Eric, he was called. He gave me his own name and the surname Parkhill, because that was where I was found: Park Hill recreation ground. And one of the ambulance crew gave me my second name – Victor, because they saw it as a victory that they'd rescued me in time. So that's me in all my borrowed glory – Eric Victor Parkhill.' He'd often wondered if his mother had already chosen a name for him – maybe something with a regal air, like George or Harold or Edward – but perhaps that, too had been swept away.

Mandy was still staring at him. 'It sounds like … like a fairytale.'

'Not many fairies, unfortunately! I have to say I'm still pretty gutted about losing all that early stuff.' The old cardi most of all. His mother might have worn it right against her skin; it would have borne her touch, her smell, maybe even a stray auburn hair. Inestimable treasure. 'And there were other important things in the box. A later set of foster-parents put in my first baby-tooth and a curl from my first haircut and, later still, someone else added all my childish drawings and poems.'

'But how on earth was it lost? The very fact it's called a Precious Box surely means it's precious, so it should have been guarded with great care.'

'Oh, everything went missing. With so many moves from place to place, it's more or less inevitable. They even lost my original records – the ones made by the child-care officer who registered my birth. Some of the information was written out again – which is why I know about the recreation ground and how I got my names. But a lot of the detail was left out, so I've no idea exactly where I was found. I mean, it could have been in the bushes, or on a bench, or' – he shrugged – 'who knows? And I haven't a clue which hospital I went to, let alone what I looked like as a baby. I suppose they only had time to jot down a rough outline, or perhaps they couldn't remember much beyond the basic facts.'

'But couldn't you have asked your various foster-parents – later on, I mean, when you were old enough to understand? *They'd* have remembered, surely?'

'No, I lost all contact with them. The first set moved away and my second foster-mother had a sort of breakdown, so I wasn't allowed to see her any more. I also had a lot of different social workers, so there wasn't just one person to ensure my records were properly looked after.'

'It sounds as if you were messed around in a quite atrocious way.'

'No, it was more a chapter of accidents, with no one person specifically to blame. OK, I admit it was rather a shambles and there were several major cock-ups along the way, but that's just the fault of the system. People always seem to have it in for social workers, but sometimes they're too young to cope, or have such a massive caseload, they get swamped in paperwork and tend to lose the plot. And their lives aren't exactly easy. I mean, people slam the door in their face, or threaten them at knifepoint, or even send them parcels of poo through the post.'

'Maybe so, but I still reckon you're exceptionally forgiving. God, if it was *me*, I'd be beside myself with rage!'

As a child, he *had* been angry, but mainly because his social workers never seemed to listen; discussed him at review meetings as if he wasn't there; made him feel he was just a 'case', a number. They'd fired questions at him when he didn't have the answers, and always sided with the staff at the home, so that even if he had reason to complain – a slap, a punch, or having to stand and face the wall in silence for two hours at a stretch – they'd say, 'Now, come on, Eric, you're probably just exaggerating.' And half the time, they were strangers, anyway, because, just as he had got to know one, he or she would disappear and he would be assigned to someone new. And he'd often had the feeling they resented him for adding to their work. In fact, he hated the word 'caseload', which turned him into a burden; a sort of heavy rucksack strapped to their long-suffering backs.

He gave a sudden grin. 'You won't believe this, Mandy, but once, I even had another boy's records in my file – instead of mine, I mean. He was called Eric Parks, so I can understand the confusion. His circumstances were entirely different from mine, but it took a while for anyone to twig, so it caused no end of problems.'

'Eric, you amaze me! I mean, you've clearly been through hell and back, and had to suffer all this monstrous inefficiency, yet you make out it's just nothing.'

Hardly nothing. She didn't know the half of it – perhaps no one ever would. There were limits to what you could actually admit. 'I told you, I was lucky. Not just because I was spared a mum who was violent or unbalanced or high on crack-cocaine, but because I had someone in my early life who saved me from the scrapheap – a woman called Miss Mays, who worked at the public library. She took me under her wing, supervised my reading and gave me a set of values I've upheld to this day. I suppose she saw I had a bit of talent but no one to encourage it, so she took a personal interest in me, stopped me acting up or playing truant. She even invited me back to her home and helped me with school projects and stuff. And she was determined to correct my accent, on the grounds that, if I "spoke proper", it would help me get a better job. I have to confess I was a common little brat before *she* came on the scene. No one had taught me manners, you see, and I'd got into the habit of swearing like a trooper, because everyone around me swore. By the time she'd polished me up, though, I was becoming quite a toff!'

Mandy was looking puzzled. 'But how could just one person effect such a transformation?'

'It only needs one, Mandy, so long as that person's really dedicated. And Miss Mays was single, with no children or dependents, which meant she could devote a lot of time to me. She was a principled woman, with a social conscience and very high ideals, so maybe she wanted a sort of … mission in life. The library was her passion, of course, but she had energy to spare and I suspect she was looking for some cause with more personal involvement. And she did genuinely believe in me and thought I had a future, which is extremely rare for any kid in care, so naturally I responded. It wasn't easy, mind you. Often, I felt caught between two worlds – her genteel, middle-class one and the rough, tough one I knew. But every time I went through a delinquent phase, she intervened in a really forceful way, and made me—'

'I'm sorry, Eric,' Mandy interrupted, 'but I just can't believe you've ever been delinquent.'

'You'd be surprised! I got in with the wrong crowd and started sniffing glue and taking gas and poppers and—'

'But you seem so … so squeaky-clean.'

'Far from it! When you're cooped up in an institution with thirty other kids, there's always someone egging you on to take drugs, or bunk off school, or nick cash from the staff, or sweets and stuff from people's rooms. I actually started drinking and smoking at the ripe old age of twelve. We used to make "prison-ciggies" from filter-tips and fag-ends picked up from the street and, as for booze, it wasn't beyond our wits to break into the local off-licence and make off with quarts of cider. But, despite my petty crimes, I knew at base that if I didn't take this one big chance offered by Miss Mays, I'd end up as a dead-end kid – achieving nothing, constantly in trouble and being excluded from school, most like.' He shuddered at the memory of just how low he might have sunk.

Mandy shook her head in bemusement. 'Well, all I can say is your Miss Mays must have been a saint, if not a miracle-worker.'

'She was both – and more besides. The only thing she couldn't do is protect me from the bullies. Bullying's rife in children's homes, and I was a natural target, being small, red-haired and bookish. And when I tried to change my accent, I was taunted so badly for "talking posh", that, in the end, I adopted two completely different kinds of speech – one for the home and one for elsewhere. It was quite tricky to keep switching between them, but I reckon it saved me a lot of thrashings! Mind you, I sometimes felt I couldn't win, because even if I brought books back from the library, I'd be set upon again and beaten up. It was fatal to like reading because then you were classed as a geek, a sissy and almost certainly gay.'

'But that's plain daft, as well as cruel.'

He shrugged. 'The same attitude's around today, to some extent. But, you know, I only became a librarian because of Miss Mays' influence. And it was the perfect job, of course. Most foundlings know zilch about their origins or parentage, so it was always a huge draw for me to be surrounded by certainty and knowledge – all those solid, indisputable facts, encapsulated in books.'

'I'd like to meet this wonder-woman. Is she still alive?'

'No, alas, though we always kept in touch. She died four years ago, and I honestly think I was more upset than anyone else at the funeral. So I *was* fortunate, you see. Most of the kids I grew up with had no one rooting for them, so it wasn't really surprising if they messed up their lives and went to the bad. And a lot of the girls got pregnant and often had their babies taken into care, just as *they'd* been, earlier. And some went on the game as young as twelve or thirteen, simply to make a bit of pocket money.'

Mandy got up and walked slowly to the window. 'I feel thoroughly ashamed,' she said, tracing a squiggly pattern on the cold and misted pane.

'Whatever for?'

'Because I've been so spoilt in comparison – I mean, coming from a happy, normal family, with two loving parents and a whole tribe of other relatives, to prevent me going off the rails. I wasn't even *allowed* in a pub till I was officially eighteen!'

Yes, he thought, most normal folk took such things for granted: their family tree, family photos, family traditions; even their genetic inheritance. It required an imaginative leap to envisage how it felt to have no idea who you were, where you came from, or what sort of people your parents were. His mother might have been a duchess or a slag; his father a CBE or a thug. When the other kids said casually, 'My dad's a builder; my mum works in a hair-salon,' he could hardly add his own version: 'My dad's a mystery; my mum's an unknown quantity'. Indeed, sometimes, as a child, he had felt so insubstantial he'd become a sort of x-ray picture, with no colour or solidity and with all his bones and innards vulnerably exposed.

Suddenly he caught sight of the clock; horrified when he saw how late it was. He'd been banging on for hours and they hadn't had their lunch yet, let alone their supper. The omelette would be ruined; Mandy's plan for a cosy little meal in bed totally disrupted. 'Mandy, I'm so sorry. I must have bored you rigid, going on about myself like that, when it's *your* life I want to hear about.'

'No, mine's the boring one! Yours is just … amazing. And that ambu-lance-man was right, you know. You *are* a Victor. I mean, to have gone through all that trauma unscathed makes you a true hero.' Returning from the window, she pulled him up from the sofa and put her arms around him. 'Darling, I want to hear much more – every single detail of the story and how—'

He scarcely heard the rest of the sentence. It was the 'darling' he was fixated on; rolling it around his mouth; sucking it like the most delicious sweet. He was 'darling' again – and, even more momentous – for the first time in his cowardly life, he was a victor and a hero.

chapter ten

Eric padlocked his bike and stood looking up at the huge, fortress-like building opposite, suppressing a shudder as he recalled the gallows here, dismantled only in 1993. The thought of it induced a choking panic, as if *he* were the hapless bloke being bound and gagged and hooded; the noose closing round his neck, as he prepared for the dizzying drop. And, yes, it could have been him, he reflected – just as he, too, could be banged up here with the other 1400 men. His whole background and experience had taught him that those inside and those out were separated only by a hair's-breadth, and whether you were fêted as a good, upstanding citizen, or condemned as so-called scum, was often just a matter of circumstance and fate.

Having unstrapped his case from the carrier on his bike, he crossed the road, dwarfed by the intimidating presence of the massive ramparts now rearing up in front of him. Pausing for a moment, to try to get his bearings, he located the main prison entrance up a flight of steps. However, once he'd humped the heavy case to the top, he was instructed to go down again and report to a second, smaller entrance, up a different set of steps. He was already feeling somewhat disoriented as he entered a bleak and featureless lobby and joined the queue at reception.

'Yes?' said the man behind the glass security-panel, when, at last, it was his turn.

'My name's Eric Parkhill and I'm here to attend the prison book club.'

The bloke checked through the visitors' book, only to shake his head. 'There's no paperwork for a Mr Parkhill, which means you're not expected.'

Eric frowned in consternation. 'But I confirmed my visit yesterday – with the prison librarian, Abi Ayotundi.'

'Abi's not here.'

'Not here? But he's running the group this evening and he arranged to meet me an hour and a half before.'

'Sorry, he's not on the premises. That's the information I've been given.' The man consulted his book again. 'In fact, there's no paperwork for the book club either, so I reckon you must have got the date wrong.'

'Look,' said Eric, irritably. 'I spoke to Abi in person less than twenty-four hours ago. And I've put off another engagement, in order to be here this evening.'

Despite the man's dismissive shrug, Eric stood his ground. He'd be damned if he'd cycle all the way back to Vauxhall, on one of the coldest days of the year. 'Can't you ring through to the library and see what's going on?'

With an audible sigh, the guy picked up the phone. 'No reply,' he reported; a note of almost glee in his voice. 'I'd say they've all gone home.'

'Well, *I'm* not going home. I was invited here for five o'clock and I want this sorted out.'

'In that case, you'll have to wait. I can't keep all these people hanging around.' He indicated the queue that had built up again in the last few minutes. 'Take a seat over there.'

Reluctantly, Eric moved away and sat on the only chair – an uncomfortable thing in rigid plastic and positioned opposite the open door. Cold night air was blasting in from outside, threatening to numb his hands and feet, but, as he got up to close it, the man behind the desk yelled out a reprimand.

'Hey! We leave that open deliberately, to keep the exit clear.'

Eric returned to his seat, fuming inwardly, He had expected a slightly warmer welcome, having gone to quite some trouble selecting books for the group, and turned down free tickets from Mandy for a special screening of *Mamma Mia*! tonight (not quite his cup of tea, but who cared, with her beside him?) Except the subject of Mandy was strictly banned for the duration of the evening, since it would only distract him from the job in hand. He actually regretted having confided in her at all, because of the storm of insecurities his confession had unleashed. Always before, he had kept a lid clamped firmly on his past; using suppression and concealment as tools to help him cope. But since prising off that lid, he seemed to be swamped in a toxic overflow, bubbling up from childhood. And he had made himself more vulnerable by revisiting those memories, as if he had shed a layer of insulating skin.

He could certainly do with insulation in this icebox of a lobby, where he continued to sit for an unaccountably long time, watching various people take their turn at the desk. He envied the fact that they seemed to be expected and were treated with civility, not as intruders or impostors. Eventually, he concluded that he must have been forgotten and so went back to reception, to remind them of his existence.

There was now a second man on duty, wearing the same uniform of white shirt and smart black epaulettes. 'Know where Abi is?' the first guy asked his colleague.

'Nope!'

'And know anything about a book club?'

'Nope!'

A third guy suddenly materialized from a small room at the back. 'Yeah,' he said. 'That'll be the lady from Roehampton University. She runs the club, along with Abi. In fact, I'm sure I've seen the paperwork.' He grabbed the book and began riffling through the pages. 'Yeah, here we are – Linda Lewis.'

'That's her!' Eric cried, relieved.

'But it doesn't start till six-thirty – that's what's written here.'

'I know, but, as I keep explaining, Abi asked me to meet him beforehand, which means you should have my name too.'

'What *is* your name?'

Eric spelled it out again, beginning to feel distinctly Kafkaesque.

'No, nothing here under Parkhill.'

The second guy now leaned over and consulted the book himself 'That name rings a bell. Yes, Eric Parkhill. You're meeting Abi at five.'

Which is what I've been trying to tell you for the last half-hour, Eric refrained from saying, pointing out instead that it was now twenty-eight minutes past.

'And Abi's not here anyway,' the first bloke chipped in, helpfully.

'Is he the sort of person likely to forget?' Eric asked, with some anxiety. He had not yet met the fellow; had no idea whether he was reliable or not. All he knew was that Mr Ayotundi was six-foot-three and Nigerian.

'Couldn't say.' Another casual shrug. 'If I was you, I'd simply sit and wait. Nothing's happening till six-thirty, so let's hope this Linda person turns up then, and you can check the whole thing out with her.'

'Well, perhaps I could sit somewhere a bit warmer.'

The man looked dubious. 'Have you got identification?'

'Yes. I was told to bring three different forms.' Eric pushed his debit card through the slot in the glass partition, followed by his medical card and a recent electricity bill. For normal mortals, a driving licence or passport would have sufficed, but he didn't possess either, and even his birth certificate was one he preferred to conceal.

Several minutes passed, while all three items were studied with a high degree of suspicion. 'OK,' the bloke said, finally. 'Though I'll need to keep this until you've left the premises. *And* your mobile phone. And if you're carrying a pager, or any type of Chubb keys, leave those with me, too, please.'

Eric handed over his keys and phone. What next? His shirt and trousers?

'Right, go through that sliding door behind you.'

The door in question appeared to be locked, resisting all attempts at entry. Eric rattled the handle – in vain. Apparently even an insensate door was determined to keep him out.

'Hang on!' the fellow called from the desk. 'If you give it time, it'll open automatically. Don't force the thing or I'll be in trouble.'

Once he did get through, Eric found himself in a second lobby, a little larger and warmer than the first, but equally uninviting; containing nothing but a couple of chairs and a row of metal lockers. Again, he took a seat, aware that his stomach was rumbling. Getting here by five meant he hadn't had a minute to grab a cup of coffee, let alone a sandwich. Yet he realized now that he could have taken his time; found a nice warm café and eaten a leisurely meal.

As he sat resignedly waiting, suitcase at his feet, legs twisted round the chair-rungs, he was suddenly reminded of arriving at Grove End, as an uprooted kid of seven. They, too, had kept him waiting; hadn't been expecting him; had muddled up his paperwork. All at once, his horror at the first sight of the building came surging, seething back; a grim, forbidding pile, with stern stone walls and air of real malevolence. 'Go away!' it seemed to shout. 'You're not wanted here, not welcome.'

But he wasn't wanted by his foster-parents either, which meant it must be *his* fault that he'd landed up in such a prison of a place. His foster-mother had shouted at him constantly; his foster-dad dished out whacks and blows, but at least they'd been his mum and dad, and at least it had been home. The huge, stony-hearted building could never be a home – he knew that in his gut – and, once he'd crossed the threshold into the oppressive entrance-hall, with no carpeting or cosiness and very little light, he felt he'd been swallowed up for ever.

Having been marched along to an office, he was told to wait outside while they tried to sort out the confusion, although he had to wait on his own, because his social worker was chafing to dash off somewhere else. He sat for what seemed hours, sending up a desperate prayer that it would turn out to be a mistake and he could return to the house in Cedar Road. Whatever its deficiencies, that small, shabby semi was familiar and safe; not hideously scary like *this* hateful institution.

His prayer remained unanswered, as did most prayers, he found. When, at last, he was called into the office, he was confronted by a big-boned, frightening female, who barked instead of talked, and had very short, straight hair and seemed more like a man.

'I'm Mrs Barnes. I run the home. Your key-worker will be Alison, but she's off sick today, so Tracy will look after you – although she's only here till five, then Kenneth will be on tonight. Tea's at five-thirty, and your bedtime will be half-past eight, and we'll need to get your bedroom sorted out and see about the ...'

She spoke so loud and fast, he couldn't take it in, and was also worried by so many different names: Mrs Barnes, Tracy, Kenneth, Alison – would they all be cruel?

'Now what's your date of birth, Eric? And where do you go to school? And have you any brothers or sisters? And...?'

Each time he tried to answer, she had rushed on to another question – although she should have known the answers, since they were all written in his file. But perhaps it had gone missing, as things always seemed to do, because the whole time she was talking she was searching through a pile of papers that overflowed her desk. Never once did she look at him, although he was actually quite glad, because he knew she'd have the sort of eyes that could pierce through skin and bone.

Then, suddenly, the phone rang and she kept shouting at the caller and saying it simply wasn't good enough and she didn't intend to stand for it. And, once she'd banged down the receiver, she seemed surprised to see him there still, and began asking him the very same questions she had put to him before. When he was finally let out, another scary person appeared, to show him round the house; her big black shoes click-clacking along the corridors.

'This is our playroom, Eric.'

He had stared in at the scuffed lino, the lack of any toys. No one had ever played here – that was very clear – but then grown-ups always lied. Next, they'd gone down a dark passage, which led into the kitchen. Kitchens should be small and warm and kind, not vast and cold and cruel. And they should smell of frying bacon or hot cakes, not of disinfectant and boiled cabbage.

This one even had a mousetrap in the larder. *He* was a mouse – a tiny, power-less creature, with a steel trap closing round him, about to crush him to a—

'Excuse me, are you Eric Parkhill?'

A small, fair-haired man, dressed funereally in black jeans and a black anorak, came rushing over, clearly out of breath. Eric made a desperate effort to leave Grove End behind; to reinhabit his adult self and try to work out who this was – certainly not a six-foot-three Nigerian. 'Yes,' he said, jumping to his feet. 'But—'

'Great to meet you, Eric! I'm Sam – Sam Hodgkinson, and I'm standing in for Abi tonight. I'm afraid he was rushed to hospital in the early hours this morning. I'm really sorry to keep you hanging about. I hear you've been waiting ages.'

'Don't worry – not a problem. But that's bad news about Abi. Is he going to be all right?'

'Yeah, fine. It was appendicitis. But they operated straight away and he's doing well, the hospital says. But look, let me show you the library. You've been sitting here quite long enough.'

'Yes, I've brought some books for the group.' Eric gestured to the suit-case by his chair.

'Shit! You can't take that inside. We'll have to go back to security and have it checked.'

Eric's suppressed a sigh, guessing – rightly – that there'd be more delay and more suspicion.

'Are you taking those books out with you again?' the balding bloke enquired – the one who'd originally given him short shrift.

'No. They're for the men.'

'Yes, but will you be taking them with you when you leave?'

'I've just told you – no.'

'So you're giving them to someone inside?'

Couldn't they understand plain English? 'Yes, to the members of the book club.'

'Be that as it may, you're forbidden to take cases into the prison.'

Eric bristled. Having risked life and limb transporting them on his bike, he was determined they should reach their destination. 'Well, I'll put them in a carrier bag. Would you have one somewhere?'

'You can't take bags in, either.'

At this point, Sam intervened, having spotted a small, see-through plastic crate on top of a cupboard by the door. 'Mind if I take over?' he asked Eric.

'Delighted.'

Opening the case, Sam began unloading the books into the crate, ignoring the remonstrations of Baldie's younger colleague, who clearly regarded books as the equivalent of bombs. Then, leaving the offending case at the desk, Sam somehow obtained clearance to pass back into the second lobby through the automatic door. There, he handed the crate to Eric, pulled up his anorak to reveal a bunch of keys chained around his waist and unlocked a narrow door that led out again into the cold night air. Yes, definitely Kafkaesque, Eric thought. All that kerfuffle, yet here they were outside once more, apparently back to square one. He followed Sam down some steep stone steps and across a concrete yard, where the wind blew with such icy force, his eyes watered and his nose ran, although it was impossible to do much about either, weighed down as he was by the books.

He had soon lost all sense of direction, as they crossed several other bleak and chilly yards and proceeded through a further series of doors. Progress was necessarily slow, since Sam had to unlock each door, then lock it again behind them. Finally, they found themselves inside, although the harsh, colourless surroundings of the prison proved little less daunting than the intimidating yards, with their razor-wire and lowering walls.

Then he came upon the cells and froze; the row upon row of small locked doors evoking another flood of memories. *He* had been incarcerated when he'd run away from Grove End; hauled back after just two hours and condemned to 'solitary'. Never to this day, had he forgotten the sheer terror of not knowing if he would ever be released; his mounting claustrophobia as he paced his own small 'cell'; the sense of utter powerlessness as his panic-stricken cries echoed through empty space and he began to fear that the other kids had all been evacuated, and he was the sole prisoner in the huge, hostile torture-house.

Sam was chatting to him affably as they continued along the corridor, although he scarcely heard a word. By opening up to Mandy, he'd crash-landed back into childhood and seemed unable to escape its dark, entangling coils. Swapping denial for disclosure had plunged him into turmoil, undermined his defences, left him disturbingly out of control.

Indeed, everything he witnessed here seemed another grim reminder of Grove End. The group of prisoners, queuing for their evening meal of stodgy stew and dumplings, jolted him straight back to the dining-room the first day he arrived. He could hardly believe the uproar: aggressive kids engaged in fisticuffs, and even chucking food across the room. Then, more commotion as the staff weighed in with shouts and threats, only to be defied by one recalcitrant little tyke. He'd sat cowed and silent, as a much older lad, Hussein, kept viciously kicking his legs throughout the meal. And, even when he was used to the chaos, it had been difficult to eat much, because the bigger boys would either nick his food or bait him for being small and shy. In fact, throughout his childhood, he'd felt continually ravenous, although even if he had munched non-stop, no amount of food would have ever filled the hole. Once, he had even sneaked to the local shop and bought himself three large, crusty loaves; gobbled the lot in one famished feeding-frenzy, yet still felt empty inside.

'There are five wings in all,' Sam was explaining, 'each with four landings and all built to the same plan. The Vulnerable Prisoners' Unit is separate, with its own library and its own prisoner orderly, and it also has a book club, very similar to ours. But I'm afraid I won't have a chance to take you there, as we're already pressed for time.'

'That's OK,' said Eric, again frantically attempting to haul himself back to the present. But the mention of the Vulnerable Prisoners' Unit set off new disquiet. That unit housed mainly sex-offenders and, as a kid growing up in care, he'd come in for his share of sexual molestation, not only by the older boys but by ancient Uncle Frank. Christ, he thought, Uncle Frank might actually be *here*; arrested, at long last, and serving his sentence a matter of mere yards away! Not that he'd ever shopped the bloke – indeed, never admitted to a single soul what had transpired between the pair of them. He'd felt far too guilty, too embarrassed; feared people might imagine he'd liked the things he did with Frank, when in truth he had detested every minute.

It wasn't easy to say no, however, because the weird old guy was kind, not cruel; gave him sweets and even money, and took him for long rides in his big, black, fancy car. And he always kept his promises, whether it was taking him to a football match, or buying him new books for Christmas. He never turned up late, as other grown-ups did, or forgot to *buy* the presents, like his foster-mum and dad. He wasn't a real uncle, of course; just someone who had once waylaid him when he was walking back from school. None the less, he was the only person in the world who actually listened to his every word; gave him undivided attention, so that he would almost feel like a kid who mattered – at least before the dirty stuff began.

Sometimes, though, he'd felt so ashamed of that dirty stuff, he had longed to confess to Alison, or even to his social worker, and get Uncle

Frank sent packing. Then the creepy man wouldn't lie in wait for him and coax him into his car. But they were bound to say he was lying, if only to protect themselves from blame. *They* had all the power, and often used to twist his words to mean something else entirely, such as 'trouble' or 'attention-seeking'. Besides, if the other kids should ever get to hear, he would be called a poof and a pervert and bullied even more.

Of course, when he'd left the home, he could have gone public and sought recompense, reprisals, but he had never once considered it. The word 'abuse' labelled you a victim; kept you chained for ever to the past. And it was much the same with therapy. Why rehearse such shaming incidents, dig them up again, pick off the healing scabs that, mercifully, had begun to form? Wiser far to block the whole thing out; pretend it hadn't happened and get on with life as best he could. And that strategy had succeeded, more or less, until just three days ago, so now he cursed himself for departing from his lifelong habit of drawing a prudent veil across the past.

'When they first arrive, the men are sent to E-wing, for assessment. And that gives them a chance to find their feet before they're moved to another wing.'

Sam's words were both a rebuke and a reminder: a rebuke because he was miles away – once more – and a salutary reminder that he was here for the sake of the prisoners; not to obsess about himself. Indeed, he was well aware how many of these inmates shouldn't have been banged up in the first place: psychotics, schizophrenics, drug addicts, ex-servicemen – maybe even sex-offenders, in some cases. He knew as well as anyone that a quarter of the prison population had been in care as kids, and nearly half of the under-twenty-ones. Didn't that speak volumes in itself? – one injustice added to another. And the systems had things in common: a lack of cash, overworked or uncaring staff, a whole raft of often irrational rules and a culture of abuse. Children's homes and prisons were both closed and secret worlds, full of misery, frustration and thwarted, wasted lives. He burned to reform both systems, yet how the hell would one puny individual ever have the power?

As they passed the last straggle of prisoners collecting trays of food, he was uncomfortably aware that he and Sam were the object of close scrutiny. Several of the men were casting them distrustful glances; a mixture of resentment and hostility. And was it any wonder? They must always feel a sense of envy, if not bitterness, towards those lucky sods who could control their own existences and come and go as they pleased. He'd felt much the same towards the kids at school who weren't shut up in institutions where every aspect of their lives was strictly regulated, and escape was near-impossible.

A couple of prison officers were standing by the servery and only now did he notice how prominent their keys were; a constant reminder to the inmates that, given one false move, they could be locked up even longer than usual. Again, he was struck by the absence of colour: the men mostly wearing drab or muted clothes; the staff in sober black and white; the walls a dingy cream; the floor a nondescript beige. He now regretted having worn his yellow sweater, which seemed crassly bright in so sombre an environment.

'Of course, many of the men come to Wandsworth just to be categorized,' Sam was explaining now, as they continued along the corridor. 'Then they're sent off to a different gaol. Very few stay longer than six months – which makes it hard to run the book club.'

Before Eric could reply, he was startled by the sound of thrashing wings. A pigeon had been trapped in the confining space and was flying frantically from wall to wall in its effort to get out. However, it was simply banging into things and becoming still more disoriented. *He* had been the same, he thought, when he'd tried to run away again – this time from a second home, called, ironically, The Haven – only to be punished with even more restrictions.

Sam ignored the bird completely, as if used to desperate creatures pitting themselves against implacable odds. Besides, they had now reached the library, at last – a true oasis, compared with what they'd seen so far: well lit and brightly painted, with the consoling presence of books on every side.

'Where shall I put this?' Eric asked, indicating the crate.

'Oh, just here on this desk. And thanks a lot for bringing the books.'

'Well, these are just some extras for the group. I've sorted out a selection of stock for the library, which will be coming by van, as usual – a good sixty or so, I'd guess. And I chose things that Abi suggested: crime novels, of course, but also poetry collections and books on chess, and arts and crafts, and travel books and …' It had struck him as poignant that these caged and corralled men should travel in their minds to far-flung lands.

'Sounds great! So many books go missing, new supplies are more than welcome. We must lose up to fifty every week. I suspect most of them are just lying around in the cells, but no one's got the time to do a search. Besides, a good few of the officers regard books as an unnecessary privilege, so they're hardly likely to waste precious manpower trying to track them down.'

Eric had heard about the problem of bolshie prison officers, who might refuse to escort the men from their cells to attend the book club meetings, either from laziness or spite, or because they opposed the library on principle. His natural instinct was to crack down on such conduct; become more involved in general, so that he could sit in on prison-management meetings and argue the prisoners' case, but he just didn't have the authority, alas.

'Coffee for you, Eric?' Sam had moved to a small office at the back, and was bustling about filling the kettle and searching for clean mugs.

'Thanks. Two sugars, please.'

'Then I'm going to have to leave you for a while. I didn't know I'd be helping out this evening, so I need to do a few things first, to get myself prepared. Is that OK with you?'

'Yes, fine.'

He was relieved, in fact, to be alone, so that he could rehearse his little spiel. He wanted to explain to the group his hopes of raising money to fund a writer-in-residence, as well as author-visits – a crime-writer, he felt, would go down rather well. Then, he'd outline his plan (already worked out with Stella) of supplying children's books for those men who were fathers, to send to their kids back home.

Yet, as he sipped his coffee, his mind refused to stay on books and authors, but kept straying back to Mandy. Although she had expressed her admiration for him, she might have been hiding her true feelings, out of pity or good manners. And, anyway, that initial admiration might well have changed already to disquiet or dismay. After all, even many liberal people regarded kids who grew up in care as feckless, unreliable and basically inferior. And foundlings were worse still; considered in past ages the lowest of the low – shameful bastards, resulting from their mother's 'sin'. And, even in these enlightened times, illegitimacy remained a stigma. Besides, what about her family? Might *they* not hate the thought of her consorting with a rootless man, who might be carrying 'bad' genes, the son of a criminal, a hooker, or a junkie?

Of course, he hadn't breathed a word about the sordid sexual stuff, for fear Mandy might well shrink from any further contact with someone 'tainted' and 'polluted'. Yet that was another problem in itself. Concealing something so significant hardly squared with his deep longing to be totally upfront with her and become her genuine soulmate. Or was that just an empty dream now? Perhaps he'd ruined his own chances of any continuing relationship by revealing even a fraction of his past. And those awful things he'd said about being a common little brat, engaged in petty crime, seemed increasingly misguided if his aim was to impress her.

He jumped as Sam came back in, jolting him back from his obsessive thoughts for the umpteenth time this evening. He'd vowed *not* to think of Mandy, yet here he was, failing once again in his duty towards the prison and the group.

Sam, too, seemed less than happy. 'Now Linda's been delayed,' he said, frowning in annoyance. 'The men will be here in just five minutes, yet she's stuck in traffic, would you believe? So, what I think we'd better do is introduce you first and have you chat to them about your plans, then move on to the book club proper, once she actually arrives. Any objections, Eric?'

'None at all.' He was actually glad to be put on the spot, since that might concentrate his mind, at last. He'd behaved woefully, so far; present in body only; not in mind or spirit; his normal strict professionalism scattered to the winds.

'I'll just prepare the coffee for the men. We're expecting ten this evening. Some of them will know each other, but three are new to the group – Stewart, Craig and Terry – so perhaps you'd keep an eye out for them.'

'Of course.'

Hardly had Sam returned to his back-office to fill the kettle and find more mugs, when an officer appeared, accompanying a skinny, dark-haired man, dressed soberly in jeans and a grey sweatshirt.

With a curt nod in Eric's direction, the warder turned on his heel and disappeared, leaving the man standing stiffly at the door.

Eric went over and introduced himself. 'Are you one of the newcomers?' he asked, with a friendly smile.

'No, I've been at least three times. Though I can't say I've seen *you* before.'

The tone was wary, even hostile, but Eric was used to that. The reading groups he ran also had their share of members who needed time to thaw. Having asked the fellow's name (Kevin), he tried to break the ice by broaching the subject of this evening's book, *The Girl with the Dragon Tattoo*.

'Sorry. Haven't read a word of it. *You* try reading when you share a cell with a nutcase. There's never a moment's peace. Even at night, he keeps moaning and groaning or shouting out in his sleep.'

'I do sympathize, believe me. It must be so hard to concentrate.'

'I'd say!' Kevin was now unbending slightly. 'Though I suppose I should count myself lucky. One of the blokes on B-wing was murdered by his cell-mate.'

Eric was wondering how to respond to such a statement, when Kevin suddenly opened up himself.

'Anyway, I don't come here just for the books. It's the only place I can forget about being in prison and sit and chat with people, like I used to do outside. It's a sort of escape, I suppose; makes me feel less cut off. Mind you, at first I thought it was really naff, getting together to talk about a book. I mean, I've never been a reader, or had books at home as a kid. But we often start discussing – you know, important things, like justice, or divorce, or whether it's brave to top yourself or just a coward's way out. Last month, we got so heated about suicide, we almost came to blows!'

Eric nodded encouragingly. Wasn't this the reason he was here: to give men like Kevin some tiny means of 'escape', and to widen their horizons, if only for a couple of hours and if only once a month?

'And I did finish one book, way back in July. *Man and Boy*, it was – about this bloke who messes up his marriage, then makes a song and dance about bringing up his kid alone. He ought to be in here, then he'd know the difference. Life's on hold for us. I'd do anything to be living with my son again, getting him his breakfast, taking him to school. But the bloke in the book sees all that sort of stuff as just a chore. It made me mad, to be honest. I wanted to keep telling him – listen, for someone who's locked up, it's a real blessing to share life with your kid.'

'Yes, I must say I agree. So how old's your son?'

'Just six. Jack, he's called and he's already quite a—'

Unfortunately, Eric had to interrupt him, since the rest of the group were now arriving, escorted by a surly-looking officer. But Kevin's words echoed through his head. Erica would be with him in just over eleven weeks, and, yes, it would be 'a real blessing' to get her breakfast and share his life with her, if only for a shortish time. However flaky he might feel today, he did have his precious freedom; did have his precious daughter. And, all at once, the sheer magnitude of those two facts seemed to release him from the cellar of his past, as if a door had been unbolted and he was streaking out to light and air and able to breathe free. At last, he'd stopped his fruitless agonizing and did definitely feel better – almost normal, for God's sake – and determined to play a useful part in making some small difference to this group.

But, before he went to greet them, he made a mental note to ensure that Kevin got a good supply of children's books – for Jack.

chapter eleven

Should he have aimed higher, Eric wondered anxiously, as he opened the oven door to check on the roast chicken? After all, he was cooking for a semi-pro, so perhaps he should have pulled out all the stops and served up something fancy such as venison or grouse. Except his elementary culinary skills wouldn't stretch to preparing game – even if he'd had a clue where to buy it. And what about the starter? The melon slices, bought ready-cut from Sainsbury's, were hardly likely to impress. Mandy was used to gourmet meals, so she would probably be expecting an elaborate home-made terrine or some high-falutin soufflé. Although, even if he had spent all week laying on a ten-course banquet, it wouldn't divert attention from the basic squalor of the flat. Despite his heroic efforts yesterday, cleaning the place from top to toe, it really required a fairy godmother to effect a total metamorphosis.

He started as the doorbell rang. Not Mandy, surely – she was always late, he'd discovered. Well, if it *was* a fairy godmother, his wish-list was at the ready: a penthouse in Park Lane; a king-size bed with built in massage-function; a dial-a-feast from Gordon Ramsay and …

'Mandy!'

'Well, don't look so surprised. You invited me for dinner and here I am – though late again, as usual. I'm sorry, darling, honestly. I just can't seem to get my act together when it comes to time.'

'Actually you're early.'

'I thought you said seven.'

'No, eight.'

'Shit! I do apologize. Want me to go away again?'

'Not likely!' It was so fantastic that she still seemed keen; hadn't subsequently decided that a foundling with a chequered past should have no place in her life, it was all he could do not to kidnap her and keep her here for ever. He pressed himself against her, trying, for once, not to get a hard-on, as he inhaled her musky scent; felt the luscious contours of her body beneath the cuddly coat. It was vital to stay in chef mode – at least until he'd served the coffee.

Finally withdrawing from the embrace, she picked up her wicker basket and took out a large glass bowl. 'I've made us a sherry trifle, as my little contribution to the meal.'

Having carried it into the kitchen, he stood gazing in admiration at the rosettes of whipped cream, studded with whole blanched almonds, crystallized violets and chocolate curls. 'Mandy, this puts me to shame! I just can't compete in the cooking stakes. And I'm still feeling bad about you coming here, when—'

'Eric, *will* you stop apologizing! You spent the whole of last week telling me how grotty your flat was and' – she paused to remove her coat, then made a lightning tour from sitting-room to bedroom – 'all it needs is a bit of jazzing up. I could make you a new bedspread, if you like, and a nice bright throw for the sofa, with a few contrasting cushions. And I'm a pretty dab hand at painting, so if you want me to slap some colour on these walls … What do you think?'

'I think,' he whispered, kissing her again, 'that you're the most amazing woman in the world.'

'Well, actually, I *have* been rather amazing! You'll never believe what I've managed to track down.' Rooting in her bag, she withdrew a large white envelope.

His mind was still on furnishings; relieved by the thought that when Erica came over, the flat would be transformed – not that he'd mention Erica just now. Although Mandy knew about his ex-wife and daughter, he didn't want to labour the point so early in their relationship. She herself had never married or had children – came 'without baggage', as she'd put it, which to him was quite extraordinary. A woman of her charm should have had swarms of men queuing up to claim her, from the age of seventeen, so how could she have reached thirty-five without a permanent partner?

Lord, he thought, he was neglecting his duties as host! He should be pouring her a drink, offering her some nibbles. So, having ensconced her on the sofa with a glass of wine and a saucerful of nuts, he dashed towards the kitchen, to turn the oven down. They must spin out their drinks a while, to allow time for a few long, impassioned kisses.

'Don't disappear!' she called, extracting a sheet of paper from the envelope and waving it in front of him. 'Come and sit beside me. In fact, you *ought* to sit down before you look at this. It may be a bit of a shock.'

MIRACLE BABY SURVIVES! the headline shrieked, and beneath it a picture of a tiny infant cradled in the arms of a triumphantly smiling elderly man, clad in a smart uniform and cap.

'That's *you*, Eric, with the other Eric – the park-keeper who found you! Isn't it incredible?'

He didn't trust himself to speak. His first instinct was to shut his eyes; close his ears; even bolt out of the flat. All the pain and uncertainty of his past seemed to be crashing in dangerous waves about his head.

'Don't you think I'm clever? I just couldn't get your story out of my mind and I knew I had to help you in some way. So I went down to Croydon Library and managed to see their archivist, who told me the local papers were now on microfilm, and gave me the roll for the *Croydon Advertiser*, January to March, 1964. You'd told me the month of your birth, but not the actual date, but it's only a weekly paper, so it didn't take long to scroll through all the February editions and – bingo! – there it was. Do read it, darling. It's riveting.'

He had to force himself to take hold of the sheet, but the type began blurring on the page, so that he couldn't decipher so much as a word. He himself had worked in Croydon Library for close on twenty years; been friendly with their archivists, familiar with the records, and could have found this paper easily, years and years ago – in fact, had been on the point of doing so a hundred-thousand times. Yet, in the end, caution had always prevailed. He knew at some deep level that it was essential *not* to investigate, in case something he read should implicate his mother.

What Mandy didn't understand was that there were two types of abandonment: the caring kind, when the mother wanted desperately for her infant to be found, so she would leave it well-wrapped up in a public place such as a hospital or shop, where there were people around who would immediately take action. The opposite kind was akin to infanticide, when the baby was asphyxiated in a plastic bag, or plonked in a dustbin and left to die amidst the trash, or shoved into a toilet-bowl, to drown. Admittedly, none of the latter had happened to him, but none of the former, either. All he knew was that he'd been discovered in a recreation ground, which sounded decidedly dodgy. Such a place might well have been deserted on a bitter February morning, and it would also have litter-bins and toilets, where an infant could be summarily dumped. It was crucial to his peace of

mind that his mother remained a kindly, caring person, not a callous criminal, so wiser to keep his fantasies intact than start searching out hard
evidence.

'I mean, it gives you all the information you said you wished you knew.
See that.' Mandy jabbed her finger halfway down the column. 'It says you
were taken to the Mayday Hospital, so that's one of your questions
answered. Of course, I went straight on to see it, from the library, although
it was quite a little trek. The present hospital looks newish, but there's one
wing left of the old building – the one where *you'd* have gone.' She
rummaged for her mobile, clicked it on. 'I took a lot of photos, darling, so
you'd get the feel of the place. Actually, I reckon it looks nicer than the new
hospital – sort of faded brick, but with loads of character.'

It was all he could do not to push the phone away. They were going far
too fast. His early history was being excavated, fact by fact by fact, and all
he felt was panic. Suppose he couldn't handle the turmoil of emotions this
knowledge might evoke? It had been bad enough in the prison, last week,
and since then he'd been extremely careful not to risk another disorien-
tating state.

'And do you know why it's called the Mayday?'

Before he could answer, she had plunged straight on again. 'There are
several different theories, in fact, but the one I like best is that it comes from
the French distress-call, "*M'aidez!*" And that's wonderfully apt, don't you
think? I mean, they *did* help you, Eric – saved your life, most probably. Oh,
and by the way, I've written down most of the stuff I'm telling you. You see,
I thought it would be a great idea to re-make your Precious Box. Then we
can put in all the information, as we gradually get hold of it, and the photographs, of course, and this article in pride of place. And the nationals may
have also run the story, so if we go to Colindale, we can check their records,
too, and gradually build up your personal dossier.'

She paused for breath, but only for a second, clutching his arm in excitement. 'And, listen – there's even better news. I was determined to dig a bit
deeper, so I asked if I could have a word with someone at the hospital who
might let me see the records from the sixties. The receptionist tried several
different departments, and there was a whole lot of palaver while they put
me through to various bods, but they all told me the same thing – they never
keep records that far back. Eventually they let me speak to the data-protection manager – a lovely man called Oliver Birch, who actually came down
to see me and was more helpful altogether. I showed him the piece in the

Advertiser and said I was a close friend of yours and that you were longing to discover more about your—'

She was interrupted by the noise of banging, vibrating through the ceiling in a series of sharp hammer-blows. At least it gave him an excuse to stay silent, since he'd just realized, with a jolt, that her detective work was totally his fault. He *had* given the impression of someone desperate to know about his origins, unaware how threatening it would feel to be actually faced with the facts.

Mandy glanced up with a grin. 'Those must be the neighbours you told me about – the DIY fanatics!'

'Dead right!' he said, glad to change the subject. 'It beats me how they can still find things to do, when they've been hammering and drilling ever since I first moved in. We'll probably hear the other couple soon – shrieking at each other or hurling crockery about! Hey, darling, do drink up. You haven't touched your wine.'

Mandy, however, refused to be diverted, either by her wine or by the neighbours, and merely raised her voice above the din. 'Well, this Oliver chap confirmed that, after eight years, all records are destroyed, but he said one of the present staff might know a much older nurse – you know, someone retired but who still lived in the area and would remember back to 1964. And, bless his heart, he promised to ask around – said he'd send a memo to all the nursing staff and, if a name did come up, he'd drop that person a line. He said he's not allowed to give me their details, because of data-protection issues and stuff, but he can give *mine* to them, and leave it up to them whether they get in touch or not. And he thought it was quite possible – you know, someone old, with nothing much to do except sit and watch TV, might welcome the chance to revisit such a drama from their past. So, who knows, darling, in just a week or so, you might be face to face with one of the nurses who actually held you in the first days of your life!'

He seized his glass and drained it in a few choking gulps, while he struggled through a maelstrom of emotions. One part of him ached to meet such a person, so that he could discover what he'd been like as a baby: a bawling brat, or a charmer; a clingy, sickly infant, or a stout-hearted little fighter? Perhaps it was downright stupid to put his head in the sand; refuse to take this chance to fill the gaps. Certainly he was deeply touched that Mandy should have gone to so much trouble purely on his behalf – all the more so because her approach was such a contrast to Christine's. The latter's uptight, conventional family had regarded the idea of a foundling as suspicious and unsavoury, so his wife had followed their lead in sweeping the whole thing under the carpet. When people enquired, she had sometimes even pretended that both his parents had died young. And yet, strange as it might sound, that felt safer, somehow. Admitting you'd been dumped could turn you into a piece of rubbish – dross, to be discarded.

'I just wish you could meet the park-keeper, as well, but he must be dead and gone by now. It says here that he was sixty-three when he found you and very near retirement. But Oliver did suggest a few other things. Apparently, there's this outfit called NORCAP, who help people trace their origins and have a separate group specifically for foundlings.'

Yes, he knew about NORCAP but, once again, he'd concluded that the dangers in the search might outweigh the benefits. But couldn't he change his stance? Did he have to be so stubbornly determined to leave things under wraps? He sat wrestling with himself, but the maddening noise reverberating overhead made it impossible to come to a decision.

Mandy, though, seemed unfazed by the racket and, after a quick sip of wine, returned to her account. 'And he mentioned a Foundling Museum – in Brunswick Square, I think he said. Apparently, it's quite well-known. Have you ever heard of it?'

Certainly he had, but its very name was enough to reignite his former reservations. He had never had the slightest wish to see those pathetic 'exhibits'. In the past, most foundlings had died, whether in the workhouse or the famous Foundling Hospital. Bastard kids had been treated like dirt; fed on watery soup; sometimes even forbidden to speak, or known simply as girl fifty or boy ninety, without so much as the distinction of a name. *Royal* bastards were different, of course. Charles II's illegitimate sons had all been created dukes. But for a commoner like him, the whole concept of illegitimacy remained a source of shame.

'And he said, if you agree, we could send out an appeal on the Internet – you know, does anyone remember the "miracle baby" of 1964? Or we could put leaflets through people's doors in the local Croydon area, or—'

Absolutely not. Having spent his life concealing his past, he had no intention of broadcasting his foundling status to the world. None of his colleagues at the library knew about his origins – not even Stella, who was close friend as well as colleague – but if Mandy went full steam ahead, it would soon be the hottest gossip in the staffroom.

She nestled closer; put a protective arm around him. 'Darling, are you OK? I thought you'd be over the moon, but you seem – well, sort of weird

– almost as if you don't even want to listen. Yet it's such a touching story. I actually cried when I read it, thinking about your mum and how she must have felt. I mean, she obviously cared about you deeply, leaving you in the warm like that, in the park-keeper's cosy little office, right in front of the stove—'

'*What*?' He gripped her arm so hard, she flinched. 'Mandy, what did you just say?'

'Well, the stuff about your mother. You've read it, haven't you? It's all here, in black and white.' Retrieving the printout from the sofa, she pointed to the second paragraph.

He took it from her with shaking hands. Even now, he didn't dare believe her until he had seen those crucial words with his own eyes.

'See?' She pointed over his shoulder. 'They reckoned she must have slipped in with the baby while the park-keeper was out on his rounds. And apparently that was quite a feat, because the office was behind a wall, with big double gates, kept strictly locked. And, anyway, there'd have been other staff around – gardeners coming and going, and people working in the glasshouses – who would pounce on any trespassers if they were discovered in the private yard. So, of course, the old boy was completely gobsmacked when he came back in and found a new-born baby by the stove. You were wrapped up in three cardigans, it says – not baby-size, but big, warm, cuddly ones.'

'*Three*?'

'Eric, what's wrong with you today? You're meant to be a librarian, yet you seem to have forgotten how to read! You haven't taken in a single thing, as far as I can see.' Shaking her head in bewilderment, she slumped back against the cushions and took refuge in her wine.

He was now struggling to control his tears. Those cardigans, the stove, the little haven of the office – all superseding images that could have been so different: naked infant flesh turning slowly blue in a germy metal litter-bin, or decomposing in a clump of thorny shrubs. Mandy had given him treasure; banished his worst fears.

'I … I've taken in absolutely everything,' he managed to stammer out, at last. 'And, Mandy darling, I just don't know how to thank you. I'd never have found this article without you.'

'Well, it was dead simple, actually. In fact, I'm completely at a loss to know why you didn't do it yourself, as soon as you left care – or even years before.'

No, she couldn't understand – nor could anyone. 'Did you *go* to Park Hill – see the office and everything?'

'No. I was fearfully late by then. I'd promised Beatrice I'd help out in the café and she kept texting me to see where I was. But surely you must know the place, when you've lived in Croydon so long.'

'I've, er, never actually been there.'

'Why on earth not? Weren't you curious?'

Curious – of course – but it came back to the same issue of his mother. Why would she choose to leave him in a recreation ground – such a scrappy, unromantic sort of place? If it *had* to be outside, then why not Lloyd Park, which was gracious and extensive, or Coombe Wood, with its historic house and grounds? Better not to know, he had invariably concluded.

'But you must have been to Mayday.'

'Never. The only time I landed up in hospital, it was the old Croydon General, to have my tonsils out.'

'Listen, darling' – Mandy gripped his hand – 'why don't we go on a sort of odyssey together? You know, visit Mayday and Park Hill and take lots of photos and collect anything we can for your Precious Box. I've already started making the box and I have to say it's quite a work of art – just you wait and see.'

As he bent to kiss her, she suddenly leapt up to her feet. 'Something's burning, Eric! Either that, or the flat's on fire.'

'No, it's not the flat, it's dinner! Oh, my God – it'll be charred to a cinder by now!'

He rushed out to the kitchen, opened the oven, which was belching clouds of smoke, and withdrew the blackened, shrivelled chicken-corpse.

Yet, as he stared down at the wreckage, he found himself grinning like a loon. They could always feast on trifle, after all. The only thing that mattered at this moment was the fact that his mother had wanted him to live; had braved high walls, locked gates and even possible arrest, to ensure that her beloved son was left somewhere safe and warm.

chapter twelve

'It's absolutely nothing like I thought.' Stopping in his tracks, Eric glanced around at the sweep of grass, stretching as far as the eye could see; the well-established trees and glossy shrubs – a green oasis, tucked peacefully away from the soulless office-blocks. 'So much larger, for one thing. And nicer altogether – more like a proper park.'

'Well, they changed the name from Park Hill Recreation Ground to Park Hill pure and simple.' Mandy was busy taking photographs, snapping away from every angle. 'And you'll never guess when – 1964 – the very year you were born! I reckon they wanted to upgrade you.'

He laughed, although the sound was almost jarring in his present state of mind. It was incredibly emotive coming here for the first time in his life – the very place his mother had left him; cutting the cord, for ever. Was it as cold then as today, he wondered, picturing the unhappy girl not only terrified and weakened after the birth, but also frozen stiff? All the years he'd lived here, he'd been desperate to believe that she had deliberately remained in Croydon, so she could watch her son grow up – brushing past him in the street; sitting next to him on the bus; mouthing a silent goodbye as he went into school each morning; a silent hello when he emerged again, at four. And while he'd imagined her observing him, he, too, was seeking her. Any red-haired woman, at least fifteen years his senior, invariably attracted his attention. Could *that* one be his birth-mother? And should he pretend to trip and fall, so that she would pick him up, console him, reveal herself, at last?

'Look!' said Mandy. 'Roses in bloom. Amazing in mid-January!'

He was tempted to pick one and twine it in her hair – although one would be poor recompense for the sheer trouble she had taken today. She deserved a whole nursery-full of roses, not only for arranging what she called this 'pilgrimage', but for coming with him and giving him support.

Without her, he would never have found the courage to venture here at all.

A flurry of seagulls went soaring overhead; their white wings a reproof to the leaden greyness of the sky. Just minutes ago, they had seen a couple of parakeets, and several self-important crows were strutting around, calling to each other with deep-throated, rasping caws.

'It's almost like a little wildlife sanctuary.' Mandy took a photo of two squirrels, chasing each other up a tree.

He nodded, profoundly relieved that he could ditch his long-feared image of some crummy recreation ground and replace it with this charming pleasure-garden. He was also glad it was so central. OK, Lloyd Park might be better known and larger, but it was further away from vital public services, so a tiny infant might well have died while waiting for the ambulance.

'And we seem to have the place to ourselves. I suppose most sensible people are indoors in the warm.'

'Look,' he said, suddenly anxious on her behalf, 'we can call a halt now if you're cold.'

'I wouldn't dream of it! I want to see absolutely everything, especially the place where you were found. It's such a shame the actual building was demolished.'

Not a shame – a tragedy, he felt. Everything connected with his mother should be preserved for ever, as vital monuments.

'Mind you, that Polish guy I spoke to in the Parks Department gave me a pretty good idea of what it used to be like. He hadn't a clue himself, of course, because he's only in his twenties. But he made a few enquiries and managed to track down an old chap called Ken, who'd worked at Park Hill as a gardener in the old days, and remembered the original office really well. It was called a bothy, then, apparently, and, although it was fairly basic, the old cast-iron stove made it incredibly warm, Ken said, and could have kept a whole brace of babies alive!'

'Lord!' He clutched her arm. 'You mean, he was actually there when I was found?'

'No, unfortunately not. He left in 1963, although, of course, he heard about it later, on the grapevine. But what he couldn't understand was how your mother ever smuggled you in, in the first place, when the office was barred to the public and behind a high brick wall.'

Because, thought Eric, I meant so much to her, she was willing to brave anyone and anything – a tiger fighting for its cub.

'Anyway, the present ranger's office is on roughly the same site, so I'll take some photos of that, to go in your Precious Box, along with all the rest.'

Even now, he couldn't quite believe that she should care enough to remake that box – and remake it in such splendid style: silk-lined, velvet-covered and decorated with glass beads and fabric flowers. The original, he suspected, would have been plain and functional.

'Oh, this must be the walled garden.' Mandy pushed open a small metal gate beneath a yellow-brick arch. 'The Polish chap told me it was used for growing medicinal plants. And, look, more flowers in bloom – primula and winter jasmine. I'm sure that's a hopeful sign, Eric – you know, that spring is on its way, and better times for you.'

'They're so much better already.' He stopped to kiss her, as he had been doing all the morning. 'I can't tell you what it means that you should involve yourself in all this stuff.' She probably didn't realize that, never before, had another human being taken such an interest in his past.

'It's so quiet in here,' she whispered, pausing for a moment to listen to a chaffinch tuning up, 'we could be in the country. Did I tell you this whole area used to be a deer park? And used by the Archbishops of Canterbury, no less, who apparently hunted here for yonks. You're getting grander by the minute, Eric!'

'Right, that deserves another kiss!'

'Get away! You'll have to wait till tonight.'

She pranced off through the gate, he running to catch up with her, and they walked arm in arm up the hilly path. The beeches, birches and cherry trees were now giving place to evergreens and firs, and even a cedar and an impressive-looking monkey-puzzle tree. Yes, he liked the grandeur.

'Hey, there's the ranger's office!' He stopped dead; took in the scene: a flat-roofed, featureless building, positioned beside a long green metal barrier, with a gate set in the middle. 'Could that be the gate my mother went through?'

'No, the old brick wall was pulled down, and all the buildings behind it, including the bothy, alas. If only the ranger was here, he might have unlocked this entrance for us, so at least we could see the site, but, if you like, we can come back when he's on duty. What's important, Eric, is that your mother must have stood here, on this exact same spot, preparing to sneak in with you.'

He shivered at the thought, but, although his hands and feet were numb, his mind was white-hot with emotion, as he pressed close against the barrier, picturing it as a high brick wall and admiring her determination in allowing nothing to stop her. He maintained a solemn silence, to pay homage to her memory, yet wordless words kept forming on his lips; things he longed to say to her: how he understood her desperate situation and how alone she must have felt; how he didn't blame her; never had and never would, and, if she could bring herself to get in touch, the long gap didn't matter; they could bridge it in a trice, if she would only seek him out.

His natural inclination was to stay here the whole day, soaking up her traces, communing with her silently, but he was aware of Mandy beside him, stamping her feet to try to warm them up. She must be freezing cold and also ravenous. They'd been out since early morning, first visiting the old wing of Mayday Hospital, and then the streets and houses where his various sets of foster-parents had lived. Mandy had urged him to knock and introduce himself, in case any were still there, but he had resisted the idea. Not only was it more than likely they would have died or moved away, but he had no desire to risk arousing painful memories, and had only gone in the first place because she was so keen to see his home-ground.

'OK, time for lunch now, Mandy, before you die of hypothermia!'

They strolled back down the hill; his mind still on his mother, wondering by what cunning means she had gained entrance to the bothy, and where she'd gone and what she'd done, once she'd left him there. Was she totally alone in the world? Did she have money or a job? And what about—?

'Eric, are you sure you don't want to see Grove End? I mean, if we're making a record of all your early life, shouldn't we include it?'

'No!' he said, more brusquely than he intended.

'But it's been turned into an old folks' home, so it'll probably feel less threatening now.'

Determinedly, he shook his head. Whatever the iniquities of foster-care, living in an institution had been infinitely worse – that sense of being a 'charity' child, often hungry, always bullied; with nowhere to go in the holidays and nothing much to do except envy all those other kids who could go back to their families for Christmas, or the lucky few who were taken to the seaside in the summer. If he and Mandy visited Grove End, the horrors would surge back: those countless times he'd cried himself to sleep – or failed to get to sleep at all – because a kid in trouble was being brought back late by the cops, or the whole house being searched for some other child who'd gone missing. In fact, the memory alone had rekindled the experience of lying wide awake, while tramping feet and angry voices re-echoed through the corridors. His only consolation then had been the fantasy that he was living in a *real* home, with a real mother sleeping just across the landing.

'What about the other place – the Haven?'

'That was demolished a good ten years ago – thank God!' However sympathetic Mandy was, there were limits to her understanding. 'Haven' was more the word for her own childhood home, where she and all her sisters had each had a room to themselves, and were allowed friends to stay and sleepovers, and where they would invite whole tribes of relatives for big, jolly family Christmases.

'Well, you just have to show me the library. You can't say no to that.'

'I shan't – don't worry. The library's the best place in Croydon, as far as I'm concerned! But how are we doing for time?'

Mandy consulted her watch. 'Fine. We're due at Violet's at three, and it's almost half-past one now, so if we find somewhere quick for lunch, we should be quite OK.'

'Let's settle for a pub, then, and grab a pie and a pint.' He needed a drink before this next emotional encounter. In fact, he had put up some resistance to the idea of meeting Violet, since it sounded just too highly charged. But Mandy had insisted, on the grounds he needed solid, factual memories, instead of baseless fantasies, to give him a more rooted sense of identity.

None the less, it was all he could do not to order a double Scotch along with his pint of bitter, just to ratchet up his courage.

'Cheers!' he said, nudging Mandy's leg with his, as they sat side by side on the tatty brown banquette, gradually thawing in the fuggy warmth of the pub.

She grimaced, as she inspected her cider. 'Ugh! This glass is smeary.'

'Want me to get you another.'

'No, don't worry. There's such a crush at the bar.'

'It's funny you like cider,' he said, letting his hand creep up her thigh. 'I haven't touched it since I got filthy drunk on a huge bottle of the stuff. I was barely fourteen and being physically held down by a bunch of kids at Grove End, who forced me into swallowing close on half a gallon.'

'Honestly, every time you talk about that place, it sounds more like a Borstal! But perhaps I'm just naïve. I mean, I've never met anyone before who's ever been in care. I presume there are fewer of them, anyway, these days, if so many homes have closed?'

'Well, there must be a good seventy thousand still going through the system. They're called "looked-after" children now, but that's really only window-dressing. I'm sure most of them don't feel properly "looked after" – or "cared for", come to that.'

'The whole thing's so unjust! I mean, from what you say, they need more help than anyone, yet they end up getting zilch.'

'Yes, but don't forget some are pretty tough nuts – villains, rather than victims. Although even the victims often end up as villains – ironically, as the result of being in care. And I'm not sure villains is the right word anyway, when you think what a rotten start they've had, with parents-from-Hell who neglect them or keep them away from school. Almost no one in care leaves the system with any qualifications.'

'And yet *you* got – what was it – nine O-levels? Twice as many as me, yet I had it really easy.'

The difference, he refrained from saying, was that Mandy didn't need to prove herself. With her secure and loving background, she could afford to be easy-going and unambitious; try her hand at a whole range of different jobs: waitress, nanny, florist, artist's model. And if none of them worked out – well, she had doting parents to tide her over a tricky patch or support her next venture, be it jewellery-making or speciality cakes.

'I've told you, darling, it was all down to Miss Mays. If she hadn't kept my nose to the grindstone, I'd have probably landed up on the dole – or worse. It's not exactly easy to study in a children's home, let alone revise for exams. There's so much noise and chaos, and the other kids would punch you up, if they found you with your nose in a book. But I had the refuge of the library and could study there in peace. Miss Mays even supervised my work and set me mock exam-papers, to give me confidence. But, more important still, she treated me like a *normal* child – one who had feelings and should be taken seriously. And she made it clear that I was worth some time and energy, so I felt I had to make some effort in return.'

'But I thought you said you were continually moved from pillar to post, so how come you stayed in touch?'

'Oh, I was only moved within the borough, so *she* remained a constant. And that meant all the more to me, because the staff at the home seemed to be always coming and going. And, even when they were there, they spent half their time filling in forms, rather than interacting with us kids.'

'Well, I can't wait to see where your famous Miss Mays worked. Eat up, darling, then we can get off.'

'It's OK, I've finished.' He pushed his plate aside. Today's emotional rollercoaster had left him with scant appetite.

The cold slapped them in the face as they emerged from the over-heated pub and turned into the High Street, on their way to the town hall.

'Wow! What a fabulous place.' Mandy stood gazing up at the Victorian clock-tower and the handsome building adjoining it, with its stained-glass windows and carved stone frieze.

'Yes, it's a big Arts Centre now, as well as the new library, but, in my day, the adult library was behind us in Mint Walk. That's where I worked for twenty years. But the children's library was *here*, on the site of the present entrance hall. It's a pity it's Sunday, otherwise I could take you in.' He peered through the locked and barred glass doors, seeing only an empty lobby, but, in his mind, transforming it into a treasure-house of books.

'It's funny, I can feel the spirit of Miss Mays still hovering around the place. She used to let me help with little tasks – you know, like sticking date-labels into new stock, or putting books back in their proper places. She'd tell me where they went and why, so I was learning all the time. And sometimes she'd take me upstairs to see Braithwaite Hall, which was the reference library in those days. You can see how grand it is' – he stepped back a pace or two and pointed to the storey above – 'just from the outside. But inside it's even better, with a huge hammer-beam roof and a minstrels' gallery and stained-glass figures in the windows, depicting high-flown things like "Thought" and "Art" and "Science". They use it for weddings nowadays, and concerts and what-have-you. But I used to imagine it was my parents' home and the three of us lived in all that splendour and owned shelves and shelves of leather-bound books, and had troupes of minstrels singing to us non-stop.'

'Honestly, Eric, you seem to have spent your whole life in a fantasy-world!'

'Well, it's often a darned sight better than the real one.'

'I disagree. In fact, my goal, as far as you're concerned, is to try and show you that real life can be pretty good.'

'You're showing me already. Here, give us a kiss.'

'Well, only a quickie. We ought to leave for Violet's now.'

His elation immediately switched to apprehension, which increased to wild proportions as they made their way to Frith Road and found themselves, at exactly 3.01, standing on the well-scrubbed step of a small, neat terraced house.

The door was opened by a spry but elderly woman, with soft, white, this-tledown hair and sharp eyes that belied her age.

'Eric!' she exclaimed, holding out a welcoming hand. 'I recognize you by the hair. It's exactly the same shade as when you were a baby.'

He laughed, relieved that she'd broached the awkward subject straight away. He'd imagined a stressful silence, or endless pussyfooting about, before any of them confronted it.

'And you must be Mandy. Lovely to meet you both. Do come in and sit down. It's perishing out there!'

They followed her into a small, chintzy room, overstuffed with furniture and crowded with china ornaments. An old-fashioned gas-fire popped and purred in the hearth, giving off a cosy orange glow.

'I hope you don't mind cats?'

'I love them,' Eric said, making for the chair already occupied by a well-upholstered tabby, whom he transferred to his lap. Any cat brought a pang of loss for Charlie, but Mandy was already on the lookout for Erica's new kitten. 'And Mandy likes them, too.'

'Well, this is Caesar and he's seventeen, which is almost older than me!'

They all laughed again, and Eric actually felt himself relax, as he sat stroking Caesar's fur.

'We'll have a cup of tea in a wee while, but I thought we'd get down to business first, since Mandy says you're very keen to know something about your first few weeks of life.'

'Well, I have to admit it's all a bit of a blank.'

'You're lucky that I remember it so well.' Violet settled back in the chair, her thin, blue-veined hands clasped loosely in her lap. 'But then it was quite a big event, what with the police and the ambulance-men turning up at the hospital, and the old park-keeper at the head of the whole cavalcade, holding you as if you were Baby Jesus Himself! We had quite a job prising you from his arms. Apparently, he'd recently suffered the loss of a grandson, and he obviously saw you as a replacement – sent by God, he claimed. If the police hadn't intervened, I reckon he would have spirited you off home!'

Eric sat dumbstruck. A whole new life-story was opening up – a doting, elderly park-keeper as Dad.

'Anyway, you were rushed into the maternity ward, where I happened to be on duty, and my heart went out to you immediately. You were such a dear little thing, with your bright red curls and your big blue eyes looking up at me as I cuddled you.'

'You … you cuddled me?'

'Of course. All the time. I knew it was important and, fortunately, you were healthy enough not to have to go into an incubator.'

'But I thought I was very small.'

'Well, just under six pounds, but very hale and hearty. Of course, you had all the proper medical tests, and the paediatrician checked you over carefully, to make sure you hadn't suffered any harm. And he was the one who calculated your approximate date of birth as two days previously.'

'Yes, February 13 – that's on my birth certificate.' A peculiar birth certificate, with no parents' names or details.

'He reckoned your mother was probably very young, because teenage mothers tend to have low-weight babies. And the cord had been roughly cut, so she probably gave birth alone, without a midwife in attendance.'

He drew in his breath, the usual pity he felt for his mother intensified still further.

Violet smoothed the skirt of her dress – obviously a 'best' dress, put on in their honour. 'Actually, the park-keeper wasn't the only one who wanted to take you home. I felt such a bond with you, Eric, that I'm afraid I got quite shirty if anyone looked after you but me. And, even on my days off, I'd come in to see how you were and feel jealous of the staff on duty. You see, I was already in my thirties and unmarried, so I knew I might not have children of my own – which, sad to say, I never did. I suppose a motherless child and a childless mother naturally gravitate towards each other. And you certainly seemed to take to me – far more so than to any of the other nurses. I always got the biggest smiles and coos! Mind you, I had to fight off a fair bit of competition. You'd become the star of the unit. The police had put out an appeal for your mother to come forward, so your story was public knowledge and people began sending in teddy bears and toys and cards and things. One dear old soul – she must have been all of ninety – spent half her pension on a rocking-horse. In fact, you must have had more presents than any baby in the world!' Violet smiled, remembering. 'And the older Eric kept turning up, telling anyone who'd listen the story of how he found you and gave you his own name, and how God *meant* for you to be saved.'

'Perhaps He did,' Mandy murmured, almost inaudibly.

Violet reached out to switch on a table-lamp, as the light outside was fading. 'I knitted you a bear myself, and made it a little hat and scarf. Your foster-parents took it home – Arthur, it was called, after my late father – so maybe you still have it? *And* the rocking-horse.'

He shook his head. If only. 'So I stayed in quite a while, then?'

'Yes, it must have been a good four weeks. They didn't want to discharge you until you'd put on weight – which didn't take too long. In fact, I'll never forget giving you your first bottle. You suckled at a quite frantic rate, then, when you'd finished, you looked around, as if to say, "Yes, that was nice, but how about some more?"'

'He's not much different now,' Mandy laughed.

'Well, in that case, I'd better fetch the tea. And I could do with a cup myself. I'm not used to talking quite so much!'

Mandy jumped to her feet. 'Let me help.'

'No, it's all prepared. I just need to re-boil the kettle and wheel the trolley in.'

'I'll do that,' Eric offered.

'What, and disturb poor Caesar? He'd never forgive me. He's enjoying all that fuss.'

Once Violet had left the room, Mandy came over and squeezed his hand. 'Aren't you glad you came?'

He nodded. More than glad – enchanted. He now had the crucial knowledge that he'd been pampered, cuddled, fêted, fed – showered with love, in short. Even more important, he'd learned the fact, unknown before, that he'd spent two whole days with his mother.

As they heard the wheels of the tea-trolley trundling along the passage, Mandy jumped apart from his embrace.

'So when are you two getting married?' Violet asked, manoeuvring it through the door.

'He hasn't asked me yet,' Mandy said, with a mischievous grin.

He stared at her, confused. Had she told Violet they were *engaged*? Was she expecting a proposal? Surely not, when they'd known each other less than a month.

'No, we're just good friends,' Mandy added, 'as the celebrities tend to say!'

'Well, Eric *is* a celebrity. Look, here's a picture from *The Times*, no less.' Violet took a yellowed press cutting from the lower shelf of the trolley and held it out to them. It showed a picture of a young, slender, dark-haired nurse, holding a surprised-looking infant, swaddled in a shawl. 'You were a bit thrown that day, bless you, with all the photographers milling round and the flashbulbs making you jump. It was quite an event for me, as well. I had my hair done specially. It's not often that I get to meet the Press.'

He took the cutting from her, handling it with reverence. This was an original – faded, tattered, flimsy – and thus more precious than a printout.

'Pity it's not in colour. Then you could see your hair. It's most unusual, you know, for babies to be born with bright red hair. Future redheads are normally blond, as infants, or with just a reddish tint. And you had these brilliant blue eyes, like—'

'I always thought they were rather pale and boring.'

'Get away with you! You were a really bonny baby – everybody remarked on it. And, look, more cuttings here – from the *Telegraph*, the *Mail* and the *Express*.'

'Fantastic!' Mandy said. 'I'd planned to get all these myself, so you've saved me a long slog to Colindale.'

'Well, you're welcome to take them home, if you want.'

Eric craved to drink in every word – *now*, this very minute – not wait till he got home; wished he could be rude enough to turn his back on the other two and ignore his role as guest.

'But we mustn't let our tea get cold. Milk and sugar for you both?'

Mandy answered for him. He was still gazing at the four very similar photographs, struck by the devoted way Violet was holding him; his face against her cheek; her arms circling him protectively.

'And I hope you'll try my home-made sponge. This is quite a treat for me, you know. It's ages since I've had anyone to tea.'

'Well, you must come and visit us,' Eric offered, forcing himself to look up from the cuttings, 'if it's not too much of a trek.'

'Not at all. I'd love that. In fact, I wanted to stay in touch with you right from the beginning. But I heard you'd been adopted, so I didn't think it right to interfere.'

How ironical, he thought. Had she known that both adoptions had actually fallen through, she might have remained a presence in his life – a sort of loving aunt, perhaps.

'I've thought about you so often, and wondered what became of you. I was truly sad you never found your birth-mother, but you mustn't think that people didn't try. The police checked out all the midwives in the area, and all the doctors who'd been doing antenatal work, and they put out calls for anyone who might have seen a woman with an infant, especially in the Park Hill district. But I'm afraid to say all their efforts drew a blank.'

She paused to cut the cake; pass them plates and napkins. 'And, while the searches were in progress, the gifts for you kept pouring in. Of course, the one thing people wanted to give you wasn't in their power to give – your mother. I suspect she was too frightened to come forward. It's a criminal offence to abandon a baby, so she might have feared she'd be arrested, although in point of fact such fears were pretty groundless. Even in those days, people had some understanding that a poor young girl might have felt abandoned herself and simply acted out of panic.'

Eric deliberately started reading the *Telegraph* account; unwilling to hear another word about his mother's tragic predicament.

'*Eric Johnson, 63, a local park-keeper, had the surprise of his life just yesterday, when he came back from his rounds to find a newborn baby lying in front of the stove in …*'

Mandy and Violet were talking – he could hear them somewhere, far away – but *he* was in the bothy, being picked up by fatherly Eric; held securely in strong and loving arms.

'Now, I'm just going to refill the teapot.' Violet eased herself from her chair. 'And give Caesar a drop of milk.'

As the cat sprang off his lap, Mandy came to sit beside him, squeezing his arm affectionately. 'Isn't this just great? And we can probably get a load more stuff. Why don't we have a bash at tracking down the police who conducted all those searches, and the ambulance-men who brought you in, and maybe even the photographers? Some of them are bound to be alive still. We could try the National Archives in Kew. Or there's this special "search" service, I've just discovered, run by the *Daily Mail*, which helps you find—'

He clasped her hand, uncertain what to say. However grateful he might be for her enthusiasm, some instinct made him want to call a halt. There was enough to digest already, without going any further. Besides, whatever she might say, fantasy had its value. Safer, for one thing, and easier to control.

Fortunately, before he had time to reply, Violet came back in; refilled their cups, cut more cake, then went across to the bureau, looking slightly shame-faced. 'I'm afraid I have a confession to make. I stole something that belonged to you, Eric, and it's high time I gave it back.'

Eric stared in bewilderment. What on earth could she have nicked? The rocking-horse? A teddy-bear? No, she was holding out an envelope too small to contain a toy.

'I should have given this to your first foster-mother, to be passed on to your adoptive parents, so I've felt really guilty all these years, keeping it myself. I suppose I wanted to cling on to some part of you, once you'd vanished from—'

'Eric, look!' Mandy interrupted, as he withdrew a small blue plastic band from the envelope. 'That's your hospital wrist-tag – and just perfect for your Precious Box!'

Eric peered at the tiny writing on the label: 'Eric Victor Parkhill', he spelled out – a relic from the first chapter of his life. And that chapter was infinitely better than he had ever dared to hope. So wasn't it time to live in the present now – with Mandy – and leave the past behind?

'I hope you'll forgive me, Eric, dear?' Violet murmured anxiously. 'All I can say in my defence is that you've always had a place in my heart – and always will, even more so now.'

He jumped to his feet and gave her an impulsive hug, pressing her bony body into his, and, suddenly, tears were sliding down her face and *he* was crying, too – although whether from joy or sorrow he really couldn't say.

chapter thirteen

Eric bounded into the children's library and gave a quick glance round. Not too busy, good! – and no one actually waiting at the desk. 'Got a minute, Stella?'

'Not really.'

'Half a minute, then. I've just come up with this brilliant notion – a project based around Remembrance – and I want to share a few ideas with you.'

'Fire ahead.'

'I'd like it to be a joint project, involving children and their parents and people in the community. We could get the kids to interview the old folk, ask them for their memories of the Second World War, and what their dads and granddads might have done in the Great War. Then we could see if we could take them to the Cenotaph and the Imperial War Museum, and also visit a few local war memorials. I thought it might encourage them to think about why we have memorials at all, and how they personally would like to be remembered if they'd died in battle somewhere.'

Stella looked up from her computer, at last. 'Oh, Eric, darling, you're always coming up with some new brainwave! I mean, what about your music therapy scheme? Trevor shot that down and—'

'He didn't. He says he's still considering it. In fact, he mentioned it the other day.'

'Well, the Family History thing, then. We poured our hearts and souls into that, yet it never got off the ground.'

'Only because no one was prepared to give us the budget and, anyway, the—'

'Whatever the reason, it was still a lot of wasted work. And *this* idea sounds equally time-consuming, especially trying to organize school visits.'

'Look, forget the slog – it's valuable education. A lot of them know zilch about the two World Wars – and I don't mean only the children. Just yesterday, a woman asked me if the Battle of the Somme was part of the Crusades!'

Stella gave a non-committal grunt, her attention on the screen once more.

'We can try to get the parents to help their kids with the research – bring in the Local History library, too.'

'Eric, can we discuss it later?' Stella eyed a group of lads now waiting to get their books stamped and doing their boisterous best to jostle him out of the queue. 'Listen, how are you fixed after work? If you're free, why don't we meet in the pub?'

He hesitated, unwilling to mention Mandy – again.

'OK.' Half an hour wouldn't hurt. Mandy wasn't expecting him till later. 'See you there at six.'

He returned to the Information Desk and took over from Harriet, although in between answering queries, his mind kept sneaking back to Armistice Day, working out the logistics of the project. If they based it on one school, they'd need to contact the head teacher before the Easter break, so that work could start in the summer term and be finalized the following autumn. Then any displays or performances could be put up, or put on, the first two weeks of November.

By the time he joined Stella in the Dog and Duck, his brain was fizzing over with new plans. She, however, seemed more cautious altogether.

'We'd need to see if there's any funding available, but we can't count on them approving the idea.'

'Why not? It ticks all the right boxes. And, if we get the ESOL kids to research their own countries' activities during both World Wars, it also covers diversity.'

'OK, OK, just give me time to think about it. I've a lot else on my mind.'

'We could make it very hands-on, if you want. The older kids could take photos of the memorials and do sketches in the museum, and the younger ones make poppies and—'

'Do we have to discuss it *now*, Eric? Why can't it wait till next week? I've had a shitty day and frankly I'm exhausted. I'd rather just relax, OK, and chat. I never seem to see you these days.'

'You see me every day.'

'In passing.'

'We had tea at the same time yesterday.'

'Big deal! When did we last go out together – have a meal or see a movie, the way we used to do? Frankly, you're so obsessed with Mandy, I never get a look in.'

He flushed. All too easy to neglect a former friend, now that dazzling sex and dizzy love were transfiguring his life. 'I'm sorry, Stella – honestly. Let's make a date for next week. Is Tuesday any good?' (Mandy was out on Tuesday, visiting one of her sisters.)

Stella giggled suddenly. 'God, don't remind me of Tuesday! I'm meeting this weird chap from a new dating site I've joined.'

'So why meet him if he's weird?'

'Well, he can't be as bad as the last one.' She raised her voice against some rowdy fellow shouting orders at the bar. 'I haven't told you about Peter, have I? Well, he was *Brother* Peter for the last twenty years – a Cistercian monk, of all things, looking after pigs on some godforsaken island.'

'Heck! Did he turn up with straw in his hair?'

'No, he just looked shabby and sort of lost. Apparently, if you leave a religious order, you receive precious little support. You're just cast adrift, with no proper skills or training and barely a penny to your name.'

'Couldn't he farm pigs somewhere else?'

'Well, he happens to live in Hackney, which isn't exactly swarming with the creatures. And I'm not sure he liked farming in the first place. But the worst thing was, he hardly said a word. Cistercians take a vow of silence, so I suppose he was completely out of practice. I kept starting conversations and he'd answer "yes" or "no", and that was that. And he kept fidgeting and clearing his throat, and was so tense I thought he'd explode. I imagine he hadn't been out with a woman since before he joined the order at eighteen – maybe not even then. And, of course, he'd have taken a vow of chastity, as well, so even if I'd lured him into bed, it would have ended in disaster.'

'Honestly, Stella, you do have rotten luck. Remember that bloke who turned up to meet you in Country and Western gear?'

She shuddered. 'Melvyn, you mean? How could I forget? He must have been twenty stone, yet he was wearing the full works – cowboy hat and boots, leather chaps, bandanna round his neck. We were in this rather conventional bar and everyone was staring. I could have died with embarrassment.' She paused to sip her drink, frowning at the memory. 'At least Peter didn't show up in his habit – or with a tonsure, come to that. Actually,

I'm seriously thinking of giving up this whole dating lark. I mean, look at you – you found Mandy just by chance and I'm sure that's the best way.'

'I'd love you to meet her, Stella. I know you two would get on.' Although it would put him in a quandary: Stella still knew nothing about his background as a foundling and, if the two women got together, Mandy was bound to bring it up. Which meant he must confide in Stella – soon – otherwise she might feel left out, or, even worse, betrayed. 'Why don't you come over to dinner, one evening, to her flat in St George's Square? She's a fantastic cook, apart from anything else.'

'OK. I suppose I don't mind playing gooseberry.'

'Tell you what, I'll ask her to set you up with some gorgeous hunk – maybe one of her wealthy clients. In fact, she's making a cake this evening for a forty-something City banker and I happen to know he's single.'

'In that case, he's bound to be gay. Anyway, I thought all City bankers had gone bust.'

'Not this one. He owns a racehorse, apparently.'

'Well, if he's that high-powered, he wouldn't even look at me.'

'I'll tell him you spend half your time hobnobbing with famous jockeys at Sandown Park.'

'Yeah, when I'm not removing bits of soggy chewing-gum from the latest *Harry Potter*.'

There was silence for a moment – apart from the chink of glasses and a cheerful buzz of conversation from other customers. If he had any sense of decency, he would stay with Stella longer, since she was clearly feeling low. In fact, wasn't this the perfect time to come clean about his origins; get it off his chest, at last? Yet, if he embarked on such an emotive subject, he might never get away and his whole mind and body burned to be with Mandy. In the end, he compromised; bought Stella another drink and a so-called 'healthy' salad, but kept the conversation safe and superficial, before finally admitting that he ought to make a move.

'OK. Sorry if I was grouchy. I'm probably just plain jealous. I mean, there you are, over the moon with your soulmate, while I'm still on my tod.'

He gave her an affectionate kiss, knowing he would feel the same. The whole world should be jealous of his sheer amazing luck.

'Sorry, darling,' Mandy said, coming to the door in a frilly gingham pinny. 'I'm running late, as usual. But you're very late yourself. In fact, I was beginning to get worried. Normally, you turn up on the dot.'

No point trying to explain that his obsessive punctuality was part of a general insecurity that regarded disruption to most travel plans as more or less inevitable. A terrorist attack might halt all means of transport; an inconvenient heart attack delay him in A & E, or apocalypse strike at any second.

She took his coat and ushered him into the sitting-room. 'Just as well you *weren't* on time, because I'm seriously behindhand with the cake. Why don't you sit and watch the box while I finish in the kitchen?'

'I'd rather sit and watch *you*.'

'OK, but I'm doing really fiddly icing, which means I have to concentrate. So strictly no kisses, Eric.'

'Would I dream of kissing you?'

'Actually, I have to say you're rather a fabulous kisser. So many men get it wrong. They're either too violent, or too slobbery, or their breath smells of garlic – or worse.'

He loathed it when she mentioned other men. He was already harbouring strong suspicions about Oliver Birch, the data-protection manager at Mayday. She had let slip last week that the creepy bloke had taken her out to lunch, which seemed odd in the extreme. Why the hell should she need to see him again, when he'd already given her the contacts she required? And it wasn't as if he lived next door; Croydon was quite a trek. Besides, meeting for lunch suggested a certain intimacy that made him want to murder the presumptuous little geek. All week, he had tried to picture him as an ancient, balding windbag, who could bore for England about all seventy-five sections and sixteen schedules of the Data Protection Act, but, for all he knew, the guy might be sex-on-legs.

He followed her into the kitchen, awestruck by the sight of the cake – although 'cake' was an inadequate word to describe such a work of art. It was made in the shape of a racecourse and covered with lush green icing, to represent the turf. The track itself was edged with a trim white fence, and dotted with miniature horses and authentic-looking jumps. There were even spectator-stands and boxes and a tiny winning-post.

'Mandy, it's out of this world!'

'Not bad. The client's a racing fanatic, so it should go down all right. I'm just annoyed with myself that I had to buy the horses. If I'd had the time, I'd have made them out of marzipan, but you know me, Eric – always rush, rush, rush!'

'How on earth did you make the jumps?' he asked, peering at a creditable Beecher's Brook.

'Oh, that's easy. Those chocolate sticks called Matchmakers come in very handy, and I managed to get some *white* chocolate ones, for the fence. As for the brook itself, that's just a Fox's Glacier Mint, melted in a double-boiler and poured on to a marble slab. Once it's set, it looks very much like a little strip of water. Since I started on this lark, I've learned a few tricks of the trade. For instance, ice-cream cones, placed upside-down, make rather effective turrets for a castle. Hey,' she said, wheeling round to face him, 'it's *your* birthday in a fortnight. Do you fancy a castle-cake? Or how about a library? That would be a challenge – all those fiddly books!'

Could she be serious? To have all that time and trouble lavished on his birthday belonged in the realm of fantasy. His childhood birthdays had been either non-events, or had ended in disaster. None of his various foster-parents seemed capable of remembering the date, with so many other foster-kids jostling for attention. Admittedly, he'd always had a birthday cake at Grove End and the Haven, but it took only a fight or some random act of violence to halt the celebrations, and the whole bunch of them, guilty and innocent alike, would find themselves banished to their rooms.

He watched Mandy pipe green rosettes around the base of the cake, impressed by her dexterity. Perhaps he should set her up a website, so she could put her business on a more professional footing and display her wares to the world. He longed to be of use to her; repay her for the fact she had transformed his life so radically. He couldn't tear his eyes away as she continued with her task; enchanted by her frown of concentration and by the tip of her pink tongue just showing between her teeth. Deliberately, he fixed his mind on the Remembrance Sunday project, trying to dredge up new ideas, in the hope that war and carnage might keep his mind off sex.

It was she who broke the silence, looking up for a minute, as she licked a drool of icing from her fingers. 'Actually, I'd like to arrange a proper party for you. I was mulling it over yesterday and I think we ought to hold it on the fifteenth, not the thirteenth. I know it's stupid to be superstitious, but the thirteenth is a Friday, which makes it doubly unlucky. And, anyway, you were found on the fifteenth, so that's the day to celebrate, rather than your birthday. Besides, the Sunday would be easier for my family. I want you to meet them, Eric, and this would be the perfect chance. The only problem is, it's a terrible squash if everyone comes here, so it might be an idea for me to host it at my parents' house in Sussex. There'd be room for the whole tribe, then, and—'

'Hell!' she muttered, breaking off, as a spurt of icing cascaded from the nozzle and zigzagged down one side of the cake. 'Look, I mustn't talk or I'll only get distracted and muck the whole thing up. Can you read the paper or something and we'll discuss it later on?'

It was no hardship to be quiet – although in his mind trumpet fanfares were blaring out, full-volume. All this time, he had remained absurdly anxious that Mandy might prefer to keep her family away from him, in case they disapproved. But now, it seemed, his birthday would be a genuine family affair. The date was immaterial. What mattered was the celebration, which seemed set to surpass all the lame and low-key birthdays of his life.

'Do you know,' said Eric, tugging back the duvet which had slipped on to the floor, 'whales and human beings are the only two members of the animal kingdom that make love face to face?'

'Whales don't have faces, do they?'

''Course.'

'Do they do it doggy-style, as well? I liked that best today.'

'It was all fantastic,' he whispered, letting his hand linger on her breast. Normally, when making love, his fears and problems still churned away at some level. Only with Mandy did they vanish altogether, as he entered a new world whose only purpose was pleasure; whose only language was gasps and cries, and where the only thing that mattered was becoming so much part of her that he lost his own boundaries and temperament. Mandy was ultra-sweet and super-special, like one of her own cakes, yet she also had a wild streak. Indeed, his body bore her marks – purple love-bites, clawings from her nails – as if he'd been tattooed; branded as her love-slave.

He nuzzled against her hair, which was powdered here and there with the odd sprinkling of icing-sugar and smelt of lemon shampoo. He could pen an ode in praise of all her smells, especially the faint, tantalizing odour of her pussy: somewhere between Feta cheese and lilac.

All at once, she sat up; arms folded across her chest. 'Eric, there's … something I want to tell you – something really important.' She seemed embarrassed, suddenly, speaking in a jerky fashion and turning her head away. 'It's … wonderful news, in one way, yet a hell of a shock, I must admit.'

Immediately, he imagined the worst: she'd been offered a job by some filthy-rich tycoon, to make cakes for him on a permanent basis, but the bastard lived in Sydney – 10,000 miles away, or perhaps she'd won the

Lottery and was now a millionairess and thus completely out of his reach, or been accepted on some cookery course that just happened to be based in the Far East.

'Well, spill the beans.' The jokey tone was totally at variance with his impending sense of loss.

'Thing is,' she mumbled, deliberately not looking at him. 'I'm ... pregnant. With your baby.'

Dumbfounded, he stared at her, hardly knowing what he felt. Delight, terror, pride and incredulity were stampeding through his mind in such dizzying succession, the result was total confusion.

'I suspected something was going on, so I bought a pregnancy-testing kit and did the test this morning. And it was ... positive.'

'Surely it's too early for a test?' he asked, ashamed to hear how cold and almost businesslike he sounded. He should be whirling her round in excitement, whooping in sheer relief that, far from losing her, they were now inextricably bonded.

'No. They're much more sensitive these days. In fact, they can pick up a pregnancy before a woman's even missed her period. And it's actually thirty-two days since we first made love.'

'But ... but I thought you were on the Pill.' Why was he being so damned negative? Because he himself had been remiss? Never, once, in thirty-two days, had he mentioned contraception, and, of course, on New Year's Eve itself, the sex had been so stunningly sensational, no way would he have stopped to indulge in a bout of risk-assessment or fumble for a condom.

'I assumed you'd be pleased,' Mandy said, accusingly. 'Yet you seem to be saying I was careless – even blaming me, for God's sake.'

'I'm not. I'm *not*.' He reached out to squeeze her hand. 'I'm just ... overwhelmed, that's all.' How could he explain the clash of contradictory emotions – the elation of being a father again; creating another person who actually shared his genes and could be counted as true family; and the importance of this new lasting tie with Mandy. Yet also the huge worry of it all – not just the financial hassle of paying for two children when he was already strapped for cash, but the anxiety about fatherhood in general. Having never had a father himself, nor any other male as role-model, he had experienced the deepest apprehension when Erica was born. And now that his marriage had collapsed and his only child chosen not to stay with him, but accompany her mother to Seattle, his sense of inadequacy had grown. Suppose Mandy left him, too, and took the baby with her? After all, she knew nothing of the very fears that had driven his ex-wife away. And, added to the turbulent mix, was Christine's own experience of childbirth: she had almost died in labour, suffered months of post-natal depression, and lost all interest in sex once she had given birth. Could he really afford to take such risks with Mandy?

'Well, you still haven't said a thing, Eric.' She snatched her hand from his. Her body was flushed from love-making, but her face was cold and closed. 'Do I take that to mean you want me to get rid of the kid?'

Blood rushed to his cheeks. 'How could you even *think* such a thing?'

'It's obvious, isn't it? The way you've reacted – with silence and suspicion.'

'Listen, Mandy, you can't possibly believe that someone with my history would ever be pro-abortion? The only reason I'm here at all is that my mother didn't choose that option. And, of *course*, I want your baby.'

'*Our* baby.'

'Our baby, yes. I'm thrilled about it. But the news took me by surprise and I need a bit more time to digest it. I mean, I didn't think you even wanted children.'

'I've wanted them for years. But not with just anyone. It had to be the right person.'

All his fears came swarming back. How the hell could he be 'right', when he was neither wealthy nor good-looking and, worst of all, ruled by irrational terrors? Mandy would hardly want a spineless wimp as father of their child; someone forced to renounce whole acres of experience that normal people enjoyed without a qualm. And could she ever comprehend the sudden dread that overwhelmed him sometimes when he grappled with the fact that man knew almost nothing – despite all the 'knowledge' in all the libraries in the world – and was adrift in an incomprehensible universe, infinitely beyond his grasp. She would simply laugh; tell him not to be so serious.

'If you really want to know, Eric, I'm feeling pretty lousy. I mean, it's actually quite frightening being pregnant – and a thousand times worse when I'm not even sure if you want to go ahead.'

God, what an insensitive lout he was! *She* was the one actually carrying the child and faced with the upheaval of pregnancy and childbirth, yet he'd been wallowing in his own existential angst, without sparing her a thought. Was he behaving like his *own* father, who had presumably run off and refused to be involved? The thought was so horrific, he began covering her with kisses, frantically moving down from lips to breasts to belly, thighs and toes. Then, easing himself on top of her, he whispered, 'It's the best news in the world, my love.'

And, suddenly – miraculously – it was.

chapter fourteen

'Happy birthday, Eric!'

'Happy birthday!

The phrase had been repeated so often, he was coming to believe that today truly was his birthday. And Mandy was right: it did feel better to celebrate the day that he'd been found; the one day of his life he'd been something of a celebrity.

A tall, flame-haired woman was making her way towards him; a slightly older version of Mandy.

'I'm Prue,' she said, dispensing with formality and giving him a hug, 'the eldest of the sisters.'

'Ah, yes, I've already met Angela and Karen, so now the trio's complete. And I have to say we redheads are out in force today!'

She laughed. 'Did you know that less than two per cent of the entire human population have red hair, so we truly are remarkable?'

He forbore to say that redheads had a reputation, dating back to the ancient past, for unbridled sexuality. Was that why sex with Mandy was invariably sensational – because they were redheads to the power of two?

'It's a pity we don't live in Holland,' Prue continued, warming to her theme, 'because there they hold a Redhead Day – a festival for people with naturally red hair. Mind you, it has to be the genuine article – no dyes or tints allowed. Hey, why don't we all attend this year, just for a lark? Holland isn't far.'

Much too far for him – and, if he was forced to board a plane or ferry, far from being a lark – so he simply gave a non-committal smile. He already knew about Redhead Day – part of the stash of useful and useless facts, amassed in his long years as a librarian. He also recalled the intriguing fact that medieval stained-glass artists used the urine of pre-pubescent, red-haired boys to thin their oxide paint, but perhaps that wasn't quite the thing to mention in this company. Anyway, Karen had now joined them and the conversation turned – again – to his origins.

'I think it's terribly romantic being a foundling, like something in a fairy-tale.'

Hardly romantic, he reflected, and not many happy endings. Despite the clutch of famous foundlings – Oedipus, Moses, Romulus and Remus, Heathcliff and the like – most abandoned infants were unwanted, undistinguished bastards.

'But do you honestly have *no* idea,' Karen persisted, looking him in the eye, 'who you are or where you come from? I find that quite incredible!'

Incredible, maybe – romantic definitely not – but how would Karen react if she knew that her own sister was expecting a foundling's child? There was no more chance to speculate, however, because someone else was approaching: a much older woman in a smart, green, silky dress.

Ah, there you are, Eric! I couldn't see you in this crush. I'm Frances, Mandy's grandma.'

He shook the small, gnarled hand, surprised by the strength of its grip. Clearly a feisty lady. Even her shock of coarse white hair had the thickness of a horse's mane. Perhaps she, too, had been a redhead in her youth – like Mandy's mother, Joyce, whose hair had dulled and faded but was still unmistakably auburn.

'So how do you like the house?' she asked. 'I used to live here myself, you know, until it was too much for me to manage.'

'I love it!' Whenever he'd drawn a house in his childhood, it had always been something along these lines – set in idyllic countryside, with a thatched roof, oak beams and roses round the door – just because it was so different from the reality he knew. He glanced through the latticed windows at the view of rolling hills beyond, which even a sullen February sky couldn't do much to spoil.

'Where's Mandy?' Frances asked, scanning the crowded room. 'She seems to keep disappearing.'

He looked anxiously around. Last time he'd seen her, she'd been in the kitchen, knocking back the wine. All that booze couldn't be good for the baby – not that he could mention it in public. The baby was their secret.

'I'm starving, Mum,' Tim complained, running up to Karen, accompanied by Joyce. 'When are we going to eat?'

'Not till six.'

'That's ages.'

'We'll have the cake before that. Pretty soon, in fact.'

'How did Auntie Mandy make the cake,' Tim's sister, Rose, enquired.

'It was a real labour of love, I can tell you.' He was only too happy to talk about the subject, since he found it deeply touching that so stupendous a creation had been made solely in his honour. 'She bought the bookshelves from a dolls'-house shop, and made the books herself, from marzipan, which she dyed with some sort of food-colouring, to make it look like leather. Then she used gold paint and gold metallic markers for lettering in the spines.' It was too complicated to explain that Mandy had even included the book, *Tom Jones* – as a little in-joke between them – and made a marzipan Miss Mays, complete with tiny pince-nez. 'And the library ladder was part of a set of bunk-beds, which also came from the dolls'-house shop.'

'I wish she'd make *me* a cake,' Rose said longingly.

'Well, perhaps she will,' Eric dared to venture, 'if you ask her really nicely.'

'Mum, I'm too hungry to wait for the cake,' Tim wailed, jigging up and down.

'OK, help yourself to something from the fridge.'

'I'm sure that child's got a tapeworm,' Joyce remarked, once Tim had rocketed off. 'He's always ravenous.'

'Don't be silly, Mummy,' Karen muttered irritably, moving away to speak to someone else.

Mum, Mummy, Mamma ... Eric was always super-conscious of such words; words in extensive use today, with four generations present. He was also very much aware of the natural bond between the mothers and their children; that unspoken sense of belonging and security. As a kid, he'd been forced to call all his various foster-mothers 'Mum', which had struck him as bogus, even at the time, since surely there could only be one mother. Besides, those 'mums' had so many children, continually coming and going, how could any one child be truly special, truly loved? And, once he'd left each successive 'home' and been carted off to yet another address, new kids would always take his place and he'd be instantly forgotten. A real mother wouldn't forget her son.

Having excused himself to the others, he went in search of Mandy; found her in the kitchen still, pouring herself another glass of wine. Could *she* be nervous, too, he wondered, because he was on trial here as her boyfriend and might be judged unworthy? Worse for him, though, surely.

Fortunately, she put down her glass and rummaged in a drawer for matches. 'Let's light the candles now, OK? The kids are getting restive.'

'Yes, fine by me.'

Once back in the lounge, she clapped her hands for silence. 'Right, we're going to cut the cake and drink a toast to Eric, so if you could all gather round the table....'

The process took some time, as the more ancient of the guests had to be coaxed away from their comfy chairs by the fire, and various squabbles between the children sorted out with at least a token show of justice. Eventually, however, both young and old were assembled in the centre of the room.

'Damn! Some of these refuse to light.' Mandy discarded her third match and tried to straighten the recalcitrant wicks.

'I'll help,' Helen offered, flicking on her lighter.

A cheer went up once all forty-five candles were successfully alight. Eric felt embarrassed by so many – surely five would suffice – but, when it came to the matter of his cake, Mandy had refused all compromise.

'Right, blow!' she urged, standing close beside him.

'*I* want to blow the candles out!' Rose whimpered.

'No, it's Eric's birthday, not yours,' her mother reproved in a whisper.

'We'll light them again,' Prue said diplomatically, 'and all you children can blow them out together, OK? But Eric has the first turn.'

'If you blow them all out at once, you get a wish,' another child reminded him.

He was so determined to get that wish, he puffed out his cheeks like a hamster and blew with all his might; exhaling in a gigantic sigh, until every single candle was extinguished. The wish itself never varied – regardless of whether he had a cake or not – that his mother would actually turn up on his birthday, in person, in the flesh. It could happen. Couldn't it?

'Well, have you wished?' Joyce asked.

He nodded. Birthdays had always been difficult because of the crushing disappointment when there was no sign of his mother, and not even so much as a card in the post. Couldn't she track him somehow; find out his address? He added his usual silent sub-wish: if she didn't actually turn up, then he craved for her to think of him on each and every birthday – and to do so until her death.

Mandy's father, Harold, an ex-army chap, who still preserved his military bearing, now stepped up to the table. 'I'd like to propose a toast to Eric – to wish him a very happy birthday and welcome him to our home today.'

'To Eric!'

'Eric!'

'Speech!' someone shouted.

'Oh, no! Let me off. I'm not much good at speeches.'

'Just a few words, Eric – please.'

He could hardly refuse Mandy's father, nor his imperious tone of command, as if the old chap were back in the army, issuing orders to a rookie.

He cleared his throat and searched for inspiration, longing to make some announcement that would instantly improve his standing; make him more of a catch. If only, like Tom Jones, he could declare himself of noble birth and thus heir to fame and fortune. Or that he was off to die a glorious death in the service of king and country, as Tom had also done. Harold would surely be impressed by *that*. But since he was less likely to win his military spurs than shit his pants at the faintest sound of gunfire, he decided to settle for a simple vote of thanks. 'I'd just like to—'

'Mum, you said *we* could blow the candles out!'

'Sssh, in a minute, Harriet. Uncle Eric's speaking now.'

'Uncle' was a definite advance, and surely meant he'd been accepted; that this whole extended tribe were actually *his* family – or at least on the way to being so. The thought was so delightful, he immediately gained new confidence and began pouring out his appreciation of the house, the party, the whole occasion and, finally, of Mandy. 'I've never been one to believe in Fate, but I'm coming to think that some kindly power must have directed my steps to All Hallows Church on Christmas Day. Because that was the start—'

Suddenly, he was interrupted by a loud hiccoughing from Mandy. Some of the children began to snigger and he was so embarrassed, he stumbled over his next few words. 'Actually, the … the encounter could well have been doomed. I … I bumped into her, you see, and—'

A second bout of hiccoughing, and he had lost the thread entirely. The children were now laughing out loud, which was hardly conducive to speech-making. She, however, appeared totally unfazed and quite happy to take centre-stage herself.

'Shit!' she giggled, clapping her hand to her stomach in an overtly dramatic gesture. 'I keep getting these awful hiccoughs. I suppose it's because I'm pregnant.'

'You're *what*?' Prue asked, swinging round to face her.

'Oh, Lord, I shouldn't have said! It's meant to be a secret. I promised Eric I wouldn't breathe a word.'

His cheeks were flaming as every eye turned to look from Mandy to him. Why in heaven's name had she blurted out the news like that, when they had agreed to keep it secret? It was far too soon to go public. The baby was barely established and, anyway, they'd planned to tell her parents first, in private; not broadcast it to all and sundry. Indeed, her revelation had already caused a stir. There was a babble in the room, whispered conversations, although he had no idea what anyone was saying. They might all be deeply shocked; regard him as feckless and irresponsible, putting Mandy in the family way when he had known her only six short weeks. They'd assume he'd taken advantage of her; might well gang up against him as an inconsiderate lout. Her father, in particular, was bound to take a Draconian line.

Mandy, though, seemed completely unrepentant and was still hiccoughing and giggling, as her sisters crowded round her.

'I ... I'd better get you some water,' he stuttered, making a wild dash for the kitchen. He just had to escape before the execration started; couldn't bear to hear himself condemned as a sordid, selfish seducer.

chapter fifteen

'He was a loony, though, wasn't he?' Graham said disparagingly, tipping back on his chair.

'No more than any of us,' Rita observed.

'Speak for yourself!'

'I am.'

'Look, let's get back to the poem' Eric urged. 'It's a very famous work – one of the best-known of the—'

'But it's not exactly a laugh a minute,' Graham interrupted. 'I come here to feel better, not bash my brains out in despair. And it's a crappy title anyway – "*I Am*". What's *that* supposed to mean?'

'Well,' Eric began to explain, 'he's lonely and confused and losing his sense of identity, so he's trying to remind himself that he still exists and still has—'

'And we're meant to find that uplifting?' Graham asked, with a sneer.

'*I* think it's very moving,' Alice countered. 'And all the more so when you consider that he wrote it when he was locked up in an asylum – with manic-depression, wasn't it?'

'Yeah, same as me,' said Rita. 'Only now it's called bi-polar.'

'Why all these saddoes?' Graham demanded. 'Gerard Whoever-it-was Hopkins made me want to top myself. Then we had Sylvia Plath, who literally stuck her head in a gas-oven – and good riddance, I'm inclined to say. And now it's fucking miserable John Clare.'

'Language!' Eric warned.

'OK, but the point still holds. Why the gloom, for God's sake?'

'Because depression's part of life,' Warren retorted, 'so it's better faced head-on.'

'Anyway, a lot of poets find healing in their work,' Sue added. 'In fact, I've just started to write myself, so I know it can be therapeutic. And, actually, I love the poem, whatever Graham says. Can we hear it again, Eric?'

Thank God, he thought, for Warren and Sue. The rest of the group had been difficult today – lethargic or distracted, and a couple downright truc-ulent. A fierce argument had even broken out, about the rights and wrongs of confinement in mental institutions – a touchy subject in this particular company. 'OK, Donna, would you like to read it this time?'

Donna cleared her throat, shuffled her feet, flicked back the curtain of long, dark hair that fell across her eyes, and finally began.

> *I am: yet what I am none cares or knows*
> *My friends forsake me like a memory lost,*
> *I am the self-consumer of my woes.*

Listening to the desolate words, intoned in Donna's downbeat voice, Eric was again aware how totally out of synch he was, not only with the dejec-tion of the poem, but with the low spirits of many of those present. He had established the group originally in the hope of helping people struggling with addiction, mental illness, bereavement and the like. And he had delib-erately chosen poets who themselves had suffered, or come close to despair, so that their words would touch a nerve and offer consolation. Of course, when he'd first proposed the scheme, he'd been feeling pretty desperate himself, and thus naturally in tune with the dark mood of the works. Yet now his life was totally transformed and, in truth, he felt a hypocrite, expounding John Clare's torment, while he himself was sitting smugly on cloud nine; elated by the momentous fact that Mandy's entire family had accepted her pregnancy with delight – indeed, relief.

'We've been telling her for ages,' Prue had said, giving him a hug, 'she shouldn't postpone motherhood too long. She never took much notice, though, until *you* came on the scene. You're the only man, Eric, who's ever made her see sense!'

> *Into the living sea of waking dreams,*
> *Where there is neither sense of life or joys …*

Donna's voice jolted him back to the poem, although he felt only still more guilt that while John Clare found no pleasure in life, his own mood bordered on the euphoric. His former doubts about fatherhood had dwin-dled, and even the financial situation no longer looked so grim. Mandy had suggested that he move in with her and split the rent – an alluring prospect to exchange his seedy basement for a stylish top-floor flat, and actually save money in the process. Also, his maintenance payments for Erica would be substantially reduced once his second child was born. Admittedly, Erica herself might feel a little jealous; maybe even see the baby as a rival for his love, but that was bound to pass, if he handled it with care. In fact, she had always wanted a brother or sister, so might actually welcome a step-sibling.

All at once, he realized there was silence in the room. He'd failed to notice that Donna had finished reading – indeed he'd barely taken in a single word of the poem. That was seriously remiss. In fact, the group's unfocused mood today was probably his fault, since he himself was finding it so hard to concentrate; his mind more engaged with weighty personal questions: should he propose to Mandy and, if so, when – next month, next week, tomorrow? Would her family expect it? Was he even ready to marry again so soon? And if he was going to be a husband and a father, should he aim for promotion; try again for a manager's job, despite his dislike of the role?

Looking up, he saw every eye focused on him, in expectation, puzzlement. Once the poem was re-read, he normally gave a little spiel, pointing out various things they might have missed first time. Quickly, he jumped in. 'Now, you'll have noticed in that final stanza, the poet longs for the innocence of childhood and what he sees as the peace of death. He's sunk pretty low, to a state of utter misery, but there *is* some hope of redemption, as he imagines a sort of paradise, where he can be free and—'

'Do you reckon he was feeling suicidal?' Alice asked.

'Well, he had a lot to contend with – that's for sure. He was extremely poor as a child, and had to scribble his verses on odd scraps of grocer's wrapping paper, and he wasn't even properly fed. He grew up to be barely five foot tall, probably on account of malnutrition, and developed all sorts of health problems. And, on top of everything else, he had eight children to feed and clothe, by the time he was forty-odd.'

'Heavens above!' The new member, Beryl, gave a rueful laugh. 'I only have the two, yet they're a handful, even so!'

'And I suppose it must be difficult,' Warren remarked, rubbing his chin reflectively, 'being a poet at all, when you're the son of a farm-labourer.'

Eric nodded. 'Yes; he didn't really belong in either world. He was no longer a peasant, yet felt out of place in literary London, where he was viewed as a bit of a bumpkin, And he also—'

'Isn't it time for our soup?' Graham interrupted, yawning hugely, then cracking all his finger-joints in turn, as if to indicate his boredom by sound as well as gesture.

Marjorie peered at her watch. 'Fifteen minutes *past* time,' she confirmed – the only words she had spoken throughout the session.

Hell, thought Eric, he was truly losing his grip! Normally, he kept a strict eye on the clock and stuck carefully to schedule. In just the last few days, though, time had taken on new dimensions – the nine months of a pregnancy; the two months until his lease expired and he could move to St George's Square; the four weeks till Erica's visit, when he planned to tell her about the baby and hoped she would forge a close relationship with Mandy. 'I'd better go and see what's happened. Maybe Helen's been delayed.'

It was a relief to leave the room. He was in need of a brief respite to pull himself together; reflect on why the group had been so much less successful today and why Graham, in particular, was in such a bolshie mood. Could that be his fault, too? Perhaps he was exuding an air of smugness that might well alienate a chap who happened to be homeless, epileptic and struggling to come off drugs? And the fact that Barry, Lee and Hannah had all recently dropped out was also a bad sign. Maybe he needed to reformulate the group's basic aims and structure; get feedback from existing members as to a possible new format.

As he walked towards the staffroom, struggling between self-reproach and elation, he bumped into Stella, just returning from her lunch-break.

'How's it going, Eric?'

'Well, to be honest, not that brilliantly. I think I've lost the plot a bit today.'

'I'm not surprised. It's a wonder you can concentrate at all, with all this drama going on in your life.'

He noted the edge to her voice. Last night, he'd invited her for a drink, for the specific purpose of revealing his foundling origins, at last, and also confiding the news of the baby. She had reacted to both bombshells with uncharacteristic coolness; annoyed, perhaps, that he'd concealed his background during all the years they'd known each other, and probably jealous of Mandy's pregnancy, since she herself had always wanted children.

He and Mandy had discussed it later, in bed, and decided to ask her to be godmother – or maybe *un*godmother, in light of her agnosticism. At least it would build a connection between her and the new child; make her feel less excluded, more part of his new family.

'Hey, there's something I want to ask you, Stella. Would you have a minute after work?'

'May do,' she said grudgingly.

'OK, I'll recheck at ten to five and see how things are going.'

He dashed into the staffroom and found Helen visibly flustered; trying to heat the soup, wash up mugs and butter rolls, all at the same time.

'Oh, Eric, gosh, I'm sorry! You must have been wondering where on earth I'd got to, but all hell broke loose downstairs. A gang of boys came racing in from the street, with this savage-looking dog, and no one could control them. We rang the police, but they took an age to come, so I had to stay there, with Harriet, to try to sort things out, which is why I'm so behindhand. Actually, I'm surprised you didn't hear the racket.'

He shook his head. 'Not a thing.' Sequestered in the study-room upstairs, he'd been blithely unaware of what must have been a very nasty incident. Not his fault, of course; none the less it returned him to his senses. He was meant to be a professional, and had no right to let his personal life take precedence over the interests of the group. His mind was in turmoil today, a joyous, jangling tumult of future plans and challenges – Mandy, Mandy's family, marriage proposals, engagement rings, Erica, the new baby, the move to St George's Square – but he made a silent vow that, after the soup-break, he would consign the whole imbroglio to temporary oblivion and focus solely on John Clare's problems, not his own.

He picked his way with care between the sludgy piles of snow, in danger of measuring his length on the pavement, where the puddles had frozen into mini-skating rinks. The succession of snow, rain, sleet and floods over the last few days had made it impossible to use his bike and he was missing his normal exercise. His energetic workouts with Mandy provided perfect compensation, although tonight he was on his own at Vauxhall, catching up with admin work: a local government report to read on recent service developments, and an assessment to write on his outreach projects and how he planned to expand them.

In fact, it was hard to shift his mind from work, as he continued his zigzag progress to the tube. He was still assessing the performance of the group, which, fortunately, had rallied in the second half. Indeed, considering the weather, it was something of a miracle that nine of the usual fourteen members had managed to show up at all, and might even be seen as proof of their dedication. And Sue had stayed behind to show him some of her poems, and told him that these meetings were more helpful for her personally than any other therapy she'd tried. On the other hand, Nadirah had remained silent throughout the session, despite his frequent attempts to draw her out. He suspected she was only semi-literate; none the less, he was determined to persevere. Growing up in care had left him with a burning wish to change the general consensus that poetry was 'difficult', inaccessible and the exclusive preserve of intellectuals.

'Damn!' he muttered, dodging back from the kerb to avoid a swash of muddy water thrown up by a passing car. Soon, he was soaked to the skin, as yet another snow-shower pursued him in a whirl of stinging flakes. At least he didn't suffer from chionophobia: fear of snow. All those way-out phobias – fear of buttons, beards, shadows, stars, the number eight, even garden peas – made him feel exceptionally courageous. He could confront a beard or a button without so much as a tremor; multiply eight by eighty-eight without missing a single heartbeat; greet his shadow like a dear old friend, and eat garden peas for England. Perhaps Mandy's calming influence was making him less panicky, although, admittedly, it hadn't yet been tested. If she were to suggest a swim in the local pool or a trip in a hot-air balloon, he'd break out in a cold sweat and run shrieking from the room.

Indeed, as he approached the entrance to the tube, he felt his usual apprehension about going down in the lift, especially one so crowded. He glanced at the impassive faces, all deliberately avoiding eye-contact. Did *they*, too, fear the horror of being trapped for claustrophobic hours in a metal box suspended between floors? And the tube was even worse. Each time it stopped in the tunnel – which it did with spiteful frequency – he experienced a choking sense of panic. Yet the people all around him didn't seem the slightest bit concerned, and were reading, chatting, even dozing, for God's sake.

Only back at street level could he breathe again with any sort of ease, knowing he was safe from fatal crashes, terrorist attacks, burial alive, or a repeat of the King's Cross fire. In fact, emerging at Vauxhall, he almost welcomed the treacherous pavements and the sheeting, blinding snow, because at least he wasn't coffined underground.

It was a relief, though, to get in, remove his sodden coat and make himself a warming cup of tea. He had barely swallowed the first sip, when his mobile rang – Mandy, with good news.

'I've found this adorable kitten – and a ginger one, would you believe? I know Erica will love him. And, by the way, I've decided to make her a birthday cake – something really special – so you'll need to tell me what her interests are and what sort of thing she'd like.'

He never ceased to marvel that, once he was talking to Mandy, he became another person. The cowering wally on the tube had instantly expired and, in his place, was a bloke so cool and calm he could take a job as a tube-driver; work night and day in sewers, mineshafts, subterranean tunnels.

Then, when Mandy told him she loved him – which she invariably did, at the close of every phone-call – he could settle down to work with new energy and verve; mobile close at hand, though. She had promised to ring back, to let him know when they could collect the kitten, which was at present down in Sussex.

There was a call within five minutes, and he picked it up with an antici-patory grin. 'Mandy, I forgot to tell you Stella's priceless joke about – *Who*? Oh … Christine – sorry, I was expecting someone else.' His voice changed from velvet to barbed wire. This was the woman who had cheated on him; a fact he found it difficult either to forgive or to forget.

'I'm afraid I have bad news, Eric.'

'Oh my God! Not Erica? What's happened?'

'Don't panic. She's OK – well, physically she is. Emotionally, it's a different story. Her periods have just begun and it seems to have had a dire effect on her. She loathes the whole business, and doesn't *want* to be a woman, or grown-up, or anything. Yet, on the other hand, she's behaving like a trollop.'

'A trollop?' He sprang to his feet, half-anxious, half-indignant. 'What on earth d'you mean?'

'I'm sorry, I can't go into it now. It's eleven in the morning here and I had to leave an important meeting in order to get hold of you. And, anyway, that's not why I rang.'

'So why *did* you ring?' His mind was churning: Erica a woman, yet hating the very thought of it. Despite the fact this was a strictly female issue, he must do all he could to help.

'Christine, are you still there?' he asked, suddenly aware of the silence the other end.

'Yes.' Another pause. 'Look, this is a bit … awkward to explain, espe-cially over the phone. But Dwight's divorce has come through, at long last, so, you see, we … we planned to marry during the Easter break, when Erica would be with you in England. We thought it would be better if she wasn't at the wedding. She's not herself these days; flares up at the slightest thing, or sulks for hours on end. In fact, she and Dwight have almost come to blows on several different occasions, so we didn't think it wise to include her in the …'

As the sentence petered out, Eric felt a shameful twinge of *Schadenfreude*. However generally superior the rich, successful Dwight might be, the guy had clearly made a total hash of relating to a loving and lovable stepdaughter.

'Anyway,' Christine added, 'he has to go to Hong Kong, to see one of his top clients, so we thought the best idea would be to get the business out of the way, then stay on in Hong Kong and have the wedding there – make it a completely private ceremony, so Erica doesn't feel she's missing out on something close to home.'

He nodded in relief. He could well understand how upset she might feel to witness her own mother making solemn vows to another man. He, too, felt excluded; even jealous, for God's sake. Christine's wedding marked the final, official end of his own marriage. He had now lost his wife for ever. It was too late for her to change her mind; return to him and give him a second chance.

'OK,' he said, disoriented by the depth of his resentment. Shouldn't he have left all that behind, now he had a new relationship? 'That's fine by me,' he said, determined to focus on his daughter rather than on himself. 'In fact, if you want me to have her for longer, I'd welcome the chance.'

No response.

'So long as her school doesn't mind, of course. And if they *are* a bit concerned about her missing lessons, I can set her up a programme of work, supervise her homework – all that sort of thing.' He had already Googled her school and obtained the exact details of the syllabus, and was now enjoying the challenge of tutoring himself in a wide range of her subjects.

'No, Eric, I'm afraid you can't.'

'What do you mean? I'm up to scratch in most things – not Spanish, or earth sciences, but I can always ask around and—'

'She's … not *coming* to England, Eric.'

'What?' The word came out as a yelp of pain.

'She's changed her mind and refuses point-blank to make the trip. Actually, I suspect she's trying to get at Dwight and me, hoping we'll be forced to change our plans. If you really want to know, she's being quite impossible, and Dwight's near the end of his tether. There's no way we're going to cancel the wedding and we certainly can't afford to mess this client about. He's Dwight's most important customer, and a touchy sort, in any case, who's easily offended. Besides, we've made all the arrangements, booked the hotel, paid a fortune for the wedding. So there's only one solution: *you'll* have to come over here and look after her while we're away.'

A cold, clammy hand closed around his heart and began squeezing, squeezing, squeezing. Slowly, he lowered himself back into his chair, already feeling dizzy and dry-mouthed. 'But ... but you know I can't fly.'

'I'm sorry, that won't wash. I had to put up with your ridiculous fears all the years we were married, but Dwight is far less tolerant. He finds it incomprehensible that you can't – or won't – get on a plane, and says I shouldn't encourage what he regards as just a feeble excuse. I mean, he and I are burdened with the full responsibility for Erica, while you faff about thinking you're heroic because you see your daughter for two weeks every two years.'

'That's totally unfair!' he shouted, roused to anger now. 'You haven't even *been* in the States two years. And the fact she couldn't come last summer was nothing to do with me. She was ill, for heaven's sake, and, in any case, we'd arranged for her to be with me a whole six weeks, not a measly fortnight. And I was gutted when she couldn't make it, and—'

'Forget last summer. We're talking about *now*. This is a crisis, Eric, and we need you to pull your weight. You can't just shrug off your duty as a father.'

'That's the last thing I want. In fact, if Erica's such a burden, let her come and live with me – permanently, I mean. Then you and Dwight can be free to jet off anywhere you please.'

'She doesn't *want* to go to England. I thought I'd made that clear. I can't force her against her will. And, actually, both Dwight and I think it's utterly preposterous that your phobias – or whatever you happen to call them – should have to rule everybody's lives.'

'They ... they don't.' It sounded unconvincing, even to his own ears. He had restricted Christine all the years of their marriage; refused point-blank to travel outside England; refused to drive a car, or even learn to swim. And Erica had also been affected, of course.

'I'm sorry, but I have to go. I'm needed at this meeting, but I'll ring again tomorrow – seven p.m. your time, if that's OK. But, before I go, I want to make it absolutely clear that we're expecting you in Seattle, fears or no fears. Dwight and I are leaving for Hong Kong on Saturday, 28 March, so you must be here by the Friday, at the latest, OK? And, remember, you need a passport. I've no idea how long it takes to get one, but I strongly advise you to apply first thing tomorrow, in case of any delays.'

Please, God, he prayed, let the delays be endless, then I shan't—

'And you'd better have a look at flights and prices. BA fly direct, but it'll cost you. If you're willing to change flights at, say New York or Chicago, you'll probably save a fair bit. Anyway, I'll leave the arrangements to you. All I need is the date of your arrival.'

Before he could say another word, she had bid him a curt goodbye and put down the receiver. He gripped the arms of his chair; knuckles white with tension. He *couldn't* fly. It was physically and mentally impossible. The mere thought of it had turned him into a wreck. His hands were clammy-hot, despite the chill of the flat, and he could barely breathe for the obstruction in his throat. Ten minutes on the tube this evening had left him close to panic, so how could he endure being cooped up in a plane for ten hours minimum? Any plane was a death-trap; could crash, explode, be targeted by hijackers and terrorists. All the air-disasters of the last few decades were now playing on the wide-screen of his mind, in sickening detail and gory colour: Lockerbie; 9/11; the jumbo-jet ripped open at 29,000 feet, the summer of last year; the landing on the Hudson River, just five weeks ago. He closed his eyes; saw the crowd of hysterical passengers huddled on the wing of the swiftly sinking aircraft, awaiting rescue by frail and perilous boats. He was as scared of water as of planes, and, if it was women and children first, he was bound to drown – if he didn't die of terror first.

Nor had he forgotten the fatal crash in Buffalo, a mere six days ago; the plane dropping from the clouds and nose-diving into a house, killing every passenger on board. He had watched the all-consuming flames on the television News, and could feel those flames now scorching through his body, burning him to ash.

He reached out for his phone. He had to speak to Mandy; share this news with her.

No. He snapped the mobile shut again. How could he let her see him in this state? Both Dwight and Christine were contemptuous of his fears, so she might feel felt the same. He would lose her, like he'd lost so much already – his birth-mother, his foster-mothers, his wife, his daughter, even Charlie – and now beloved Mandy, too. And it wasn't just his fears that would appal her, but the fact that, if he did go to America, she might regard that as a betrayal, in that he'd be putting his first child first. Besides, did he really want to involve her in the whole messy business of an angry ex-wife and a sulky adolescent daughter?

Erica's photo was standing on his desk; her childish face and guileless smile reproaching him. Too easy to dismiss her as a sulky adolescent, when she was still only a kid of twelve and, for all he knew, might be deeply distressed. Why was she refusing to come to England, when he knew full well she'd been looking forward to it? And why should she mind so much about starting her periods? Could she be anorexic; want to remain a child for ever? He'd read about girls who starved themselves to death in the hope of avoiding puberty and all the challenges of womanhood. It was his duty as her dad to support her in this crisis, yet *how*, for heaven's sake, when she lived 5,000 miles away?

He picked up the photo, discomfited still further by her direct and trusting gaze. Dwight and Christine saw him as uncommitted father, and there *was* a grain of truth in that – latterly, at least. He'd become so besotted with Mandy, other things had faded in importance, including, to his shame, Erica herself. Mandy he would phone or text every hour of every day, yet he hadn't rung his daughter for a month. OK, there were problems – the time-difference, for one thing, and the fact that if he did ring, she was often unavailable. But that should have been a warning that something might be wrong. Instead, he'd shrugged it off, assumed she was out with friends, when the reality could be darker altogether. By the sounds of it, she was seriously depressed. And, knowing Americans' love of medication, she might be put on Prozac or some other unsuitable drug, unless he was there to intervene. Which meant he *had* to go and see her; play his part in sorting out the mess.

Yet every fibre of his being was telling him 'impossible': the sickness in his stomach, the churning in his gut, his pounding, throbbing headache, the wild, arrhythmic capers of his heartbeat. Desperate, indecisive, he began pacing round the flat, pulled between fear and responsibility; Erica and Mandy; his daughter and the new child; his duty and his stupid, phobic self. Pausing for a moment at the window, he stared out at the snow, mesmerized by the swirl and spin of the flakes; wishing *he* could be a snowflake: something insentient and transient, which would melt away to nothing.

Suddenly, on impulse, he grabbed his keys and ran full-pelt from the flat, slamming the door behind him and resolving to stay out all night. He would keep walking, walking, walking, just to calm the tumult in his mind and, if he froze to death, or fell and broke his back, well, that was infinitely preferable to getting on a plane.

chapter sixteen

Eric stared at the computer screen, overwhelmed by the enormous choice of flights. The price-range alone varied from a modest £266, return, to an astounding £9,172. First Class, of course, was for millionaires and thus not even on his radar, although he would willingly shell out nine grand, just not to have to fly – indeed settle for lifelong penury if it would let him off the hook.

He zoomed in on the cheapest fare, but found it was hedged around with restrictions and had to be booked three months in advance. Even the day you travelled seemed to make a difference to the cost, and certainly the time of year. There was also a perplexing choice of airlines – at least seven different carriers – an equally confusing choice of airports and a variety of routes. Christine had advised him not to fly direct, simply on grounds of expense; what she *hadn't* told him was whether he should change at Amsterdam, Chicago, Toronto, Dallas, New York or Minneapolis.

Just looking at the different options magnified his fears. And the fact he'd been awake all night meant his mind was quite unequal to the task of cutting through the mass of detail and reaching a decision. Having blundered around for several hours in the freezing cold and funereal-dark, he'd finally come back in at two o'clock in the morning, feeling yet more overwrought.

It was still only five a.m.; the black, murky sky pressing against the windows echoing the blackness in his mind. Fear itself was terrifying. Suppose he panicked in the plane and tried to force the doors? Or, worse, lost control of his bladder or his bowels? Even before he boarded, there might be total chaos at the airport. He'd read about it frequently: baggage-handlers' strikes, conveyor-belts breaking down, huge delays caused by fog or storms; hysterical crowds of passengers forced to wait whole days for flights in conditions not that different from third-world refugee camps.

Subjected to such stress, perfectly normal people could snap, so how would *he* survive? And, even if he found the courage to actually get on the plane, it might be grounded on the tarmac for petrifying hours, with no way of getting out or off.

He darted into the bathroom. His bowels were already loose, from anxiety alone. How would he endure such mega stress-levels for five more weeks, without cracking up, collapsing? He might even lose his job. No way could he go to work this morning and function in his normal fashion. He would have to call in sick, yet the very thought appalled him. He was renowned for his good attendance-record; his determination to struggle in, even with a stomach bug or cold. If only he had some genuine illness; something physical and simple, which people could understand. Even cancer seemed preferable to this paralysis of fear. At least it would arouse a little sympathy, whereas if he tried to explain that he'd rather cease to *exist* than have to fly, he would simply be laughed to scorn. He longed for a switch that would turn him off; snuff him out like a candle; end his mounting panic.

His haggard face stared back at him from the reflection in the mirror: dark circles etched beneath his eyes; tongue, furred; skin, ashen-grey. If Mandy were to see him, she'd be shocked – although he couldn't *let* her see him, or it would all be over between them. No one could love a person who had more or less disintegrated on account of one transatlantic flight.

He barged out of the bathroom, his anxiety still greater as he tried to think of excuses not to see her. He'd better pretend he'd gone down with some infectious disease that posed a threat to her pregnancy. The more lethal threat was the one to their relationship, unless he found some instant cure.

Dragging himself back to the computer, he Googled 'Fear of Flying'. A host of different sites came up, offering every type of remedy: hypnosis, psychotherapy, desensitization, neuro-linguistic programming, cognitive behaviour therapy. There simply wasn't time for such long-winded techniques and, in any case, he had little faith in any of them. Cognitive behaviour therapy might be flavour-of-the-month, but it worked on the principle that most terrors were irrational – a principle he challenged root and branch. Fear was not only rational, it was also perfectly natural in a terrifying world. Many people deluded themselves by imagining they were protected by a benevolent, all-powerful God, or by persisting in the inane belief that nothing bad would ever happen to *them*. His own strategies had always been acceptance and avoidance. He could accept his fears, just as long as he didn't have to face them. But now all that had changed.

Beat the Fear of Flying with a Virgin Atlantic One-Day Course!

He peered at the small print. The course included a fifty-minute flight, which was clearly self-defeating, since he would die of terror on that flight and so never get to Seattle.

Except he had to go – there wasn't any let-out. He couldn't leave Erica with casual friends or neighbours, when she was already disturbed and might find her mother's absence a further source of grief. Indeed, he was partly to blame for her present troubled state. Divorce was notoriously bad for children, and it was his fears and inadequacies that had contributed to the break-up of the marriage.

Turbulence Explained …

The very word made him dizzy and the details were worse still. *You may feel as if the plane is falling from the sky, but, although this is uncomfortable, it isn't dangerous.*

Not dangerous? Who were they trying to kid?

Just after take-off, you may hear thumping and whirring sounds …

No, he wouldn't hear a thing. Long before take-off, he would have collapsed into a coma.

Rest assured that pilots are trained to land in an emergency, even if all the engines fail. The landing may be scary, but you are likely to survive.

'Likely to'? What was *that* supposed to mean? Leaping from his chair, he dashed back to the bathroom and voided everything inside him – not just the contents of his bowel, but the entire length of his intestines; his liver, lungs, kidneys, heart and spleen. If he were as badly affected as this when he was actually on the plane, he might have a shameful accident. There were bound to be queues for the toilets, or they might be out of order, as they often were on trains.

Horrified at the thought, he crawled back to his computer, desperate for some miracle cure.

Cure your Fear of Flying in Under Twenty Minutes!

Well, that was indeed a miracle – or else simple blatant hype. If the claim were actually true, it would mean he could go to work today; spend the night with Mandy, as arranged, and pass the next five weeks in a state of blissful calm.

He skipped the details to find the cost: £499.99. Which meant each of those twenty minutes would set him back £25. He could hardly justify shelling out so much, when he believed in miracles no more than in God.

Still shaky from the runs, he scrolled down the list of options to find something more affordable.

Conquer your pteromerhanophobia with these three simple steps:
Control your breathing.
Relax your muscles.
Stop thinking negatively.

Yes, but how, for pity's sake? If he could master those three steps, there wouldn't *be* a problem.

Suddenly kicking back his chair, he strode into the bedroom and stretched full-length on the bed. At least he had to try; not give way to utter hopelessness. Relaxing and deep-breathing wouldn't cost a penny, and there was just the smallest, slimmest chance that they could transform his full-blown panic into normal – and endurable – disquiet.

Thank you for calling the Identity and Passport Service …

He groaned at the recorded voice. Flesh-and-blood people answering any call these days were as rare as unicorns.

If your inquiry relates to the cost of a passport, please call our fees-information line …

The question of a fee hadn't even crossed his mind, although, in fact, the costs of this whole trip were increasing by the minute – not just the basic fare, but fuel surcharges and airport taxes, transport to and from both airports, travel insurance (exorbitant) and at least twenty grand for all the anti-fear courses obviously required before boarding any flight.

If you wish to book an appointment for our one-week fast-track or one-day premium service, please press 2 …

One week? One day? Part of him still desperately hoped that it was too late to get a passport – the perfect excuse not to have to make the trip. But that was shamefully selfish. He should be glad, for Erica's sake, that the service was so quick.

Palms sweaty, he pressed 2.

Due to the high volume of calls, all our operators are busy. Please wait and we will answer your call as soon as possible …

Mobile in hand, he paced around the flat, listening to the same frustrating message repeated over and over.

Due to the high volume of calls …

The whole world must be wanting passports, which only proved their folly. Each time he scanned the travel pages, he was astonished by the lunatics willing to sit coffined in a plane for up to thirty hours, and all for the dubious pleasure of seeing Ayers Rock or Alice Springs or whatever. Virtual travel was so much easier, not to mention safer. He could take a tour of Alice Springs without getting up from his chair, and the only thing that might crash would be his computer.

Thank you for your patience. Please continue to hold …

Patience? He was getting so worked up, he would start shrieking abuse at the disembodied voice, if he held on any longer.

He grabbed his coat, his keys, his wallet, and braved the snow once more. Far better to go to the Passport Office, in person, and speak to someone real. Since it was only at Victoria, he could walk there in under thirty minutes. The roads were still too icy for cycling, and the tube was out of the question in his present frenzied state. Even the slightest risk of a breakdown or emergency might tip him over the edge.

At least it was now light, and no new snow had fallen. Indeed, the day was reasonably bright, a fitful sun shining on the slush. Two other major blessings were that his bowels had settled down, at last, and Trevor had taken his 'sick-call' with no trace of either suspicion or annoyance. 'Mm, that sounds really nasty, Eric, so don't rush back to work until you're feeling a hundred per cent.'

A hundred per cent? Was he kidding?

As he picked his way along Kennington Road, his mind kept switching between Erica and Mandy, torn between their opposing needs. All the treats he'd planned for Erica had now shrivelled into dust, of course: the theatre tickets, booked last week; the birthday party with her former friends; the boat trip down the Thames …

He felt a deep affection for the Thames – below him now, as he made his way across Vauxhall Bridge. He could ask for nothing better than never having to move too far from London. Seattle would be alien – a soulless city full of skyscrapers, with no history or tradition. Just the thought of being somewhere strange filled him with foreboding; a legacy of the constant different placements in his childhood. Having never had a settled home, never known when he'd be moved again to some strange and scary place, with yet another set of strangers, he'd been left with a profound desire to stay put and put down roots.

As he trudged along Vauxhall Bridge Road, he tried to think more positively. He wasn't actually being torn up from his home-ground and transplanted to foreign soil – or at least only for three weeks. It was just a one-off visit and, before the end of April, he'd be back again, secure and safe.

Don't kid yourself, he thought, you've *never* felt secure and safe.

He switched his mind deliberately to the problem of the kitten, simply as a distraction technique. He'd promised Mandy to look after it at his place until it was properly house-trained, but apparently it couldn't leave its mother yet, so he'd be departing for Seattle just a fortnight after it arrived. Could you train a cat in a fortnight? Kittens, he reflected, were luckier than foundlings, in that they spent longer with their mothers; were fed with mother's milk and cuddled up with them at night.

Sighing, he cut through Warwick Way to Belgrave Road and continued on to Eccleston Square. The Passport Office was at number 89, although there was no sign of it, either there or anywhere. In fact, all the buildings in the square were gracious porticoed houses, very similar to Mandy's. Thank God she'd accepted the story of his 'illness'; even offered to come round and nurse him – an offer he had speedily declined. He hated lying to her, but the alternative was losing her – infinitely worse.

He traversed the square again, in case the numbers weren't in sequence, but still couldn't find any sort of building resembling a Passport Office. Just then, however, he saw a woman emerging from her flat and dashed up to ask for directions.

'Oh, everyone gets lost! It's actually in Belgrave Road.'

'But the address is given as Eccleston Square. See, it's written here.'

'I know – it's crazy. I can't tell you how many people I've had to redirect.'

Cursing, he retraced his steps and found it within minutes; an ugly modern structure made of concrete and green glass. The warm fug inside was welcome, but he was immediately accosted by a big, burly bloke, wearing a black uniform, who barred his way as if he were a terrorist armed with a clutch of bombs.

'Do you have an appointment?' he barked.

'Er, no.'

'We only see people with appointments.'

'Well, I'd like to make one – *now*, please.'

'You can't make appointments here.'

'Well, where do I make one, then?'

'It's not my job to give out information.'

'Thanks a lot. That's helpful!'

'If you have enquiries,' the fellow said, ignoring Eric's sarcasm, 'you can speak to the receptionist.' He pointed to the far side of the foyer. 'Over there,' he snapped.

There was a queue to see the receptionist – not the female he'd expected, but a balding guy with a nose-stud and a tattoo.

'Are you applying for a first-time passport or the renewal of an existing one?'

'First-time.'

'In that case, you'll need an interview.'

The very word was alarming, with its overtones of job-applications and memories from decades back of case-conferences and case-reviews: loads of bossy grownups using words he couldn't understand, and only asking *his* opinion when it was too late to change decisions already made about his life. 'When?' he asked. 'And where? What sort of interview?'

'They need to confirm your identity. You can choose the office you go to, but there's only one in London – Hannibal House, Elephant and Castle.'

'OK. Can I arrange it right away?'

'Hold on! First you have to apply by post, to Peterborough. You'll need this form.' The man handed over a sizeable white envelope. 'All the instructions are in there, too – how you fill it in; what documents you need to send; the type of photos deemed acceptable. Once they receive your completed form, they'll write back within two or three weeks and—'

'Two or three weeks?' he interrupted. 'So how long does the whole thing take?'

'You'll need to allow six weeks.'

'I don't *have* six weeks. This is urgent.'

'Well, it can be speeded up if it's a matter of life and death – and I mean that literally.'

'No, not quite life and death. But I have to fly exactly five weeks from today.'

The man shook his head. 'That's cutting it extremely fine. I can't guarantee you'll get it in time.'

'But I thought there was a fast-track service?'

'Only for renewals, not for first-time passports. All I can suggest is that you use the "Check and Send" service offered by the post office. They'll go through your application, line by line, and send it by Special Delivery. At least it'll get there quicker then, and won't be returned because you've made mistakes, so you'll save time, overall. If you want more information, the nearest post office is in Eccleston Place, just up from here, on the right.'

The queue in the post office was twice as long as that in the Passport Office. Eric stood, fuming with impatience, as various doddery pensioners conducted their maddeningly slow business at the counters, or, in one case, dropped the entire contents of a handbag on the floor. He darted over to lend a hand, retrieving various objects, including two half-eaten chocolate bars, a sheaf of lottery tickets, a box of indigestion tablets and a packet of cat-de-fleaing powder. The old crone thanked him profusely, although it did little to lessen his frustration at losing his place in the queue.

Cashier number four, please….

Cashier number two, please….

Would it ever be his turn? Perhaps he should get a prescription for Valium – or something twice as strong – not just to calm him on the flight, but for all these stressful pre-flight chores. No. If he was heavily sedated when the plane crashed, he wouldn't make it to the emergency exit or be alert enough to propel himself down a chute. Besides, if he arrived in Seattle doped up to the eyeballs, Christine would write him off as a completely unsuitable father.

Cashier number five, please….

He rushed over to the counter, but within minutes he was totally confused, since the clerk informed him categorically that he didn't need an interview and didn't have to go to Hannibal House. All he had to do was apply by post, to Peterborough, and he should receive his passport within two weeks.

'But they told me at the Passport Office I wouldn't get it within *five* weeks.'

'Hey, Adrian!' The clerk shouted at the guy sitting at the adjoining counter. 'Know anything about Hannibal House – having to go there for an interview?'

'Yeah, I think it's some new thing. But there may be certain exemptions. I suggest your customer returns to the Passport Office and asks them for more info.'

Groaning, Eric walked back the way he'd come, only to take his place in yet another queue. The balding bloke had vanished; replaced now by a younger man, with bedraggled, greasy hair.

'The post office don't know what they're talking about. They're not trained in this line of work. And, in any case, if you use their "Check and Send" service, they'll charge you an extra £6.85, on top of the standard fee.'

'What *is* the fee?'

'£72.'

Eric did more calculations in his head. Any hopes he might have had of saving for the baby, or saving for an engagement ring, were disappearing at the speed of light.

'Whereas we can check your form for nothing here.'

'So why didn't someone tell me that, before I traipsed off to the post office?'

'No idea.' A shrug.

'But are you absolutely sure I need to have an interview?'

The man screwed up his face, as if pondering the question. 'Probably,' he said, at last.

Eric suppressed a scream. There were no certainties in life, of course, but one might reasonably expect them in a government department.

'Anyway, I suggest you get the form off and wait and see what happens.'

It was snowing again as he left the building, so he dived into the nearest café; cold, confused and absolutely ravenous. Not that he could eat. Anxiety affected his stomach, as well as just his bowels. But a shot or two of caffeine would help him concentrate. The instruction-booklet for filling out the form ran to twenty-four pages of fine print.

Every year, 250,000 postal applications are rejected or delayed because of simple mistakes....

He could just imagine Christine's scorn if he cocked up the procedure. He was already deeply anxious about getting the passport in time, since the booklet stated clearly that new applicants should allow six weeks. And *his* case might take longer, on account of his being a foundling, with an unusual birth certificate. If Dwight and Christine were forced to postpone their wedding, he would be blamed in perpetuity and never live down the disgrace. The booklet also warned that if he missed his interview for any reason including illness, he might have to re-apply; fill in another form and send new photographs. The mere thought sent further spasms shuddering through his gut.

Only the section headed 'Your Particular Needs at the Interview Office', gave him any relief, since at least he didn't need wheelchair access, a hearing-loop, a carer to be present, or a private room in which to remove his niqab. However, there were further problems in that his form needed counter-signing by a professional person who had known him at least two years. Trevor would probably be classed as a professional, but he could hardly go and beg his help when he was meant to be lying in a darkened room, too ill to move a muscle. Besides, he was loath to reveal to anyone the shaming fact that he hadn't had a passport up till now. The alternative was to make an appointment with a doctor or solicitor, but speed was of the essence – in fact, he ought to post the completed form today.

'Yeah? What can I get you?' The waitress had slouched over to his table: a skinny girl, with a mane of hair twice as long as her mini-skirt. Could he bribe *her* to sign the form; pretend she was his lawyer or physician? No, then he'd be done for fraud, which would delay the process longer still while he languished in Wandsworth gaol.

Which reminded him – he was due at the prison book club in just under a month, for an event he'd arranged himself: a talk by the crime-writer, Simon Brett, about his life and work. In fact, he'd promised to ring Simon before ten o'clock this morning, to give him further details, yet had totally forgotten. And since Simon had mentioned an early dental appointment, he'd be in the dentist's chair by now and would think him rude and offhand, especially as he was doing the talk as a favour and had agreed to waive his usual fee.

The waitress was still waiting for him to answer and gave an exaggerated sigh.

'Er, sorry. A double espresso. Oh, and is there any chance you could you lend me a Biro?'

She gave him the pen from her order-pad – a blue fibre-tip – which put paid to his filling out the form. Fibre-tips, felt-tips, fountain pens and blue ink were all forbidden; a black ballpoint being the only thing allowed. Instead, he studied the instructions for the photographs, and 'studied' was the operative word, since there were seventeen separate headings, mostly prohibitions. Glare, shadows, red-eye, sun-specs – all would invalidate the photo, as would grins, frowns, raised eyebrows or hair across one's eyes. Well, at least grinning wasn't a problem. He doubted if he would ever grin again.

Once the waitress brought his espresso, he put the form away. If even a creased photo rendered it null and void (heading number eight), then a

coffee-stained form was bound to be destroyed. He should have brought
Simon Brett's book with him – the one the book club were reading this
month, in preparation for the author's visit. At least it would have
distracted him, and he could have jotted down some points of interest, so
he could take part in the discussion that would follow Simon's talk. But,
lacking a book of any kind, he reached out for the newspapers abandoned
on the adjoining table.

NATIONAL DEBT REACHES £2-TRILLION …
TERRORISTS INTENT ON MURDER STILL AT LARGE IN BRITAIN …
NEW FLU PANDEMIC THREAT ….

Every headline seemed to prophesy disaster and, even when he rifled
through the Sports section, he found it impossible to concentrate on Tiger
Woods' knee injury, or the traumatic finale of the Third Test in the West
Indies. So, when a glossy brochure fell out of the Arts Review -'Magellan's
Travel Supplies' – he picked it up, with a certain curiosity. Flicking through
it, however, only increased his angst, since, according to Magellan's, anyone
contemplating air-travel required a whole cabin-load of specialist supplies:
crease-free clothing; a folding foot-rest; every type of cushion – for necks,
backs, bums, shoulders, tailbones; a moulded sleep-mask; tamper-proof and
leak-proof bottles; an individual air-supply (a mere £119), and a travel-case
for medicines and vitamins (a snip at £20). Several items were described as
'travel must-haves' – for instance, the Slash-Proof, Snatch-Proof Security
Bag, complete with Pickpocket-Proof Security Wallet. *New* fears were being
added to all his existing ones: fear of knives, thieves, smash-and-grab, deep-
vein thrombosis (Magellan's special socks the only remedy); travel sickness
(ditto Magellan's acupressure bands) infections caught *en route* (deadly, or
even terminal, unless prevented with Magellan's Anti-Virus Flight Spray,
Carbon-Filter Masks and Push-Pen Water-Sterilizers). Well, if he sent away
for that little lot, it would add several thousand pounds to his fast-esca-
lating flight-costs.

Suddenly decisive, he slammed the brochure down, gulped his tepid
coffee, flung some coins on the table and hared off to Victoria Station to
find a photo-machine.

It was already occupied by two teenage girls, who were sitting on each
other's laps, making silly faces in the mirror, applying blusher and eye-gloss
and generally larking about. It was obvious that they weren't actually

taking photographs, and, in any case, they had left the curtain undrawn. However, he hadn't the heart to hurry them up, since they were little older than Erica and a fond reminder of his daughter. Besides, like her, they might have problems. According to statistics, many adolescents in both England and America were stressed, unhappy or even secretly self-harming, so why deprive this particular pair of a bit of innocent fun?

In fact, as he stood waiting by the booth, listening to their little shrieks and giggles, he suddenly knew he *had* to go to Seattle, however great his fears. He hadn't seen Erica for almost fourteen months, which reflected on him badly as a father. He owed it to her to make the trip and, even if he arrived more dead than alive, make it he damned well would.

Then, all at once, as if inspired by his decision, he remembered someone he could ask to countersign his passport, and a solicitor, no less. Jeremy Hugh-Jones, a former neighbour in Kingston, had moved to a flat in Wandsworth some nine months ago, and had immediately asked his help, as local librarian, for a project he was involved in, tracing the history of clay pipes. In fact, the fellow had tried his patience, forever seeking him out and taking up his time – and not just in working hours. *He* might be retired and potty about pipes, but that didn't mean everybody else was. So Jeremy owed him a favour and, although there was a danger of being recruited again as an unpaid research-assistant, it was worth the risk if it meant he'd get his passport.

Just at that moment, the girls pranced out, leaving the photo-booth free. 'We've warmed up the seat for you, Granddad,' the taller one remarked.

And, as he sat down on the, yes, warm seat, he actually managed the ghost of a smile. 'Granddad' was dead right – he had aged at least two decades overnight.

chapter seventeen

He watched as Jeremy poured the tea from a Victorian silverware teapot, circa 1869. Antique teapots were the fellow's new obsession – so he had learned to his cost. Research on hallmarks and decoration-styles had been added to his research on clay pipes, and all in return for one rushed and squiggly signature on the passport-application form. They'd been talking teapots for at least the last half-hour, yet the wretched man showed no sign of desisting.

'Did you notice the snake's-head finial?' He pointed to the top of the pot, where a silver serpent extended its tiny tongue. 'Most finials in Victorian times were screwed onto the lid, but this one's soldered, which makes it quite unusual.'

'Really?' Eric said, resolving to find some way of terminating this far-from-welcome relationship. The guy was obviously lonely, since he kept suggesting further meetings and seemed to assume they were now bosom friends.

'And this octagonal-shaped body' – Jeremy stroked the teapot lovingly – 'was introduced in the early eighteenth century but continued to be fashionable throughout the Victorian era.'

He passed Eric milk and sugar and cut him a slice of cake, with a further disquisition on the cake-plate, milk-jug and sugar-bowl, all hand-painted Early Worcester and apparently quite rare. Then, having stirred his tea, he settled back in his seat, with a sigh of satisfaction. 'Well, I must say, this is nice, Eric – almost like old times in Kingston. Oh, by the way, what happened about your passport? Did you get it in the end?'

Eric had assumed he would never ask. Clearly, in Jeremy's estimation, passports were less enthralling than teapots, creamers, slop-bowls and the rest. 'No,' he replied, with some vehemence. 'And I have to say, I'm in quite a stew about it. I'm due to leave eight days from now, which means I'll have to cancel the flight if it hasn't come by then.'

'Well, you know these bureaucrats – they always take their time.'

'But my interview was a whole nine days ago. And I told them then – *and* when I first applied – that my visit to the States was a family necessity, not a pleasure-trip, so could they please hurry up the process.' The official conducting the interview hadn't been exactly sympathetic – a suspicious, sullen type, who had taken a grim delight in nitpicking over everything.

'Well, I can only wish you luck.' Jeremy brushed a stray cake-crumb from his lip. 'And do keep me in the picture, won't you? In fact, maybe we could meet again, just before you leave.'

'*If* I leave,' Eric interrupted, quickly fabricating a raft of reasons why he'd be too busy to socialize, even if he didn't fly.

'My own flying days are over,' Jeremy remarked; proving his thick skin by barely registering the brush-off. 'Although I must have flown a good million miles in my time.'

Eric gave an involuntary gasp. Shouldn't the guy have died of terror way before a thousand miles, let alone a million?

'But, a year ago, on a flight to New Orleans, the plane was struck by lightning just as we approached the airport. We flew into this thick yellow cloud and suddenly there was a terrific bang, and the whole plane shuddered and sparks flew off the wing.'

Eric put his plate down. No way could he munch chocolate cake whilst digesting such atrocities.

'And somehow I just lost my nerve. Now I prefer to stay at home.'

'Absolutely,' Eric echoed.

'Although, one way and another, I've survived a good few horrors in my time. I remember one occasion, in 1975, there was a fire in the undercarriage as we landed at Heathrow. In those days, inflatable chutes weren't available, so I had to climb down this sort of ladder-affair, then hold it out, with the help of another passenger, for the others to escape. We were surrounded by dense clouds of smoke, and I was choking so much I could barely breathe. The cabin crew were useless – in fact, more panicked than the rest of us.'

Eric fought an overwhelming instinct to bolt out of the flat before any further disasters could be added to the list.

'And, the following year, when I was coming back from Athens, we were caught in a violent thunderstorm. The plane was thrown all over the place and everybody yelled blue murder. Mind you, snowstorms can be even worse. I'll never forget the one in '83, when I was on my way to Boston.

The turbulence was so horrendous, I assumed we were about to crash, and just sat there with my eyes shut, calling on the Lord for help. And what with engine-failure, which I've experienced on three occasions, and—'

No, he *couldn't* fly – Eric knew that now. Thank God the passport hadn't come: a blessing in disguise.

'And, of course, it's much more dangerous nowadays, with these confounded terrorists. OK, they foiled that plot in 2006 to blow up ten separate aircraft, but the buggers are bound to be planning more carnage – and on just the same grand scale, I bet!'

Eric's hand was shaking on the cup. He needed a stiff drink – or three – not this watery Earl Grey. But he was due at the prison this evening, for Simon Brett's visit to the book club and could hardly greet the author half-cut.

'And another thing – standards are much lower now among most airline staff. You won't believe this, Eric, but the other day I heard of a case where the pilot was actually rogering his co-pilot while they were over the Atlantic. But who was there to care, when most of the stewards are high on cocaine – or worse?'

Eric fought a wave of dizziness. He had been relying on those very staff to help him through the ordeal, but if they were crack-heads or sex-fiends – or even both at once – what chance was there of survival? He longed to rush straight round to Mandy's flat, bury his head in her breasts, and beg her to kiss his fears away. But how could he even admit to such fears without losing her respect – maybe losing *her*, full-stop? In fact, during the last few weeks, he'd had to invent a string of crises at work, as an excuse to see her less. Much as he craved her company, he couldn't take the risk of breaking down and confessing his mega-cowardice – when he was off his guard in bed, maybe – and revealing himself as the snivelling wreck he was.

Desperately, he shot up from his chair, strode over to the display-case and indicated one of the clay pipes. The only way to stop this bloke discoursing on catastrophes was to return him to his favourite subject. 'Is this a new acquisition?'

Needing no second invitation, Jeremy joined him by the case and reverently withdrew the pipe: an elaborate specimen, with a decorative stem and a bowl in the shape of a lion's head. 'Yes, and what a beauty! See that detail on the mane? The bowl measures a mere inch-and-a-half, yet the carving is exquisite.'

'Lovely,' Eric agreed, glancing round the cluttered room, which seemed more museum than home; stuffed as it was with cabinets and display-shelves; every inch crowded with collectables. Even when the guy had lived in Kingston, he'd been patently eccentric, and these new retirement passions had only emphasized the trait.

'Eric, I've just had a thought – why don't you join the Society for Clay Pipe Research, now you're becoming so involved yourself? We could go to their meetings together, then.'

'Well, as I said before, I *am* extremely busy, what with—' All at once, he exploded in a sneeze, followed by another and another. 'I do beg your pardon,' he tried to say, only to interrupt himself with yet more resounding '*atishoos*'.

'You should have told me you had a cold,' Jeremy said, his mood swiftly changing from affable to peevish. 'And I'd have postponed our little tea-party until you were free of germs.'

'It's not a cold,' Eric retorted. 'I'm just ... *atishoo* ... allergic ... *atishoo* ... to ... *atishoo-ooooo*.' He gave up the attempt to explain, as a dozen more successive sneezes rendered it impossible to speak. Little tea-party indeed! He'd had no desire to come here in the first place, especially on his one day off – and not even a complete day off, with his book club engagement this evening.

However, at least Jeremy's concern about catching something lethal provided a convenient escape, since when he said he'd simply have to leave, to avoid whatever allergen was lurking in the flat, the guy put up no resistance and ushered him swiftly to the door.

Having said a brief – *atishoo* – goodbye, he wheeled his bike along the street, deciding not to ride it, in case the jolting sneezes rocked him from the saddle. After ten explosive minutes with no let-up, he began to worry that he would trumpet all through Simon's talk. If only he were *normal* – someone not prone to allergies or panics; a bloke like Trevor, maybe, whose only fears were budget-cuts or failing to meet targets.

Finally, however, the sneezing petered out and, having mounted his bike with a sense of huge relief, he pedalled on to the prison. Reaching it at half-past five and thus with time in hand, he decided to go for a walk on the common, not only to calm his nerves, but to give him a chance to do some quick revision on Simon's latest paperback, *Blood at the Bookies*. In truth, he'd never been a fan of crime fiction but, even were he reading Tolstoy, the weighty issues on his mind would have fatally distracted him: the mix of hope and angst each day as he checked the post for his passport; the fear of Christine's fury if he was forced to let her down; the dilemma over Mandy. Would a 'brave' façade ensure her lasting love, or should he opt for honesty and make a clean breast of his terrors? And there were lesser concerns, as well. Who would run his reading group, while –*if* – he was away? Would any of his colleagues want to cope with the depressives, who could be unpredictable, if not downright cussed?

With a muttered curse, he yanked his mind back to murder suspects, betting shops and plot-twists; wishing someone would be kind enough to dispatch *him* in a betting shop. Death, however gory, seemed, at present, the only possible way out.

'So how do you do your research?' asked Doug – a hulking fellow, with a jowly, pock-marked face.

Eric, sitting next to him, suddenly noticed that his copy of *Blood at the Bookies* itself was stained with blood, and that there were jottings in blue biro scrawled across the pages.

'Well, my favourite method is taking people out to lunch,' Simon replied, jocularly. 'Much more fun than slaving away in a library! I'll choose someone who knows the subject well and question them over fillet steak and strawberries, with a glass or two of wine, to keep the conversation flowing. For instance, for *Death Under the Drier*, I lunched with the owner of a hair-salon and asked her to dish me all the dirt – you know, what the staff get up to, who are the vainest customers—'

'And who *are* they?' Rashid asked.

'Asian men, I'm afraid to say!'

Everybody laughed, including Rashid.

'Then, for a novel called *Dead Giveaway*, I took out a TV producer and picked her brains about television talent shows. And she told me they had an "Ugly Wall", to display photos of contestants who were desperate to appear but just didn't have the looks.'

'*I'd* be on that wall, then – that's for sure,' Doug commented.

More laughter.

Eric dared to relax. Simon's talk had gone down well and now questions were coming thick and fast. Only one of the men sat silent; a young, anaemic-looking chap, whose arms were crossed tight across his chest and who'd been staring at the floor since he had shuffled in at the start. He seemed to be giving off signals saying, 'I'm not part of this. Count me out', and had even failed, so far, to interact with any of his fellow members. Eric decided to talk to him, in private, at the close of the proceedings, in an attempt to get through his armour, and maybe offer him a book or two, to keep and read in his cell. These prisoners were all trapped, but reading might provide some means of mental escape, however limited. In fact, he'd been heartened to learn from Linda Lewis, when chatting to her before the men arrived, that previous book club choices included not just modern crime novels and thrillers, but authors as demanding as Dickens, Orwell and Scott Fitzgerald. Linda had also told him that although some members, such as Kevin, often failed to finish the book, others made detailed notes about the characters and contents that would put most scholars to shame.

'I do try to check everything carefully,' Simon continued, pushing his specs back up on his nose. 'But mistakes can still get in. For example, in *The Stabbing in the Stables*, there's an injury to a horse, but it changes midway through the book from the front right knee to the left. I only realized when the book was published, and by then it was too late.'

'It was corrected in the paperback, though,' Beverley remarked. As prison library assistant, she was deputizing for Abi tonight; himself too busy to come. 'I read them both and noticed.'

'Good for you!' Simon said, approvingly. 'I deplore mistakes, but I love attentive readers!'

'I was wondering, though, why you use amateur detectives, rather than professionals?'

'Well, there's a long tradition of amateurs, going back to Sherlock Holmes and Poirot. And, actually, it's easier for me, as author. My knowledge of police procedure is limited, to say the least, but my two amateurs aren't very genned-up, either. So I hope they and the readers can go on a sort of journey together, finding out things by stages, which makes the exposition less plodding – or so I like to think.'

'I didn't believe in their friendship, though,' Xavier objected. 'They're so different in basic temperament, would they really have hit it off?'

'They live in a small village, remember,' Rashid observed, 'so presumably there wouldn't be much choice of friends.'

'Same as us,' said Jake. 'The only company we have is our cell-mate.'

'And I'd run a mile from mine,' Doug grimaced, 'if I only had the chance.'

'You don't make friends in here, anyway,' Stewart remarked, with a touch of bitterness. 'You come in on your own and you leave on your own.'

Like children's homes, thought Eric, aware that during his peripatetic boyhood the prospect of having a best mate had to remain in the realm of fantasy, as either he, or one of the other kids he'd just dared to get to know, was moved on yet again. Besides, when you lived in an institution, there was a sense of not belonging, which clearly Stewart felt as well. Indeed, Stewart was the only man he recognized from the previous meeting in January, so, if even book club members changed so radically, no wonder the guy felt adrift. The librarians provided an anchor, of course, as did Linda herself, who brought to the group her experience and expertise as a university lecturer. She also served as an important link with the wider world outside – as *he* did, too, in fact – a reassurance to these men that they hadn't been forgotten by that world.

'What *I* didn't like,' Jake observed, returning to the subject of the book, 'was the humour. I just don't find the subject funny. I mean, we're not in here for a petty bit of shoplifting, or dealing a few Es, you know. However much we've fucked things up, we have to live with what we've done and that's no laughing matter. OK, we did the crime, we'll do the time, but prison's not exactly Butlins – right?'

Eric glanced across at him – a harmless-looking bloke, dressed not in the usual grey tracksuit, but in smart brown trousers and sweater. Whatever Jake had done, he would never dream of judging him – nor any prisoner, come to that – without knowing what had driven him to crime. After all, he himself might well have murdered Uncle Frank, had the abuse gone on much longer. And, as a boy, he had nicked a lot of stuff and also done his share of drugs – usually pressurized by older kids, or even used as a decoy. Growing up in care, you had to submit to the bullies in order to survive, and, if it involved law-breaking and a few bad trips, well, that was just the system. The fact he'd escaped both serious addiction *and* a prison-sentence was due more to chance than to any virtue on his part. And many of these men could have suffered childhoods far more gruelling than his, and then sought revenge through violence, or oblivion through drugs, so who was he to take the moral high line?

Simon was expounding on comedy, seemingly unfazed by Jake and Xavier's criticisms. Keen to redress the balance, however, Eric weighed in with some praises; glad now of his 'revision' on the common, since he could quote specific details. Anyway, quite apart from his fiction, Simon deserved an accolade, having turned up well on time, gone to obvious trouble with his talk and been endearingly good-natured and self-deprecating throughout the whole proceedings. Not all authors were so amenable, alas.

Some of those he'd invited to speak at library events had been late, or rude, or woefully unprepared.

He just wished the numbers were higher. A mere seven men were here this evening, despite the fact this was one of the biggest gaols in Europe. He'd also welcome the chance to be more involved with the group; to arrange regular author-visits, or maybe bring in a performance-poet or set up drama workshops, but, with all his other library work, he had neither the time nor the funding.

'What interests me,' said Linda, flicking back her hair, 'is that your amateur detectives are both female, unlike Holmes and Watson. I've noticed you often write about women, especially in your radio series.'

'I find it easier,' Simon confessed. 'For one thing, women talk about their feelings more than men, which gives readers more idea of who they are.'

'Your female characters all seem very strong,' she went on. 'Did you have strong women in your own life?'

'My mother was extremely strong – *and* extremely difficult! My wife is strong but less difficult. My daughter is strong and not difficult at all. My granddaughter is the strongest of the lot, although whether she'll turn out difficult still remains to be seen.'

Another burst of laughter. Eric was surprised to find himself joining in, when the day had begun in such despondent mode. And, although he felt a twinge of envy for all those women in Simon's life, he reminded himself, with uncharacteristic optimism, that *he* could have a new wife, new daughter and even, eventually, a granddaughter, if things worked out with Mandy. In fact, he had made a decision, at last – and made it this very minute. He would go round to her flat tomorrow and tell her the unvarnished truth; admit his fears in full, but stress the point that they were only *part* of him and he could compensate in other ways – through loyalty, fidelity, unwavering support for her, and constant hands-on help with the baby. Many people who'd grown up in institutions found it difficult in adult life to show any sort of affection to their kids, but he had already proved, with Erica, that he wasn't one of them. He'd been determined to give his daughter the very things he himself had lacked: kisses, cuddles bedtime stories, an involved and active parent. Tragically, and due to the divorce, all that had broken apart, but at least now he had the chance to start again, with Mandy.

All at once, the prison alarm drowned out Simon's voice – clearly some emergency, because, as well as the shrilling siren, there was the sound of pounding feet, tearing up and down the walkways underneath the library. Then, suddenly, a group of prison officers burst into the room, adding to the uproar with their jangling keys, tramping boots and crackling radios. Having checked on the small group of men, they raced out again, slamming the door and shouting to each other. Next, screams from some hapless inmate began echoing from below, curdled with the ever-frantic screech of the alarm.

'I wonder which dickhead wants to get out of Education early,' Rashid joked, raising his voice above the hideous noise.

'Poor bastard,' Stewart countered. 'I wouldn't want to be bent up by *that* lot.'

'Bent up?' Simon was clearly unfamiliar with the term.

'Three of them grab hold of you at once and pin you down, so you can't move.'

'Yeah, but the idiot doesn't need to scream blue murder. Anyway, if he'd kept his head down, no one would have picked on him, so he's only got himself to blame.'

'Come off it, Doug,' Xavier jeered. 'You're no better yourself – always having a go at the screws, then moaning when you're down the seg, in front of the governor.'

'Down the seg?' Again, Simon queried the phrase.

'It's where all the fucking idiots are held,' said the pale and hitherto silent man, finally speaking up, 'if they've been nicked for, like, making hooch in their cell.'

'Yeah, you'd know all about that, wouldn't you, Bill?'

'Piss off!'

Eric gripped the arms of his chair. The meeting was disrupted; the men no longer on their best behaviour, but distracted, even fractious; all concentration lost. Worse – chaos had erupted the very minute he'd dared entertain a hope about his personal life. Wasn't that a warning to him that such optimism was recklessly ill-founded?

Yes, that ominous alarm was shrieking on and on, seeming to underline the point that just as his youth had been subject to peril, so would be his future.

chapter eighteen

'So you see, Mandy,' Eric concluded in a rush; palms sweaty from the strain of his confession, 'I'm *not* the hero you think. In fact, I doubt if you've ever met someone so utterly pathetic – at least when it comes to flying.'

Mandy suddenly burst out laughing; the laughter sounding uncomfortably close to derision.

'It's not funny,' he retorted, stung by her reaction. 'Just because you're so cool and calm, you don't realize quite how badly fear can screw a person up.'

'Darling …' She got up from the table and kissed him on the lips. 'I'm not laughing *at* you; I'm laughing with relief. You see, I've known something was wrong for at least the last three weeks. You've been so stressed and snappy, which is not like you at all. And you didn't seem to want to see me – kept saying you were busy, even on your days off. So naturally I imagined it was something to do with me – maybe you didn't want the baby, or were having second thoughts about our whole relationship.'

He stared at her, appalled. 'For heaven's sakes, Mandy, I adore you! And, of course, I want the baby. OK, I admit I had some qualms at first, but only because I feared you might go off me, once you realized what a coward I am – hate the thought of the father of your child being such a loser.'

She shook her head so vehemently, her auburn curls bobbed and jounced in protest. 'You're *not* a loser. Thousands of people are scared of flying – it's one of the most common fears. I'm lucky in that I actually enjoy it. I was bitten by the travel bug very early on and I'd jet off anywhere and everywhere without the slightest qualm. So, if it would help in any way, I'd be happy to come with you to Seattle.'

'C … come *with* me?'

'Why not? I've no job to tie me down. I just won't take on any new cake orders for the time we'll be away and, as for the café, Barbara will have to cope without me. I'm only there on a casual basis, anyway.'

'But you can't fly if you're pregnant.'

''Course you can. Everybody does – well, except for the last month, maybe, when it might be a bit dodgy. In fact, I'd enjoy the trip immensely. I've been to Boston and New York and Philadelphia, but never to the West Coast.'

He put his spoon down, having spent a good ten minutes trying to finish his dessert. In fact, he had done scant justice to any of the meal. His *coq-au-vin* had been seasoned with dread; his pavlova garnished with terror. Mandy couldn't take away that fear (nobody and nothing could, short of a total brain-transplant), but if she were with him on the flight – her experience and confidence steering him through the whole ordeal – he might just be able to cope.

'In any case, you've been saying how important it was for me to meet your daughter, and if she's not coming over here, well, I'd better make her acquaintance in America.' Having collected up the dirty plates, Mandy went into the kitchen to make coffee.

Would Erica object, he wondered, with a twinge of apprehension; perhaps want him all to herself? And what about Christine's reaction if he turned up with a girlfriend in tow – and a pregnant girlfriend at that? So what? He would only see her for one short evening, before she and Dwight departed for Hong Kong. And, as for Erica, the two of them could still do things on their own, while Mandy went off sightseeing.

'To be honest, darling,' Mandy said, returning with a pot of coffee, 'the only thing that worries me is the cost. I haven't told you yet, but yesterday I took myself to Top Shop and blew two weeks' rent on maternity clothes. I just got carried away!'

Although jolted by such extravagance, he didn't begrudge her anything. After all, she'd just become his personal "Beat Your Fear of Flying" course, and none of those came cheap. '*I'll* pay your fare – that goes without saying. I wouldn't dream of you coughing up yourself, when you're doing me a favour.' He did some calculations in his head. He'd managed to get a reasonable price for the flight, but doubling it would still prove a major strain. Yet, if he had to go cap in hand to Bill Gates himself and beg a personal loan, he would do it gladly to have Mandy as his sky-marshal. 'I hope you don't mind, but we won't be flying direct. We have to change at Minneapolis.'

He had made the booking suddenly, impulsively – and probably quite irrationally – after days and days of dithering. True, flying via Minneapolis was cheaper, but also longer, less convenient and, indubitably, more frightening, with two take-offs and two landings. He sincerely hoped that neither of the planes would be Boeing 777s, which, according to the headlines last week (Friday the thirteenth, of course), all had a fatal engine-flaw and were thus liable to crash. And he just couldn't forget the atrocities Jeremy had listed. All that gruesome detail had stopped him sleeping last night, and been preying on his mind all day at work. Was it wrong, indeed immoral, to inflict such danger on Mandy? 'D'you object to two flights?' he asked her, wishing they could simply opt for a day-trip to Southend.

''Course not. In fact, I'd like to see Minneapolis.'

'I'm afraid we won't see much of it – just three hours hanging about, waiting for our connection.'

'That's OK. I love airports – all those gorgeous shops!'

'Talking of shopping, promise me you won't go to any expense as far as the flight's concerned. I insist on buying all the stuff you need.'

'What stuff?'

'You know, special gear for flying – lightweight cases with swivelling wheels and security locks, and crease-proof clothes to travel in, and—'

She laughed. 'You don't need any of that. I always travel in ordinary jeans and take my old battered suitcase.'

'I don't even own a case. Christine took them all. And somehow I've put off buying one. I suppose I'm trying to pretend this whole thing isn't happening.'

'I'll lend you one, don't worry. What I *am* concerned about is whether you'll manage to get me a seat – next to yours, I mean. With only a week to go, both flights may be full by now.'

The thought sent shudders down his spine. But even if it took him the whole seven days to secure seats side by side, he must and would succeed. 'I'll sort it out, I promise,' he said, feigning a breezy confidence. 'So put the twenty-seventh in your diary. Oh, and by the way, is your passport up to date?'

'Yes, I renewed it last year.'

'Mine's only just arrived – literally this morning!' It had been an extraordinary moment, holding in his hands a document he'd assumed he would never own. In fact, it had seemed like a rite of passage joining him to the normal, adult world. 'I've been shitting bricks imagining it wouldn't come in time.'

'Eric, you must stop all this worry! Even your concerns about being a father are totally unjustified. You'll be great – I know you will. You're the kind of guy who doesn't mind mussed clothes or sticky fingers, and who'll happily teach a kid to read and write, and mend its toys and bandage knees and stuff. Some men are just so vain and self-absorbed, all they care about is their clothes, or their career, or their progress in the gym.'

He all but purred as Mandy praised his attributes as dad – a welcome change from Christine's gripes about his 'uselessness', because he couldn't drive Erica to school or even take her for a swim.

'Hey!' Mandy gripped his arm. 'I've just had an idea – about the baby. Why don't we ask Violet to be godmother – not as a religious thing, but as someone who'd be close to it and take a special interest and—'

'But I've already asked Stella, and in exactly that same sense. I told you, didn't I?'

'Yes, but can't we have *two* godmothers?'

'Mm, bit tricky. Stella was so pleased to be involved, I wouldn't want to steal her thunder, especially as she's rather down at the moment.'

'Well, perhaps Violet can be a sort of stand-in grandma – almost a relation on *your* side, if you like, to make up for my huge family.'

'Brilliant! Let's ring her tomorrow and find out how she feels.'

'Pity you're working all weekend, or we could have gone to see her in person. It's been ages since – hold on – is that my mobile? Damn! I left it in the kitchen.'

He could hear her through the open door; caught the words 'Oh, *Oliver*, how nice!' Oliver? Why the hell was the bloke ringing her so late – indeed, ringing her at all?

He jumped up from the table, hating the thought of eavesdropping, but driven by sheer jealousy to try to listen in. Although what he heard was far from reassuring: flirtatious giggles on Mandy's part and a worryingly intimate tone, as if they knew each other well. And then she closed the kitchen door, which was even more suspicious. What could she be saying that he wasn't meant to hear? Maybe they were planning an assignation – not lunch, this time, but a cosy little evening together. No, that was downright stupid. If she was pregnant with his child, she'd hardly be pursuing another man. Did he have to be so insecure, especially when she'd just been singing his praises? Except that made it more upsetting, in a way. Why couldn't she come back in and continue the conversation, rather than linger in the kitchen with some upstart?

He waited in a fever of impatience. Her sitting-room, normally so colourful and comfortable, now seemed dark and menacing. He took his coffee over to the sofa, only to push the cup away. It tasted bitter, tainted; the dregs gritty in his mouth.

'Who was that?' he asked, the minute she did return – what seemed like centuries later.

'Oh, just a friend.'

'I heard you say "Oliver".'

'Yes, that's right.'

'You mean the Oliver at Mayday Hospital? How long has *he* been a friend?'

'Oh …' She flushed. 'He was so helpful when I went there, we've become quite pally since.'

Pally? Sleazy images began flooding through his mind: Oliver peeling off her clothes; fondling her breasts; giving her so wild a time, his own performance paled into insignificance. Yet if she did abscond with Oliver – or anyone else, for that matter – it would be entirely his own fault. This last month, his behaviour had been inexcusable. Not only had he invented dead-lines in order not to see her, he had also kept her in the dark; hadn't so much as mentioned his summons to America, the whole business of the flight, or the nerve-racking wait for his passport. Instead, he'd flared up at the slightest thing; snapped and even shouted; been totally obnoxious, in short. No wonder she'd assumed he had doubts about their relationship and didn't want the baby.

All at once, he knew he had to act – resolutely, instantly – or he might lose her *and* their child. He fell to one knee on the carpet; gazing up at her face. 'Mandy, will you … will you marry me?'

The mantel-clock seemed to tick out every second with a cruel and mocking torpor. Why hadn't she replied? Was she trying to find the words to say she wasn't sure; that what she felt for Oliver could no longer be denied and that she needed time to sort out her emotions?

He became increasingly aware of the crick in his neck; the hardness of the floor beneath his knee. How ludicrous he must look to any outside observer. Indeed, if she turned down his proposal, he would have made himself a laughing stock.

Then, suddenly, she whispered, 'Yes, Eric, darling, I will.'

He catapulted to his feet; hugged her, kissed her, waltzed her round the room. To hell with that stupid prison-alarm! To hell with air-disasters! Jeremy had been exceptionally unlucky, whereas *he* would be exceptionally lucky – in fact, the luckiest guy in the whole wide world, now that Mandy had agreed to be his wife.

'I wanted to buy you a ring,' he said, stopping his mad dance, at last, if only to pause for breath. 'But I didn't dare to go ahead until I knew what your feelings were. You see, I was terrified you wouldn't want to hitch your-self to such a pathetic waste of space.'

She led him to the sofa and clasped both his hands in hers. 'Don't call yourself a waste of space. It's demeaning and untrue, darling. OK, you may be more prone to fear than other people, but that's completely understand-able in light of what you've been through. How could anyone survive those constant moves from pillar to post, without feeling insecure? You had no real settled home, remember – never even knew who your parents were. And maybe the circumstances of your actual birth affected you, in some way. Your mother must have been scared stiff, going into labour all alone, and perhaps you picked up on that instinctively, even in the womb. I know *I'd* panic if I had to cope on my own – most women would, I'm sure. Eric, listen – I'm telling you now, I want *you* there at the birth, as well as all the midwives they can spare!'

'I'll be there – you can count on it.' He was determined not to miss this baby's arrival in the world, as he'd had to miss Erica's, to his deep and lasting regret. As a foundling, he lacked the vital details of his own birth – the time, the place, the circumstances – and thus felt a deep desire to witness the delivery of any child he fathered.

'Christine had a Caesarean,' he told her, 'so I was marched out of the labour-ward and made to sit in some dreary waiting-room. She was a special case, though. She'd already had three miscarriages and had to take enormous care all through the pregnancy. That's why I can't help worrying. I mean, are you absolutely positive it's safe for you to fly? I don't want you taking the slightest risk.'

'Stop fussing, darling! I'm as fit as a fiddle – never been ill in my life. And Prue told me just the other day I'd probably sail through my labour because of what she calls my "child-bearing hips". Actually, I suspect she was just saying I was fat.'

'Of course you're not fat. Your hips are incredibly sexy – rounded and voluptuous and—' He unzipped her jeans; eased them down, and began kissing those voluptuous hips; letting his mouth move gradually lower and lower.

'Let's go to bed,' she gasped.

'No – can't wait – want you here and now!' Dragging off his own clothes, he flung them on the floor behind him. All the tension of the last gruelling month had reached crisis-point this evening, yet now had been miraculously resolved. Mandy was actually accompanying him to America! Even more amazing, they would soon be husband and wife. He burned to make love to her with all the joy and triumph such assurances deserved; with such extremes of passion, she would have no strength left for Oliver, and with such devoted tenderness, it would celebrate their committal to each other, for better, for worse; for richer, for poorer, and, yes, till death did them part.

'Mandy, that was just … fantastic!'

'The best ever – honestly. I'm so glad to have you back.'

'What do you mean?'

'Well, these last few weeks, I simply couldn't get through to you. It was like you were living in a different world.'

'I was – the world of fear. It *is* another planet, where all the usual pleasures and distractions mean nothing any more.'

'And you mean to say that fear's completely gone now?'

He laughed. 'Well, I wouldn't go as far as that! Let's put it this way – after I've made love to you, I feel so incredibly brave, I could apply for my pilot's licence and still not turn a hair!'

'In that case, we'd better do it on the plane – join the Five-Mile-High Club!'

'No problem. I won't need an invitation.' He stroked her breasts, noticing how full they'd become; larger now and weighty, as he cupped them in his hands. He loved to imagine her breast-feeding – a real turn-on in itself. Because of Christine's mastitis, he had never seen his daughter breastfed, but, when it came to this new baby, he was eager to be part of the whole ritual; maybe pleasuring one breast himself, while—

'Good God!' he exclaimed; all erotic images instantly dispelled by the sound of a key turning in the lock. 'Someone's coming in to the flat!'

Mandy leapt off the sofa, making a grab for her shirt. 'Stay here!' she hissed, as she rushed out to the front door.

He froze in shock. Who in heaven's name would have a key? The caretaker? The landlord? No. Neither would let himself in, without checking it was convenient – least of all so late. He could hear a man's deep voice. *Oliver*, he thought! Had the bastard turned up unannounced, thinking Mandy was alone? If so, she was conversing with him clad only in a skimpy shirt.

He listened in a paralysis of jealousy and indecision, then realized she was speaking in a frightened and defensive way, with no trace of the flirtatious tone she had been using on the phone. It must be someone else – perhaps a previous tenant, who'd retained his key for some peculiar reason. Or maybe an out-and-out crook, who'd deliberately had a key cut, so he could come and case the joint. If Mandy were being threatened, or was in any sort of danger, he must act – immediately.

Naked as he was, he hurtled out to defend her, stopping in his tracks at the sight of a tall, rangy bloke, dashingly dark and stylishly dressed in a black leather jacket and obscenely tight black jeans – decidedly not a hitman or a thug.

The man swivelled round to look at him, his expression darkening in fury. Then, wheeling back to Mandy, he all but spat at her, 'So *this* is why you don't want me to come in! What the fuck's going on, you promiscuous slut?'

Eric faced the guy head-on, determined to protect Mandy from such appalling rudeness. 'Who the hell do you think you are? Get out – this instant! Mandy's my fiancée and I won't stand for her being insulted like this.'

'Oh, so you're engaged now, are you?' the bloke said, with a sneer, ignoring Eric completely, as he turned again to Mandy. 'Well, congratulations on finding another father for your baby! Though it's a pity you didn't tell me. I could have saved myself a journey.'

'Yes, I … I thought you were in Haiti,' Mandy stuttered. Her face was deathly pale, and she was cowering against the wall.

'I *was* in Haiti, but I came back earlier than planned – and just as well, it seems, otherwise I'd never have known what you get up to behind my back. I was fool enough to imagine I could trust you. You see, the reason I returned was to tell you I'd be willing to give you the benefit of the doubt. But my first instincts were obviously right, you two-faced slag!'

'How dare you speak to Mandy like that?' Eric cried, outraged. 'And what the hell d'you mean about her finding another father for her baby? *I'm* the father, I'll have you know!'

The guy gave a mocking laugh. 'So now we have three poor saps, all with a claim to paternity. Well, that's news to me, I must say! Mandy was forced to admit I might be one of two, but I didn't realize she'd deceived me twice.'

'For God's sake, Brad,' Mandy said, suddenly springing to her own defence. 'You said you didn't want a child. Well, Eric does. So leave him alone, you bastard!

'Mandy,' Eric said, with an icy calmness that belied his racing heart. 'Who *is* this guy? And what's going on?'

'Yes, maybe it's time for some introductions,' the guy said, with a grim smile. 'You're Eric, so I gather. I'm Brad – Brad Sunderland. Though I doubt if Mandy would have mentioned me – not if she was hoping to pass you off as the baby's father.'

'I *am* the baby's father,' Eric repeated. He would say it over and over; keep reiterating it all damned night, if necessary, until this jerk realized it was true.

'Can you prove it?'

Eric hesitated, embarrassed to be discussing his sex-life with a stranger. 'Do you really need all the intimate details?'

'Yes, I think I do in the circumstances.'

'Well,' said Eric, flushing, 'I … I had unprotected sex with Mandy on New Year's Eve. A month later, she took a pregnancy test and found she'd conceived that very night.'

'Amazing!' Brad jeered. 'There's just something you don't know, you poor mug. Mandy told me she was pregnant two whole weeks before that. And, yes, she had a pregnancy test, but that initial one – I remember it distinctly – was done on December the fifteenth.'

Eric steadied himself against the wall. He hadn't even known Mandy on 15 December. This couldn't be happening; must be some sort of nightmare. 'So … so, if you're the father, why did you abandon Mandy, piss off to Haiti and leave her on her own?'

'It wasn't a question of "pissing off",' Brad retorted. 'I happen to be a photographer and a work assignment came up in Haiti – a much longer job than my usual sort of thing: four months' travelling the country, recording voodoo rituals and suchlike. And I have to say I was bloody glad to accept, so I could get the hell out of England and leave the whole mess behind. You see, Mandy here is quite the little schemer. Mind you, it took me a while to twig, because although we've been together three years, we've never shared a pad. I value my independence, so I've always kept my own place – a flat in Clerkenwell, which doubles as a—'

'Never mind your living arrangements,' Eric interrupted. 'I'm totally confused by these allegations you're throwing around. Could you start at the beginning and fill me in, OK?'

'No!' Mandy pleaded. 'Eric doesn't want to hear this stuff.'

'The poor sod *ought* to hear it, since you've dumped him in the shit.'

Poor mug. Poor sod. Eric bristled at the insults, yet still couldn't quite believe what this odious man was saying. There must be some mistake. Or maybe the bloke was lying, for some reason of his own.

'Perhaps we could sit down,' Brad said, irritably, 'I've had enough of standing around in a cramped and chilly hall.'

'No,' Mandy begged again, 'I don't want—'

Too late. Brad had already barged into the sitting-room and stood a moment surveying the scene; his face screwed up in an expression of disgust. Eric felt doubly mortified, realizing how sleazy it must look: sofa-cushions dumped on the floor; two discarded pairs of jeans, lying inside-out; his scarlet Y-fronts intimately entangled with Mandy's black lace bra and pants. She was now frantically trying to cover herself; grabbing her jeans and dressing in desperate haste. No way would *he* get dressed – demean himself by fumbling with zips and buttons, while Brad looked on derisively. He already felt at a definite disadvantage; not only naked, but less distinguished in every way than this sleek and striking intruder. However, he seized the throw from the sofa and wrapped it round his body; wishing he could simply vanish from the earth.

Brad flung himself into a chair. 'OK,' he said in an acrimonious voice, 'let me put you in the picture, Eric. Around the middle of October, Mandy decides to come off the Pill, but she doesn't bother to inform me of the fact. A month later, I find out, and, yes, I'm pretty bloody furious. She knows full well I don't want kids. In my line of work, I'm forever on the move and I don't fancy being tied down – or not yet, in any case. I mean, if a job comes up I like the sound of in, say, Bangkok or the Congo, I drop everything and go.'

Yes, of course you do, Eric muttered under his breath. A he-man and a jetsetter snaps his fingers at any sort of danger; doesn't need chaperons and straitjackets and mega-supplies of Valium, just to get him through one puny flight.

'Well, to cut a long story short, we had a flaming row and Mandy slammed out of the flat and went to some drunken party on her own. OK, we made it up, and she promised to go back on the Pill until I'd had more time to sort out what I felt about the whole business of a family. Then, exactly four weeks later, she tells me she's pregnant with my kid. She just happened to conceive between stopping the Pill and restarting it. I was stunned, of course, but I did the decent thing – told her I'd pay for the kid and accept my responsibilities as father. I can't say I was exactly delighted by the prospect, but I reckoned I could handle it – well, until one of my close friends told me he'd seen Mandy actually shagging some bloke at that famous party she went to on her own. They were having it off in one of the bedrooms, he said, where he'd gone himself, to crash out. It seems everyone was legless that night and, in fact, Mandy told me later she was so rat-arsed she hadn't even known what she doing. Well, that was her excuse, but it didn't change the fact that the baby she insisted was mine could just as well be his.'

'*Stop* this!' Mandy implored, now slumped on the sofa, with her head in her hands. 'It's nothing to do with Eric.'

'It's everything to do with him. You were already six weeks pregnant when you and he first screwed, so no way could this kid be his. Yet you were willing to deceive him – tell him a quite flagrant lie and think no one would find out.'

Eric drew the throw closer round his body, aware that he was shrinking – in size, in strength, in status. He had become a puny cuckold; a bare-arsed figure of fun; a poor mug; poor sap, poor sod.

'Anyway,' Brad continued, springing up from the chair again, in obvious agitation, 'while I was in Haiti, I had time to mull things over and, once I'd simmered down a bit, I tried to see things from Mandy's point of view. She's five years older than me, and I knew she wanted kids, so maybe I'd failed to understand all that stuff about women's biological clocks. And she did seem truly sorry about sleeping with the other bloke; said she'd only done it because she was so gutted by our quarrel, she just got pissed out of her mind and—'

Yes, thought Eric bitterly, remembering Mandy drinking at his birthday party; announcing her pregnancy in public, when they'd agreed to keep it secret; allowing her whole family to congratulate him on what he was forced to realize now was a completely fraudulent fatherhood.

'And I don't mind admitting I missed you.' Brad had stopped by the sofa and was addressing her directly. In fact, giving her a sexy leer, Eric noticed with another surge of fury. All Brad had missed was the shags – that was bloody obvious.

'So I thought "what the hell, why cut off my nose to spite my face?" I'll do what I promised originally – accept the kid and pay for it, even if it's not my own. But not now – no way – not after what I've seen tonight. I mean, for all I know, Eric may be one of a whole string of men you've been screwing here, when you thought I was three thousand miles away.'

A whole string of men. The phrase was like a punch in Eric's face. Yes, what about that slimy Oliver? Was *he* another candidate for the hapless role of father?

'Well, thank Christ I've stumbled on the truth before committing myself to umpteen years of childcare. I doubt we'll ever know who the sodding father is, but at least it's not my problem any more. I wash my hands of the whole damned thing – and that's my final word, Mandy. I've seen you for what you are now – a lying, deceitful, scheming, little bitch!'

Mandy gave a cry and dashed towards the bedroom.

'Hold on a minute!' Brad said, intercepting her. 'I shan't be using *this* again!' He hurled the door-key into her hands then turned on his heel and strode out, only pausing to shout, "Good luck, Eric! You'll need it.'

chapter nineteen

Eric shuffled along the path. He had grown old in just the last two days – no longer a thrusting lover, a soon-to-be-new-father, but now a discarded piece of trash, like the stained and greasy McDonald's cartons he'd seen flung down near the entrance to the park. Yet everything around him was young and in its prime: trees glazed with pollen or unfurling into new green leaf; daffodils exploding in full-throated golden triumph; clouds of blackthorn blossom frothing in bridal white. Pigeons were cooing and courting; other birds pairing up or busy building nests. He alone seemed solitary, surrounded as he was by lovers strolling hand-in-hand and family groups with little bands of kids. Clearly, mothers and grandmas had been coaxed out of doors, in droves, in honour of Mothering Sunday – a day he had always detested, when the whole damned land went gaga over mothers. Was *his* mother feeling disgruntled because she hadn't received a lavish bunch of flowers? Well, if she'd only thought to get in touch forty years ago, she would have had lorryloads of flowers, by now, and he'd have been treating her to lunch today. Except he couldn't bear her to see him in his present abject state: a failure, with no love-life and no future, destined to be on his own for ever.

He screwed up his eyes against the glare; resenting the sun for shining with such fervour; hating the baby-blue sky, simply for its colour. Maybe his mother had gone on to have a brood of other children and had simply written him off as an error of her youth. Was he crazy to have idealized her, when she could just as well be subnormal, stupid or criminally insane? He had never forgotten Rory, one of the kids at Grove End, who'd been removed from his mother when little more than a toddler, on account of her LSD addiction, and didn't meet her again till the age of thirteen. Imagining she'd be totally cured and thrilled to have him back, the reality was cruel: he had come face to face with a ravaged old hag, who displayed no emotion whatever, beyond a sense of bafflement that her baby had grown up.

He was so deep in thought, he all but collided with an elderly woman and her equally ancient dog.

'Excuse me, but do you have the time?' she asked.

'Yes, just coming up to half-past twelve.' The strength of his voice surprised him. Shouldn't it be a croak now; an old codger's bronchitic wheeze? He was glad of the interruption, though, since it had roused him from his introspective brooding. Self-pity was quite odious and he had no right to inflict it on Stella, who'd been kind enough to invite him to lunch, knowing he'd always hated Sundays on his own and that, following Mandy's bombshell, this particular Sunday would be hellish in the extreme.

He ambled to a stop beside the lake, where more kids were larking around; more young couples sitting entwined on the benches, kissing and embracing. Moving closer to the water's edge, he watched a drake pursue a duck with merciless determination; bite its neck to hold it down underwater; then rape it, more or less. Sex in the animal kingdom seemed so short and unsatisfactory, if not downright violent; a total contrast to his long, tender nights with Mandy. New Year's Eve had been the first and best, because so unexpected; so rapturously triumphant. Of course, *now* he realized that her sheer randiness and lust had been nothing more than a deliberate ploy to ensnare him. Her baby required a father – and required one pretty fast. She hadn't time to select a better candidate, so she had set out to seduce him; apparently regardless of the fact she would then be forced to deceive him throughout his lifetime, *and* the child's. His own personal Dewey Decimal system was now completely overturned, so that everything was wrongly filed: 'love' under 'self-interest'; 'passion' under 'calculation'; 'trust' under 'duplicity'; 'fatherhood' under 'cuckoldry'.

An eccentric-looking female, dressed in a summer frock and wellingtons, began feeding the birds with a whole, large farmhouse loaf. More and more avian hopefuls came flocking in, to grab their share of the spoils; geese and coots and tufted ducks paddling full-speed across the lake; gulls and pigeons swooping down from above. Soon, a cacophony broke out – honkings, squawkings and quackings, accompanied by angry flappings as one bird fought another or tried to drive it off. Eric surveyed the scene in silence, aware that it was an echo of the turmoil in his head: one emotion battling with another – love and desire for Mandy, followed by sheer loathing of her treachery; deep longing for the unborn child mixed with hatred for its every cell, because it had been fathered by some pick-up.

His mind drifted to Tom Jones, who had also been unfaithful; rogered a whole raft of women, yet, despite all the betrayals, still achieved his happy ending: marriage to Sophia. Was there any point in being loyal, he wondered, bitterly? Or maybe, unlike Tom, he was simply destined to lose the things that mattered. After all, the pattern had been set in childhood where no relationship ever lasted long. Each time he found a 'mum' or 'home', a modicum of love and safety, it had been snatched away and he'd been packed off somewhere else.

Aware that he was indulging in more nauseating self-pity, he turned his back on the birds and continued along the path until he reached the sub-tropical gardens. His attention was caught by a group of presumably vulnerable plants, swathed from top to bottom in straw and polythene, to protect them from the elements, and looking like Egyptian mummies standing upright in the flowerbed. He himself was in need of similar wrappings; thick and bulky bandages to bind his wounds; swaddle his raw feelings; cocoon him from the sharp winds of grief and loss. And they would be even more effective on the plane; shrouding his eyes and ears, so that he wouldn't see any terrifying void opening up beneath him; hear any dangerous engine-noise, or the sounds of an impending crash. And those lengths of twine that girded the plants would tie him down securely in his seat, prevent him running amok or leaping up in panic every time the plane lurched.

Taking a diagonal route across the sports field, he noticed a dead fledgling, fallen from its nest; the naked, embryonic form reminding him of the baby again. He kept wondering whether Mandy would have left him if, like Christine, she had suffered a miscarriage. Did she only value him as useful dad-material: someone – as she had pointed out herself – who would be unfazed by messy kids and, in that one respect, preferable to Brad? A snazzily dressed photographer wouldn't welcome sticky fingers besmirching his designer clothes, nor would he be running baths or reading bedtime stories if he spent half his life abroad. The question was uncomfortable; prompting another in its turn: had Mandy ever loved him for himself?

Averting his eyes from the pathetic little corpse, he headed for the Albert Gate and for Stella's garden flat, which was in this northern stretch of Albert Bridge Road, right opposite Battersea Park.

'Hi!' he said, giving her an affectionate hug. He had neglected her of late; too obsessed with Mandy to socialize with his loyal, long-standing friend.

'Great to see you! Have you left your bike somewhere safe?'

'I'm not on the bike. I ... decided to walk.'

'It's quite a trek from Vauxhall.'

'Not really. And it's such perfect weather ...' The sentence petered out. He refused to confess that, having cycled all his life, he had lost his nerve two days ago. *All* his fears had mushroomed in those last racking forty-eight hours. Mandy thought him courageous for riding a bike at all, since she regarded it as more hazardous than driving. And, indeed, the very prospect of getting on a bike now filled him with alarm. Even day-to-day living had become fraught with new and indefinable dangers, no matter where he went or what he did. And neither the scented, spring-like air in the park, nor the general mood of Sunday relaxation had done anything to assuage his sense of menace and precariousness.

'Well, come in and have a drink. How are you, anyway?'

'OK.' Why burden her with all the details? The sleeplessness and headaches, the sick, churning feelings in his gut were all clearly stress-induced and thus of little consequence.

She ushered him in, took his coat, poured him a glass of wine. Settling into a chair, he glanced around at the familiar, high-ceilinged room. Prior to meeting Mandy, he had always envied Stella this light and spacious flat, yet now it seemed dull and drab, in comparison with Mandy's place. It was as if he'd become addicted to Mandy's brilliant colours; her riot of cushions, pictures, paper flowers; her exotic fabrics and unusual ornaments.

'Aren't you drinking?' he asked, as he took a sip of wine.

'No. I've given up booze for Lent.'

'What, you've suddenly seen the light and become a Born-Again?'

She laughed. 'No fear! It's more a slimming thing – saving on calories and detoxifying and all that sort of stuff.'

'Hell! That doesn't bode too well for lunch. What are we having – celery sticks and lemon juice?'

'Don't worry – it'll be proper food. Though, when it comes to cooking, I can't compete with Mandy, as you're very well aware. And, talking of Mandy, I have to say, I think the way she's treated you is absolutely disgusting!'

He said nothing; unwilling, even now, to hear her attacked – the woman he had once adored.

'I mean, deceiving *you*, of all people, when she must have known how much a baby's parentage would matter, after your own experience.'

He took refuge in his glass, secretly acknowledging Stella was right, but unable to admit it.

'What's the matter, Eric? I thought you *wanted* to discuss all this?'

'Mm, I do. But … but I can't help thinking of the dreadful state she must have been in. I suppose she didn't dare to tell me the truth, in case I just pushed off. The irony is, if only she'd been honest, I would have probably stayed around – you know, accepted the fact that it was someone else's kid, but still helped her bring it up. In fact, I keep wondering if I should do that – put the baby's interests before my own wounded pride. The child needs a father, as I know better than anyone.'

Stella sprang to her feet in indignation. 'Are you out of your mind? If she'd deceived you over something so important, how could you ever trust her again?'

'Yes, but look at it from her point of view. She comes from a very traditional family that has no truck with single parents, let alone with women who sleep around. If they were ever to twig that two different men could be the father of her child, and she hasn't a clue which one, they'd be truly scandalized. Her sisters are all conventional types, happily married, with children of their own, and they're always urging her to settle down to motherhood and marriage.'

'I don't know how you can defend her, Eric. None of that is any excuse whatever.'

'OK, maybe I *can't* defend her, but what about the kid?'

'It's the kid I'm thinking about – I mean, the callous way she didn't seem to care that it might find out you weren't its actual father and be absolutely devastated. Remember the case in the paper, just a week or two ago – that fourteen-year-old whose whole life fell apart when she discovered that the man she'd always called her dad was nothing of the sort?'

Yes, he did remember, In fact, he'd actually discussed the case with Mandy, who'd pretended to share his horror at the sham. 'There doesn't have to be deception,' he said, desperate not to dwell on her wounding, brazen hypocrisy. 'Once a child's old enough to grasp the facts, you can make it clear that you're not its biological parent, but that you love it just the same. What worries me especially is that neither of the baby's two possible fathers is willing to take responsibility, so it'll grow up fatherless. And, according to the statistics, that'll affect its life quite badly, which is why I feel I ought to step in myself. I mean, I could be its dad, in the sense of caring for it day-to-day, and paying for its keep.'

'Eric, *no*, I've told you! Why should you scrimp and save for someone else's child, while Mandy arses around, bringing in no proper sort of income, and probably laughing behind your back?'

He noted Stella's vehemence. Perhaps she simply wanted him single, so they could see much more of each other, as they had done, prior to Mandy. Were anyone's motives ever really pure?

She returned to her chair, slumping down in an aggressive sort of fashion. 'All she's done is use you and abuse you, and you're far better out of it. To me, she's just a scheming little bitch!'

'That's exactly what Brad called her.'

'No wonder! She deceived him, too, remember. Even coming off the Pill, without asking what he felt about it, to me is unforgivable.'

'Yes, but she was longing for a baby. And she's nearly thirty-six, which is old when it comes to—'

'*I'd* like a baby, too, and I'm three years older than her, but that doesn't give me the right to treat a man as a sperm-donor, then bamboozle him about it.'

He forced a laugh, feeling both uneasy and disloyal, but attempting to lighten the mood. 'Well, she certainly had to lower her standards when she settled for *me* as father, instead of Brad. He's fifteen years younger, to start with, ten-foot tall and drop-dead gorgeous. And, instead of being a dreary librarian, he's a famous—'

'Librarians aren't dreary,' Stella cut in, incensed. 'I won't have you running them down. Any halfway decent librarian does far more for the community than some jumped-up paparazzo chasing after second-rate celebs.'

'He's not that kind of photographer. According to Mandy, he's an idealist and a visionary who travels to Third-World countries and records war and famine and poverty and stuff.' If it weren't so tragic, Eric reflected, it would be jolly nearly comic: a fearless he-man on the one hand, spending three months in Haiti, surrounded by gun-runners and rioters and risking kidnapping and death-threats. And, on the other hand, a snivelling wimp, too scared to board a plane, and paralysed with terror even in a lift.

Only now did he realize that, if Brad hadn't cut his trip short, he would have been expected back in England at the very end of March. Had Mandy only agreed to accompany him to Seattle because she was frightened that her ex-lover might confront her, and was thus glad of an excuse to disappear? All the things that had seemed so kind and caring on her part were now open to a different interpretation. The way she'd helped him research his origins could be seen as a selfish desire to know more about her baby's ancestry. Even her sexual wiles and avidity might just have been a ruse to bind him closer, so he'd never leave her in the lurch.

He thought back to New Year's Eve again, and the dramatic fireworks display. All that magic and radiance had been so much empty dazzle; rockets burning out in seconds to spent and blackened trash. And the noise had sounded very close to gunfire – perhaps a warning of the hostilities to come. 'Happy New Year!' the crowd had yelled in triumph – mass delusion, he realized now. Why should *this* year be any happier than last?

'Let's eat,' said Stella. 'I'm starving. All I had for breakfast was half a measly grapefruit.'

'You'd better watch it, or you'll fade away to nothing.'

'No such luck. I put on weight just by *breathing*.'

He followed her to the table, which she'd laid with an embroidered cloth and a vase of daffodils. He was grateful for her trouble, yet when he cut into the stodgy lasagne, burnt black around the edges, he felt a sense of aching loss for Mandy. He missed her creativity, along with everything else; the way she could turn food into an art-form, or a flat into a treasure-house. His Precious Box, made with all her usual skill and style, was just such a work of art, but suppose she decided not to return it, out of misery, or spite?

The thought of losing all its contents – those vital and irreplaceable links with his past – was so upsetting, he all but groaned aloud. But he just *had* to shift his mind from Mandy, if only in fairness to Stella. He'd already been over and over that fatal Friday night in exhaustive, painful detail, yet it still seemed quite impossible to think of anything else.

Fortunately, Stella herself switched to a new topic – although hardly a very cheerful one. 'By the way,' she asked, 'how d'you reckon you'll do in this year's appraisal?'

'Badly – that's for certain! What about you?'

Well, I always find it a bit awkward talking about my own performance, but actually I'm not so bothered this year. I feel I've met all my targets, so—'

'Gosh, I wish I had your confidence. I'm pretty sure mine'll be a disaster. These last few weeks, my mind's been all over the place and Trevor's well aware of the fact. He's bound to give me a lower grade than last year.'

''Course he won't! He knows damned well how good you are with customers. *And* incredibly punctual and always willing to try new things and go the extra mile. And your group's been a great success – brought in new people and upped the issues. It's only because you're depressed that you're seeing things in a negative light. I bet you anything you like you get at least a "B", if not an "A".'

'Well, I'm preparing myself for a "D", which would make even a "C" seem good.'

'Eric, if you get a "D", I'll eat my hat. I'll even eat Harriet's revolting old brown beret. Anyway, let's change the subject, if you find it such a drag. Have you had any more ideas about the Remembrance Project?'

'Mm, a few.'

'Me, too. In fact, I think we ought to discuss it before you leave for Seattle.'

'Right. Fire ahead.'

'Not now. I draw the line at working on my one day off.'

'OK, but remember I'm only around for four more days, and I'll have to get off sharpish on the Thursday, to do my packing and stuff.' He gave a hollow laugh. 'Packing, huh! I don't even have a case.'

'I'll lend you one – no problem. Take it with you when you leave.'

'Thanks.' He recalled, with pain, that it was Mandy's case he'd planned to borrow – although *any* case sitting in his flat would only be a panic-inducing reminder that, this coming Friday, he would actually be on the plane. The mere thought made him break out in a sweat.

'Right, when are we going to meet, then? Is tomorrow any good?'

'Probably. We'll need more than just ten minutes, though. I want to go over the poems for my group.'

'Shit! Don't remind me, Eric. Poetry's simply not my thing and I'm bound to make some awful gaffe.'

'You'll be great – don't worry. Anyway, who else can I ask to run the group? Kath's too inexperienced; Trevor far too busy; Harriet opposes it on principle and Helen's on leave that week.'

'I'll manage, I suppose. Though I'll be jolly glad to see you back.'

'Not as glad as I'll be – just to *be* back.'

'But aren't you looking forward to seeing Erica?'

'Yes, course. It's just …' He hesitated; had no wish to burden Stella with the whole raft of his fears, on top of all the other stuff. 'I'm a bit nervous, I suppose, about how she and I will relate to each other, after all this time. Christine said she was playing up, even being bolshie and—'

'Sound like typical teenage behaviour to me. I wouldn't be too fussed.'

'And I'm not sure how I'll feel staying in the same house as Dwight – you know, seeing him and Christine in a clinch.'

'Oh, come on, Eric, they won't snog in front of you!'

'Let's hope not. And I'm not the world's best traveller,' he added, with a casual laugh, 'so I'm a bit uptight about the journey. The whole thing didn't seem so bad when I thought Mandy would be with me, but now …'

'Oh, Eric, you poor love! I can't come with you to Seattle, but I will come to Heathrow. In fact, I'll lay on a snazzy limo to take us there in style – my treat. I insist. Which Terminal are you going from?'

'Four.'

'Shame! Five is so much nicer.'

He shrugged. Could any Terminal be 'nice'?

'And, from what I hear, they're renovating Four, so it's all a bit of a mess. Never mind, I'll stay with you till you have to go through security. We'll have lunch together, if you like, and—'

'No, the flight leaves in the morning. I have to be at the airport soon after seven-thirty.'

'Well, breakfast, then.'

'Honestly, it's sweet of you, but …' Impossible to explain that no way would he be able to eat – or chat, or joke, or lounge about, or behave in any normal sort of manner. Even the mention of Heathrow had sent immediate spasms sputtering through his gut, so that he could barely swallow another mouthful of lunch. He was absolutely adamant that nobody – not even a firm friend like Stella – should witness his sheer panic at the airport. 'I'll be fine,' he said, gritting his teeth in the semblance of a smile. 'In fact, I'll imagine I'm another Brad, jetting off without a qualm to some Third-World trouble-spot. Yes,' he said, warming to the theme, 'Why settle for somewhere as tame as Seattle? Don't expect me back before Christmas, at the soonest, Stella. I've changed my plans – this minute – and I now intend to plane-hop from Zimbabwe to Islamabad, then on to the Sudan, with a lightning tour of Afghanistan and Iraq, an unscheduled stop in Palestine and … and …'

The next destinations petered out in a cul-de-sac of stuttering, then, all at once, his voice skidded to a total halt, as he was racked by choking sobs.

chapter twenty

Eric stopped to check the wheels of Stella's case. They had been jamming since he set out from home, slowing him down as he manoeuvred the case along the puddled streets. Not that he was in danger of being late, since, at 4.55 a.m., the tube wasn't even open yet. The journey to Heathrow took roughly fifty minutes; *he* had allowed two hours, for fear of hold-ups or emergencies – and because he couldn't bear another second pacing sick and shaky around his flat.

The rain drummed against his back as he bent to investigate the wheels. He was so wet already, he hardly cared about a further drenching, but what did concern him was whether the downpour would affect the flight. Did planes have windscreen-wipers and, if so, could they cope with such relentless rain? And wasn't there a danger of the aircraft skidding on the runway?

The case appeared unmendable – probably shared his own reluctance to make the journey at all. Having gone down with a filthy cold, his natural instinct was to creep back into bed and hibernate for the next few weeks. He pitied the poor people sitting beside him on the plane; feared they might erupt in air-rage if he coughed and sneezed all over them. He had dosed himself with aspirin, Lemsip and Benylin – together with Imodium for his over-active bowels – but there was no remedy for his mounting terror at having to board a plane.

He continued along Kennington Road in the grudging pre-dawn light. The shops were closed and shuttered, and an air of gloom seemed to hang across the area, as if spring had lost its confidence and retreated back to winter. Crossing the road, he could barely see his whereabouts in the driving, sheeting rain, and was relieved to reach the shelter of the tunnel that led to Vauxhall Station.

'Spare some change, please?'

He fumbled for his wallet and placed a two-pound coin on the calloused, outstretched palm. Despite the pitiable state of the beggar's clothes and person (matted dreadlocks; rags tied round his feet), he would gladly have swapped lives with him. Better to be destitute and homeless than faced with a thirteen-hour flight.

'God bless you, sir!' the bloke called after him.

If only. What comfort there must be to believe in an all-powerful God who would ignore all other problems in the universe – war, famine, global warming, economic meltdown – in order to concentrate His efforts solely on the welfare of one Eric Victor Parkhill and on the safety of one transatlantic flight.

Emerging from the tunnel, he humped the case down the flight of steps to the tube. The entrance was still locked and barred, but at least he was in the dry now, and could blow his streaming nose, working through almost his entire supply of tissues. He also used the time to re-check his ticket and passport, which he'd done several times already during the short walk from his flat, continually worrying that someone might have nicked them. He ought to have purchased one of the theft-proof pouches advertised in that catalogue, but he'd been feeling too downhearted to buy anything at all, save a few presents for his daughter. Only now did it occur to him that he should have made more effort to impress her – *and* Christine, of course – by dressing with more care this morning. They hadn't seen him for fifteen months and might be suitably appalled to come face to face with a creased, dishevelled hobo, whose skin had erupted in an unsightly rash – stress-induced, no doubt.

Well, that was the least of his problems. The female on his mind at present was neither Erica nor Christine but Mandy – especially the horror of their meeting on Monday, when he had turned up, unannounced. He'd been missing her so fiercely, he'd gone round to her flat to suggest that he should act as the baby's father in all respects except the biological. However, he had found her, not alone, but entertaining the mysterious Oliver Birch – a fairly ordinary sort of chap, in cold reality, although he'd hated him on sight, of course, for no other reason than he was hobnobbing with Mandy. She insisted that he 'just happened to be passing' – a likely story at ten o'clock at night and when the fellow lived in Croydon. Presumably she was softening him up, in the hope he'd play the role of father number four – a wiser choice than Brad, maybe, since he was at least a decade older and did look rather fatherly. Well, good luck to him, the shit!

The whole devastating encounter had forced him to conclude that Stella was right and he couldn't live with a woman he would never be able to trust. The problem was, he still adored her, and that love was like a blockage in his heart; a thwarted and frustrated love, with no outlet and no access.

He was glad to see a member of the underground staff come towards the barrier and start unlocking the metal gates. All this hanging about only encouraged gloomy introspection. As he lumbered through the entrance with his case, another of the staff wished him a cheery 'Good morning!'

Nothing very good about it, except at least there wasn't a tube strike, and he hadn't gone down with diphtheria or scarlet fever, just a piddling cold. And he had to admit he was feeling relieved about his recent appraisal. To his intense surprise, Trevor had congratulated him on a successful and productive year and said he'd be recommending a grade of B-plus. Of course, the assessors might disagree and mark him down when it came to the final result, which meant he would lose his higher bonus, or even …

His speculations were interrupted by the arrival of a train. Jumping on, he felt not a little conspicuous, with his sodden trousers clinging to his legs and his hair dripping water down his neck. Not that there was anyone to see him. He was alone in the carriage – apart from a suspicious-looking package, directly opposite his seat.

He eyed it warily, recalling the endless warnings about unattended packages. And this one did look dodgy: a cardboard box, with no address or label, loosely tied with several lengths of string. Could it truly be something dangerous, like a bomb? If so, he ought to welcome it, as it would provide the perfect let-out; blow him to bits before he had to fly. On the other hand, he might lose a leg – or two – be mutilated beyond repair and end his days in a home for paraplegics. Perhaps it would be wiser to get out.

Seizing his case, he crept towards the doors, making as little disturbance as possible, for fear any sudden movement might detonate the device. But, as the train rattled into the station, he remembered it was *Mandy's* station – Pimlico. Suppose she were on the platform, giving Oliver a last, lingering kiss, after a night of steamy sex together; waving him off as he staggered back to Croydon.

Bullshit! Of course she wouldn't be up at five; nor out in such lousy weather. But, as he was about to alight, the doors slid shut, imprisoning him with the package again. And, indeed, as he watched, it seemed to change before his very eyes into a living, breathing terrorist – bearded, turbaned, heavily armed and about to shoot him through the head. He waited for the blinding flash; the ear-splitting explosion, but the only noise was that of the train rattling into Victoria, where a crowd of people got on, including a mother with her baby. If there *was* a genuine risk, he ought to act responsibly and try to avert the danger. Leaping out of the carriage, he began running the length of the platform, the rickety case juddering behind him, as he tried to reach the driver in time. He must beg him to take action – apply the emergency brakes, to halt the train. However, just as he drew level with the driver's cab, the doors slid shut once more and he was left stranded on the platform.

He slumped on to a bench. He was probably overreacting – as usual. The package could well be harmless: a stack of leaflets, waiting to be distributed, or a parcel of books someone had left behind by mistake. Surely a bomb would have exploded by now, and the whole network would be closed, with staff and police pouring on to the platform to escort passengers to safety. Whereas there was nobody in sight save a few harmless-looking people on their way to work.

As soon as the next train came in, he lugged his case on board again, found a seat, took out his book and vowed to sit and read, instead of behaving like a human jack-in-the-box. And if Osama Bin Laden himself got on, armed with a grenade-launcher and a Kalashnikov, well, he wouldn't even look up from the page.

LIFTS TO DEPARTURES.

The sign alone was enough to send his panic-levels soaring. There was no escape – nobody and nothing could save him now from having to depart.

He trundled the baggage-trolley into the lift, and stood leaning against the wall, for support. He had always been scared of lifts, but at least they didn't take off into the stratosphere and climb to 30,000 feet. He cast an envious glance at the woman standing next to him. Being male had definite disadvantages, due chiefly to the strain of living up to the qualities required: bulldog courage, heroism, maverick self-sufficiency. Women had it easy in comparison; could get away with being scared of lifts, or mice, or spiders – or of any damned thing, actually. Fear in them was excused as sweetly feminine, whereas in men it was plain pathetic.

As the doors opened to let him out, he was appalled to see a jostling mass of passengers crowding every inch of the space; with long queues snaking from each check-in desk, and a general air of chaos and confusion. Stella had assured him that, since British Airways' move to Terminal Five, *this* terminal would be comparatively empty – at least until more airlines moved in, later in the year. So he was completely unprepared for the scene that met his eyes, or indeed for the sheer ugliness of the place. It resembled an outdated industrial warehouse; the low, oppressive ceiling cluttered with lumbering pipes and hideous steel fans. Whatever the perils of air travel, he had somehow imagined it as glamorous – the preserve of rich sophisticates who expected stylish surroundings. Yet he had walked into a dump, with no comfort, no amenities and very little natural light. The only window was sited at the far end of the concourse, and did nothing to alleviate the air of dingy claustrophobia.

Well, he thought, venturing out into the mayhem, he wasn't here to appraise the aesthetics. He had better bite the bullet and join one of the long queues.

Feeling like a new boy at some vast, confusing school, he went up to one of the airport staff and asked him where to go.

'If you're flying InterWest Airlines, sir, you need to check in at Zone A, but I'm sorry to inform you that the baggage-system has developed a fault, which means all flights are subject to serious delay.'

He stared at the man in horror. He would miss his connection and be stranded in Minneapolis. Although his insurance would cover an overnight stay, what it couldn't do was alleviate Dwight and Christine's wrath if he failed to turn up in time, when they were due to leave for Hong Kong tomorrow. Suddenly, the claims of that insurance policy began echoing in his head: Catastrophe Cover, Hijack, Mugging, Personal Accident. No, he couldn't go through with this – the dangers were just too overwhelming. Even the prospect of a night on his own in some alien motel in Minneapolis filled him with near-panic.

'We're doing everything we can to fix the problem, sir, but, of course, a backlog has been building up, which is the reason for the queues and all the—'

'OK, I understand,' he interrupted tersely, 'but which way is the chemist?' He was now desperate for more Kleenex, highly embarrassed by the fact that his nose was running into his mouth, like some snotty little kid's.

'I'm afraid all the shops are closed at present, sir, during the current renovation. There *is* a branch of Boots in Arrivals, one floor down, but I strongly recommend that you stay here and check in.'

'I *have* checked in – online.'

'Yes, but you still need to drop off your bags and have your passport checked, so I suggest you make your way to Zone A, sir.'

Humiliated by his constant need to sniff, he squeezed between the crowds; jabbed by the sharp corners of other people's luggage, or rammed by pushchair-wheels. Finally, he joined the queue at the far end of the terminal, remembering, with relief, that he'd packed a spare shirt in his flight-bag, assuming he would sweat so much on the first flight, he'd need a change of clothes for the second. That shirt would have to function as a handkerchief, however disgusting the prospect.

As he shuffled slowly forward in a stop-start, stop-start fashion, he noticed a young couple passionately embracing, just a few yards off. They were clinging to each other, kissing almost manically as they said a last goodbye. He could hardly bear to watch, since it served as a reminder that he hadn't said goodbye to Mandy – just shouted incoherently as he slammed out of her flat.

After half an hour of queuing, surreptitiously mopping his nose on the shirt, he began to understand why passing through Heathrow was said to be as stressful as being mugged at knifepoint. So why did people travel? Presumably the majority were flying for pleasure (an oxymoron, surely), or at least had *chosen* to fly, which seemed equally inexplicable. Yet, according to recent forecasts, more and more quite ordinary folk would be travelling further and further. Why was he so different; so unable to participate in common human pleasures? And why was he feeling so alone, despite the press of people milling round? Without his usual props – his flat, his job, his daily routine – he was like a hollow tree; an empty shell of bark, with no solidity or sap; no inner core.

At last, he reached the desk, although the sharp-suited woman behind it did little to reassure him. No, she couldn't say whether he'd catch his connection or not; all she could suggest was that he listen to the announcements. He'd been doing that, non-stop, but the maddeningly upbeat recorded voice had provided no real information; just apologized for the disruption and repeated the assurance that they were doing all they could to solve the problem. Perhaps the delay would give him time to dash down to Arrivals and invest in some paper hankies and a box or two of lozenges to dislodge the stash of razor blades embedded in his throat. But, no – the woman at the bag-drop desk directed him to another queue, this time for Security, where he was issued with a plastic bag, to put in any liquids he was carrying.

'I've already done that,' he objected, having spent twenty minutes yesterday studying the small print about the dimensions of the plastic bag, and any containers that went into it, along with the pedantic definitions of what constituted 'liquids'. He understood, of course, that such precautions were intended to prevent jihadists from smuggling liquid explosives into perfume or shampoo bottles and then blowing up the plane. But, according to Jeremy, nothing could actually stop them and, in fact, another air atrocity was almost guaranteed to happen, so long as such jihadists saw their mission as divinely ordained.

Once he had rummaged for his plastic bag and looped it over one finger, he was told to join yet another queue. Queue number three was at least different in its format, in that it wound its zigzag way between lengths of tape strung between blue posts. He found himself behind a woman carrying a baby, and pregnant with another child. Every mother and baby he saw only underlined his aching sense of loss, and again he felt choked with grief as he traipsed along between the posts, like a refugee in transit.

When he finally reached the head of the queue, he was ordered to proceed to desk number one – where there was, of course, another queue, although a shorter one, admittedly. All the other passengers seemed to know the ropes, and appeared to be undressing – or partly, anyway – putting their coats and jackets into black polystyrene trays, along with other items like their belts and keys and phones. He, the fumbling novice, was holding everybody up, as he tried to follow suit, yet still managed to disgrace himself by failing to put his flight-bag on the conveyor-belt.

Once he had complied with all the procedures, he was directed through the security arch; seriously alarmed as a loud bell rang and an official came striding over and began running his hands up and down his body; even between his legs. He was then instructed to remove his shoes – pathetic, sodden things, and clearly objects of intense suspicion, since they were put back through the x-ray machine by one of the security staff. Could someone have planted drugs on him while he was waiting in the various queues? All his childhood experience of being a pawn, at the mercy of those in authority, came flooding back as he stood mortified and shoeless; an object of suspicion, already attracting curious stares. His clothes were still wet and soggy; his nose running like an urchin's. Then, as now, there was nobody to plead his case; no one who believed him, even though he knew full well that he hadn't committed any crime.

But still they hadn't finished. A second little Hitler appeared, armed with some sort of metal-detector, which was dragged across his body, with obsessive thoroughness. They must be looking for lethal weapons. Would he be forbidden entry to America; even locked up in a cell?

Nothing was said; no explanation given. He was simply frogmarched to the end of the conveyor-belt, where yet another official investigated his flight-bag, taking everything out, object by humiliating object – the Imodium, the Senokot (only *he* would need both); the fluffy black toy cat (Stella's good-luck gift to him); the three separate books on overcoming panic; Mandy's scarlet thong. He had packed the thong as a memento of their fantastic sex and because, if he didn't have her with him in person, then at least he had this one small thing that had sat against her skin, still bore her intimate smell. But, of course, the security staff would assume he was a pervert who liked to dress in woman's underwear.

However, the fellow's interest seemed fixed on something else. 'What's this?' he barked, seizing on a brightly coloured package.

'A present for my daughter.' Erica's other presents were in the case, but this one was too fragile: a heart-shaped pendant, made of Venetian glass.

'All presents are subject to screening and searching,' the official told him sternly, 'so they have to be carried unwrapped. Would you unwrap it and show me the contents, please.'

Reluctantly, Eric prised off the gift-wrap and the layers of tissue underneath, opened the box and showed it to the bloke. The guy all but snatched it from him and took out the delicate heart; handling it so roughly Eric felt almost more assaulted than when he himself was being searched, as if his own heart was being torn from him and crushed. And, even after it was grudgingly returned, the officious hands continued to probe remorselessly the innermost crannies of the bag, finally unearthing a packet of tampons, which Stella must have overlooked when she cleared it out for him.

By now his cheeks were scarlet, especially as several other passengers had been observing the whole procedure and continued to watch, with interest, as tampons, bowel-aids, fluffy cat, scarlet thong *et al* were shoved summarily back in the bag.

'OK,' the guy said curtly, 'you're free to go.'

He was almost surprised to be released. Growing up in care had left him with scant respect for justice, since he'd been invariably found guilty, regardless of the facts. Yet, here he was, actually walking free and, indeed, once he'd reclaimed his possessions, he found himself in more congenial surroundings than the drab and functional area he had mercifully escaped. What was strange, however, was that he appeared to be in a shopping mall, rather than an airport. He had expected to see the actual planes, but there was no sign of any aircraft, nor anyone to ask for help, except a crush of passengers, all busy with their own concerns. Scanning the departure-boards, he saw that almost all the flights bore the word 'delayed', including his own, to Minneapolis. Yet despite what had seemed like hours of queuing, it was still only half-past eight, so there was still some frail hope of catching his connecting flight.

Having bought a stack of Kleenex, he prowled aimlessly around; too sick to eat or drink; too anxious to sit still, but too keyed up to do any further shopping. However, everyone he watched seemed to be gorging, guzzling, browsing, buying. *He* was a different species, lacking their robust digestions and laid-back temperaments; their ability to forget the fact they were about to board a death-machine. Just last Friday, he'd been stupid enough to read an account in the paper – written by plane-crash survivors, no less – the horrors of which made even Jeremy's experiences pale into insignificance. Snippets of their testimony were still shuddering through his head: '"Brace for impact!" the captain announced, then we hit the water and skidded to a halt, like the worst car-wreck you could possibly imagine ...' 'The plane slammed down, bounced up, came back down on its nose and began to cartwheel ...' 'The aircraft broke into five sections and I was knocked unconscious. When I came round, I was hanging upside-down from my seat-belt ...' 'Then there was an almighty crunch, which was the port-wing catching a tree. The next thing I knew was waking up in hospital. I'd lost an eye and my nose, and broken my spine, shoulder, jaw and ankle....'

Retching, he made a dash for the men's toilet, found an empty cubicle and crouched above the bowl; emerging half-an-hour later, deathly pale. Only then did he notice a sign for a multi-faith prayer-room and was tempted to go in search of it. The way he felt at present, he would convert to *any* faith – Muslim, Hindu, Buddhist, Christian, Sikh – if it could save him from the flight. The longer he hung about, the worse his sense of dread, but every time he checked the departure-boards, his flight was still marked 'delayed'. Delayed by how *much*, for Christ's sake? Couldn't they give details? Surely other passengers must be anxious about missing their connections, although all those he could see seemed totally unfazed; some even laughing and joking. He could no more laugh than train as a matador. But then, even as a boy, he had been over-serious; a wary child; old before his time; not interested in sport or toys; only in books, because they could transport him to another world. And books had been his friends – the only friends, in fact, who wouldn't let him down, or sneak on him behind his back, or be moved to other placements, just as he'd got to know them.

So why didn't he go to Smith's and find himself a book that truly *was* a friend – not a self-help manual that only served to emphasize his fears, nor a stodgy novel, like the one he'd been struggling to read on the tube – but a magical tome that would whisk him to a realm where no one flew except fairies and all endings were guaranteed happy?

Queue number five. Worse than all the others because he was queuing now to board. And, outside the large windows, were – at last – the planes – terrifying objects, far too large and cumbersome to fly. How could such ungainly Titans wing their way across the vast Atlantic, then from one side to the other of the whole huge American continent? Although he might never reach the far side – not today, in any case – but only get as far as Minneapolis. The plane had been due to leave at 9.40, and it was now 11.05. True, he had some time in hand at Minneapolis, but that time was slowly ebbing away, and all the extra stress of whether or not he would make it, had reduced him to a wreck.

The book he'd bought was useless, for all its seductive style, since he couldn't concentrate on even the first page. Nor could he strike up a conversation, because, despite standing in this long, long line of so-called fellow humans, he felt cut off from every one of them. And so tired, he could collapse. It wasn't just the lack of sleep, but the exhaustion of fear itself; the way it sapped and undermined you; made every moment fraught. However, this particular queue he would gladly stay in for ever, so long as he never had to reach the officials at the end of it, who were directing passengers down a ramp that must lead out to the plane. Yet every second he was drawing nearer, nearer – and every second fighting the temptation to turn tail and run the other way; not stopping till he was safely back in Vauxhall.

Somehow, he stood firm though and, within cruel minutes, drew level with the desk.

'Where are you staying in the United States?' the uniformed hulk demanded, peering closely at his passport.

Eric's mind went blank. Such was his state of terror, he couldn't recall his ex-wife's address; could hardly even remember his own name.

'I asked you where you were staying in America?' the man repeated, drumming his fingers irritably on the desk.

'With my … my daughter.'

'I need the address.'

Eric started fumbling in his flight-bag. He'd stowed the address in one of the pockets, if he only knew which one. After what seemed like hours of scrabbling, accompanied by more finger-drumming from the increasingly impatient bloke, he finally located it and passed it across the desk, not trusting himself to speak.

As the man studied it in silence, Eric plunged once more between abject fear and hope. Perhaps, even now, he would be forbidden to travel – the most enticing, glorious prospect in the world.

'OK, go on through.'

He stood rooted to the spot. Proceeding any further was physically impossible.

'Move on, please! You're holding people up.'

It was a miracle his legs could actually function, let alone lead him down that treacherous curving ramp – a passage into Hell. His heart was thumping; his mouth dry and full of gravel, as he staggered further on, into some sort of corridor, then stopped dead in his tracks, suddenly confronted by a group of what looked like stewardesses. Surely this couldn't be the plane? Didn't he have to go outside, on to the tarmac, and mount a flight of steps, with the great flying-machine towering high above him? He had seen it often on television – dignitaries like presidents and popes walking up those steps into the aircraft. Yet there *were* no steps, no aircraft – he had simply reached the end of a corridor.

'Welcome aboard!'

He was being greeted not only by the stewardesses, but by an important-looking bloke, rigged out in braid and epaulettes. Indeed, judging by their effusive welcome, he might well have been a long-lost friend, rather than someone who detested airline staff on principle.

And, yes, he was *on* the plane, although he couldn't understand how he had ever got there. Indeed, his first impression was one of total shock. It was nothing like the huge metal monster he'd seen parked outside the windows, but hideously small and cramped, like an overcrowded bus. Almost every seat was taken; the passengers squashed up, with no room to stretch their legs, or barely breathe. Some were standing in the aisles, and he had to struggle past them, as he was directed by a stewardess, further on and further on, to what must surely be the worst seat on the plane, right bang in the middle of the aircraft, with rows of heads in front of him and rows of heads behind.

'That's your seat,' she smiled, pointing to the centre of the row.

'But I booked an aisle seat,' he protested, already feeling trapped and claustrophobic, 'and in the last row at the back.' He'd studied the seating-plan with the utmost care; choosing a location near the toilets, in case he had to throw up, and close to the emergency-exits, so he could make a speedy getaway.

'I'm sorry, sir, but according to your boarding-card, this is the seat you've been allocated.'

'No, it certainly isn't. My seat was 44 J.'

'I'm afraid you should have explained that when you checked in, sir.'

He'd been too petrified at that stage even to think about seats. 'Would it be possible to move me?' he asked, with increasing desperation.

'I'm sorry, no. Seat 44 J is already taken. And I must ask you, sir, to kindly sit down, as we're getting ready for departure.'

Aware that people were listening in, he squeezed, with considerable difficulty, past a hugely overweight guy, who patently needed *two* seats to accommodate his massive thighs. Just his luck to be sitting next to such a fatso, which would make escape extremely difficult. His neighbour on the other side was a woman in a niqab, with only the slits of her eyes showing – possibly a man in disguise. Jeremy had told him that violent criminals sometimes managed to evade arrest by donning burkas or niqabs; relying on the laxness of security staff, who often failed to make them remove their veils, for fear of being labelled Islamophobic. Eric seethed at the injustice. *He* had been subjected to a virtual striptease, whereas the individual beside him might be carrying a gun or bomb beneath those flowing robes.

'Mum, look at that man's hair!' a voice behind him shrilled. 'It's nearly the same colour as Pippa's carrot puree.'

'Ssssh, Katy, don't be rude.'

Eric swivelled round to see three small fry in the row behind – the girl who'd spoken, her younger brother and a babe-in-arms (Pippa, presumably), together with their harassed-looking mother. He smiled at them through gritted teeth; bracing himself for more comments on his appearance – his rash, for instance: 'nearly the same colour as tomato soup'.

However, the next assault was physical in nature, as, the minute he sat down, one of the kids began kicking the back of his seat, jarring him quite painfully with each repeated thump. But before he could object, he was overtaken by a monstrous sneeze that seemed to echo through the plane.

'Terribly sorry,' he muttered to his neighbours. 'Do excuse me. I've gone down with a cold.'

'You shouldn't fly with a cold,' the fat man remarked, with obvious disapproval. 'You could rupture an eardrum and, believe me, mate, that's the most god-awful pain! And it can leave you permanently deaf.'

'Really?' Eric muttered, almost wishing he were deaf already, so he didn't have to listen to yet more flight-induced disasters.

'Yeah. A friend of mine flew with a bad cold and never really recovered. He's suffered with balance problems ever since – even spent two weeks in hospital.'

Hospital, thought Eric, was where *he* should be, right now. All his bodily functions had gone into manic overdrive. His heart-rate had reached danger-levels and, at any moment, would simply shudder to a stop. He prayed it would happen before take-off, so he could be whisked to the safety of a morgue on *this* side of the Atlantic. He was also sweating so profusely, he might have been sitting in a sauna rather than in an air-conditioned plane. Nor could he shift his mind from airline-carnage. In addition to Jeremy's atrocities and the unspeakable catastrophes depicted in *The Week*, he'd also read lurid reports of two plane-crashes, this very Monday, occurring within minutes of each other: the first in Montana, the second in Tokyo. And the latter crash had been caused partly by strong winds – exactly the same type of wind forecast for today.

He cast an anxious glance at the Muslim, who was sitting preternaturally still. Wasn't that suspicious in itself? If he were a notorious gangster, wanted by the police, naturally he'd want to avoid attention.

'Please fasten your seat-belt, sir.' A passing stewardess had stopped at the end of their row and was gesturing to his lap.

'Er, yes, of course.' How did the damned thing do up? It appeared to have only one end, unless he was sitting on the other, which would account for the pain in his buttock.

'Though you might be more comfortable, sir, if you took off your coat.'

Only then did he notice that no one else was wearing coats. No wonder he was suffocating – although even stark naked he'd be sweating. He struggled to his feet. It wasn't easy to remove a coat in such a restricted space, but, fortunately, the stewardess relieved him of the garment and stowed it safely in the overhead locker. She even leaned across and helped him with his seat-belt, clearly realizing what a greenhorn he was. Could he really be the only person on a 300-seater plane who had never flown before? Certainly, everyone in his line of sight appeared enviably at home, so he used the ruse he had relied on in Security, and copied what they were doing: extracting earphones, eye-mask and some glossy magazine or other from the pocket on the seat in front.

And it was not the only reading matter, since a steward was now coming down the aisle, distributing copies of the *Daily Mail*. He waved his away with a vehement 'No thanks!' These last few days, every time he'd so much as glanced at a paper, some new horror caught his eye; not least an article (in the *Mail*, no less) about the debauchery of airline staff. Yes, Jeremy was right. Apparently, the stewards were often drugged or drunk on duty, or having it away in the toilets with each other.

'Ladies and gentlemen, this is your captain speaking …'

Was *he* drunk, Eric wondered, or maybe stoned out of his mind, or shagging his co-pilot?

'Welcome aboard this Airbus A330 to Minneapolis St Paul. Our flying time is just over nine hours, and we shall be cruising at …'

As Eric tried to shift his mind from dissipation to the details of the flight, another sneeze tickled in his nose and exploded in a resounding '*Atishooooooo!*', despite his frantic efforts to abort it. Sneezing with an allergy might be frustrating and inconvenient, but sneezing with a cold rendered him a genuine source of infection – as his neighbour lost no time in pointing out.

'Bloody hell!' the bloke exclaimed. 'You should be home in bed, mate, not spreading your germs to us poor sods.'

'I really do apologize. I assure you I wouldn't fly unless it was absolutely necessary.'

'What, is someone ill or dying, then?'

Eric nodded. *He* was ill and dying, so it wasn't exactly a lie, Anyway, he had to appease this fellow, otherwise he might be subject to twenty-stone of furious attack.

'Very sorry to hear that. My name's Phil, by the way.'

'Oh, hi … I'm Eric.'

He prayed no more conversation would ensue. Chitchat was impossible in his present state of mind and, besides, he might somehow start confessing all his terrors and then be duly mortified. He'd discerned long ago that other people regarded fear as fundamentally selfish; a narcissistic focus on one's own footling little qualms, rather than a wider concern for the ills of all mankind. Although shamed by such accusations, he was also well aware that he *did* care about humanity; *did* make constant efforts to shift his attention from his pusillanimous self, yet it made not a shred of difference. In fact, he suspected Mandy was right. Somehow his mother's own desperation had been imprinted on his every cell from the moment he drew breath, so that nothing he could do ever dented his sense of vulnerability at being cast adrift in such a capricious world.

However, to avoid any risk of further exchanges with his (probably fearless) neighbour, he buried himself in the magazine, *High Life*, which seemed full of celebrity interviews and advertisements for luxury trinkets. But who in their right mind would want to read about Angelina Jolie's love-life, or decide between a Rolex watch and a pair of Gucci sunglasses when death stared them in the face?

'Hello again, ladies and gentlemen, this is Captain Cooper, with an update. I'm sorry to announce there will be a further delay to your flight, because we're waiting for a replacement part to …'

Eric clutched Phil's arm so hard, he left red marks.

'Steady on! What's up, mate?'

All colour had drained from Eric's face. 'Didn't you hear what he said? A piece must have fallen off the plane.'

'Don't be daft! He said a replacement part for the in-flight entertainment system.'

Eric barely heard. In his mind, he was watching the plane break up in mid-air, as other parts slowly came adrift and the whole thing crashed to earth.

'You know, for the movies and TV and stuff.' Phil gestured to the tiny screen in front of him.

'Oh … I see.' He had assumed those little screens were some security device, scanning every passenger throughout the duration of the journey. After all, if the authorities were so Big-Brother-like, the idea made perfect sense.

The baby behind him suddenly started screaming – a wail of profound despair, entirely appropriate in the circumstances. Shouldn't everyone be crying, when, any minute, they would meet their doom? Take-off and landing were the most dangerous of all procedures, according to reports. Indeed, one of Monday's crashes had occurred when the plane was landing, and there had been countless other disasters as planes tried – and failed – to take off.

'Thank you for your patience, ladies and gentlemen. I'm afraid it's taking a little longer than we anticipated to replace the missing part.'

Patience? The kids were kicking the back of his seat again; the infant was still shrieking and his knees were jammed uncomfortably against the seat in front. In fact, he was developing cramp in his thighs, although he almost welcomed any new and different pain, as a distraction from the risk of death-by-terror.

He was also increasingly uneasy about the Muslim's almost creepy stillness. She *was* a female (as he'd realized from her hands and from the presence of, presumably, her husband – a hirsute and swarthy bloke, slumped glumly on her other side); none the less, there was something distinctly unsettling about her total silence and rigidity, as if she were made of stone, not flesh. Attempting to be friendly, he flashed her a nervous smile, but the problem with a niqab was that you had no idea if its occupant was smiling back. Unlikely, judging by the hostile eyes. If only he was sitting next to some gorgeous, sympathetic woman – a Mandy-clone, who would let him hold her hand; bury his face in the shelter of her breasts.

'Hello again, ladies and gentlemen. This is Captain Cooper speaking. I'm glad to report that we now have the aircraft doors closed, which means we're in the system to depart....'

Eric gripped the arms of his seat, fixing on that one word: 'depart'. His overwhelming instinct was to leap up from his seat, tear along the aisle and demand to be let out. Only the thought of Christine's scorn, Dwight's fury and Erica's distress kept him buckled down.

And now a female voice was speaking. 'Ladies and gentlemen, this is to remind you that all mobile phones and electronic devices must be switched off before departure.'

Departure. There it was again. No word in the whole lexicon could induce such sickening dread. Yet, although he was primed for catastrophe – every cell of his body on the highest possible alert – there was a strong sense of anticlimax, since nothing actually happened; no revving of the engines; no sudden movement forward; only a ripping sound from Phil as he tore open a giant-sized bag of crisps.

'Here, mate, help yourself.'

'Er, no thanks.' The smell of grease and vinegar only added to his discomfort. Any minute he'd throw up.

'Ladies and gentlemen, Captain Cooper again. I'm extremely sorry to announce a further delay. We are, in fact, fully ready for departure, but our pushback tractor has disappeared, so I'm afraid we'll have to wait till it arrives.'

What the hell was a pushback tractor, and how could it 'disappear'?

Perhaps this flight was fated and everything that could go wrong *would* go wrong, finally ending in apocalypse. The omens were certainly bad. The baby's wails had become a screeching caterwaul that split his head apart. And the kids behind were not only kicking his seat but quarrelling and fighting; their slaps and shrieks providing a noxious descant to the jaunty music now playing over the speakers. And, on top of everything else, the cramp in his thigh was spreading down his leg in stabbing jolts of pain. He needed desperately to get up and walk about, but the way he felt at present he would probably never walk again, but spend his future as a quaking blob – not that he could count on there *being* any future. And, once they were airborne, he certainly wouldn't dare to move a muscle, for fear of overbalancing the plane. If passengers began milling around, the strain on the aircraft might prove just too great. For all he knew, the cabin floor might be fragile, especially with great hulks like Phil putting it at extra risk.

He glanced at one of the stewards as he came striding down the aisle. He looked anxious, didn't he, as if something grave was preying on his mind? Perhaps all the staff knew full well that flight IW 103 was fatally imperilled, but, of course, were forbidden to divulge such fears. And the weather itself would give additional cause for concern. Heavy rain had been forecast all day, and might well become torrential and, once they were over Greenland, there would be no end to the hazards: sleet, snow, ice, fog, thunder, lightning—

Another announcement interrupted his thoughts – not the captain this time, but a different male voice, sounding inappropriately upbeat. 'I'd like to introduce myself. I'm Andy, your senior flight attendant. I wish you all a pleasant flight and—'

A pleasant flight! Another oxymoron and one so patently absurd, it was all he could do not to yell out an objection.

'In a moment,' the cheery voice continued, 'the crew will be demonstrating the safety procedures used aboard this Airbus A330 aircraft. Do please give them your full attention.'

He watched nervously as a couple of stewardesses took up positions in the aisles and began performing some sort of dumb-show, while a recorded voice spelt out horrors so unfathomable, he all but retched again, in panic.

'If the cabin air-supply fails, masks like these will drop down from the panel above your head....'

'Your life-jacket is located under your seat. In the event of a landing on water....'

'Do not inflate your life-jacket until you are outside the aircraft ...'

'A light and a whistle are attached for attracting attention....'

Even if he stoppered his ears, he couldn't avoid this catalogue of disasters, since they were illustrated, in grotesque detail, on the little screen in front of him: people struggling into life-jackets, putting on masks, or – more hideous still – sliding down an escape-chute. Only now did he realize that Jeremy was actually a hero – the way he had helped his fellow passengers down a highly dangerous ladder, whereas *he*, the pitiful coward, could never, ever, go within a mile of an escape-chute. Where would those poor hapless victims land: in the heaving waves of the merciless Atlantic, or impaled on the peaks of some barren, snow-bound mountain-range?

He shut his eyes; tried to blank out the warnings; felt an overpowering desire to take up the foetal position – become nothing but an embryo, with an undeveloped brain, devoid of any feelings whatsoever.

But, Christ! The plane was moving – and moving backwards, not forwards, which meant something must be seriously amiss. If any aircraft took off backwards, the result would be catastrophe.

Then, suddenly, it stopped, having travelled only fifty yards. His fists were clenched so tightly, the nails were clawing into his palms, simply from the tension of not knowing what was going on. Would they depart or wouldn't they? Centuries had passed since he first got on the plane, yet they seemed no further forward on their journey.

'Ladies and gentlemen, in preparation for departure, please ensure your tray-tables are stowed, your seat-backs are in the upright position and your seat-belts are securely fastened. Cabin-crew, take your seats for take-off.'

Could this be it? Or just another false alarm? Certainly, the plane was creeping forwards, but with tantalizing slowness; just inching along, as if the engines had failed and it was already losing power. Perhaps the long delay had made the pilot so edgy, he had muddled the controls.

Then, all at once, it gathered speed and began hurtling along the runway at such a petrifying rate, he grabbed hold of Phil and clung on to him in extremes of panic, ignoring the bloke's protests; ignoring everything but the rattling, roaring, shaking sensations vibrating through his body. And, suddenly, the plane lifted off, with a horrendous sort of lurch and shudder, and he braced himself for death; whispering a farewell to his daughter; hoping desperately she would remember him, for ever. They were climbing now – higher, higher, higher – but any second they would go into a nosedive and crash-land on the tarmac. As he waited for that terrifying impact, he lost all remaining vestige of control; became a dribbling, trembling, sobbing wreck; his sole resource to merge himself with Phil; blunt his fear in that anaesthetizing bulk.

Furiously, Phil pushed him off, shoving him back in his seat, with undisguised aggression. 'I could have you up for assault, you know, manhandling me like that! What's the *matter* with you, you snivelling piece of shit?'

Eric scarcely heard; was in some sort of coma; deaf and dumb and paralysed. Somewhere, far away, though, things were going on – announcements, movements, voices – but indistinct and vague. He remained crouched down in his seat; catatonic, drugged; no longer part of the sentient world.

Only a painful jabbing in his arm brought him slowly back to consciousness. With supreme effort, he forced his eyelids open, to see Phil's big, blubbery face looming close to his.

'Look, sorry I was rude, mate. You took me by surprise. Are you OK, or should I call for help?'

Still confused, Eric glanced around him, then, gradually and gropingly, registered the miraculous fact that the plane was in the air still; hadn't plummeted to earth and hit the ground. He looked along the rows of heads; all 300 totally unscathed; no flames, no charred remains, no sickening wreckage scattered far and wide. Somehow, they had overcome extinction. And, even more miraculous, he was *flying* – actually flying. How could he have failed to realize how astounding the experience was; how you left behind the dingy earth and soared up to this celestial realm; defying gravity and casting off all normal human limitations. Man had longed to fly since he first crawled from the slime, and now he, Eric Victor Parkhill, had achieved it, at long last; had cheated death, survived – and been spared for just one reason, so that he could fly again, again.

Snapping his seat-belt open, he squeezed past Phil, with a torrent of apologies, and began tearing down the aisle to the rear end of the plane, making for a window where he could actually see out, with no passengers or seats beside it.

Without the slightest tremor, he pressed his face against the glass. There, before him, lay a majestic bank of cloud, as dazzling-white as snowdrifts, and gilded by the sun. The rain had vanished; the grey, sullen skies had gone; replaced by shimmering light. He was like God, on the first day of creation, beholding the beauty of His universe. These clouds were pristine, unpolluted by any taint or stain; newly-hatched, new-born.

As he watched, the snowdrifts slowly transformed themselves into a tranquil sea of cloud, with foamy, swan-white breakers rolling gently in. He felt no fear – no fear of sea, or water; no fear of anything. Which meant he, too, had been reborn. And, suddenly, he realized that dawn would just be breaking in Seattle, so he was flying from light to light; overcoming darkness, including his own personal dark night.

Wonderingly, he continued gazing at the shining stretch of undefiled cloud-ocean, and – not caring who might hear – let out a whoop of sheer, ecstatic triumph.

chapter twenty-one

The taxi-driver stopped again and peered out through his window at the street-sign. Clearly, he was lost, having been proceeding – or rather *not* proceeding – in aimless sort of circles for the last twenty minutes or more. Why, thought, Eric wearily, had he turned down Christine's offer to meet him at the airport? Any awkwardness or bitterness at being driven by his ex was as nothing in comparison with this slow, frustrating journey. And it would have cost him not a cent, whereas the cab-fare would be astronomical. He had certainly never realized how far out Christine lived. The bright lights and stylish tower-blocks of Seattle had long since been left behind and he was now in prosperous suburbia, cruising around a maze of streets that all looked much the same, although the houses themselves were distinctive, sharing only a sense of spaciousness and style.

Let me get out and walk, he longed to shout, as they rounded yet another corner that seemed to lead to nowhere. But the driver spoke no English and all communication, so far, had been limited to the fellow's curses (completely indecipherable, but clear in their intent) each time they took a wrong turning. Besides, he would cope no better on his own; traipsing around in the dark and cold, looking for 6521, 82nd Avenue South-East – surely the most soulless address on record. And why so many house-numbers? Surely there couldn't be 6520 other dwellings in Dwight and Christine's street? Obviously, the system was quite different from the English one and, indeed, never had English street-names seemed so comforting and friendly: Pudding Lane, Parson's Green, Puddle Dock, Peartree Gardens – and those were just the Ps. Yet England seemed achingly remote, as if it had been expunged from the map, or simply sunk beneath the sea. Indeed, he felt as if he'd been banished to a limbo where no one else existed save him and the small, swarthy bloke sitting in the driver's seat, because, although lights were on in all the houses, there was no sense of any human life, and almost no traffic on the roads.

He started as the driver let out a sudden shout. Despair, or jubilation? Eric couldn't tell. All he knew was that they'd stopped once more, right beside a street-sign that said '81st Avenue South-East'. Which meant 82nd Avenue must, presumably, be close. The guy was consulting a map, but his cartographic skills appeared to be no better than his English. When he got home – *if* he got home – Eric vowed to hug every single cab-driver in London, to congratulate them personally on their skills, their expertise.

He rummaged in his flight-bag for the least soggy of his Kleenex; now reduced to re-using the old, wet, crumpled ones. Yet, although his nose was streaming, at least the sneezing had stopped and, in his present mood, he was grateful for the smallest of small mercies.

Having blown his nose till it was sore, he settled back against the seat and closed his eyes. According to his body-clock, it was four o'clock in the morning and all he craved was the oblivion of sleep. Counting his journey to Heathrow and this trip from Tacoma airport, he'd been travelling for sixteen hours – or sixty, or 600. Time had lost all meaning and, although he'd set his watch to Seattle time and knew at some vague conscious level that it was getting on for ten in the evening, all calendars and clocks no longer made much sense.

He had almost succeeded in dozing off when another yell roused him from his torpor. Even without a common language, he could tell it was a victory-call. The excited driver had his head stuck out of the window and was gesticulating wildly at the sign: 82nd Avenue South-East. Success! Now it was simply a matter of finding number 6521 – although 'simply' wasn't quite the word, since the street was frustratingly long and it was difficult in the murky-dark to make out any house numbers at all.

Yet, once they'd finally pulled up outside the house, and he'd handed over a veritable king's ransom, his overwhelming instinct was to get back into the cab and spend the entire night (morning?) continuing to meander round the streets. Because, faced with this self-important house, with its columned porch and general air of grandeur, he felt himself visibly shrink in status and importance. How could Erica ever come and stay with him, in his cramped and poky flat, when she was used to such palatial surroundings?

Hoisting his flight-bag over his shoulder, he forced himself to walk up to the front door; noting the extensive garden, with its shrubs and flowerbeds and clumps of stately conifers, and becoming more and more miserably aware of his crumpled clothes, his pimply rash and his red and swollen nose. He prayed that Erica would open the door. At least his darling daughter would be less critical than Dwight; might even be glad to see her dad, after so long an absence.

'Eric, for heaven's sakes! We've been worried sick, wondering where you'd got to. We expected you two hours ago. Couldn't you have rung?'

Not exactly the warmest of welcomes and, indeed, as he stared at his ex-wife, he was overwhelmed with a maelstrom of emotions: love, hate, regret, resentment, embarrassment and grief. This was the woman he had married, bedded, worshipped, lost. Yet she seemed to be a stranger: slimmer and more glamorous than ever he remembered her, as if she'd been remodelled and revamped. The girl he'd met more than twenty years ago had been plumpish, darkish, prettyish and shortish. But all those 'ishes' had been outlawed, and this new streamlined version was emphatically thin, fashionably stylish, and now had dramatically black hair. She even looked as if she'd grown three inches, in her high heels and pencil skirt and general air of sophistication.

'What happened?' she demanded, ushering him in, with, he felt, very little grace. 'We've been waiting for you to call all afternoon.'

'I'm sorry,' he mumbled. 'My mobile doesn't work outside the UK.' That itself was a point against him. Any serious traveller would own the most expensive model, fully operational in every country from Tibet to Timbuktu.

'But couldn't you have rung from Minneapolis?'

'No, there wasn't a spare moment – and I mean that literally. The first flight was delayed and it was touch and go whether I'd make my connection or not. I had to queue for hours in Customs and Immigration and the queue hardly seemed to move at all, yet time was ticking on and …' When he'd finally reached the desk, he'd been interrogated and fingerprinted by a sinister armed officer, who'd then photographed the iris of his eye and continued to question him relentlessly. Far from being welcomed into America, they had made him feel a cross between a leper and a terrorist. 'I only caught the flight by the skin of my teeth and if I'd stopped to find a phone, I'd still be stuck there, overnight! Then I was delayed again at Seattle. They lost my luggage, would you believe, which meant hanging around for ages in yet another queue, then filling in these forms and—'

'Gosh, what bad luck!' Christine sounded slightly kinder, at last. 'Did they find it in the end?'

He shook his head. 'They reckon it was left behind at Minneapolis, or maybe it never left Heathrow. No one seemed to know.' The news had been a shock, almost visceral in its impact. Losing his possessions had increased his sense of being an alien or refugee, stripped of all he owned. Half-expecting to be issued with a set of prison clothing, he had received instead a so-called overnight kit, containing a toothbrush, basic toiletries and what he assumed was nightwear; the latter comprising a gigantic T-shirt, big enough for a behemoth and blazoned with InterWest logo, and a pair of pants so minuscule they would have left an elf indecent.

'That's rotten,' Christine said, with what seemed like genuine sympathy. 'But not to worry – Dwight can lend you pyjamas and shirts and anything else you need.'

'Thanks,' said Eric, with a marked lack of enthusiasm. Since Dwight was six-foot-six to his own five-foot-ten, he would be obliged to trail around with flapping trouser-bottoms and with his hands engulfed by the shirt-sleeves. 'Then, to cap it all, the taxi driver didn't seem to know the way and—'

'Was he black?' Christine interrupted.

'No,' he said, wondering if his once-liberal wife had suddenly become a racist. 'Mixed race, I'd guess.'

'Well, any shade of black or brown, they hate coming out to Mercer Island. No blacks or Asians live round here, you see, so they resent it as a white preserve. But what I'm dying to know, Eric, is how you coped with the flight itself? I mean, all these years you've refused to fly, telling me it was literally impossible, and now you've actually done it! Was it as bad as you feared?'

'No,' he muttered, unwilling to discuss the matter, which he had been mulling over for the last six or seven hours. His brief moment of euphoria, when he'd become like God surveying His creation, had soon been swamped by fear again, once they ran into bouts of turbulence.

'Told you so!' Christine exclaimed, unable to desist from crowing. 'All that fuss you made, for heaven's sake, and quite unnecessarily, it seems.'

'Told you so' was itself grounds for a divorce, and too simplistic anyway. In fact, his mind was in a turmoil on the subject, lurching between pride in his achievement at having overcome a phobia, and deep dread at the prospect of having to board another plane. Admittedly, none of Jeremy's horrors had materialized, and here he was alive and in one piece, yet the thought of hurtling through the air again in an aluminium coffin brought him out in a cold sweat. But, no point trying to explain – least of all to

Christine. She had always felt at home in the world, firmly rooted and secure, so how could she understand his ever-present sense of the precariousness of life itself?

'Actually,' he remarked, 'I think flying's a gigantic con; almost like a form of cattle-transport. I mean, there you are, a captive victim, stiff and cramped and achy and pinned down in your seat, and they keep plying you with booze and playing soppy movies, to lull you into thinking that the experience is pleasurable and—'

He broke off in embarrassment as Dwight swept into the room, looking maddeningly suave in dove-grey trousers and a soft suede cardigan the colour of wet sand.

'Welcome to Seattle!' he said, extending a well-manicured hand.

Eric proffered his own clammy, snot-smeared hand, which was all but crushed to pulp in Dwight's pincer-strong handshake. 'I really do apologize,' Eric said, fumbling for a Kleenex, as his nose began to run again. 'I've gone down with this rotten cold, and I'm just hoping you don't catch my germs.' He imagined Dwight and Christine coughing, sneezing, snuffling throughout their marriage ceremony, and realized to his shame that he wouldn't give a damn.

'I'm never ill,' Dwight said dismissively, as if illness were a form of moral weakness. 'I just don't have the time to waste, lying around in bed.'

Feeling doubly reproved, Eric followed him into the sitting-room, trying not to gawp at its sheer size and splendour – not one sofa but three, all in spotless white leather; a huge black dining table, with a dozen matching chairs, and great splodgy black-and-white oil-paintings echoing the colour scheme.

'What a lovely house,' he murmured, feeling a mixture of awe and envy. Each of those paintings probably cost more than the annual rent on his flat.

'Yes,' said Christine, arranging herself decoratively on one of the three sofas, 'we had it totally remodelled, inside and out – which took some doing, I can tell you! We were never on our own, what with the architect and project manager practically taking up residence, then a load of design consultants trooping in, along with colour-psychologists and various other experts they co-opted in their turn.'

What, he thought, was a colour-psychologist and how had he managed all his life without one?

'We were awash in samples, swatches and colour charts, until the place looked like a shop! And every single step of the way, there were decisions to be made. Even the shade of white for the walls in here became a major issue. I wanted a slightly creamier tone, but they told me that was passé and brought me so many different varieties of ultra-trendy whites, I began to go cross-eyed! And, even when they'd finished, we still weren't home and dry, because then it was the turn of the landscape gardeners – six of them in all. They transformed the yard from a wilderness, but – my God! – the fuss they made. I almost went insane!'

Eric swallowed. 'What a hassle,' he said lamely, glad he didn't share the problems of the rich. Stella was *his* design consultant – told him off if he teamed a blue shirt with a green sweater. And he was still perplexed by how white could be 'ultra-trendy'. Surely white was white.

'Oh, you haven't heard the half of it. You see, just when we thought—'

'Hold on,' he said, before she could elaborate further on loft-conversions or lighting consultants or the latest input from some *feng shui* expert. 'Where's Erica, for goodness' sake? I hope she hasn't gone to bed already. I just can't wait to see her!'

He noticed Dwight and Christine exchange a glance. 'I'm afraid she's not here,' Christine said, defensively.

'Not here? But I've just travelled three thousand miles to be with her!'

'You'll see her in the morning, Eric. She's staying the night with a school-friend.'

'But *why*?' he asked, suspiciously. Were they deliberately keeping her away from him?

'Because – well, it's complicated.'

What sort of answer was that? 'Couldn't we fetch her back – now I'm here, I mean? I know it's late, but—'

'No, the house is in May Creek, which is a good twenty miles, there and back, and I don't fancy trekking all that way at ten o'clock at night. Her friend's one of the few kids who live off-island but still attend the school. They made a special case for her, because her father works for a Mercer Island company and drives her in each day. And, anyway, they plan to move and should be our near-neighbours by the summer. But at present they're—'

'Forget the geography,' Dwight interrupted. 'We should be dealing with the important issues.' He turned to Eric; a new edge to his voice. 'I know you're tired, but we need to put you in the picture – and this evening, if you *don't* mind.'

Tired was an understatement. His whole body ached and throbbed; his mind begged to drift away – away from problems, complications.

'But, first,' Christine offered, 'let me get you something to eat. You must be starving.'

'No, they fed us well on the plane.' In fact, he had barely touched the lukewarm pasta and stodgy cheesecake served on the first flight, nor the pastrami sandwich and blueberry muffin doled out on the second. However, he wouldn't dream of asking Christine to cook for him at this hour – if she *did* cook, that is. They probably had a culinary consultant for all that sort of thing.

'Well, how about a drink?' Dwight went over to the bar – yes, a genuine bar, straight out of a voguish cocktail lounge; black, with six white bar-stools, in keeping with the colour-scheme. 'What would you like? There's vodka, gin, Tequila, bourbon, or I can rustle up a pretty decent apple-martini or a mojito or …'

Eric hesitated. What the hell was a mojito? A pint of bitter was more his sort of thing, but it might seem rather naff.

'Or if you prefer Scotch on the rocks, I have a ten-year-old malt whisky – a present from a grateful client.'

'Yes, great!' All things considered, he needed a stiff drink. It wasn't exactly easy sharing a space with his ex-wife and her patently superior spouse-to-be. Dwight dwarfed him, in every sense, and, rather than accept his swanky Scotch, his natural inclination was to thump the man over his sleek head with one of his kitschy bar-stools.

'Cheers!' he said, joining Christine on the sofa and wishing his own personal consultant would effect an instant makeover, rendering him worthy of the room, rather than a blot on its perfection. Never had he felt so totally inadequate. Dwight's skin was lightly bronzed, as if he'd just returned from a trip to the Bahamas, whereas his own was red and scaly from the rash. And while the wretched guy glowed with health, he himself was a germy, aching, weary lump of flesh, fit only for the dump. His rival's teeth were dazzling white and superbly straight and even – as indeed were Christine's – making his own gnashers seem yellowed and misshapen. And his absurdly carroty curls seemed all the more unruly in contrast to Dwight's enviably straight hair, which looked as if it had just been coiffed and blow-dried, and would never erupt in dandruff, or turn manic in the rain. Most galling of all, the bloke was a mere two years older than him, yet had achieved success in every field, with this extensive, ritzy property, three cars in the garage and a portfolio of shares that would make his own National Savings seem utterly pathetic. And, of course, he came from a normal family, with a mother, father, sister, brother and two sets of grand-parents, so that Christine wasn't forced to conceal his origins.

'Cheers!' Dwight echoed, spread-eagling his athletic limbs in a modish steel and leather chair that resembled an exhibit in a design museum.

There was silence for a moment – a tense, uneasy silence. He kept expecting Dwight to embark on the 'important issues', but the guy said nothing more, and even Christine only enquired about his job.

'Oh, it's much the same as ever. Although we're quite excited about the new Wandsworth Town Library that's opening in the summer. It's a listed building, actually, so it was a real challenge to adapt it, but the whole place looks amazing now.' As if either of them could care.

'And how's your own work going?' he added, hardly able to believe that he and Christine were talking in this footling manner, like two odd acquain-tances, rather than as a couple who had shared a life, a bed. His natural instinct, were he alone with her, would be to open his heart and admit his faults and failings; tell her how deeply he regretted allowing his terrors to cramp and choke the marriage; that perhaps he could overcome them (having made a start, with flying), and be granted a second chance. He imagined taking her and Erica back with him to England, beginning afresh, re-establishing their family.

Yet, even as the thought took root, he realized it was hopeless. How could this new Christine ever settle for the old life; the lack of funds and cramped horizons, and why should he expect her to renounce all the recent bounty she'd amassed? It was *over* – as he had known full-well at the time of the divorce. Yet some part of him had always craved to reverse that cruel decree and – now that he'd lost Mandy, too – he was tempted to hark back to the past and try to salvage what was clearly irretrievable. Better to face the fact he had failed – failed twice over, with Christine and with Mandy, and that he might never find another woman, or be part of a proper family.

Silence again. He gave a surreptitious glance at his watch: 10.20, Seattle time. If they didn't bite the bullet and embark on the subject of Erica, they might never get to bed tonight. And, since neither Dwight nor Christine had brought it up again, he had better take the initiative himself. 'So what's going on with Erica?' he asked. 'Why has she been banished from the house?'

'Don't be silly,' Christine frowned. 'It's not a matter of banishment. We simply thought it best if we left tomorrow without her being here.'

'But won't she be upset if you just sneak off without saying goodbye?'

'We've said goodbye.'

'But why all the secrecy? Surely it's not good for her.'

Christine sighed in exasperation. 'Look, she's upset about the wedding, so we decided—'

'You mean, she wants to be there herself?'

'Far from it!' Dwight said, testily. 'She'd rather we called the whole thing off.'

Christine bit her lip. 'Listen, Eric, we've decided on the plan, so let's stick to it, OK? Once we've left for the airport, Kimberley will bring her over. She's the mother of Erica's new friend, Brooke, and, to be honest, a total airhead. In fact, Brooke's a bit of a problem herself.'

'Like mother, like daughter,' Dwight put in, taking a sip of his Scotch.

'I mean, we're grateful to her, in one way, because it took Erica a while to make new friends at school and she and Brooke have really hit it off. But I have to say she's a precocious little miss and a bad influence, I fear. So, while we're glad she's found a mate, we can't help wishing it was someone rather different.'

'But what happened to her other friend – you know, Kelly – the one who owned a horse and—'

'Kelly's history, Eric! She dropped Erica a month ago and, I'm afraid to say, in a very hurtful manner, which only added to the problems, of course. Anyway, maybe you could talk to her and try to help in some way. To be honest, I need a break from the whole damned thing, and Dwight does, too – in fact, even more than me. It's really been getting to us these last few weeks.'

'I'll say!' Dwight screwed up his face in an expression of acute distaste.

'So, from tomorrow morning, she's all yours, Eric. Which should give you a chance to see what's going on. Maybe you can persuade her to confide in you, and, of course, you'll also need to keep a careful eye on exactly what she's doing – how long she spends on Facebook, for example, and who she's seeing and where she plans to go. And don't let her stay out too late, even if she argues the toss, and be sure you have the address and phone-number of anyone—'

'OK,' he cut in, irritably. He wasn't a total greenhorn when it came to parenting and this advice was kindergarten-level.

'Oh, and I've left a load of food for you both. The fridge and freezers are full to overflowing, so don't worry about that side of things. And if you want to take her into Seattle for a movie or a meal or whatever, all you have to do is—'

'Hold on a minute. Never mind about movies. You say she's in this awful state, so what if she turns bolshie? How am I meant to deal with it?'

'That's your problem,' Dwight said, coldly. 'It's time you took some responsibility. *You're* her father, Eric – not me – although I try hard enough, for God's sake.'

Swallowing his pride, Eric accepted the reproof. Clearly, he was out of date with regard to Erica's friends and other pressing issues in her life – reason enough to reproach himself. 'I'll do my best,' he mumbled.

'But first we need to bring you up to date.' Christine shifted in her seat, swirling her juice round and round her glass. 'There's something we haven't told you yet – the main thing that's bugging Erica, in fact.'

'Well?' he said, awaiting elucidation in the long, awkward pause that followed.

Christine put her glass down and locked her fingers together. 'I'm … I'm pregnant, Eric.'

He stared at her, dumbfounded. She had never wanted another child, despite his own desperate wish for more; always warned him of the dangers of a second pregnancy: miscarriage, morning sickness, a second labour as traumatic as the first, ending in a caesarean and months of post-natal depression. And she was older now – forty-two – so surely the risks would be greater still. He glanced at her flat stomach. *How* could she be pregnant, when she looked almost painfully thin? And why should the news have upset him quite so fiercely; plunged him into a turmoil of jealousy and bitterness, together with a sense of racking loss? The reason was glaringly obvious: all those years, she had refused to have a second child with him, so it was harrowing to learn that now she had gone ahead to have one with the odious Dwight. It might have been less devastating if his own hope of being a father again hadn't just been overturned by Mandy's treachery. She had cuckolded him, unfathered him, and all his pain at her deceit began choking through his mind once more, adding to his resentment of Christine's own good fortune.

'Well, aren't you going to say something?' she asked.

'Congratulations.' The word was ashes in his mouth. 'When's the baby due?'

'The end of September.'

His own child – or what he'd thought was his child – would have been born at the end of October. It was as if he himself had suffered a miscarriage and was now empty and in mourning.

'I have to say we're absolutely delighted. It'll be Dwight's first child, you see.'

She and Dwight exchanged the smuggest of glances. Thumping the cad with a bar-stool was no longer punishment enough; he couldn't rest until this hateful, boastful super-stud was ripped to pieces and fed to ravening sharks.

'Unfortunately,' Dwight said, giving him an oily smile, 'Erica doesn't share our delight.'

Eric made a supreme effort to focus on his daughter rather than on himself. If *he* was so upset, was it any wonder that, Erica, too, should find the news distressing? 'So when did she find out?' he asked, trying to keep all emotion from his voice, whilst seeing hateful images of Dwight's superior sperm swimming up triumphantly to merge with Christine's egg.

'We told her just a week ago,' Christine said, leaning back against the cushions, 'and I'm afraid she reacted very badly. For one thing, she thinks I'm too old to have babies and seems to finds it almost disgusting.'

'And to make things worse,' Dwight added, 'she resents the fact the child is mine. You may not realize, Eric, but your daughter isn't exactly my number-one fan. As I said, I've done my best – leaned over backwards to try to get her onside, but I seem to be fighting a losing battle.'

'I see.'

'Actually, you *don't* see,' Christine remarked. 'She's not the Erica you knew. She's changed out of all recognition.'

'But how? When? Why didn't you tell me all this before?'

'We did tell you – several times – but you never seemed that concerned.'

The accusation stung. Had he become so involved with Mandy, so cock-ahoop about his (apparent) second child, he'd stopped bothering with his first? He let out an involuntary groan, taking refuge in a Kleenex and blowing his nose so long and hard he began to feel light-headed.

'Listen, Eric, that's a really lousy cold you have. And you must be dead-beat after the journey. Why don't we call it a day and go to bed? We can have another discussion in the morning and, anyway, I'll need to show you how the heating works, and how to set the burglar-alarm and all that sort of stuff. We're not leaving till eleven, so there should be plenty of time. Right now, you need some rest – and so do we, for that matter. Our flight tomorrow is nearly eighteen hours, so we ought to get an early night. Not that it's particularly early,' she added, glancing at her watch.

Thank God, he thought, he wasn't flying to Hong Kong. Another flight so soon would finish him off.

'I'll show you to your room, OK?' Christine said, getting up. 'But, first, are you sure you don't want something to eat – a little bedtime snack, maybe?'

He shook his head. His stomach was a war-zone.

'Or another drink?' Dwight proffered the Scotch again.

'No, thanks.' Although seriously tempted to settle for drunken oblivion, it would be most unwise to greet Erica tomorrow with the mother of all hangovers.

Having said a curt goodnight to Dwight, he followed Christine upstairs; astounded by the guest-room, which was bigger than the whole of his flat and contained a four-poster bed, with an elaborate canopy and hangings, and twisted barley-sugar bedposts in what looked like real mahogany. Never had any bed seemed so wildly inappropriate. Four-posters were for lottery-winners, honeymooners and royals, so how could a loser and a loner sleep in such princely grandeur?

'Do use all these closets,' Christine said, gesturing to a whole wall of cupboards, in the same wood as the bed. Had she forgotten he had lost his luggage? Apart from the contents of his flight-bag, he had nothing to put into them.

Next, she showed him the guest-bathroom, which was not far off the bedroom in size, and had a gleaming marble floor, twin basins, side by side, and what Christine called an 'infinity tub'.

'What's that, exactly?' he asked, surveying the huge circular bath, free-standing in the centre of the room.

'It means you can fill it right up to the top and it won't ever overflow. The excess water goes into a special channel, so there's no risk of any spillage.'

But *why*, he thought, would you wish to fill it right to the top? Weren't they into saving water over here?

'And you can bathe by candlelight, if you like.' She pointed to a brace of candles, set in wrought-iron candlesticks and arranged on a marble shelf beside the bath. 'They're safe, too. They can't burn down or catch fire. There's also a stereo system, if you fancy a bit of music. The CDs are in that rack there – everything from grand opera to pop.'

He tried to imagine bathing to a soundtrack of Verdi or Wagner, but the imaginative leap was too great. He couldn't even get radio reception in his basement bathroom at home.

'Towels in here,' she continued, opening yet another cupboard to reveal a stack of towels so extensive they would have done credit to Harrods' Linen Department. Bath, candles, towels and walls were all in the exact same shade – what he'd describe as brownish, although no doubt the colour consultants would use more resonant words.

'And if you need a robe, there's a couple hanging on the door there – his and hers.'

His and hers. If only. There was room for two in the bath; room for four in the bed; ample room for someone special in his heart. Yet never had he felt so achingly alone; so far from everything familiar and safe.

'I'll just fetch some pyjamas and shirts and stuff. Anything else you want?'

Yes. He wanted to be back in his tiny Vauxhall bathroom, with its scuffed lino on the floor, its stained and cracked white bath, and to be sleeping in his own small, cramped divan, with its lumpy mattress and saggy springs.

Christine returned with a pair of real silk pyjamas, four poncy-looking shirts, a cashmere sweater and a pair of sleek white trousers that would make him look, frankly, gay. 'I've brought the smallest things I could find.'

'Thanks a lot!' he bristled, feeling himself instantly shrink to dwarf-size. In fact, he had no intention of wearing Dwight's clothes, even if they did fit. With any luck, the airline would return his case in the morning – hopefully before Erica arrived. Until then, he would stick to his own gear, however creased and grubby it might be.

'By the way, I've left you a list of phone-numbers – everything from plumbers to physicians – and our neighbours will be happy to help, if there's anything you need. And Kimberley, too, although she's further out, of course. But Erica knows the ropes, so you should manage perfectly well – at least as far as the practicalities are concerned. So I'll say goodnight for the moment, and we'll liaise again tomorrow. Sleep well, Eric. Sweet dreams!'

Sleep well. Never had words seemed so ironically inept. He hadn't slept at all – let alone well, yet now it was 2 a.m., and he felt completely knackered, having been awake for three nights running. He loathed those prats who blithely said, 'If you're tired enough, you'll sleep' – a claim he had frequently disproved. Besides, anxiety and shame didn't make for a restful night, and he was feeling both on account of Erica: her unhappiness, her resentment of

Christine's pregnancy, his own comparative neglect of her. And, despite the fact he was lapped in utter luxury, that only made things worse. The four-poster was claustrophobic; the lowering wooden canopy reminding him of a coffin-lid and the heavy velvet curtains shutting out all light and air. Every time he closed his eyes, new, disturbing fears began churning through his mind – fear of the dark, of suffocation. The coffin-lid was pressing down; the curtains had become a shroud, binding tighter, tighter.

Sitting up in terror, he struggled out of bed, fighting his way through the obstructive, weighty hangings, and pressing every light-switch in the room: ceiling lights, cupboard lights, bedside lamps, lighting round the mirrors. The glare was merciless, but better that than the darkness of death.

'For God's *sake*!' he muttered. 'Get a grip.' No wonder Christine had left him. Would any normal person put up with such a wimp?

Desperate to regain control, he stretched out on the floor. Perhaps he could sleep there instead. At least he wouldn't have that oppressive sense of being stifled and shut in, nor would his skin be irritated by the beaded, sequinned linen. Sequins on bed-sheets really was a step too far.

After only five minutes, his limbs were aching, making sleep impossible once more. Countless times in childhood, he had lain awake like this – whenever he was moved to another so-called home, and had to get to know a new foster-mum, or find his way around a new, confusing building. Or maybe he dared not close his eyes because some brute or bully who shared his room might pounce in the night and insist he tossed them off, or try to smother him with a pillow, or cut off all his hair with painful jabbing scissors, stuff the curls halfway down his throat, then deride him as a sissy if he cried.

Trying to dispel the painful memories, he got up again and began prowling round the room, unable to avoid the mirrors, which reflected him six times over: a ludicrous figure, clad in the voluminous airline T-shirt that stopped just short of his hairy knees. Who needed all those mirrors – or works of art in a bedroom; huge abstract things the colour of dried blood? Even being in a guest-room seemed all wrong. He *wasn't* a guest, but a relative – Erica's biological father, for God's sake. Guests weren't family and had to observe the niceties and be on their best behaviour; couldn't get up and raid the larder, as he was severely tempted to do, just to find some comfort-food and fill the void inside him. His identity seemed to be crumbling away, and he was shrinking into nothingness, unravelling, disintegrating....

Close to panic, he flung open the cupboard where he had stowed his flight-bag, took it out, with shaking hands, and rummaged through the contents, grabbing Stella's black cat and Mandy's scarlet thong. Perhaps they might possess the power to restore him to himself – make him friend and lover again, functioning human being. He took both back to bed with him; laid the thong on his pillow, and tried to imagine Mandy lying there beside him; still his beloved fiancée and carrying his child. Then he held the cat close against his chest; turning it into Charlie, the old feline friend who had helped him through the divorce; Charlie no longer lost in the uncaring streets of London, but restored and resurrected.

At least, he thought, closing his eyes in complete and utter weariness, the three of them were safe here from the bullies and abusers.

chapter twenty-two

'Bon voyage!' Eric called, feeling a curdled mix of relief and apprehension, as the limousine purred away, with Dwight and Christine waving a stiff goodbye. In truth, it was good to see the back of them, although, of course, there was a downside: he was now on his own, in charge of a huge house and soon to be responsible for a disturbed and wayward daughter. He waited till the car had turned the corner, noting with a twinge of resentment how different it was from his *own* cramped and undistinguished cab. This was a sleek stretch-limousine, big enough for a tribe.

Nor could he help envying the fact that the pair were leaving to get married. He, too, should have been planning a wedding; arranging a honeymoon – not as exotic as theirs, maybe, but still deeply gratifying. The loss of Mandy had left a scar so red and raw, he doubted if it would ever heal.

Walking back to the columned porch, he was aware that, in the light of day, the place looked even more imposing and seemed to shrink from him in disdain as he entered the stylish hall. Although was it any wonder, when he was still bunged up with a cold and wearing yesterday's grubby, crumpled clothes? The first thing he intended to do, now he had the house to himself, was put his gear in the washing-machine and give it a quick press, so that he would be fit (well, fittish) to meet Erica and Kimberley.

Having stripped to the skin, loaded the machine and girded himself in the towelling robe from the guest-room, he embarked on a tour of the house. Christine had already showed him round, a couple of hours ago, but he needed to get his bearings before his daughter turned up, to ensure he knew where everything was kept. Beginning in the kitchen, he marvelled again at its size. The walk-in pantry alone would almost house a family and was filled to the gunwales with a huge array of food and drink, mostly in giant-sized packets, or bottles so large they would have doubled as effective coshes. He had counted a dozen different cereals, twenty salad-dressings, six varieties of peanut butter (crunchy, smooth, whipped, organic, reduced fat and low-salt; all in jars as big as Ali Baba's), and every type of tea from Earl Grey and jasmine to Red Bush and camomile. He had to keep reminding himself that a mere three people lived here, since clearly they had stocked up for a siege. The fridge was panelled in Brazilian cherry-wood, to match the kitchen-cupboards, and had double doors, like those of a church, which opened to reveal a cornucopia of goodies. How would he and Erica ever consume all those cheeses, yogurts, salads, sausages and fruits before they were past their sell-by date? And still more supplies awaited them in the three – yes, three – freezers, each crammed to the brim with a variety of ready-meals, vegetables, pizzas, waffles, ice-creams and frozen gateaux.

Another thing that struck him was the number of dining-tables – a large one here in the kitchen, in addition to the black one in the sitting-room, the glass-topped one in the dining-room and the wooden one on the deck outside, adjoining the large barbecue. As someone who was quite content to eat his meals on his lap, it did seem a tad excessive, and he wondered if they were used in turn, on some sort of rota system.

Equally excessive was the games-room, which housed a ping-pong table, a pool-table, a free-standing air-hockey game, a plasma TV with a screen so large it took up one whole wall and a variety of gym-equipment, including a treadmill, two exercise bikes and a rowing-machine. Well, if time should start to drag, he could always embark on a fitness programme; develop a few muscles to impress his library colleagues.

The games-room led into the garage, itself so massive it could have played a major part in solving London's housing crisis, and containing not only the three cars – one of which was Dwight's new toy, a Porsche Carrera Cabriolet – but also a snowmobile, a speedboat, three gleaming new bikes and a whole battery of tools. Could you hate a man on account of his garage?

Yes.

Dwight and Christine each had a separate office, with elaborate swivel-chairs and such a profusion of cupboards they could have set up a stationery business and serviced the whole country, coast-to-coast. Examining their state-of-the-art computers and elaborate stereo systems, he couldn't help thinking of the children he'd grown up with – kids from sink estates, where the lifts were permanently broken, the stairwells stank of piss, and gangs of teenage yobs roamed the place at night, armed with knives, or worse. And even nowadays, for that matter, close to where he lived himself, families of immigrants were crammed in, ten to a room, with elementary kitchens and dodgy sanitation. Perhaps Dwight and Christine could give up part of their house and turn it into a centre for those behind with their rent, or fighting off the bailiffs, or faced with sleeping rough.

Hitching up his robe, which seemed designed for a giant – was *nothing* small in America? – he continued his tour upstairs, taking in the laundry-room and the three additional bathrooms: Dwight's, Christine's and Erica's; the first boasting a four-poster bath. When he got home (*if* he got home), he must indulge in a little carpentry; carve a canopy and barley-sugar posts over his own shamefully basic bath, to add a touch of class.

Distracted by some photos on the landing, he stopped to look at one of Erica taken several years ago, and wondered, as he often did, if she resembled his own father in appearance – that mysterious figure, who, for all he knew, could have been dark or fair, tall or short, Mr Average or an Adonis. It was always harder for him to imagine that his dark-haired daughter took after his mother, who had invariably been a redhead in his fantasies, but he liked to think that perhaps Erica had inherited her nose or mouth or face-shape, or some of her characteristics.

Mooching on to the master bedroom, he gazed in at the huge expanse of satin-covered bed and suddenly pictured Dwight making love, with consummate expertise and skill, while a passionate Christine moaned and writhed beneath him in extremes of ecstasy. He was revolted by the thought, yet couldn't stop the succession of images throbbing and thrusting through his mind. The flagrant couple were probably at this very moment snogging in the taxi; indulging in some practice before the honeymoon.

No such excitements for him; only a session at the ironing-board. Christine had seemed flummoxed when he asked her where the iron was; told him his guess was as good as hers, since Malinal took care of the laundry, and she herself hadn't ironed so much as a handkerchief since moving to the States. He'd eventually tracked it down in the laundry-room and, in the absence of Malinal – a Mexican maid, apparently, and due to turn up tomorrow – got to work on his shirt and jeans.

Having dressed in the still damp garments, he studied himself in the brace of mirrors. No, not a pretty sight. His rash was still unsightly, his nose still red and swollen, dark circles were etched beneath his eyes, and the shirt looked, frankly, cheap – at least compared with Dwight's. Reluctantly, he went to fetch his hated rival's dove-grey cashmere sweater, knowing he had to make an effort not to disappoint his daughter too severely, since she would now be used to Superman and comparisons were odious.

Although far too big, the sweater did effect a minor transformation – he now looked almost classy, for God's sake! He made a mental note to ask Santa Claus to stuff a cashmere jumper in his Christmas stocking, along with a cashmere face-mask to conceal any future rashes.

Next, he inspected the bathroom-cabinet (almost the size of a wardrobe) and picked out anything and everything that could add a little polish: Sudafed to dry up his runny nose, brilliantine to tame his hair, mouthwash to sweeten his breath and a good dousing of Dwight's aftershave to bring women flocking in droves. Who was he kidding? His sex-life was probably over now, for ever.

Once coiffed, groomed and scented, he checked the time once more. He'd had his eye on the clock all morning, counting down the minutes until Erica arrived. Still half an hour to go, so he decided to ring the airline and enquire about his lost luggage. It took him an age to get through, and then he was passed from one department to another, with long waits in between, spent hanging on, listening to maddening muzak. And all for no result. No, they hadn't located the case; no, it wouldn't be coming today; no, they couldn't say exactly when; yes, could he ring again tomorrow, to check?

Only when he put down the phone, did he realize quite how tired he felt. A combination of sleeplessness and jet-lag, together with the stress at being so far away from home, had reduced him to a zombie. He made himself a coffee, after a long tussle with the Espresso machine, which, complex as it was, would have done credit to the biggest branch of Starbucks. Taking his cup out onto the deck, he listened to the silence; a silence so profound, he found it almost disorienting. Living in Vauxhall, he was so used to noisy neighbours, shrilling sirens, droning planes and a cacophony of building works, the hush here was almost uncanny in comparison. There was no traffic noise, no crying babies or barking dogs; indeed, no sign or sound of another living soul. Far from welcoming the peace, it seemed to emphasize his isolation, as if every person in this whole quiescent suburb was confined to a monastic cell and barred from communication. He'd assumed he'd be staying in Seattle proper, with all the buzz of a big city, the sense of connection and community, the vital reassurance that bustling human activity was going on around him.

Wandering back inside, he tried to sit and read, but found it impossible to concentrate on anything beyond the fact that, in roughly seven minutes, he would be face-to-face with his daughter. It was stupid to be nervous, yet he was so desperate to make a good impression that when, eventually, a car drew up, he rushed out to the porch in a state of excessive agitation.

He stopped dead in his tracks as he saw her. His daughter? No, impossible. The Erica he remembered had been a little girl, still three months short of twelve, with a naked face, straight, dark hair, a flat chest and a boyish figure. So who was this outrageous little sexpot, with streaked and blonded curls, a layer of heavy make-up and pert new breasts, emphasized by some sort of push-up bra? His gaze travelled from her crop-top to the expanse of naked midriff, on display for all to see, then down to her skin-tight jeans, designed to draw attention to her newly rounded hips. Trying to disguise his shock, he walked unsteadily towards her, opening his arms in a hug.

'Hey, watch my hair!' she muttered, dodging his embrace.

He swallowed. Hardly a fitting welcome for a Dad, especially after an absence of fifteen months. But, before he could say a word, the woman who had brought her home extended a scarlet-taloned hand in greeting and flashed him a dazzling smile.

'I'm Kimberley,' she said. 'It's great to meet you, at last!'

So this was the airhead Dwight and Christine had mentioned, but at least *someone* was pleased to see him. His daughter hadn't even said hello, or given him so much as a peck on the cheek, and was now standing in sulky silence, jabbing at the ground with one ill-fitting, high-heeled shoe, which looked as if it had been borrowed from a grown-up. The Erica he'd known had worn battered trainers, or flip-flops.

'Yes, good to meet you, too,' he said, daunted by the woman's sheer good grooming. She, too, was over-made-up, with bee-stung crimson lips, heavily mascara'd lashes that reminded him of miniature iron railings, and hair so lacquered, primped and volumunized, she must have spent the morning at the salon. 'Do come in,' he urged. 'Can I offer you a coffee or a drink?'

'Oh, I just love your English accent! It's exactly like Christine's. But, no, I mustn't stay, thank you all the same. I've left Brooke on her own. But let's get together very soon, OK? You must come over for dinner and meet my husband, Ted. Or we could take the girls out, if you want; maybe drive into Belle Vue or Seattle and see a movie they'd like.'

'Yes, great idea!' He stole another glance at Erica; still unable to believe that she could have metamorphosed into this shameless little Lolita, and how in heaven's name Christine could have permitted it.

'You have my number, don't you, Eric? Don't hesitate to ring if there's anything you need. In fact, why don't I phone you tomorrow, to make sure everything's OK?'

'Fine,' he said, feeling so far from fine he was tempted to cling on to this female and keep her there by force, so he wouldn't have to be alone with his transformed and sullen daughter.

''Bye!' Kimberley called, returning to her car – a huge, truck-like monster in an incongruous powder-blue. 'Have fun!'

Fun seemed hardly likely, judging by the way Erica was dragging her feet as she walked into the house; shoulders hunched; eyes down.

'It's wonderful to see you, darling.' He was determined to act the loving father, whatever her own attitude might be.

'Yeah, well.'

'Yeah, well,' wasn't exactly a promising start, but he persevered, trying to conceal the sense of hurt he felt. 'Did you enjoy your time with Brooke?'

'Has Mum gone?' she asked suddenly, ignoring his own question, as if it were beneath contempt.

He nodded. 'She sent you her special love.'

'Love?' She pronounced the word with a mixture of bitterness and sarcasm. 'Dwight's the only one she loves.'

'I'm sure that's not true.'

'And how would *you* know? You haven't seen her for yonks. Or me.'

Her undisguised resentment resulted in a surge of guilt. Now that he was with her, it did indeed seem terribly remiss that he should have allowed his fears to stand in the way of maintaining the relationship. True, she'd been ill last summer, which had wrecked the plans for her visit to see *him*, but that was no real excuse. 'I'm sorry. I should have come before. It's totally my fault.' He needed to apologize, own up about his failings, and also give her time to thaw, to readjust, get to know him again. Nor must he forget that she was the child of a divorce, which obviously brought a raft of problems and was – again – very much his fault. 'Look, why don't we sit down and have a bit of lunch or something.'

'Not hungry.'

'Well, how about a drink?'

'OK,' she said, grudgingly.

'What d'you fancy?'

'Diet Coke.'

He hoped she wasn't on some dangerous diet, as all young girls seemed to be, these days, although he had absolutely no intention of nagging about food or drink. Having fetched a Coke from the fridge, he poured himself a beer and joined her at the kitchen table. Now that he was sitting close, he noticed the acne beneath the make-up and the badly bitten nails, as if the half-fledged adolescent was showing through beneath the 'adult' exterior, and remembered, with compassion, how hard it was to be thirteen. 'Now I *am* here, darling, let's try to make the most of it, OK? There's so much I want to know – how you're getting on at school and—'

'School's shit!'

'I thought you liked it?'

'Not now. I don't fit in. I get teased for being English and wearing the wrong clothes and stuff.'

'How do you mean, "wrong"?'

She let out an impatient sigh, as if he ought to understand without it being spelt out. 'Listen, Dad, I was used to wearing uniform and being at an all-girls' school and—'

'But you said you were looking forward to mixing with boys and choosing what to wear. You *wanted* to go to the States, remember – thought it sounded exciting and—'

'I've changed my mind, OK? I admit it did seem cool at first, but I knew nothing about America and even less about their schools. And, to be honest, I find the clothes thing a real drag. I have to decide what to wear, every single day, which isn't as easy as it sounds. I'm always worried about people making fun of me.'

'Surely they don't do that?'

'Oh, all the time! Like, to start with, they're all taller than me and prettier and have loads more clothes, in any case. And Kelly's just the biggest bitch. She used to be my friend, but now she makes me feel like a piece of shit. She had this make-over party and I was the only one in the class she didn't invite.'

'What's a make-over party?'

'Oh, you know, Dad – where you get your face and hair done, and people give you advice on how to make the best of yourself and how to dress and—'

'Aren't you a bit young for all that?'

'Young? No way! Half the girls at school have been having manicures and facials since, like, the age of eight. When they heard I'd never shaved my legs, let alone had a leg-wax, they thought I must be kidding.'

'But doesn't Mum object?' he asked, truly shocked that eight-year-olds should be frequenting beauty salons, rather than climbing trees or playing hide-and-seek.

'Not really. And, if she did, it would just be hypocritical, because she's always having pedicures and fake tans and stuff herself. She even has a personal shopper who picks out all her clothes. The only thing she *does* object to is the way some of my friends get up, like, two hours early and use all that extra time just doing their face and hair. And, of course, they're really good at make-up – unlike me.'

'But, darling, you don't *need* make-up.'

'I do – to cover the zits.'

'You can hardly see them, honestly.'

'Who are you kidding? I look gross!'

'Don't keep putting yourself down. You've always been attractive and—'

'Attractive, with this acne? You must be blind or something.'

He gave a nervous laugh; intent on lightening the mood. 'Well, look at me, covered in a rash!'

'Yeah. I noticed. Is it infectious?'

'No, just stress. Listen, darling, I know it's hard, but it's best simply to put up with things like spots and rashes and just accept that eventually they'll go.'

'That's easy for *you* to say. Suppose I'm stuck with them till I'm twenty or something?'

'You won't be, Erica.'

'Oh, by the way, I'm not Erica any more. I've decided to change my name.'

He stared at her, appalled. *His* name; the name that bonded them, and which had given him such pride when she was born.

'It's a man's name and I hate it.'

He swallowed. 'So what are you going to call yourself?'

'Carmella. That's feminine and pretty and makes me feel less of a weirdo.'

'Erica, you're not a weirdo, and there's nothing weird about your name. It's a perfectly good name.'

'Well, I don't think so. Anyway, I'm Carmella from now on, so will you please stop calling me Erica.'

'OK, Carmella, then. Does Mum know you've changed your name?'

'No. I only decided yesterday. Me and Brooke discussed it last night, for hours. She hates her name, as well, you see, but she hasn't come up with a new one yet. It takes time, you know, to choose.'

'Well, shouldn't you tell Mum before you go ahead?'

'No point,' she shrugged. 'She wouldn't give a shit.'

'Of course she would. You're her daughter, for heaven's sake! She takes an interest in everything you do and—'

'Dad, you're *so* out of date! The only person she cares about now is Dwight. And, actually, it makes me puke the way they slobber all over each other, as if I wasn't there. I suppose you know she's pregnant, do you?'

'Er, yes.'

'Well, don't you think it's disgusting?'

'Erica – sorry, Carmella – when people love each other, they naturally want to have children together. Just as *we* did, with you. When you were born, Mum and I felt our marriage was … you know, complete. You were the most wonderful thing that ever happened to us and—'

'Don't change the subject. I'm talking about Mum, not me. And you haven't a clue what she's like these days. I hardly ever see her, for a start. She's either at work, or out at the salon, or entertaining loads of boring people – mostly Dwight's gruesome friends. And, as for Dwight, he's a total shit.'

'Do watch your language, darling. You shouldn't keep saying "shit".' Despite the reprimand, he was secretly delighted by her description of his hated rival, although he made a heroic effort to defend him, knowing it was his duty as a parent. 'Look, whatever else, he's given you a really luxurious life. I mean, this lovely house and the sailing trips and riding lessons and holidays and things. Doesn't all that count?'

'It might do, if he didn't hate my guts. And, of course, when the baby's born, he'll probably want to push me out completely. I mean, he's really, like, *old*, yet he's never had a kid before, so he's bound to go all gaga over his precious brat and I'll just be in the way – even more than now.'

'I'm sure that's not true, Erica – Carmella.'

'You keep saying you're *sure* about things, but actually you don't know what you're talking about. And, if you really want to know, Dad, most of this is *your* fault. If you and Mum hadn't split up, we'd still be living in Kingston and I'd be back at my old school, with all the friends I had then, and I'd never have laid eyes on Dwight, or had to come to this rotten country, or—'

'Darling,' he said, feeling extremes of shame and guilt, yet also a sense of mounting irritation. 'I wish I could change the past. I hate to see you so unhappy and I'd do anything I could to try to make it up to you.'

'It's a bit late for that, isn't it? You should have made some changes before everything went wrong – agreed to travel, for one thing, so Mum and I could go abroad, like everybody normal does. You don't realize, Dad, what a total freak you are. When I first told Brooke about your fears and stuff, she just couldn't believe that Mum would ever put up with it. No wonder she fell for Dwight and couldn't wait to have a different life. OK, I loathe the guy, but he's pretty cool, you have to admit – even the way he looks. I mean, you never had your teeth fixed or bothered to buy decent clothes, so you can't blame Mum for wanting a bit of style.'

Horrified, he sat in silence. She was *ashamed* of him – that was glaringly obvious. He was a total freak, with no dress sense and bad teeth.

'But, even at that late stage, you could have, like, taken a stand; not let yourself be pushed around and agree to a divorce you didn't want. And *I* didn't want it, either. It was horrible for me. I just felt caught in the middle, while you two got all angry and emotional. I kept hoping you'd stand up to Mum and make her change her mind, but the thing is, you're just totally weak.'

Still, he didn't say a word. What was there to say? He was feeling even more guilty, yet also indignant and insulted. Forget the teeth, the clothes, his lack of cool. What really stung was the 'totally weak'. But how could he contradict her, when he was well aware that his whole upbringing had made him submissive? Throughout his childhood, he'd had no say in his life, no vestige of control, no room for negotiation, either with the grownups or with the other kids, let alone in relation to his absent mum. He couldn't make his mother *want* him; make her return and take him home. He couldn't even choose to be good – his natural inclination – because the bully-boys insisted he be bad; join them when they bunked off school, or nicked fags from the jobbing gardener. And, as for the staff, they had all the power and, since he couldn't change the outcomes or the decisions that were made about him, he had gradually lost hope and simply surrendered to authority. What his daughter didn't understand was that it required confidence to take a stand and, because kids-in-care were stigmatized as dirty, feckless and inferior, they soon lost all self-belief. Yet, if he mentioned any of that, it would only seem as if he were trying to excuse himself. Perhaps he should take a stronger line with her; prove he *wasn't* weak.

'Now, listen to me a moment, Carmella. Whatever I did or didn't do, that's over now and we have to try to deal with the present situation. I admit I haven't seen you for ages, so, yes – you're right – I don't understand what's going on, but maybe you can fill me in over the next few weeks. And, now they've given you this extra time off school, we ought to use it to go out together – perhaps see a bit of Seattle, take in a few movies or museums.'

'And how are you going to get there?' she asked, contemptuously. 'That's another thing that made Mum mad – the fact you never learned to drive. I mean, how pathetic is that?'

'Surely there's a bus?' he said, ignoring her sneery tone, however wounding it might be.

'Look, buses may be OK in London, but they're nothing like as frequent over here. *Everyone* drives in the States, so they don't bother to lay on any decent sort of service. And, if you weren't so useless, Dad, you could borrow one of our cars, instead of expecting me to hang about at bus-stops.'

He fought a sudden urge to slap her. OK, she had her grievances, but she was also a spoilt brat, and he was outraged that she should call him useless, when she hadn't the slightest comprehension of how deeply fear could sabotage a life. Taking a long, slow draught of his beer, he tried to calm his anger. 'OK, forget the bus. How about doing something local?'

'And what do you suggest? There's nothing much round here – well, a few lousy restaurants, maybe, and a Starbucks and a sandwich-bar – big deal! And the shops are pretty crap. There's only, like, a supermarket, a drug-store, a dry-cleaner's and—'

'Well, why don't we walk to the supermarket? It's a lovely day and I need to stock up on T-shirts. The airline lost my luggage, you see, so—'

'Dad, the thought of buying T-shirts at QFC isn't my idea of a fun day out.'

'OK, let's go to Starbucks and treat ourselves to ice-creams.'

'I'm nearly thirteen, you know, not eight,' she said, giving him a withering look, 'so there's no need to bribe me with ice-creams. In any case, I can't go anywhere. I promised to ring Brooke.'

'But you've only just seen her.'

'*So?*' she countered, insolently. 'Are you trying to tell me I can't phone my friends?'

'No, of course I'm not. But why don't we have lunch first?'

'I've told you, I'm not hungry. Kimberley made us pancakes for breakfast, and breakfast wasn't that long ago. They get up late at her place. So, if you'll excuse me, Dad …'

Wincing as she slammed the door, he sat with his head in his hands, remembering how he had fed her as a baby: the countless bottles he had given her during the long stretch of time that Christine had been ill with mastitis or laid low with depression. He had burped her, changed her nappies, laid her in her cot; sung her lullabies until she had settled down to sleep; got up in the night, every time she cried, and walked back and forth, back and forth, with her cradled in his arms until she gradually calmed down. If only it were that simple now. If only he could hold her in his arms – calm her, feed her, be important to her. Yet, judging by her attitude, they might never be that close again.

Not only had he lost his longed-for second child, it appeared he had also lost his first.

chapter twenty-three

'Carmella!' he called. 'Kimberley and Brooke are here.'

Erica came rushing down the stairs, displaying an enviable enthusiasm to see her friend – again. If only *he* could rouse the same responsiveness. She and Brooke embraced, as if they hadn't seen each other in years, instead of just yesterday evening. His first sight of Brooke last night had been almost as much of a shock as his first sight of Erica. The pert little miss was in essence a miniature version of her mother, with the same scarlet nails, blonded hair and over-made-up face. Indeed, he strongly suspected that Erica had copied her new sexy style from this mother-and-daughter duo. However, whereas Kimberley was wearing puce-pink pedal-pushers and a sequinned silver top, the two girls were in riding gear: figure-hugging jodhpurs and knee-length riding-boots. He found his eyes straying back to Brooke; horrified to realize that her curvaceous little figure had aroused definite sexual stirrings in him.

He turned to Kimberley, desperate to distract himself from the troublingly precocious nymphet. 'Do stay for a coffee this time,' he urged.

'Well, it'll have to be a quick one. We've got a long drive ahead of us.'

'Don't worry, it's all ready. All I have to do is pour it.'

'OK, great! I'll just bring Chandra in.'

Chandra? The maid? A babysitter? Brooke's younger sister? No, Brooke had only an older brother, away at college, at present.

While he waited for elucidation, he fetched Diet Cokes for the girls and offered biscuits (cookies), which they both refused, too busy giggling and chatting. Although one part of him was hugely relieved to see his daughter lively and vivacious, another part was gutted that her attitude to *him* should be so entirely different. Indeed, he was still smarting from the rejection of being told there was 'no point' in him coming today, and that it would be 'babyish' for him to watch her ride. Accompanying the three

of them to the Flying Horseshoe Ranch, which was set in gorgeous countryside, apparently, seemed infinitely preferable to spending the day alone.
However, Erica had made it clear she didn't want him there and, even now,
had disappeared with Brooke, presumably to her bedroom – strictly out-
of-bounds to *him*.

'This is Chandra.' Kimberley announced, reappearing with a dog in her
arms – the smallest dog he had ever seen; an exotic-looking creature,
dressed in clothes identical to Kimberley's.

A dog? In clothes? He blinked and looked again. Yes, a sequinned silver
top and puce-pink pedal-pushers, with the addition of four, pink, matching
bows in its long, white, silky hair. Being careful not to disturb its coiffure,
he reached out to pat its head and was rewarded with a series of shrill,
protesting yaps.

'She's the love of my life,' Kimberley enthused, smothering the dog with
kisses. Where did that leave her husband, he mused, wondering if the poor
guy got a look-in? 'Would she like some water?' he asked. 'It's quite a humid
day.'

'Oh, no! She only drinks from her own special bowl and only bottled
water, sourced from natural springs. I find Volvic's the best. It's filtered
through volcanic rock, so it's a hundred per cent pure. They're a very delicate breed, you know, shihtzus, so I have to be extremely careful. All the
food I give her is strictly organic and she can't touch carbs in any shape or
form, because they tend to leave her gaseous and bloated.'

He had been about to offer Kimberley the biscuits, but perhaps she, too,
didn't touch carbs. And would the coffee meet her exacting standards, or
should he have made it from bottled water? Nervously, he poured her a cup,
passed her cream and sugar.

'No, thanks,' she said, waving both away. 'I'm on a diet. Aren't we all?'

No, he thought, we're not. And surely it was bad for Brooke and Erica
to be surrounded by adults who saw food as the enemy. Ladling cream into
his own cup, he motioned Kimberley to a chair, where she settled back with
Chandra cradled on her lap – a Chandra still yapping fortissimo. 'Maybe
she'd like to explore the garden?' he suggested, hoping for a little peace and
quiet, but Kimberley looked deeply shocked.

'I wouldn't consider such a thing! There are just too many risks –
poisonous plants, for instance, or crap from other dogs. I prefer to keep her
close to me, then I know she's safe.'

It seemed a waste of four perfectly good legs, although he had no intention of arguing the toss. 'So where do you get her clothes?' he asked, with genuine interest, having never seen such extraordinary gear in any type of shop.

'There's this fabulous little boutique in Belle Vue, which sells matching designer outfits for dogs and cats and their owners.'

'*Cats?*' he goggled, trying to imagine his lost, lamented Charlie clad in pedal-pushers. How the devil did these poor animals pee if they were bundled up in trousers? And Chandra's bladder situation would be still more dire, if the pampered little creature was forbidden to leave her mistress's lap.

'Absolutely. Most cats love dressing up as much as dogs. Chandra just adores her clothes and, every morning, she sits up on her hind legs, begging me to get her dressed. She has these really darling outfits, which cost nearly as much as mine, would you believe? I must spend a good five-thousand dollars a year, keeping *au courant* with the latest doggy fashion trends. And another five-thousand at the Pet Pavilion. She has "pawdicures" and massages and blow-dries and, if we're going somewhere special, they spray her fur with gold and silver glitter, or even dye it fuchsia-pink – using strictly organic vegetable dyes, of course.'

'Heavens!' he exclaimed, busy working out the sums in his head. Ten-thousand dollars a year – roughly £7,500 – would pay for a part-time library-assistant, to help with community projects, or create funding for vital literacy courses, especially useful for his group, or replace the old, worn furniture in the Study Room and …

'She even has her own cute little closet, with these tiny silk-padded hangers. And you should see her party dresses! One's an exact replica of Marilyn Monroe's favourite cocktail-dress. You wore it for your last birthday party, didn't you, my precious?' she added, now addressing the dog.

Chandra yapped an obedient 'Yes!', but Eric was rendered speechless. A birthday party for canines?

'What a shame you weren't here just a few weeks earlier, then you could have come. It was a really special day, Eric. We invited all her little doggy friends and I ordered two fantastic cakes – one for the doggies and one for their owners – both totally free of any kind of flour, or other nasties like preservatives. The doggy one was made in the shape of a big, pink, juicy bone, and contained nothing but organic salmon, organic chicken breast, a little touch of …'

He let the list of ingredients waft over him. Actually, birthdays were a painful subject, with his daughter's less than a fortnight away. She had turned down every suggestion he'd made to celebrate the occasion. No, she didn't want him to take her out to dinner, or take her bowling, or ice-skating – or take her anywhere. She had her own private plans, and could he please stop going on about it?

However, he ought to switch the conversation to his concerns about the girls – another tricky issue, but one that needed tackling. 'Kimberley, forgive me changing the subject, but I am a little worried about Erica. In England, girls her age don't generally wear make-up. Is it common over here? And don't parents take a stand or…?'

Kimberley sipped her coffee reflectively. 'I'd say it's very common, although, of course, it depends a lot on the individual girl. Some don't bother with even the faintest dab of lip-gloss, while others go in for the full works. My Brooke was always extraordinarily mature. Even as a toddler, she took an interest in how she looked and I encouraged that, deliberately. I think it's important for girls to make the best of themselves.'

'But isn't there a danger in them' – he paused, a tad embarrassed – 'you know, being over-sexualized, when basically they're children still?'

'Brooke's thirteen-and-a-half. I don't consider her a child. She's well on her way to womanhood, so I feel she needs to prepare herself; learn how to dress, look after her skin and hair and nails, create an immaculate polished look and stay slender, of course, through careful calorie-counting.'

'It seems, well … rather sad, though, for them to be worrying about their faces and figures when they could be just enjoying life.'

'Oh, they do enjoy it – immensely. Brooke gets a real buzz from coming shopping with me. Right from when she was little, our trips to the mall have helped to bring us close. I guess you could say we bonded in the fashion boutiques! We often flick through magazines together – you know, like *Vogue* and *Glamour* – and we always book joint sessions at the beauty salon and have sun-bed sessions side by side. You may not realize, Eric, but my daughter has extremely strong ideas about the image she wants to create for herself, and I support her two hundred per cent.'

He gagged on the word 'image' – its falsity, its shallowness – but this determined fashionista was still in full flow.

'And your Erica's the same – at least *now* she is, although I have to say she did need a little help at first. It was Brooke who alerted me to the fact that some of the girls were ribbing her about the way she looked, so I decided to step in and lend a hand. Poor Christine's up to her eyes with that demanding job of hers and all the travelling she does, but I'm at home all day, so I have plenty of time to spend with the girls. And, actually, it's given me enormous pleasure to help Erica find her feet, establish a basic beauty regime and work out her own individual style.'

Eric sat in silence, struggling with different emotions: anger with Christine for apparently neglecting their daughter; resentment towards Kimberley for encouraging these barely-teens to buy totally unsuitable attire and slather their faces with gunge, yet also a certain gratitude that she had cared enough to help Erica survive the hurtful teasing. He burned to state his own views about the superficiality of focusing on looks, but realized it was pointless, since for Kimberley they were paramount. None the less, it made him mad that children should be subjected to constant commercial pressures and encouraged to believe that following fashion and keeping up with trends were more important than developing ideals or working for some worthwhile cause. What, he thought, with sudden wry amusement, must she think of *him*, dressed as he was in his tatty old jeans and a T-shirt from the local thrift-shop, with BORN WILD emblazoned across the front – a somewhat inappropriate claim for a bloke as cautious as himself?

'Erica's just fine now,' Kimberley observed, waving a superbly manicured hand in his direction, 'so there's no need to worry on that score. And Brooke's been very good for her, you know – helped her with all sorts of things.'

He could guess what things those were – eyebrow-plucking, leg-waxing, powdering and primping. Didn't Kimberley see the dangers of turning schoolgirls into nymphets? If *he* could feel aroused by Brooke – and the very notion appalled him – what about less scrupulous blokes, who might go ahead and act on their brute urges? But he could hardly bring up such a delicate subject, so, returning to his duty as host, he offered her more coffee.

'Absolutely not! Coffee's a major health-risk. New research has shown it can do more damage than heroin.'

'Well, how about some juice?' he suggested, draining his own cup. Despite his high coffee consumption, he wasn't yet in need of rehab – or so he had assumed till now.

'It's kind of you to offer, but the high acid content of fruit juice is murder for my tooth-enamel. I find it safer to stick to iced green tea, which is better for my health in general.'

Lord, he thought, if she was so concerned about her health, would she sue him for grievous bodily harm if she happened to catch his cold? Fortunately, the Sudafed had dried up the secretions and, although his nose was still red, she might put that down to a penchant for the hard stuff. Actually, he could do with a double whisky right this minute, but since all beverages, hard or soft, were clearly lethal for her, he might as well change tack.

'By the way, there's something else I want to ask. I wondered what you felt about both our girls deciding to change their names? I must admit, I'm not too happy.'

'Oh, it's just a bit of fun, Eric. They're exploring different identities, that's all. Brooke wants to be a fashion model, so she's considering names like Jordan and Marisa, and where's the harm in that?' Kimberley gave a tinkling laugh. 'The irony is, I named her after Brooke Shields, thinking she'd be a good role-model for any daughter with high aspirations. I mean, Shields was famous from such an early age. She started modelling as a baby of eleven months and was earning ten thousand dollars a day by the time she was fifteen. But, of course, *my* Brooke thinks her namesake is totally old hat and is much more into superstars like Miley Cyrus and Paris Hilton. And, as for Erica,' she added, 'I guess calling herself Carmella makes her feel she's a Spanish prima donna and, if that helps to boost her self-esteem, it can't be a bad thing.'

Didn't this woman realize, he thought, with irritation, that a change of name could go much deeper and actually be a statement of defiance? In Erica's case, it appeared to be a deliberate move to dissociate herself from *him*, and perhaps a way to challenge Christine, too, since she, of course, had helped to choose the name. But why enter such troubled waters with a featherbrained female who couldn't see beyond the obvious? And, in any case, Chandra had started yapping again, with an even higher decibel-count.

'You're just the perfect alarm-clock,' Kimberley cooed; the dog responding with another volley of yaps. 'She always knows when we ought to leave and she's exactly on time, as usual, aren't you, my little precious? So, if you'll excuse us, Eric ...' Kimberley stood up; her coffee almost untouched, apart from a crimson lip-print branded on the rim of the cup. 'It's a good hour's drive to the stables, so we'd better make a move. The girls usually ride locally, but Brooke begged me to take them to this particular ranch and I hate to say no to my daughter. And it's quite a famous place, you know, with fantastic trails through the pine forests and ...'

As Kimberley continued to rhapsodize about the forests, mountains and valleys, he felt even more excluded; confined to tame suburbia while the others explored this wider landscape.

'Expect us back by seven, but, you never know, we may run into traffic, so I'll call you if we're delayed, OK?'

Seven! The empty hours yawned and dragged in prospect, and this was only day two. How would he endure three endless weeks if Erica was so determined to go off on her own? Tomorrow he must sit down with her and insist that she saw sense. It was patently absurd for him to have travelled all this way, only to have her deliberately avoid him. Yet her contemptuous opinion of him as freakish, weak and badly dressed had undermined his confidence; made it hard to be assertive. Each time he vowed to reason with her, her injurious words would stop him in his tracks. Why should she even *want* to see a father she despised?

'I'll just get Brooke and Erica,' he said, alerted by the 'alarm-clock', which was now barking in full-throated protest, while its mistress stood waiting by the door.

Having called the girls down, he accompanied them out to the car, watching as the dog was strapped into her special seat – a fancy affair, complete with fur rug, silken cushion and individual seat-belt. Erica and Brooke sat beside her, in the back, still deep in conversation.

'Enjoy yourselves!' he said, feeling a pang of loss and loneliness as the car pulled away and vanished round the corner. Neither girl had turned round to wave goodbye.

However, hardly had he gone inside when another car drew up, and out stepped a slim, young woman with long, dark hair rippling down her back. Eric watched with interest. Had Fate taken pity on his solitary state and sent him a gorgeous playmate? Certainly, she was walking towards the house, as if she were expected, and the radiant smile she gave helped alleviate his joyless mood.

'You Eric?' she enquired.

'Er, yes,' he said, admiring her trim figure and appealing lack of make-up. A naked face, at last.

'Me Malinal.'

'Oh – I see.' The maid! Not much chance of dalliance if she had the whole huge house to clean. Besides, he was thrown by her sheer style. The word 'maid' suggested some underprivileged, shabby soul who would shuffle in on foot, not a well-dressed woman driving a snazzy car. None the less, he did his best to detain her, ushering her in to the kitchen with his most persuasive smile.

'How about a coffee? I have some brewed and ready. Why don't we sit down for a bit, so you can tell me all about yourself?'

'Please?'

A look of total incomprehension crossed her elfin face. A language problem, clearly. Should he spend the next three weeks doing a crash-course in Mexican? Failing that, he would have to rely on gestures, so, having pointed to the coffee pot, he picked up a clean cup and made a drinking motion.

Vehemently, she shook her head. Perhaps she shared Kimberley's conviction that coffee turned you into a junkie, or simply had too much to do to sit about partaking of refreshment. Presumably the latter, since she donned a pair of rubber gloves and began attacking the kitchen surfaces with impressive application.

He persevered, however, using shorter sentences and spelling out each word with careful clarity.

'Where – do – you – live?'

'Have – you – known – Christine – long?'

'How – often – do – you – work – for – her?'

The only response to all three questions was an air of even greater puzzlement, accompanied by a distinctly dismissive shrug. Fate had let him down – again. Not only was he in her way, but they couldn't even communicate. In fact, he was beginning to feel awkward in her presence: he the leisured vacationer, drifting around with nothing to do, while she slaved away with bleach and cleaning-cloths. He considered offering to help, but doubted if she would welcome his assistance, or indeed his company. Crazy to imagine he would have any chance of attracting her, when he was a good two decades older. And, in any case, she probably had half Mexico in passionate pursuit.

All hope of romance fading, he removed himself to Christine's office, taking advantage of his ex's offer to borrow her computer in her absence. He was tempted to email all his friends back home, but what the hell could he say? He was having a fabulous time? How great it was to see his daughter again? And how exciting to be in Seattle amidst the bright lights and the skyscrapers?

Instead, he Googled 'Daddy-Dates', a dodgy-sounding project he had read about in this morning's *Seattle Times*, in which fathers 'dated' their daughters, partly to spend time with them on an intense, one-to-one basis and so get to know them better, but also to ensure that their daughters were well treated on any future dates with boyfriends. By setting an example of attentiveness and respect, the fathers primed the daughters to expect the highest standards from all subsequent men in their lives. To tell the truth, the word 'date' made him nervous – too sexualized again – and, in any case, he detested the thought that Erica might be going out with boyfriends when she was still so young and vulnerable. Suppose her drink was spiked with a rape-drug and she ended up pregnant – or dead? However, there was just the smallest chance that the site might recommend some outings or excursions that would actually appeal to her.

But, scrolling down the list of suggested 'dates', his spirits sank lower with each one.

Take her to the mall and let her choose her favourite outfit.

Useless. She was already doing that with Kimberley and Brooke, so she would hardly want Dad to tag along.

Take her sailing on the ocean, or boating on a scenic lake.

And supposing she fell in? With a non-swimmer for a dad, she would almost certainly drown.

Take a drive to the beach and swim by moonlight.

Brilliant. *He'd* be standing shivering on the strand, while she dived in, alone.

Teach her how to fix the car, change the oil and tyres.

Perfect if he *had* a car, or had ever learned to drive.

Call it a 'Mystery Date' and so heighten her anticipation.

Anticipation? She was bound to turn it down, as she had his other suggestions.

Next, he consulted the booklist. *The Dads and Daughters Togetherness Guide* might be helpful if she actually wanted to be with him and, as for *Strong Fathers; Strong Daughters*, that was a non-starter for a dad she'd dismissed as 'totally weak'. In fact, he was beginning to feel more and more inadequate – not to mention guilty. If Erica ended up an addict or no-hoper, he would be to blame, since he was well aware that children involved in a divorce were more likely to fail at school and develop drug and alcohol problems.

Kicking back his chair, he got up from the desk and began pacing round the room. It was so hard to be a father. Was he meant to be a friendly mate, or a moral anchor, or a rigid disciplinarian, or combine a bit of each? Although, he had to concede, it was probably equally hard to be a teen. He had gleaned a lot about teenagers from working in the library; come to see that many of them were self-righteous yet self-loathing, judgemental yet insecure, brash yet idealistic. And while they could be secretive and sullen, they also tended to overreact hysterically to every emotional hiccup and frustration – which was what made him loath to discuss the whole fraught issue of Christine's pregnancy. On the one occasion he'd mentioned it, Erica had slammed out of the room, so, since then, he'd held his peace. None the less, he did feel an obligation to try to assuage her fears on the subject. Maybe it would be wiser, though, to wait until their relationship was on slightly firmer ground – if it ever was.

Another matter on his mind was if and when to give her the pendant. Anything heart-shaped seemed wildly inappropriate, when her own heart was cold and closed. And her other presents were still in Stella's case, which had not yet been delivered, despite another phone-call.

Wearily, he picked up the receiver and dialled the number once more, experiencing the usual delays as he was instructed by automated voices to press one, two, three, four, or five, then passed from pillar to post again, whichever one he chose. And, even when he was eventually connected to a real flesh-and-blood InterWest employee, she could shed no useful light on the whereabouts of his case.

'It may never have left Heathrow, sir. Or, alternatively, it may have got as far as Minneapolis and then been sent back to London.'

Great news. He'd better return to the thrift-shop tomorrow and buy more mismatched clothes. Although, if he was destined to spend the whole three weeks alone, his appearance hardly mattered – except, of course, his daughter would be judging him at breakfast-time and late evening, and comparing him unfavourably with cool and stylish Dwight.

'Cut it out!' he muttered, venturing downstairs again for another glimpse of Malinal, who was now on her hands and knees, scrubbing the kitchen floor. Her position afforded him a brilliant view of her arse, but unfortunately she caught him gawping and scowled with such displeasure he made a speedy getaway.

He also decided to get the hell out and take himself to Seattle. Sightseeing was a more productive occupation than pestering a girl who hadn't the slightest interest in him. Whatever Erica might say, there *were* buses to the city, and he could hardly return to England having failed to see a single famous landmark.

He was just sorting out his keys and wallet, when there was a loud ring on the bell. The gardener? The butler? The latest colour consultant?

He opened the front door to find a matronly woman standing on the step, clad in a smart dress and jacket; her wispy white hair puffed up round her head in a dandelion-clock coiffure.

'Hello,' she gushed. 'I'm Peggy. And I bet you're Eric, with that hair! Christine told me it was red, but I didn't realize what a distinctive red.'

He nodded, curtly, weary of comments about his hair, which had been going on since babyhood.

'I live opposite,' the woman continued. 'And I thought I'd just stop by to see if you'd like to come to church. It's a lovely service, Eric, and I know you'd really enjoy it.'

That he doubted strongly. 'Well, actually,' he said, desperate for a get-out, 'I was just about to leave for Seattle.'

'But how are you going to get there? Christine said you didn't drive.'

'It's OK, there's a bus.'

'A *bus*?' In her mouth, the word sounded like a cross between a brothel and an abattoir. 'Oh, you couldn't get a bus, Eric. It will take for ever, especially on a Sunday. Anyway, it's no fun for you being on your own, and I know Erica's not here. I saw her leave about half an hour ago, with that little friend of hers, both of them in riding clothes, so they'll obviously be gone some time.'

His first instinct was to protest; indignant at the thought of this woman spying on him from just across the street. Would his every move be scrutinized; his nosy neighbour get to know that he was rarely with his daughter? He was so used to living in London, where you could be murdered in your flat without anybody noticing, let alone offering help, he found the idea of a close-knit community distinctly disconcerting. What else had Peggy seen – his lascivious expression as he ogled the maid's bum?

However, he remembered his manners and invited her in. If she were a friend of Dwight and Christine, he wouldn't want it known that he'd left her standing on the step or – worse – shut the door in her face.

Having ensconced herself in a chair, she continued her persuasion-campaign to inveigle him into church. 'Our pastor is really awesome, Eric. I'd love for you to meet him.'

'Awesome' seemed unlikely. In fact, it was a source of irritation to him that Americans should use the term so frequently, and even for ordinary people and run-of-the-mill events, whereas *he* reserved it for phenomena such as Niagara Falls, tsunamis, or God Himself – were He to exist.

'And, although he's not a Pentecostal, he does believe in the Prosperity Gospel, which *I* support wholeheartedly.'

'I'm afraid I've never heard of it.' He slumped back on the sofa, steeling himself for a proselytizing session.

'What it means,' she said, leaning forward earnestly, 'is that God wants for us to be rich.'

Now he was genuinely puzzled. 'But I thought the whole essence of Christianity was just the opposite – you know, all that stuff about camels and eyes of needles. And how about the passage in the Gospel where Jesus tells a rich man to sell everything he possesses and give the proceeds to the poor?' Which Peggy had patently failed to do herself, judging by her house – as big and swanky as Dwight's – and her decidedly upmarket clothes. But perhaps there *weren't* any poor in this ultra-prosperous suburb.

'No, Eric, you don't understand. Jesus was merely telling the man to turn his solid assets into liquid ones. The more prosperous you are, the more it proves God loves you.'

In which case, he concluded, God couldn't love him much.

'Although you mustn't think it's all one-way. I give a lot of money to the church, but God never fails to repay me – a hundredfold and more. And, if other Christians feel they're not adequately rewarded, all it means is that their faith isn't strong enough.'

A pity, he thought, he wasn't more opportunist, then he could augment his annual pay-packet simply by suppressing his religious doubts.

'Actually, poverty is the work of Satan, so no way could Jesus approve of it. You only need to look at Barack Obama. His family were so dirt-poor, they had to rely on food-stamps to get by, but look at him now! God raised him from nothing to the highest position in the land – or in the world, for that matter.'

Surely, he reflected, it was Obama's own hard graft that had brought him to the White House, rather than divine intervention, but he refrained from further argument; glad that he and Peggy at least shared an admiration for the Democrats. 'Yes, my English friends were thrilled he won. We had quite a celebration on election night.'

'Thrilled? *I* was appalled! My faith determines my politics – always has and always will – and McCain stands for family values, so, of course, he got my vote. I don't know whether you realize, Eric, but Obama supports infan-ticide.'

'That's a bit of an exaggeration, if you don't mind me saying so. He may be pro-choice, but—'

She wagged an admonitory finger; her face expressing deep disgust. 'No way is it an exaggeration. On three separate occasions, he opposed the law that said if a child was born alive during a botched late-term abortion, the doctor must do all he could to save that baby's life. Which means Obama was forcing tax-payers to subsidize cold-blooded murder.'

Eric shifted in his chair. Sex, religion and politics were hardly ideal subjects for a first meeting with a neighbour. Clasping his hands together, he clamped his mouth firmly shut, in an effort to stay silent. Peggy, however, must have interpreted the former gesture as a sign that he was deep in prayer – perhaps for forgiveness or a change of heart – because, flashing him a triumphant smile, she rose to her feet and said she would be back in half an hour to drive him to the church.

'That'll give you time to change,' she added, with an accusatory glance at his T-shirt. 'I'll come by for you at eleven sharp. If we get there nice and early, I'll have time to introduce you to my friends and, of course, to Pastor Matthews. And, after the service, we all gather in the community-room for coffee and delicious home-made cakes.'

He simply didn't have the nerve to refuse – not when she had used a tone that brooked no opposition. Peggy's mission, obviously, was to hook another soul for God, so she would hardly be dissuaded from such a noble cause. Besides, in his present downbeat mood, he should be grateful for small mercies, such as delicious home-made cakes. And, after all, the Gospel of Prosperity might stand him in good stead if the assessors marked him down and he failed to get a bonus.

'Right,' he said, forcing his features into an expression of what he hoped she'd regard as piety, 'I'll be ready and waiting at eleven sharp.'

chapter twenty-four

'Welcome to our church, Eric!'

'Wonderful to meet you, Eric!'

'Honoured to have you with us, Eric.'

The warmth of their welcome was both extraordinary and gratifying. Even at this moment, he was being pressed against fragrant necks and powdery cheeks, as sundry elderly ladies embraced him with the same relief and rapture as they would the Prodigal Son. And now his hand was being pumped with enthusiastic fervour by clean-cut, well-groomed men, while other, younger parishioners flashed him beaming smiles. All the blokes seemed taller than him, and infinitely better dressed, yet it was *he* who was being fêted like a hero – such a rare experience, he was tempted to convert at once and become a regular church-goer.

And even Peggy seemed to bask in reflected glory as her redheaded, English protégé became the centre of attention; more and more people crowding round and begging to be introduced. From what he'd gathered, English congregations were distinctly on the small side, with just a smattering of mainly over-sixties, but, here, every age was represented, including teens like Erica. Perhaps he had made a grave mistake in not bringing her up with some religious structure to her life. At least a sense of Christian charity might have made her less judgemental.

'This is Eric,' Peggy beamed, to yet another pillar of the church – a formidable-looking lady with a massive shelf of a bosom and hips as wide as goalposts. 'Eric, meet Rosanne.'

Another name to add to the list he was already having trouble memorizing. Karl was the big, swarthy one; Mary-Ann the diminutive blonde; Garrett bald and freckled, but who was the sultry brunette, with her voluptuous curves and mass of raven hair, swept up on top? There were also all the titles to remember: Clark, the director of music; Debra, the church secretary; David the Youth Minister, and Arlene, the chair of the Bible Study Group.

Actually, he couldn't say a word to Rosanne, because she was clasping him so tightly against her impressive mammaries as to render speech impossible. Not that he objected. This universal approbation was all the more agreeable when contrasted with Christine's diffidence, Dwight's resentment and his daughter's downright hostility. None the less, he experienced a twinge of apprehension as people started moving from the extensive antechamber into the church itself. It was years since he'd attended a religious service, and those he recalled had been so tediously long, they called for reserves of patience he feared he didn't possess at present. However, the church itself was nothing like the oppressive pile he remembered from his childhood, with its air of doom and darkness enveloping him each Sunday in a thick, black, silent cloud. This, in contrast, was a light and airy building; its ceiling painted heavenly-blue, its large windows letting in the sun, and with cheery splashes of colour provided by the blue hydrangeas arranged along the windowsills and by the display of hothouse flowers resplendent on the altar.

At 11.30 precisely, the choir filed in, dressed in purple robes, and accompanied by the organist in a long, black, swishy gown. Despite the impressive attire, the singing was bound to be amateurish; the sort of off-key cacophony he had endured as a young boy, kneeling restive but obedient in the stone-chill, shadowed gloom. But, no – as the conductor lifted his baton, the sound that burst forth seemed to soar right up to heaven; spectacular in its purity and force. These were true professionals and the music was so uplifting, he felt transported to another realm; realizing only now how dull and uninspiring his everyday life had become.

As the last note died away, he sat, lost in admiration, wishing he, too, had a powerful voice; one that could move audiences to tears. He imagined greeting library customers with some impressive tenor aria, or dunning them for fines with the same outraged passion as Plácido Domingo in *Otello*. Thoughts of the library made him wonder how his colleagues were getting on without him, and how Stella would cope when she ran his group next week? She wasn't as used as he was to depressives and obsessives, and always claimed to have a blind spot when it came to poetry. Perhaps he should have chosen an easier poet, but his objective was to challenge them; make them see that even words they didn't understand could speak to them at some deeper level.

Pastor Matthews – whom he hadn't yet met – had moved to the front of the altar and was giving an address of welcome, half of which he had missed, of course, due to his grasshopper mind.

'No one is here by accident,' the tall, beak-nosed man continued. 'God has summoned every single one of you for some specific purpose. Please ask your-selves *why* you are in church today, and what the Lord is asking of you.'

Eric felt a ripple of unease. He'd assumed he'd been dragooned into the service by Peggy's sheer insistence, but perhaps there was some daunting Higher Purpose, about to be revealed.

Get a grip, he thought. All the adulation had clearly gone to his head and, if he didn't watch it, he would be writhing about in transports, like Paul on the road to Damascus.

Peggy nudged him to his feet for the hymn – one he'd never heard of, with a complicated tune. However, her own exuberant singing-voice more than compensated for his halting croak – less Plácido Domingo than crow with laryngitis.

After the final cadence, the pastor invited all members of the congrega-tion to turn round and greet each other. Delighted by the prospect of more enthusiastic embraces, Eric was soon happily engulfed again, as total strangers kissed him warmly on both cheeks and generally made him feel a VIP. And people were actually crossing the aisle to come and say hello to him, as if he were some new, exotic species, blown in from a far-distant planet, rather than an ordinary bloke from England.

He was almost disappointed when his fan-club drifted back to their seats and the service continued with a Confession of Faith. The words were printed on the service-sheet Peggy had pressed into his hand, so he was more or less obliged to join in, despite his feelings of hypocrisy in professing doctrines that seemed to make no sense.

'We trust in Jesus Christ,' he faltered, 'fully human, fully God.' Wasn't 'fully human, fully God' something of a contradiction in terms? Although, if there *was* a God, he owed Him a debt of thanks for the heartfelt affirmations Peggy was pouring forth, which conveniently swamped his nervous stutterings.

The hymn that followed was much more to his taste and, indeed, could have been penned with him in mind.

> *When I feel afraid,*
> *Think I've lost my way,*
> *Still You're there beside me*
> *And nothing will I fear.*

Despite the lack of rhyme and dodgy scansion, he longed for such a comforting resource: an Almighty Presence that could banish all his terrors at a stroke. Why was faith so difficult, he wondered – as difficult as love? Neither could be had to order; neither relied upon to last.

Suddenly, he noticed that four men had risen to their feet and were proceeding to the front of the church, each armed with a collection plate, which they were passing round the congregation, row by row by row. As one of the men approached, he saw with horror that the plate was full of high-value bills – twenties by the score, a good scattering of fifties and even a couple of hundreds. His cheeks were burning as he fumbled for his wallet, knowing in advance that it contained nothing but loose change. As yet, he'd cashed only one of his travellers' cheques and already spent most of that at the thrift-shop. And, to make things worse, Peggy was now extracting a whole sheaf of bills from her purse and placing them in the collection plate. Recalling what she'd said about God rewarding her a hundredfold, he half-expected to see a hailstorm of gold ingots descending on her from above. But there was only the shaming clink of his own cache of coins, as he offloaded them into the plate.

'Sorry,' he mumbled. 'Bit short at the moment.' God! Why had he said that? It made him seem a pauper, and only emphasized his difference from these well-heeled adherents of the Gospel of Prosperity. So far, he hadn't spotted a single person who wasn't well-coiffed, smartly dressed and, in many cases, clanking with jewellery. Even Dwight's cashmere sweater, which he had donned once more, in honour of the church, looked a little commonplace in this exalted company.

He was so mortified, he missed most of the sermon, although partly because his attention kept straying back to Erica. If she was so unhappy here in the States and subjected to such invidious pressures, might she not welcome the opportunity to return to England and go back to her old school? Or would any further disruption upset her even more? She would never agree, in any case, to live with such an inadequate father, nor would Christine ever permit it of course. Besides, it was bound to involve the lawyers again, which meant he wouldn't stand a chance. All the lawyers he had ever met believed children should stay with their mothers; clearly regarding fathers as an inferior species, never to be trusted.

As if on cue, the congregation began reciting the *Our Father*. By now, his mind was all over the place and he began reflecting on his own father – a pretty useless exercise, since he hadn't the faintest notion as to who the guy might be, or what he did. But supposing he had suffered from depression and Erica had inherited the gene and would never be happy anywhere? Or perhaps she'd inherited his own fears. She didn't actually seem fearful in the slightest; showed no apprehension about riding, sailing, swimming, skiing – all panic-inducing pursuits *he* avoided like the plague. But she might have secret, existential fears, even now preying on her mind, although he had scant chance of finding out when she refused point-blank to confide in him.

Another brilliant offering from the choir succeeded in suppressing his gloomy thoughts, so triumphant was the tune. And the final *Amen* was almost a performance in itself, as the word was tossed from voice to voice; sopranos chasing altos; tenors outsoaring baritones. This wasn't just a tame 'So be it', but a magisterial 'Yes!', as the entire choir affirmed, approved, avowed, in total validation. He himself had rarely said such eager 'Amens' to the happenings in his life, but been forced to acquiesce in what others decided on his behalf; be it the string of different placements in his child-hood, or the bitter losses brought by the divorce. Would things ever change, he wondered, as he tried to imagine shouting an impassioned 'Yes!' to some new and lasting love – or even to a new and fearless temperament?

His attention was shunted back to the service by a near-repeat of the sentiments he had heard at the beginning; now recited by the congregation.

> Wherever we go, God is sending us.
> Wherever we are, God has put us there.
> He has a purpose in our being here.

As if to emphasize the theme, the pastor declared in ringing tones: 'We go nowhere by accident. Christ has something specific and important He wants to do through every one of us. Be attentive to His promptings.'

Again, Eric felt on his guard, knowing he was dangerously susceptible, due to lack of sleep and worry over Erica. All too easy to believe in some Message from Above. If he didn't try to distance himself, he'd be setting up a mission to convert the Jews, or the heathen, or even entering a monastery and taking vows of chastity. Although, in truth, the latter wouldn't be so different from his present celibate state. He cast a lascivious glance at the voluptuous brunette he'd noticed earlier on, now sitting in an adjoining pew. Her hourglass figure made him feel more saint than stud and, if only the merciful Lord would cause their paths to cross, he would have better things to do than be a monk.

He was soon lost in erotic fantasies – so much so he failed to realize that the service had actually ended, until Peggy took him by the arm and steered him down the aisle, towards the door. As they made their stop-start way, the same fervent tide of well-wishers began clustering around again, asking had he enjoyed the service and how different was it from his own church back home? He hadn't the heart to tell them that the nearest he had to a church was the Dog and Duck.

'Don't you think our pastor is just awesome?' Arlene purred.

'Er, yes.'

'Well, now you know who we are and where we meet,' Debra said, clasping his arm with as much affection as if they'd just become formally engaged, 'I hope you'll be attending all our Easter services.'

He muttered something inaudible, hoping she would interpret it as a murmur of assent, although, in point of fact, he had no intention of making church a habit. He hadn't overcome the heights of terror and flown 5000 miles to spend all his time on his knees. OK, the rapturous reception he'd received was little short of a miracle, but there were limits to his hypocrisy. He could hardly celebrate the Resurrection when the whole concept of someone rising from the dead struck him as highly improbable, if not a shade grotesque.

However, he was saved from further argument by being swept along the corridor and along to the community-room, conveniently losing Debra in the crush. A long trestle-table had been set up at one end of the room, spread with a white linen cloth and heaped with cakes of every kind – a veritable patisserie.

'This is Eleanor,' Peggy said, introducing a plumpish, fair-haired female, whose ample curves were enticingly set off by a pink gingham pinafore. 'She makes the cakes, along with her lady helpers, of course.'

'Pleased to meet you,' he smiled, suddenly realizing that he had hardly eaten anything since the decidedly scanty meals on the plane.

'Do help yourself,' Eleanor urged. 'And we cater for most allergies here, so if there's anything you need to avoid, just let me know, OK? As well as all our regular cakes, we have fat-free, egg-free, nut-free, sugar-free and gluten-free.'

'Don't worry, I eat anything and everything – fat, sugar, gluten, eggs and every sort of nut – the more the merrier, in fact!'

'Oh, isn't he just darling!' Eleanor exclaimed to her band of lady assistants. 'And don't you just love that accent?'

'And what fantastic hair!' one of her acolytes put in. 'Would you mind me asking, Eric, is that a God-given colour?'

''Fraid so,' Eric grinned, although entertaining serious doubts that any actual deity had been involved in the matter.

Reaching out a tentative finger to touch his mop of curls, the woman gave a little squeal of approval. He was beginning to feel like the family pet – patted, fondled, stroked, admired and, yes, royally fed and watered. A large assortment of cakes had been piled onto a plate and pushed into his hand, while another beaming female offered him juice, tea, Coke or coffee – the latter decaffeinated, of course. It appeared that, in America, if they could remove the things that gave food and drink its kick, they would have no compunction in doing so. However, his wodge of chocolate gateau gave little cause for complaint, exploding on his tongue in a symphony of creaminess and sweetness, with even a shot of caffeine in the ultra-strong, dark-chocolate flavour.

Stuffing in another chunk, he was seriously engaged in chewing when Peggy chose that moment to introduce him to the pastor, the Reverend Marcus Matthews.

Making heroic but vain efforts to swallow the whole large mouthful, he had to rely on dumb-show in response to the reverend's greeting. He was also shamingly aware that he probably had a whipped-cream moustache and that he'd just dropped a shoal of crumbs on the floor.

'I hear you're visiting from England, Eric.'

Mumble, mumble, was all he could manage, as he continued desperately chewing, having encountered an intractable piece of nut that wouldn't seem to go down. Nut-free might have been wiser, after all.

'And how did you find our service?' the reverend continued imperturbably.

'Er, awesome!' he gasped, disposing of the nut, at last.

Another man had now joined their little group – a bloke so big and bulky he made Eric feel a dwarf.

'I don't quite understand the terms you use in England,' he remarked. 'I gather you have High Church and Low Church. Is that correct?'

'Absolutely,' Eric said, hoping the conversation wouldn't develop into a discussion of the finer points of theology, otherwise he'd be woefully out of his depth.

'And which are you?' asked Peggy, still hovering beside him with a definite air of proprietorship.

'Er, Low.' Certainly the more truthful option, since there'd been nothing 'high' about either his birth or education.

'And what's the name of your church?' an attractive girl enquired – one he hadn't seen before, but who looked alluringly well-stacked. If only all these females were interested in his body, rather than his soul.

'Um, St Matthew and St Mark's,' he said, ad-libbing on the pastor's names. He could hardly say the Dog and Duck.

'Is it big or small?' she persisted. 'I've seen pictures of your English cathedrals, so would it be something on that scale?'

'Oh, no. Small and cosy. And extremely old.' That was true, at least. The pub boasted genuine sixteenth-century beams. 'With lots of brass and an uplifting atmosphere.' There was nothing more uplifting than a foaming pint of bitter – or three.

'Is yours a large congregation?' the reverend asked.

'Yes, it's usually pretty crowded.' Sometimes he had to wait a whole ten minutes before he caught the barman's eye.

Peggy gave a nod of approval. 'Well, that sounds very commendable – so long as you're there in person, Eric. I only hope you're not a CEO.'

He failed to see the relevance of the question. However, if she was labouring under the false impression that he earned a top-notch salary, he'd better put her right immediately, otherwise she might expect a huge donation to the church.

'Perhaps Eric doesn't know what that means,' the attractive girl put in, before he'd had a chance to reply.

'Of course I do,' he said, indignantly. 'Chief executive officer.'

Several people laughed. 'In a Christian context,' the girl explained, 'it actually means "Christmas and Easter Only" – you know, the sort of apathetic people who only think about God a couple of times a year.'

'Oh … I see.'

'What we're trying to establish' – Peggy fixed him with her gimlet eye – 'is whether *you* attend church regularly, each and every Sunday?'

'Far more than that!' he retorted. Who did this bloody woman think she was, checking on his religious credentials? 'Three or four times a week, in fact.' Frequent attendance wasn't a hardship, since the Dog and Duck was so conveniently close to the library.

They gazed at him with new respect, as someone supremely devout. However, he sincerely wished they would stop the interrogation. Not only was he bound to make a boo-boo, once the questions became more challenging, he was also being prevented from eating. The enticing smells wafting from his plate – not just chocolate, but almond, ginger and coconut – kept reminding him how ravenous he was. Indeed, he envied the troupe of little kids, blithely stuffing themselves with chocolate brownies or raisin cookies, without a care in the world. They were even free to run around the room, rather than being held captive by a bunch of pious inquisitors.

'Tell me more about your community here,' he urged, hoping that if someone else held forth, he might be able to swallow a few mouthfuls, whilst giving attentive nods.

Needing no second invitation, the pastor launched into an elaborate account of the entire history of his ministry, along with the successes he'd achieved in bringing new souls to Christ and his particular interest in the Sunday school and youth groups.

'That reminds me, Eric,' Peggy interjected, 'I've been meaning to suggest to Christine that she take Erica to Sunday school. I'm sure the child would benefit. She's growing up far too fast and it might serve as a restraining influence.'

Nonsense, Eric thought, bristling at the woman's unspoken criticism.

'It's a lovely little group,' Peggy persisted, unabashed, 'with an inspiring teacher, who's had years and years of experience. She encourages the kids to memorize verses from the scriptures and reads them Bible stories. And, in *my* opinion, that would be highly beneficial for your Erica.'

He all but choked on his carrot cake. The only verses from scripture likely to interest his Lolita of a daughter would be the Song of Solomon; the only Bible story some salacious shocker unfit for children's ears. 'She's … rather tied up with school at present.'

'But Christine distinctly told me that they've given her extra time off school, so the two of you can be together while you're over here.'

This nosey-parker Peggy knew far too much about his life and family. He searched in vain for some appropriate reply. His lying skills were patently inadequate and, besides, he despised himself for lying in the first place.

'Not all youngsters want to go to Sunday school,' a bespectacled lady observed; kindly saving him from the prospect of having to frogmarch his protesting daughter to a Bible Study class. 'But one thing, Eric, *you* shouldn't miss is our Maundy Thursday service. It's truly awesome and sometimes even reduces me to tears. All the elders of the church, along with our dear pastor here, literally get down on their knees and wash the feet of twelve members of the congregation, like Christ did at the Last Supper.'

'Yes,' said Peggy, with barely disguised smugness, 'and I'm one of the chosen twelve. Which makes me almost a disciple – or so I'd like to think.'

'We're *all* disciples,' the pastor said, sanctimoniously. 'And, actually,' he added, 'we have only eleven candidates, so far. So if you would like to be the twelfth, Eric, it would be a privilege for me to wash your feet.'

Eric removed a piece of carrot from his tooth. How on earth could he refuse what was obviously a signal honour?

'All the more so,' Matthews continued, 'because we have a tradition in this community of honouring the stranger in our midst.'

Yes, too right – he *was* a stranger here. Although unsure of the exact statistics, he knew some 80% of Americans happened to believe in God, which made him an outcast straight away. And a third of those believers claimed to be 'born again'. The phrase struck him with new force. If only *he* could have been born again – to a different mother, willing and able to keep him.

'Well, how do you feel about it, Eric?' the pastor smiled, displaying enviable dentition.

That was another thing that meant he didn't fit: a good ninety-nine per cent of Yanks appeared to have flawless teeth. But he must shift his mind from orthodontics and try to drum up some rational reason for refusing Matthews' offer. Then, all at once, he remembered, with relief, that he already had the perfect excuse – and a genuine one at that. 'Maundy Thursday is my daughter's thirteenth birthday, so I'm afraid it would be impossible for me to get away.'

'Bring her too,' Peggy suggested, most unhelpfully. 'It only lasts an hour, from six to seven in the evening, so you'll have plenty of time to celebrate before and afterwards.'

'I ... I'd need to consult her first.'

'Of course,' the pastor said, soothingly. 'But even if it's not her sort of thing, do try to be there yourself, Eric.'

Forlornly, he put his plate down, having completely lost his appetite. His feet were little better than his teeth – callused, with the beginnings of a bunion, so the last thing he wanted was for them to be on public view. And because he always sweated in any alarming situation, they were bound to be hot and fetid. The thought of this fastidious-looking pastor handling his misshapen toes had already brought a flush to his face. 'Honestly, Reverend Matthews, I just couldn't allow you to wash my feet. It would seem completely wrong – I mean, *you* an important minister, demeaning yourself like that.'

'No way is it demeaning. And please do call me Marcus. Washing the feet of my congregation is, indeed, a symbol of humility, but Christ enjoined us all to serve each other, and service is a joy, Eric. And, yes, it may be a humbling experience, but only in the best sense. It's also incredibly freeing. To abase oneself for others, as our Lord and Master did Himself, is truly the work of God.'

'No, really, you don't understand. I'd feel extremely uncomfortable.'

The pastor gave a reassuring smile. 'The great disciple Peter made exactly the same objection, Eric, but I've no need to remind you what Christ said in reply.'

There *was* a need to remind him. Any knowledge he had of the Gospels appeared to have deserted him, although he could hardly say so here. In any case, the great disciple Peter probably had near-perfect feet, having worn sturdy open sandals all his life.

'In fact, He even washed Judas's feet,' the pastor pointed out, 'to emphasize the fact that He came down to earth to minister to sinners.'

So now he was a sinner – even a traitor on a par with Judas. Well, he deserved the accusations. He had been lying through his teeth for the best part of an hour, and had also failed abjectly in all his relationships, including that with Erica. Yet, sinner or no, he was still desperate to be let off the hook. He already had reason enough to dread his daughter's birthday, without adding yet another. On the other hand, since he was destined to spend the day alone, with the birthday-girl otherwise engaged, was there really any point in continuing to resist? After all, if he was seriously worried about his feet, he could always ask Kimberley for the name of the nearest salon and book a pedicure. Yes, good idea. Why not join the Yanks in their devotion to the Body Beautiful?

'All right, Reverend – sorry, Marcus – I *will* be there on Thursday.' He suppressed a shudder as he uttered one last lie. 'It'll truly be an honour to have you wash my feet.'

chapter twenty-five

'It's a must-see, Eric – *the* symbol of Seattle....'

'You can't come to Seattle and not go up in the Space Needle....'

'The views are awesome, breathtaking....'

So what the hell should he do? Overcome his fears – new fears now, of lifts, of heights – or have to face those people at the church and admit he'd been too scared to take their advice? The Space Needle's observation-deck was nearly 600 feet high, and the elevators travelled at a dizzying rate of 800 feet per minute – facts that had made him nervous even sitting safe at home. He could, in fact, avoid the lifts if he toiled his way up the 848 steps, but there would still be a sickening sense of vertigo once he reached the top. How had he developed acrophobia, for God's sake, when he'd always prided himself on being able to cope with heights? No wonder his daughter dismissed him as a freak. Indeed, he felt the deepest self-contempt, knowing she – and everyone – would laugh him to scorn for quaking in the face of a simple tourist attraction.

'So go *up*, then,' he instructed himself, gazing once again at the beetling, daunting structure – a sort of flying saucer tethered to a gigantic pylon, towering high above him. He had been prowling round the vicinity for at least the last half-hour, determined to ratchet up his courage, yet depressingly aware that he and courage had never been natural bedfellows.

'They say it's as high as thirteen hundred and twenty candy-bars, balanced one on top of the other,' Peggy had told him on Sunday; going on to enthuse about the 360-degree views of the Olympic Mountains, the Cascade Mountains, Elliot Bay, the surrounding islands, etcetera, etcetera. He should never have mentioned sightseeing, since it had sparked off a storm of other suggestions from his enthusiastic Christian friends, urging him on no account to miss the Art Museum, Pioneer Square, Capitol Hill, the Pike Place Market and so many other places he would have to resign his job and spend a year in Seattle, just to tick them off the list.

Although, actually, he had done quite well already; devoting the whole of yesterday to viewing the city's landmarks; starting with the Central Library, whose exhilarating structure and 1.5 million books had put his modest Balham workplace in the shade. And, even this morning, he had taken in the 'Experience Music' Project and the Science Fiction Museum, just a stone's-throw from the Needle. Yet both tours had seemed achingly hollow without Erica beside him to marvel at Captain Kirk's command-chair, or join him in a jam session, complete with ready-made fans. His daughter seemed to have deliberately planned to be out all day, every day, and must even have persuaded her friends' mothers not to include him on the excursions. There was always a reason, of course. It was a 'girly' thing they were doing, or some pursuit that would bore him to tears.

Nothing would bore him, if only he could be with her, but how could he impose himself when she had no wish for his company? All he could do was hope that things would change. Today was only Tuesday, after all, which meant he'd been with her – or *not* with her – a mere three and a half days. Strange, though, how that stretch of time felt as long as three and a half months.

So what now? Did he brave the elevator and go whizzing up to the observation deck? *Yes*, was the obvious answer – except he was uncomfortably aware that, in 1965, an earthquake had jolted the structure sufficiently to send the water sloshing out of the toilets, despite the fact it had been specifically built to withstand the fiercest pressures. Were earthquakes common here, he wondered, glancing at the long line of people waiting to buy their tickets, all putting him to shame? If only he could reincarnate himself as some intrepid person: Douglas Bader, Scott of the Antarctic, Edmund Hillary.

Cloaking himself in Hillary's skin, he took his place in the queue. Now he *had* no fears. What was a mere 600 feet compared with Everest? But a brief glance at the placard, 'Take a test-drive in the sky!' sent him skulking out again. He would have to tell Peggy that the queue had been so slow to move, he'd decided not to waste his precious time standing about in line.

Disconsolately, he mooched into the gift shop. Erica's presents were still lost, along with all his gear, and the airline now suspected that the case might never turn up. They had offered compensation, of course, and, on the strength of that, he had bought himself some decent clothes, reflecting, while he shopped, on the idea of compensation. Shouldn't people be compensated for never having had a mother, or for growing up in care? Or perhaps the whole justice system should be completely overhauled; the judges made to bear in mind that while less than one per cent of children were taken into care, some twenty-five per cent of the adult prison population had, in fact, been through the care system.

Trying to switch his attention from penal reform to finding some replacement gifts for Erica, he wandered round the large, confusing store. It seemed full of expensive tat, however: musical snow-globes, light-up pens, bottle-stoppers, nail-clippers – every product either made in the shape of the Space Needle, or branded with its logo, which meant every product was a reminder of his cowardice. He stopped to look at a cat-shaped cushion, which brought unhappy thoughts of Charlie, as well as new anxiety, because he hadn't told his daughter yet that their beloved pet was lost. She had actually mentioned Charlie – twice – but still he hadn't found the guts to give her such unwelcome news when she was already feeling low. Maybe after next weekend, when Brooke and co returned to school, but she had extra leave, they would have the chance of an in-depth conversation and could discuss not only Charlie but Christine's pregnancy.

In the end, he left the shop with nothing except some postcards of the stunning view from the top: the closest he would ever get to seeing it. In any case, it was now getting on for seven, so time to return to the house – not that Erica was expected back till half-past ten. She was with Brooke again today, but at another friend's house – a girl called Barbie, of all things – for some sort of get-together, to be followed by a pop concert, out at the Tacoma Dome. The Dome was famous, apparently – one of the largest wood-domed structures in the world – although it seemed unlikely he would lay eyes on it himself.

'You'd hate the concert, Dad,' she'd told him. 'The music's so loud it'd make you deaf.'

He would gladly take the risk of deafness – indeed of blindness or paralysis – just for the chance of being with her, but it appeared he had no choice.

Once he had boarded the monorail, he sat wondering why the people here were so contemptuous of public transport. The high-speed train took only a couple of minutes to whisk him from the Space Needle to the Westlake Center Mall. And he had even found a fast, convenient bus, departing from Second Avenue and going all the way to Mercer Island Park-and-Ride, from where he could catch another bus to the square at the South End, just a short walk from the house. The entire journey from Downtown Seattle took only three-quarters of an hour. Of course, you could do it in a car in twenty minutes, and here everybody drove – as Erica herself would do, the minute she turned sixteen – and would probably despise him even more, then.

He walked from the Westlake Center down Stewart Street towards the bus-stop, now surrounded by skyscrapers; their majestic glass and steel blazing gold and scarlet in the sunset. If only Mandy were with him, he would feel less rootless in this self-confident but dwarfing city. Yet, the more he reflected on Mandy – which he did constantly and painfully – the more he was forced to admit that they weren't actually well suited. Right from the start, the idea that she was his fantasy mother – reincarnated in a younger form and miraculously available – had blinded him to other aspects of the relationship. She shared none of his passion for books, tended to laugh at his ideals, and her continual, chronic lateness would have become a source of irritation. He, too, was at fault, of course. For one thing, he should have been more open about his crippling fears, but was that really as heinous as her own decision to deceive him for the remainder of his life?

Somehow, he must leave Mandy in the past and make a real effort to move on, and also stop imagining that he would ever meet his mother, either in the flesh or in some modified version. Not that it was easy, with so many reminders of mothers: children in the street calling out 'Mom' on every hand; women pushing prams; racks of cards already in the shops for the American Mothers' Day. There was also the urgent question of his Precious Box. It would be tricky to retrieve it without re-entangling himself with Mandy, yet he knew that any contact might weaken his resolve.

Soon, the bus came lumbering into view and, having clambered on, he found an empty seat next to a comfy-looking female.

'Wonderful sunset,' he remarked, but the sole response was a stony stare. Well, what had he imagined – a loquacious heart-to-heart? OK, he was lonely, but there would be plenty of time in the future for engaging total strangers in conversations they didn't want. He wasn't in his dotage yet – forty-five, not ninety.

Better to sit and read, then he could lose himself – as he'd done so often in his life – in another, happier world, where daughters loved their fathers, mothers were real people and girlfriends never lied.

He hovered outside Erica's bedroom door, tempted to go in. In fact, nothing would induce him to invade her privacy, yet her determination to bar him access couldn't help but rouse his suspicions. Was she frightened he would find fags – or drugs – or supplies of the contraceptive Pill, or a secret diary revealing wild transgressions? She had become a stranger – no way the child he knew. When she wasn't out with her friends, she spent worrying amounts of time up here, either texting them or phoning them, or on social-networking sites. But suppose she had somehow found a way to circumvent 'parental control' and was accessing more unwholesome sites? For all he knew, some evil stranger might be grooming her for sex.

His stomach rumbled suddenly, reminding him that he hadn't eaten since breakfast, so he went downstairs to raid the Aladdin's cave of the pantry. His fantasies about cosy little suppers with his daughter, or outings to the pizza parlour, had been rapidly dispelled. And, since there was no point cooking for one, his usual fare was a handful of crisps or biscuits, and a bowl of corn-flakes or peanut-butter sandwich, eaten standing up. Even tomorrow's sit-down dinner with Kimberley and her husband, Ted, had been cancelled just this morning, because Kimberley had sprained her wrist and could neither cook nor drive. In fact, she had laid on a taxi to bring Erica back tonight, since the other mother, Virginia, had to collect her husband from the airport soon after the end of the concert, and thus would only have time to drop both girls off at Kimberley's. Apparently, Kimberley's house, being at May Creek, within minutes of the freeway, was much handier for the airport than trekking out to Mercer Island and back again.

He checked his watch – 10.10 – which meant the taxi should arrive in twenty minutes. No doubt Erica would go straight up to her room, rather than stick around and chat about the concert. However, despite the lateness of the hour, he was determined to waylay her and insist they start communicating. Just last night he'd read an article about changes in the teenage brain, which were said to account for most negative teen behaviour: lack of empathy, consideration or even risk-awareness. OK, he was willing to make allowances for her synapses being slightly off-kilter, but there were limits to his patience. However much she had shaken his confidence as a father, he refused to tolerate this stand-off the whole three weeks he was here.

Just as he was stuffing in a handful of pretzels, the phone rang and, assuming it was Erica or Kimberley, he rushed to answer it.

'Oh … Christine,' he faltered. 'How are you?'

Idyllic, by the sounds of it – a Christine on cloud nine, unable to disguise the honeymoon glow.

'Sorry to ring so late, Eric, but I wondered how things are going.'

'Fine.'

'How's your cold?'

'Much better, thanks.'

'And is Erica OK?'

'Mm.' It sounded lame even to his ears, so he added some supporting detail – about the party and the pop concert and Kimberley's sprained wrist.

'Lord! How did she do that?'

'In the gym, apparently. She was lifting weights and—'

'Typical!' Christine said dismissively. 'It's all "me-time" for that bloody woman. The only thing she cares about is making herself slimmer and more glamorous. She employs a whole gang of beauticians, hairdressers, personal fitness trainers and even …'

And who are *you* to talk, he bit back.

'She's made Brooke the way she is, of course, and that, in turn, has influenced poor Erica, and I have to say it worries me. On the other hand, the two girls seem devoted to each other, so it would be wrong to try to separate them, even if one could. But now you're there, maybe you could exert some sort of influence.'

Not a chance in hell, he thought, wishing desperately she'd end the call. No way must she discover that he had seen so little of Erica, or he would truly be in trouble. Besides, just the sound of his ex's voice was enough to conjure up loathsome pictures of her in bed with Dwight. He and *Mandy* should be on honeymoon, not Christine and her supercilious bloke.

'What time is it in Hong Kong?' he asked, having done his hesitant best to answer her shoal of questions about Erica.

'Quarter past two in the afternoon. We've just had this delicious lunch at—'

He blocked his ears; had no desire to hear any romantic, gastronomic, or – God forbid – erotic details. 'And it's Wednesday there, not Tuesday.'

'That's right.'

'I get a bit confused, what with Seattle being eight hours behind the UK, and Hong Kong eight hours ahead.' All the time-differences made him feel unsettled, and his body-clock hadn't yet adjusted, so he was still finding it hard to sleep. When finally he did drop off, he'd wake after only an hour or two and wonder where he was. Crazy to sleep so badly in what must be the most luxurious bed in the whole of the North-West Pacific.

Once he'd rung off, he went upstairs to Christine's office, deciding to email Stella again, just as a form of comfort. The messages they'd already exchanged had made him feel less isolated; kept him in touch with life back home. She had also given him the cheering news that Meryl Jones, no less –

the high-powered Assistant Head of the whole Wandsworth Library Service – had decided to champion their Remembrance Project and that, with such a formidable ally, they were now certain to get funding. He'd longed to pick up the phone and say how pleased he was, but knew Stella was bound to ask about his daughter, and felt too ashamed to admit that he was spending his time as a tourist, rather than as Dad.

And now, again, he was tempted to ring, just to hear her voice, but, again, thought better of it. In any case, he could hardly drag her out of bed at 5.55 in the morning, so, instead, he switched on the computer.

Four messages were waiting – all from her, in fact, although instead of the usual moans about some memo from management, or further details of Meryl's support, these concerned a new post – just created – for an Outreach and Community librarian at the new Wandsworth Town Library, and how the job was perfect for him and he simply had to apply.

No way. His daughter's barbs had made him extremely wary about risking further rejection. Why should anyone recruit a 'totally weak' and 'freakish' candidate?

Trevor thinks you'd be ideal and even Meryl's rooting for you. She wanted to be sure you had the details, which must be a hopeful sign.

Typical of Stella to be so optimistic. It was definitely straining credulity that someone as prominent as Meryl would be rooting for him personally. She probably wanted *all* eligible staff to have details of the post, to encourage competition. Yet Stella seemed to be assuming that he'd already got the job, since she went on to suggest that they make their Remembrance Project a joint activity with Wandsworth Town, so the two of them could still work together.

Despite his dismissal of the whole idea, he was touched by her belief in him; the way she always had his interests at heart. And the emails did remind him how valuable his work was in giving structure to his life, along with a sense of purpose and achievement.

However, he should be thinking of his daughter, not himself. She would be back in a matter of minutes now, so he decided to unfreeze one of the stash of pizzas and put it in the microwave, to be ready when she appeared. Once done, he rehearsed his lines: 'I know it's late, Carmella, but I thought we'd have a little supper together.' The Carmella stuck in his throat, but no point alienating her further by refusing to use the new name.

By the time the pizza was bubbling-hot, there was still no sign of her. Having turned on the main oven to keep it warm, he made a salad and laid the table; even twisting paper napkins into swan-shapes, Mandy-style.

By 10.50, still no daughter, and no reply from her mobile – distinctly worrying, when he had given her strict instructions never to switch if off when she was out. Having left a stern message and also sent a text, he felt concerned enough to phone Barbie's mother, Virginia, although the call was answered by what sounded like another teen.

'It's Eric Parkhill here.'

'Hi.'

'Is that Barbie's brother?'

'Yeah.'

'D'you mind if I ask your name?'

'Joe.'

'Hello, Joe. Is your mother there?'

'Nope.'

Of course – she'd be at the airport, picking up her husband. How could he have forgotten? 'Any idea when she'll be back?'

'Nope.'

'Well, do you know what time she left?'

'Nope.'

'When she does come in, could you tell her I rang?'

'Yeah.'

'Do you know who I am?'

'Nope.'

'Just say Erica's Dad. OK?'

Neither 'Nope' nor 'Yeah' this time, just a grunt as he rang off.

God, he thought, teens were a pain! Yet their blasé mothers were almost as bad. If Erica had been delayed, why hadn't either Virginia or Kimberley had the courtesy to let him know? Obviously, people were more permissive over here; didn't share his view that not-quite-thirteen-year-olds should be back home by eleven.

It was actually 11.02, so he rang his daughter's mobile once more.

The cell-phone you are calling is switched off.

He left another message anyway, followed by another text, just hoping that when she picked them up, she would realize how concerned he was. He also decided to ring Kimberley, although adopting a deliberately casual tone, so as not to seem over-anxious.

'It's OK, Eric, she's on her way. I'm afraid the taxi turned up rather late. A new driver was on and I guess he didn't know the route. But she should be with you in less than fifteen minutes.'

'Great!' His relief was so overwhelming, he could have kissed the woman – even kissed her soppy dog. 'How's your wrist?' he asked instead.

A grave mistake, since she launched into an endless disquisition on exactly what the doctors had said (doctors in the plural); how serious the sprain was and how excruciating the pain; what she could and couldn't do with that debilitated arm, and how she intended to sue the gym, because she was bound to put on loads of weight without her daily session, and had to pay her private fitness-trainer, despite the fact she wasn't using him.

By the time she had concluded, fourteen of the fifteen minutes had passed, and he began to rethink his plan of having supper with his daughter. It really was too late now and, in fact, if she didn't turn up soon, it would be time to get her breakfast, instead. Maybe the taxi had got lost, if the driver was a greenhorn, or perhaps as clueless as the one who had brought him from the airport. No – Kimberley had told him she used a highly reputable firm, and no way would she entrust either Brooke or Erica to any but the most dependable of drivers. So what the hell was going on? May Creek wasn't *that* far, especially at this time of night, when the roads were near-deserted.

He waited till 11.30, then rang Kimberley again, sick with worry now, although still trying to disguise it. Even Kimberley herself, however, sounded much less sanguine.

'I just can't understand it, Eric, unless – God forbid – there's been an accident.'

The blood drained from his face as he pictured his beloved daughter lying mangled in the wreckage of some appalling pile-up.

'I'm afraid Ted's not here tonight. He's away at a conference – back tomorrow morning – otherwise I'd ask him to drive the same route as the cab, so he could look out for signs of a crash. But let me call the taxi-firm, in case they might have heard something.'

'And we ought to ring the police. *I'll* do that, if you give me their number.'

'No, leave it to me. It's easier if I make both calls, then I'll ring you straight back, OK?'

'OK,' he agreed, although rigid with fear. Suppose Erica were dead, or so badly injured she might never walk or speak again; spend the rest of her life as a vegetable – his only child; the one person in the world who shared his genes and was flesh of his flesh. In the last few months, he'd begun taking her for granted; confident she would always be part of his life, despite the miles between them and his own panic about flying; assumed he would watch her graduate, walk her down the aisle, rejoice when she bore him a grandchild. It was probably Mandy's influence that had made him so uncharacteristically upbeat, but now he saw – with terror – all that rosy future could be wiped out at a stroke.

Should he alert Christine? No. Cruel to disrupt her honeymoon until he had the facts. There was no hard proof of any accident – not yet, in any case. Besides, he mustn't use the phone when Kimberley would be trying to get through.

Hurry, he urged her silently, each second seeming to take an hour to pass. Perhaps the taxi-firm required more time to investigate the matter, or the Mercer Island police failed to answer calls immediately. Or had Kimberley received such devastating news, she couldn't bring herself to relay it?

He paced up and down, up and down, pouncing on the phone the minute it rang, yet dreading a summons from the hospital or morgue.

'Eric, you're not going to like this, but—'

'*What*? What is it, Kimberley? Are you telling me Erica's hurt?'

'No, she's safe. Don't worry.'

'I *am* worried. Where is she, for God's sake?'

'That's the problem. We're not exactly sure.'

'Not sure? You said you'd put her in a taxi and—'

'I did. At least, I thought it was a taxi, but when Brooke heard me calling the police, she all but wrenched the phone from my hand and begged me not to speak to them. She said she knew where Carmella was and that she was perfectly OK. I asked her *how* she knew, of course, but she said she couldn't tell me. Well, that made me really furious, so I bawled her out, and eventually she confessed.'

'Confessed? I'm sorry, I don't follow.'

Long pause.

'Apparently,' Kimberley went on, now sounding both defensive and embarrassed, 'she and Carmella – your Erica – cancelled the taxi, just on their own initiative, without telling me a word about it. And, instead, they arranged for Larry to pretend to be the cab-driver and come and pick her up.'

'Larry?' He had become a witless parrot, repeating Kimberley's words. But he could make no sense of her account.

'He's a college friend of Spencer, my son. They're both at the University of Washington. Actually, I've never met the boy, which is why I didn't recognize him when he turned up at the house. I must admit, I did think he looked a little young, but he was so well-dressed and so polite and charming, it never crossed my mind that he could be anything but a bone-fide cab-driver.'

'You mean to say,' Eric exploded, incandescent with rage, 'my daughter's out with some guy you don't know from Adam? So what the hell are they doing?'

'Calm down, Eric. She won't come to any harm – I'm pretty sure of that. My Spencer's a really lovely boy, so any friend of his is bound to be OK.'

'That's nonsense!' he snapped. 'Larry's a completely unknown quantity, so how can you be sure of—?' He broke off in mid-sentence, thinking out the implications: a college student at the wheel of a car – some feckless young stud, throbbing with testosterone. 'Does my daughter know this – this' – he all but spat the name out – 'Larry?'

'Brooke said they met him just one time, in Starbucks, and apparently he took a shine to Erica.'

Eric clenched his fists. *Took a shine?* Wanted to shag her, more like.

'So the three of them hatched this crazy scheme. In fact, I suspect it was Larry's idea – you know, to give him a chance to get to know your daughter. I was really mad with Brooke, of course, and when Ted hears about it, he'll blow his top.'

'Look,' he cut in, unconcerned with Brooke or Ted or anyone but his daughter and her safety. 'Can't we phone the guy on his mobile? Ask him what the hell he thinks he's playing at?'

'Unfortunately not. Brooke doesn't have his cell-phone number. And, as I said, I've never met him. I know most of Spencer's friends, but this guy—'

'Well, ring Spencer, then. He's bound to have the number. And he may even know where he and Erica have gone.'

'Good thinking, Eric! I'll call him right away. I just hope he hasn't gone to bed.'

'Well, if he has, drag him *out* of bed! This is an emergency.'

'Try not to worry. They may just have gone for a little ride round town.'

Was this woman barking mad? A twelve-year-old in a car with a stranger, at 11.30 at night, and she was talking blithely about a little ride round town. 'Listen to me, Kimberley, if they don't turn up within the next five minutes, I intend to ring the police.'

'Please don't do that, I beg you. Brooke would never forgive me.'

Bugger Brooke, he was tempted to say. Instead, he told the bloody woman to get on to Spencer instantly and also find out the make of Larry's car, so he could watch for it in the street.

He waited in an agony for her to call him back; the clock's second-hand moving unbearably slowly. 'Ring, damn you, *ring*!' he kept muttering to the phone, snatching it up the instant that it did.

'Yeah, Spencer had his cell-phone number, but when I tried it, I only got the voicemail, so I had to leave a message.'

All the more suspicious. His daughter's phone *and* Larry's both switched off. Why, for heaven's sake? He hardly dared answer his own question.

'Still, I do have news – and good news, in a way. Spencer says that Larry mentioned taking Carmella to some pizza place at the South End of the Island. And that's only a short walk from you, so if you could get yourself down there, Eric …'

He didn't need a second invitation; only stopped to prompt Kimberley about the make of Larry's car, in case the pair had already left the pizza place and actually passed him on the road.

'A red BMW convertible.'

His fear ratcheted up yet another notch. A red sports car gave off the very worst of signals.

Not bothering with a coat, he grabbed his keys and wallet and dashed out of the house, running full-pelt along the street. No cars whatever passed him, although, when he reached the square, a fair scattering were parked there. However, he didn't stop to look at them; instead made straight for the pizza restaurant, only to find it shut. Indeed, everything seemed closed except the supermarket; nevertheless, he double-checked every restaurant and coffee-shop. No joy, except for a solitary waiter – a gangly youth of indeterminate ethnicity – standing smoking outside El Sombrero's.

Eric rushed across. 'Can you help me, please? I'm looking for my daughter. Have you seen a young, dark-haired girl – five-foot tall and wearing jeans and a pink top? She might have come in to your restaurant sometime after ten, with a boy about eighteen.'

The guy clearly hadn't understood a word and answered in an indecipherable tongue. He probably wasn't a waiter at all, but some humble kitchen assistant, without even basic English.

'Don't worry!' Eric called, next trying the supermarket; sprinting up and down each aisle, in search of Erica. A pretty futile endeavour, since the place was almost empty and, in any case, no teen on a date was likely to go grocery shopping at ten minutes to midnight.

Dashing out again, he began searching the whole square for a red BMW;

scrutinizing *every* red car, since the makes and styles of automobiles weren't exactly his strong point.

In vain.

The raw night air was bitterly cold, yet he was aflame with fear, trying desperately to dismiss the gruesome images of crashes, carnage, corpses. But he was wasting time – time that might be crucial. He must go straight home and ring the police. If it upset Kimberley, too bad. It wasn't *her* daughter who was seriously at risk.

Veering across the road, he took the short cut through Pioneer Park, stumbling to a halt as he noticed the scarlet gleam of a car. It had been driven off the road and was tucked into the parking-spot used by local dog-walkers. And, yes, it was a convertible.

A couple were sitting in the front – two shadowy silhouettes. He had to force himself not to overreact. Lots of people probably parked here at night, taking advantage of the privacy to indulge in a bit of philandering. And red sports cars were two a penny, so he mustn't jump to conclusions. He inched one step nearer; careful not to make the slightest sound, in case he was spying on a pair of strangers.

Straining his eyes, he spelled out the name on the car: BMW. Even more alarming, the two figures in the front – still blurred and indistinct – suddenly moved closer to each other in a long, impassioned kiss. Heart pounding, he crept another few paces towards them.

And then he saw her – Erica – his little girl, being kissed by some disgusting lout. He felt such extremes of rage, relief and horror, all curdled and mixed up, he stood all but paralysed. She was *safe* – thank Christ – not lying injured in the road, or naked in Larry's bed. Those facts were so precious, one part of him was dizzy with relief, yet his overwhelming instinct was to prise her from the car and really vent his fury; tell her she was never, ever to behave so irresponsibly and give everyone such cause for fear. One thing made him hesitate: the recognition that he himself had kissed girls as young as her, when he was younger still. If he ruined what could well be her first kiss – shamed her and embarrassed her in front of her first boyfriend – she might never, ever forgive him, and their already strained relationship would deteriorate still further.

He felt awkward even watching – a sneaky Peeping Tom – yet another, furious part of him felt she had lost all right to privacy and deserved only punishment. Torn all ways, he finally decided to wait just one more minute and hope desperately the guy would restart the engine and bring her safely home. *Then* he'd give her a rocket, wipe the bloody floor with her, bawl her out for breaking all the rules. Why involve this scum of a student, who would probably try to weasel out of it; pretend he'd thought Erica was older, or come up with some equally fatuous excuse?

All at once, he noticed that the pair were no longer kissing. Now, Erica seemed to be struggling, almost fighting off the boy. The sight was a match to a tinderbox. Springing forward, he wrenched open the car-door and saw, with horror, that the brazen sod was unzipped, and trying to force his daughter's head down over his erection.

Without stopping to think, he attacked the brute, bare-handed, punching him and shoving him off; using every ounce of strength he possessed. 'What the hell do you think you're doing?' he yelled.

The guy hit back, landing him a blow in the mouth. 'What's it got to do with *you*, you filthy pervert? I suppose you get your kicks from spying on innocent people.'

'Innocent? I could get you put away for this!'

'Fuck off, you arsehole!'

Reeling from another blow, Eric was forced to use his fists again, less in self-defence than in defence of Erica. Violence was totally alien to his ideals and temperament, but he would stop at nothing when it came to his daughter's safety.

But suddenly he realized she was trying to intervene and that, with all the uproar going on, he had failed to hear her panicked croak of a voice.

'Stop it, Larry. That's my ... my *dad*.'

Ignoring the blood streaming from his lip, he turned to look at her – a daughter he barely recognized: her hair dishevelled; her lipstick smudged and an expression of utter terror on her face. Was he too late? She was fully dressed, thank God, but anything might have happened. After all, she had been with this shit for close on a couple of hours.

'Are you OK?' he barked, unable to keep the anger from his voice – anger with Larry, with himself, with the whole cruel and dangerous world.

'Y ... yes.'

The word was barely audible, despite the sudden silence. The boy was looking shocked; clearly punctured by the revelation that Carmella's father had caught him in the act. But, although he'd had the grace to zip up, his loosened tie and half-unbuttoned shirt made Eric want to murder him. The only reason he desisted was for his daughter's sake. She, too, looked shamed and guilty, and began trying to explain away the incident.

'We ... we just pulled off here to ... to have a drink.'

The admission enraged him further, especially when he noticed the beer-cans on the floor of the car – empty cans, at least three or four. 'A drink? You're far too young to drink!' Then, turning on the boy, he shouted, 'How dare you let my daughter drink, or lay your filthy hands on her! She's underage – for everything. And you've no right to be drinking either – not when you're in charge of a car. You could have smashed Erica to smithereens. And it didn't seem to bother you that you might have got her pregnant.'

Larry gave a sullen shrug. 'We were just having a bit of fun.'

'Fun? I could see full well what you were up to, so don't pretend you're innocent, you scumbag! She's a minor – a child – so your behaviour's down-right criminal.'

'Dad, *don't*. Please don't.'

Despite his fury, he could hear the pain in his daughter's voice, the note of near-hysteria.

'Right,' he snapped. 'We're going home – *now*. Get out!'

'I'm OK to drive her,' Larry muttered, sulkily.

'Like hell you are! I never want to lay eyes on you again – or your fancy car. And if you ever dare get in touch with my daughter, I'll go straight to the police. Is that clear?'

Erica hadn't moved, so he all but lifted her bodily from the car, then slammed the door, with a last shouted curse at Larry. The boy accelerated off at such a rate, the car passed within an inch of them and, in trying to push Erica to safety, he lost his balance and fell backwards into the bushes. He picked himself up, brushed the bits of twig from his clothes; saw his daughter a few yards away, cowering with her head down, shoulders hunched. Gently, he approached, wrapped his arms around her, held her very close.

'Don't worry, sweetheart,' he whispered. 'I'm not cross with you – not any more. Just so long as you're all right.'

She didn't answer.

Still horrified at the thought of virtual rape, he asked again, 'You *are* all right, I hope? I mean, nothing ... happened, before I turned up? Larry didn't...?'

She shook her head. 'No. You ... you came just in time.' Then, suddenly, she buried her face in his chest and began to sob – great racking, heaving sobs, as if she were crying a whole lifetime's grief.

'Oh, Dad,' she choked, 'Oh, Dad. I'm just so glad you're here.'

chapter twenty-six

'Y ... you're bleeding, Dad.'

Eric mopped his lip again; a tide of red-stained Kleenex now surrounding him on the kitchen table. 'It's OK. It doesn't matter.'

'And a big lump's coming up on your forehead.'

'Look, what I'm concerned about is you, darling – whether *you're* OK.'

His daughter shrugged, affecting a cool he knew she couldn't feel. 'Yeah. S'pose so.'

'You haven't drunk your tea.'

The way she picked up the cup, it might have weighed a ton.

'And are you sure you won't change your mind about the pizza?'

'Told you – not hungry.'

'You're tired out – I can see that – and I should let you go to bed, but first we need to talk. It's OK, I don't intend to nag. I just want you to realize how dangerous it can be, going off with a boy you barely know.'

At last, she raised her head and looked at him; her make-up streaky from the tears. 'You don't understand, Dad. I'm, like, retarded, compared with Brooke. *She's* had a boyfriend since she was eleven-and-a-half. And the other day she asked me if I'd ever been kissed – I mean, just like that, straight out – and I felt completely gutted, having to say no.'

'Surely loads of twelve year olds haven't been kissed.'

'I'm thirteen in four days. And, anyway, it's different over here. And different from the old days. When *you* were young, people probably didn't kiss till they were, like, engaged or married.'

He had no intention of telling her that he had kissed a girl when he was ten – a decidedly inauspicious encounter. The girl in question had worn glasses, stuck together with Sellotape and, when he took them off, they fell to pieces in his hand. End of kiss. End of girl. In truth, the whole of his early sex-life had been pretty much disastrous: the bad start with 'Uncle' Frank;

284

then the bigger boys at Grove End and The Haven, who would sneak into his bed at night and demand 'services' – or else. And the much older woman he'd worshipped, at fourteen, as a kindly mother-figure, who had ended up abusing him. That particular incident he had always tried to suppress, but now the painful memory, along with all the rest, made him even more determined that Erica's own experiences should be different altogether.

'What I want for *you*, darling – not now, of course, but when you're older – is for you to meet a guy who really loves and values you. And why you have to be so careful at this stage of your life is that most teenage boys just aren't grown-up enough to treat you as you deserve. I know what guys are like, Carmella. Often, they're not thinking of the girl at all, only what *they* want. I mean, did Larry really care about your interests?'

She shook her head. 'At first, it felt really cool, being out with a college student and driving round in his snazzy car and everything. He's so different from the boys my age who are still, like, into skateboarding. And he could have had any girl he wanted, yet it was *me* he picked, and that made me feel sort of special. But ... but when he ... kissed me, it was nothing like I'd imagined. I mean, it seemed quite ... violent, yet was all slobbery, as well, and—' She broke off, blushing so furiously, he felt himself flush in sympathy.

'So maybe thirteen year olds are still a bit too young to kiss?'

'Maybe.'

'And are you brave enough to tell Brooke that?'

She shrugged. 'Dunno.'

'But at least you'll promise faithfully to be super-careful in future?'

She nodded. 'Actually' – she gave a nervous laugh – 'I feel quite scared of ... all that stuff now.'

'Well, sex *is* scary in a way. I mean, if you rush in before you're ready, you can end up in dead trouble – way out of your depth, or even pregnant, God forbid! That's why I'd like you to wait, darling, until you find the right person, and not settle for a sordid grope with some testosterone-fuelled jerk who's out to take advantage of you.'

'Yeah, but if all the others have boyfriends ...'

'I just don't believe they *all* do. And, anyway, it's terribly important to try to make your own decisions, rather than simply copying what your friends do. One of the hardest things about growing up is trying to work out who you are and what you want, and being able to resist the pressures – all those people out there desperate to convince you that you must be thin and sexy and glamorous and follow the latest trends. It's just a commercial racket, half the time. They want you to buy this or that, or splurge cash on beauty treatments or whatever, so they keep pumping out the message that if you get the perfect body and perfect teeth and hair and clothes, that's the way to perfect happiness. But it isn't true, Carmella, and you don't have to go along with it. In fact, if you do, you'll always feel dissatisfied because perfection's an impossible ideal.'

'Yes, but my friends are always buying stuff and keeping up with fashion. So if I don't do the same, I'll feel even more of an outsider.'

'Only in the best sense – being wiser than they are and thinking things out for yourself.' Was he wasting his breath? Most teens were desperate to conform, simply to be 'normal' and accepted, and just didn't have the maturity to stand against the crowd. He tried a different tack. 'You're pretty as you *are*, Carmella, and—'

'I'm not. Compared with Brooke, I'm rubbish.'

'Well, don't compare yourself! Everyone has good points, but also things they dislike about themselves – even Brooke, I bet. But if we can just accept those things, we're more likely to be happy.'

'That's easy for *you* to say.'

'No, it isn't, actually. If I could choose, I'd love to be much taller and have good teeth and hair that wasn't a joke. But I'm damned if I'm going to ruin my life wishing I was someone else.'

She looked at him, in silence – an uncomfortable sensation: being found wanting by one's teenage daughter. Should he revert to the subject of Larry; emphasize the perils of being alone with virtual strangers? No, lectures at this time of night were probably self-defeating.

She suddenly drained her tea, tepid as it was, in three successive gulps. 'D'you know, I sometimes wish I was back at my old school. When there's only girls around, it doesn't seem to matter so much how you look, or whether you have a boyfriend or not. And we weren't allowed to wear make-up or nail-varnish or jewellery and stuff, and that actually made things easier.'

'Well,' he said, choosing his words with care, 'it's not totally out of the question for you to come back to England. I mean, Mum and I would need to discuss it, of course, but if you're so unhappy over here, you could live with me, instead, and return to Tolworth Girls'.'

In the pause that followed, he allowed himself to hope, despite the raft of problems, including Christine and the lawyers. If he could somehow make his ex see sense, he and Erica could be an almost-family; he a hands-on dad again; she removed from the pressures of being sexualized so young.

And, since his job was far less punishing than Christine's, he'd have more time and energy to devote to being a parent than his busy, stressed-out ex would ever manage, with her new husband and her demanding social round. Of course, he would need to move to a nicer flat, with a decent bedroom for her and—

'No, I wouldn't fit in there either – not any more. I'm not one thing or the other; neither English nor American.'

'You seem very English to me. You've still kept your accent and—'

'Yeah, and the other girls tease me for that, as well, especially when I use the wrong word. The other day, I said "rubber" for "eraser" and they all went completely hysterical.'

He let his hand reach across the table, until it was almost touching hers. 'Darling, I do understand how difficult it is. Which is why maybe you should consider a change, or at least not rule it out entirely.'

'But the Kingston house is sold now and that was home for me. So it just wouldn't be the same.'

His dream was already foundering. He could tell from her face that she had no intention of returning. And could he really blame her? Why should she wish to swap this ritzy mansion for a poky London flat, or her five-star lifestyle for a poorer, more restricted one?

'I like it here in some ways,' she said, as if picking up on his thoughts. 'There's much more to do than there ever was in England – skiing, riding, sailing, all that sort of stuff. So I don't think it would work if I came back. And school's not *that* bad,' she admitted, with a shrug. 'I probably made it out worse than it is. The only thing that bugs me is I still don't quite fit in.'

'You're bound to need time to adjust.'

'I've *had* time. I've been here ages.'

'Only fifteen months. That's nothing. And you're doing wonderfully well.' However keen his disappointment, he could see it would be wrong to try to lure her away from a life she was just beginning to enjoy, quite apart from the little matter of Christine's opposition. 'It's always tough moving anywhere new. Everything feels strange, at first, and you don't know a soul and you think you'll never be accepted or find your way around.' *He* should know, for God's sake, after all the uprootings and dislocations in his child-hood. 'But gradually it all settles down and things slot into place. And, don't forget you've always had real courage, so you've got what it takes to over-come the problems, unlike your cowardly Dad.'

'You're not a coward, Dad – you're very brave. I only realized that tonight. I mean, the way you stood up to Larry, when he's captain of the football team and super-fit and everything. He trains almost every day, you know, and works out in the gym for hours, and the football coach thinks he could well become a pro. Yet you tackled him head-on and didn't even think about your safety. Just look at your swollen lip and all those bruises! I feel quite proud when I think you took those risks for *me*.'

He fingered the lump on his forehead, aware that it was throbbing, yet almost glad of his battle-scars, if they raised him in his daughter's estimation. 'I'd have *murdered* the guy, if he'd hurt you.'

'Yeah, I saw that.' She glanced down at the table; traced a careful pattern with one finger. 'Actually, I didn't know you cared so much.'

'Of course I care. For me, you're the most important person in the world.'

'Really?' Only now did she meet his gaze; her own eyes wary, as if subjecting his to a lie-detector.

'Yes, really. Oh, I know I should have visited before this, but I let my fears get in the way – and that's unforgivable. But I promise you I'm—'

'Dad,' she interrupted.

'Yes?'

'I … I want to say I'm … sorry.'

'It's OK. I understand. I can quite see Larry's attractions. He's tall, good-looking and athletic, so it's only natural you should jump at the chance of going out with him.'

'No, I don't mean about Larry. Well, I *am* sorry about him and causing all that crap, but I really meant I'm sorry about the awful things I said – you know, your being weak and a loser. You're *not* a loser, Dad – no way. I think I said it just to hurt you, though I don't actually know why. Sometimes, I get so mixed up, I can't even explain what I feel. And I suppose I was angry and—'

'You've every right to be. It's totally my fault that I haven't seen you for so long. Which means now we're a bit out of touch and need to get to know each other again. That may take a little while, but we could make a start right now – maybe have some supper together; talk some more and—' He was being irresponsible in keeping her up so late; putting his own desire for closeness before her need for sleep. Yet the sheer relief of being able to communicate seemed to override all else. 'I know it's ridiculously late and we ought to be in bed, but we can always sleep tomorrow. What do you think?'

'I'm not fussed. Whatever you want.'

'The pizza will be inedible by now, but I could make some scrambled eggs.'

'Yeah. Great.'

Never had he scrambled eggs so quickly, fearing she might change her mind before he had set their plates on the table. But she seemed hungry, all at once; grabbing a piece of toast from the toaster and eating it, unbuttered, standing up.

'Do you think I'm – you know, spoilt, Dad?' she asked, once they were sitting over supper, side by side. 'I mean, living in this house and having so much stuff? When *you* were, like, my age, you had almost nothing.'

'Oh, it wasn't too bad,' he said, touched that she should have thought about his life.

'It must have been terribly hard, though, not having parents, or a proper home, and being moved from place to place so often. We've never really talked about it, have we?'

'Mum preferred us not to.' It still irked him that Christine and her family should have found the subject so distasteful. 'And, of course, Grandma always hated any mention of my past.'

'Yeah, I know. But I've often wondered about my *other* grandma and why she left you in the first place? It seems so … sort of cruel. People wouldn't do that now – just dump their babies and run.'

'Well, it's much easier these days, of course, to be an unmarried mother. It used to be regarded as a shameful sin and everyone would shun you and call you a fallen woman. All the same, a few babies *are* still abandoned, although it's extremely rare, thank goodness. Only about fifty a year in England.'

'Fifty's a lot.'

'Well, in countries like Russia and China, the numbers are much higher. And even here in America, there's quite a—'

'Hey, Dad,' she cut in, suddenly, '*I* wasn't found, was I? Or adopted or…? I mean, am I truly yours and Mum's?'

He laughed. 'You're absolutely mine and Mum's. And that's as important for me as it probably is for you. You're the only blood relation I have in the whole world, or the only one I know about. We even share a name – or used to, anyway. I wasn't present at your actual birth, but I saw you minutes afterwards and when they put you into my arms, I was just – well, over the moon. I sat there, quite besotted, smiling and smiling and smiling, until I felt my face must be stretched all out of shape. In fact, if there's a league table for smiles, that one would have definitely made the championship!'

'Oh, Dad ...' She gripped his hand.

What he wouldn't tell her was that, despite his joy in fatherhood, when he finally got home, he had sunk down on the bed and wept, because seeing Christine with the baby at her breast brought home, with painful force, his own lack of any mother, and of cradling, loving arms.

Erica dolloped ketchup onto her eggs. 'So if parents feel so strongly about their babies, why ever would they ditch them and piss off?'

'Well, as I said, it's very rare, and it's usually lone mothers. Often, they don't mean to be cruel, so it isn't fair to blame them indiscriminately. They may be really desperate – young and frightened and acting on an impulse. I'm sure that was true of *my* mother. Perhaps she had no one to turn to, or came from such a strict family they'd have killed her if they discovered she was pregnant.'

Erica stopped eating and looked him full in the face. 'You *are* brave, Dad – and that's a fact. I mean, the way you, like forgive her, instead of being resentful or kicking up an awful fuss, like I bet most people would. I know I'd be seriously furious if someone had dumped *me* in a park!'

The same sentiments as Mandy's, when, on New Year's Day, he had come clean about his origins. But then neither she nor Erica – nor anybody not a foundling – could understand that rage was pretty pointless; only added harm to harm. It was essential to love your birth-mother, if only for your own peace of mind; not hate her and resent her.

'Don't you see,' he told his daughter, 'I was lucky to be found and taken in. Sadly, some kids fail to make it. They're shoved in a skip or a dustbin and simply left to die.'

'Horrible!' she shuddered.

'And it was infinitely worse in the old days. Every year, thousands of babies were abandoned in the street or left outside the workhouse. And, even when they set up foundling hospitals, the demand was so great, most of the babies died. And those who did survive might land up in some dreadful institution, with incredibly strict rules. I read of one poor kid who'd broken the no-talking rule, and had to sit in the corner and hold his tongue – literally, between his finger and thumb, and stay like that for ages. When *I* was in care, things had improved so greatly, there's just no comparison.'

'It must have been ghastly, all the same.'

He stared out at the murky darkness pressing against the window-panes; still struck by the utter silence here; no brawling neighbours, screaming tyres, no sirens shrieking through the night. 'It's strange, you know, Carmella, but sometimes growing up the hard way can actually be an advantage. There's this famous book, *A Farewell to Arms* and, towards the end, there's a sentence I've never forgotten: "The world breaks everyone and afterward many become strong at the broken places".'

She forked in a mouthful of egg; sat chewing while she pondered. 'I'm not sure what that means.'

He paused, aware of a need to shape his words. The rest of the passage was bleak in the extreme; foreshadowing the end of the book. Yet that particular sentence could stand on its own; had power and substance, in and for itself.

'Dad...?'

'Sorry. I was thinking.' He reached for another Kleenex; held it to his lip. 'I reckon it's saying we all suffer, but if we try to make sense of the bad things and don't become bitter or vindictive, we can move on in our lives and become stronger people because of what we've been through.' Was he being an arch-hypocrite in taking such a line, when someone with his weight of fear could hardly be classed as 'stronger'? And, anyway, sanitizing Hemingway was surely somewhat remiss. 'Listen, it's far too late for all this philosophical stuff, so why don't—?'

'No, wait – I'm interested. It applies to me, as well. I *was* bitter about the divorce, you see, and did resent you and Mum. But I suppose I could, like, change my view; accept what happened as just part of life and not the end of the world. Hell, half the kids at school have parents who're divorced.'

'Well, that would certainly be better than kicking against it for ever – better for *you*, I mean.'

'D'you realize, Dad, even Barack Obama's parents separated when he was two, and he hardly saw his father after that. And he had to keep moving to different homes and stuff. And he even took loads of drugs when he wasn't much older than me. But look at him now! So I suppose he's another example of that "broken places" thing. Maybe he only said, "Yes, we *can*!" because of all the bad stuff he's had to overcome.'

'You're right. I hadn't thought of that.' All at once, he recalled the pastor's words last Sunday, about everyone in the church being there for a specific purpose. Had some kind of grace descended on his daughter as a result of his own presence at the service? Hardly! There was no proof of any deity; let alone a God who would so conveniently intervene in his personal family problems. Yet he had to admit the change in Erica did seem pretty miraculous – the former hostile brat now mature, reflective and willing to engage with him.

'It's so hard, though, isn't it?' She gave a monstrous sigh; jabbed her fork against the plate. 'Actually, the worst thing for me is the baby. I know I haven't mentioned it before, but it's been bugging me ever since I heard. It's bad enough having to share Mum with Dwight, but now with, like, another kid as well.'

He felt a pang of guilt, remembering how casually he'd dismissed any fears she might have had about 'his' and Mandy's baby. Perhaps the loss, however devastating, did have some advantage, in that it spared her the painful prospect of having to come to terms with *two* babies.

He pushed his plate away. His swollen lip made it difficult to eat and everything he swallowed seemed tainted with the taste of blood. Besides, he needed all his concentration to ensure that he was saying the right thing.

'Try not to judge the kid before it's here. You might even find you like it and enjoy having a brother or sister. But it will be a big upheaval, I admit – especially when the baby's actually born. That's always a fraught time and, of course, Mum will have her hands full, so you may feel a bit left out. Hey, listen – I've just had an idea. Why don't I come over then and take you away on holiday?'

She stared at him in surprise. 'But that would mean another flight and you're terrified of flying.'

'I'd survive,' he told her, with more conviction than he felt.

'Anyway, the baby's due at the end of September and I have to be at school then.'

'But they seem pretty reasonable about you taking time out, if it's a question of a visit from a parent.'

'Yes, I know, but why go through all that crap again, when you hate the very thought of planes?'

'Because I'd like to be with you at what may be a difficult time – so long as you *want* to go away, that is, and don't mind missing school.'

'No one minds missing school, do they, unless they're seriously weird?'

'What about Mum, though? Do you think she might object?'

'No way! She's forever saying she'd like me to see more of you.'

Another surge of guilt. Whatever his terrors – and they were mounting to an uncomfortable degree – he must make this trip for his daughter's sake. 'In that case, why don't you leave it to me to clear it with the school, and think of somewhere you'd really like to go.'

'Are you absolutely sure, Dad?'

He nodded. 'Just don't choose somewhere too far away from here, please, because I don't want *two* long flights.' It was also a matter of the expense, of course, but he wouldn't mention that.

'I know – San Diego! Barbie went there on a snorkelling holiday and said it was just brilliant. I'd adore to snorkel, Dad. You see these amazing coral reefs and fantastic fish close-up – rays and perch and starfish, even sea-lions and leopard-sharks.'

He swallowed. *Sharks?* 'I think you've … forgotten something, darling.'

'What?'

'I … can't swim.'

'Oh, come on, Dad, you can learn. And you don't have to be a *good* swimmer. It's not like scuba diving. You just float on shallow water. And, in any case, you can always wear a safety-vest or hire a body-board – or both, if you're really worried.'

He tried to clear an obstruction from his throat. 'Wouldn't it be more the sort of thing you'd do with Dwight? He's the one with the boat.'

'No, it's nothing like as good round here – not as warm, for one thing, and the water's much more murky. In California, it's crystal-clear and there are more exciting fish, as well. And, anyway, I want to do it with *you*, Dad, not with lousy Dwight.'

'I just don't think it's going to work.'

'Look, you asked me what I really want to do. And now you're saying no. It'll be great, Dad – honestly. We can take underwater photos and stuff and …'

The full horror of the trip was only now beginning to dawn on him – not just swimming, but being underwater; his face covered by a claustrophobic mask; having to hold his breath while the waves closed over his head; maybe getting tangled up in seaweed and never making it back up. Yet she'd just called him brave, so how could he refuse without reverting to being a loser and a coward? 'We'll … see. OK?'

'No, it's *not* OK,' she said, slamming down her knife and fork. '"We'll see" means "No" and I want you to say "Yes". You're being totally pathetic, Dad. You just told me all that stuff about broken places making you strong, so *be* strong, for a change.'

'You don't understand. I—'

'No, I don't! It makes no sense. I mean, all those years you told Mum and me you couldn't fly, and now you *have* flown. So why can't you swim, as well? You could take lessons in your local pool from now until September and you'll be brilliant by then, I bet.'

Brilliant. She believed in him; actually wanted to go away with him, yet still he was fighting images of planes crashing onto the tarmac, or him choking to death in his snorkelling-mask and—

'So?' she demanded, getting up from the table and confronting him face to face.

'OK, yes,' he faltered.

'Promise?'

'Promise.'

'Great! Let's go online tomorrow and make plans.'

'Actually, there's something else we need to plan. In fact, I want you to promise *me* something.'

'Don't tell me. I can guess – I'm not to go out with boys till I'm twenty-five.'

'I'll settle for thirty-five! But no, I want you to save me from a Maundy Thursday service.'

'What's Maundy Thursday?'

'The Thursday before Easter, which just happens to be your birthday. I didn't tell you this before, but Peggy over the road more or less bullied me into attending church with her that evening.'

'Oh, she does that with me, as well.' Screwing up her face, Erica gave an imitation of Peggy's breathy drawl. '"Erica, it's time you went to Sunday School …" "Erica, have you thought of joining our lovely little Bible Study Group?" No thanks! Just ignore her, Dad.'

'I can't. Half the church are expecting me to show up. And, what's worse, they're planning to wash my feet.'

'Wash your feet? Whatever for? Why can't you wash them at home in the shower?'

'It's a sort of religious ritual – and one I'd prefer to miss. I'll need a good excuse, though, so if you and I had this special birthday date, that would fit the bill just perfectly. So, what d'you say – will you rescue your poor Dad?'

'OK. Anything to save you from the dreaded Peggy!'

'Oh, and talking of your birthday, I brought some presents for you, but they lost my luggage, didn't they, so Lord knows where they are! So can we please go out before the ninth and buy you a few replacements?'

'Yes, *please*!'

'There's just one I packed in my flight-bag. Hang on a sec and I'll fetch it.'

He raced upstairs; returned with the small jewellery-box, which he had carefully rewrapped, and placed it on the table.

'But I shouldn't open presents before my birthday.'

'I want you to, OK? But we'd better be fairly quick about it. If Mum knew you were up this late, she'd go ballistic!'

She tore off the wrappings, opened the box and withdrew the shimmering pendant. 'Oh, *Dad* …'

He felt a sudden doubt. She had so much stuff already – and pricey stuff at that – how could some bijou trifle make any sort of impression? 'D'you like it?' he asked, anxiously.

'I adore it.'

'I chose the heart specially,' he said, 'because it means "I love you", and that you have first place in my own heart.' Hell, this was sentimental stuff – downright naff, in fact. It might rouse his daughter's scorn, but he had to take that risk.

'It's the best present I've ever had,' she said, looping the pendant round her neck and trying to fasten the clasp.

'Oh, come on, that's way over the top!'

'It *isn't*, Dad. Here, help me do it up. I want to see what it looks like.'

Moving her hair aside, he struggled with the fiddly clasp, while she jiggled with impatience. 'Stand still!' he ordered, secretly pleased at her show of excitement. 'That's it – all done. Now turn round, so I can judge the effect.'

She faced him, half-self-conscious, half-expectant. 'Well?'

'Looks pretty good to me. In fact, damned near perfect, I'd say.'

'*I* want to see!' She darted out to the hall, to look in the large framed mirror on the wall.

He followed, watching as she stood fingering the heart, turning her head this way and that, with a smile of unqualified approval.

'It's great!' she said. 'And I love the way it sparkles in the light. Brooke will be dead jealous! I can't wait to show her – *and* Barbie.'

'Well, thank God I got it right,' he laughed. 'It was so hard to pick out something when I hadn't seen you for so long and had no idea what sort of things you like.'

'Dad, if I'd come with you to the shop, I'd have chosen exactly this.'

'In that case, give your old Dad a hug.'

Noting how shyly she approached, he was careful to hold her neither too close nor too long, for fear he might embarrass her. Yet, for him, no hug could be long enough, since he required it to express a host of different emotions: his joy in having a child at all; his concern for her happiness and safety; his regret about neglecting her, especially missing the whole business of watching her grow up; his grief at the brutal distance between London and Seattle, yet his pride in having bridged it – above all, his aching wish that the bond they had forged this evening should last until his death.

Reluctantly, he made to pull away. However loath he might be to break the contact, he could hardly continue hugging her all night. Rather, he should return to his parental duties and chivvy her to bed.

Yet, doggedly, she pressed herself against him, as if frightened he might vanish, or they might never achieve this proximity again. Indeed, he experienced a depth of shame when he realized she could have become a virtual stranger, had he stayed in England, a prisoner of his fear.

Then, all at once, she drew away and stood shifting from foot to foot; an uneasy frown cutting between her brows. 'Dad ...'

'Yes?' he prompted, worried now that she might have some new concern, something they hadn't yet discussed.

'I ... don't think I'll be Carmella any more. It seems, like, kind of ... stupid. It was Brooke's suggestion, actually, so I guess it's more her sort of name than mine. So, from now on, I'll be Erica again.'

'Fine,' he said, his non-committal tone belying his overwhelming relief. He had his daughter back, at last – in name as well as fact.

chapter twenty-seven

Eric emerged from the tube into a heavy, sleety downpour. Rain when he'd set out three weeks ago, and now rain on his return. Yet he was so relieved at having survived the ordeal and escaped totally unscathed – no missing limbs; no vacant future as a dribbling paraplegic – that he splashed blithely through the puddles on the short walk to his flat. At least he wasn't hampered by a case. InterWest Airlines had surpassed themselves by losing his luggage on the return flight as well as on the outward one. Waiting in the long, slow queue to report the second loss had delayed him by an hour or more, but he didn't care a jot. Anyway, it was Dwight and Christine's honeymoon case, and he deplored the thought of such a thing cluttering up the flat. And, as for all the stuff inside, well, there was a certain crazy freedom in simply leaving it behind.

In fact, nothing could detract from his elation at having become a seasoned traveller. Oh, he still detested flying – the cramped seats, the claustrophobia, the lousy food and long delays, the interrogation procedures that made you feel you should have stayed at home – and, yes, his terror was still there. Indeed, he had battled through extremes of it today, yet it was still a great achievement to have conquered it at all. In fact, he longed to yell at everyone who passed him in the street, 'I've flown! I've flown – for the first time in my life! And four separate flights in total. Isn't that heroic?'

And, having stopped for milk at the corner-shop, he was tempted to strike up a conversation with a customer or two, so that he could try out the unlikely words just added to his vocabulary: shuttle-buses, duty-free: escape-chutes, air-miles, cabin crew. Unfortunately, there was no one in the shop – well, apart from the man who ran it: a surly Pakistani who didn't look as if he'd be riveted by accounts of sterling courage. So, having bought his pint and a farmhouse loaf, he bounded on to the flat.

As he let himself in, he was immediately jolted by its shabbiness,

compared with the grandeur of his surroundings in the States. Where were
the works of art, the cocktail bar, the games-room, the candlelit Infinity
Bath? Not that he would miss them, nor the ridiculously pretentious bed
that had seemed always to resent him as an unworthy occupant. This was
home, however small and poky, and there was a definite sense of security in
being back where he belonged. What he did regret was no longer having
Erica as house-mate and companion. Already, he missed their long discus-
sions about whether it was wiser to settle for being a Ford – functional and
useful – rather than a high-powered Porsche, and whether fear was only
natural when the world was so incomprehensible, not to mention downright arbitrary.

'No!' she'd told him, vehemently. 'That's just a crappy excuse. Even if
you do feel fear, you have to overcome it, Dad, and say "I *can*!", like
President Obama.'

And, since her birthday outing, when, as his introduction to water-sports,
she had more or less dragooned him into kayaking on Lake Washington, she
now expected him to rise to every challenge. It wouldn't stop at kayaking,
or even snorkelling or scuba diving – that was pretty clear. It would be
ocean-racing next, or white-water-rafting, or – God forbid – paragliding.
He shook his head in disbelief. Even his daughter's faith in him couldn't
transform him quite so radically.

Having dumped his flight-bag, made some tea and gathered up the post,
he sat sorting through the pile – mainly bills and junk-mail, but also an elaborate card from Stella, saying 'Welcome back!' It touched him that she had
kept in contact throughout his three weeks' absence, as if she knew instinctively how lost he felt away from home. Yet, despite her calmer temperament,
she was more alone than he was, in a sense, having never had a spouse or
child. Would either of them, he wondered, ever meet their life-partner? The
prospects didn't look too bright and maybe it was simply time he relinquished
his romantic dreams: the hope of meeting a soulmate; the fantasy of finding
his mother. He couldn't count on a conveniently happy ending, like the more
fortunate Tom Jones, who, by Book XVIII, 'Chapter The Last', was declared
by the exultant author 'the happiest of all humankind'.

I'm away for a long weekend, Stella had scribbled on the card. *See you
Tuesday, OK?*

Unable to phone her, as he'd hoped, he decided instead to reply to her last
emails, which had remained unanswered once Dwight and Christine arrived
back from Hong Kong. It had seemed wrong to sit in Christine's office, using

her computer, rather than listen to her travellers' tales of glitzy nightlife, harbour cruises, dim-sum restaurants and all the maddening rest of it. He suppressed a yawn as he turned on his own machine; aware how stiff and achy he was, after eighteen hours of travelling, and tempted to crash out on his bed rather than pound away at the keyboard. But if he went to sleep so early, he was bound to wake in the middle of the night, when he ought to make an effort to adjust to English time. He was already somewhat confused, since his watch said eight (a.m.), while the sitting-room clock insisted it was four.

The computer seemed sluggish, as if it, too, were suffering jet-lag, but eventually it responded with a rash of Viagra ads. Whacked as he was, he knew he wouldn't need Viagra if a voluptuous female happened to waltz in, begging to be shagged – or Mandy, for that matter. It annoyed him that he should still be lusting after her – indeed, even wondering sometimes if he should change his mind and return as her live-in lover. Yet, since he knew deep-down the relationship was wrong for him, it was progress of a sort to have broken with the pattern of his childhood, when he'd been forced passively to accept things that brought him pain and grief. Maybe, when he felt less raw, they could re-establish contact, if only for the baby's sake. It still worried him that it had no acting father and, if he could make good that lack, even to some small extent, he wouldn't hesitate. And his reward would be the Precious Box, which he was determined to retrieve. Whatever her motives for making it, he was still deeply touched that she had gone to so much trouble in giving him a life-history, however rudimentary. And, once he had it back, he would guard it as a valuable possession; refuse ever to be parted from it again.

Stella's last two emails were still concerned with the new job. Apparently, no one had applied internally, not even the two most likely contenders: Eleanor at Putney and John at Battersea. And Stella said she doubted there would be many outside applicants, so she was continuing to insist that he simply had to take this chance.

No, I really don't think, he was just beginning to type, when he suddenly caught Erica's eye, rebuking him from her photograph.

'Don't be such a loser, Dad! There's no reason why you shouldn't get the job. Stop putting yourself down, and at least have a try, OK?'

He rocked back in his chair. If he *were* successful, it would mean a rise in salary – extremely useful to help fund the San Diego trip, as well as regular flights to Seattle. Now that he'd established a bond with his daughter, it was crucial to preserve it, and long-haul air-fares weren't exactly cheap. And she had promised to visit *him*, next Easter, so he really ought to move flats well before that, and again some extra cash would come in very handy.

He rechecked the original memo giving details of the job. Stella was right – it was just his sort of thing and would allow him a much better chance to realize his ideals. He could set up a new literacy project, and perhaps a Book-at-Breakfast scheme, with bacon butties to tempt the punters in, or a Brain Gym for the over-sixties and those at risk of Alzheimer's. In fact, a dozen different schemes and plans began jostling through his mind, including his long-cherished dream of establishing libraries in children's homes, which might now actually materialize. And, from all he'd heard, the new library had a definite buzz, so it should be fun to work there, especially if he got in from the start.

Of course, Stella was exaggerating the lack of competition and she could have no idea, in any case, how many external applicants there were, so someone else might pip him to the post. On the other hand, foundlings had a certain advantage in that they were used to trying harder; had been forced to make their own way without families to help, and often faced with numerous challenges from the time they first drew breath.

So, yes, he would apply, and not only for his daughter's sake, but because this new job was the obvious way to do more for the community – always his overriding interest. But best to leave his application till the morning, when he'd be fresher after a good night's sleep. So, having dashed off an email to Stella, saying OK, he was up for it, he amused himself by researching the local swimming-pools, since he had vowed to book a lesson for his very next day off.

After scanning a score of websites – everything from the Queen Mother Sports Centre to the Horizons Health and Fitness Club – jet-lag suddenly caught up with him and he could do nothing more than flop into the armchair. Closing his eyes, he pictured himself swimming fifty lengths; diving from the topmost board; becoming an Olympic swimmer; even swimming the Channel in record-breaking time. And now President Sarkozy himself was looping a gold medal round his neck, as he emerged dripping yet triumphant at Boulogne....

He woke with a start to almost total darkness – just the gleam of a lamp-post shining through his basement window and a winking icon on the computer-screen. What an idiot he was, falling fast asleep, fully clothed, in the armchair. He peered at the illuminated figures on his watch: 2 a.m., for heaven's sake!

He got up with some difficulty. His back was stiff, he had cramp in one leg and he'd developed a crick in his neck. He was also starving hungry, his stomach growling in protest, and a foul taste in his mouth.

Limping into the bathroom to get a glass of water, he recoiled at his reflection in the mirror: porridge-pale and hollow-eyed. Not exactly the rising star of Wandsworth Town new library, let alone an Olympic swimmer.

He stiffened as he heard a sudden noise. Could it be some teenage hoodlum come to case the joint? After all, he was no longer living in safe, suburban Mercer Island, but inner-city London, with its gangs of petty criminals. He stood stock-still, ears strained. Yes, there it was again – and coming from outside the door that led up to the garden; the perfect hiding-place for yobs to lurk.

God, he was pathetic! Any normal bloke would have guts enough to confront a thug head-on, instead of cowering in a heap. He slumped against the bathroom wall; all his former confidence deflating like a punctured tyre. Gold medals? Sterling courage? Was he out of his mind? He'd been seriously deluding himself in imagining he could change his life or job. He was basically so flawed, he simply wasn't equal to the challenges, whatever Erica or Stella might tell him to the contrary. A functional Ford – ha-ha! A clapped-out old nag, more like.

Somehow, though, he forced himself to creep towards the door; realizing only then that it was an animal noise and not a human one – a sort of scratching and scrabbling – perhaps an urban fox on the prowl. Relived, though apprehensive still, he unbolted the door and opened it a crack; let out a yell of joy as he identified the small, scruffy shape shivering on the step.

'*Charlie*!' he exclaimed.

With a mew of recognition, the cat rubbed against his legs in a paroxysm of equal joy. She even tried to spring into his arms, but was obviously too weak. This was a Charlie sadly changed – mangy, matted, skeletally thin and with one ear half-bitten off – yet a Charlie still triumphantly alive. How in heaven's name had an aged cat survived four whole months in such a heartless city? Yet survived she had and that feat seemed more miraculous than his own survival as a tiny infant abandoned in the park.

He carried the wet, bedraggled creature into the kitchen, first drying off her fur and doctoring her ear, before pouring her a saucerful of milk. Then he rummaged in the cupboard for the one remaining tin of cat-food he'd never had the heart to throw away; spooned some into his best blue bowl and set it on the floor. Thank God she could still eat – and with all her former gusto. He watched with satisfaction as she licked the dish completely clean; imagining Erica's delight when she visited next April and found her old friend back in residence.

Then, scooping her up from the floor, he took her into the bedroom and settled her on the bed with him; two bravehearts side by side. She, like him, had cheated death in infancy; having been taken to a refuge when found motherless and starving. And she, like him, had survived a more recent odyssey, with perils on all sides. Surely it was significant that she had returned at the very moment he was losing faith in himself, as if to remind him that, however tough the going, no way must he give up. Of *course* he had to work for his ideals; set goals, aim high; reinstate his dreams; had to make his daughter proud of him, whatever it required.

OK, there were no certainties. He might not get the job; might never be a decent swimmer, or board a plane without extremes of panic. Fear was just a given in his life – probably built into his genes. There was still hope, none the less. Wasn't Charlie proof of that?

'Yes, we *can*!' he told her and immediately she began to purr, as if expressing her agreement.

Then, all at once, and to the cat's astonishment, he broke into the jubilant 'Amen' he'd heard in Peggy's church. He sang at the top of his voice, lustily and loudly, with the full force of a choir; not caring if it woke the neighbours; not bothered if he was out of tune, just determined that the sound should soar across the vast Atlantic and on across America, until it reached the ears of his approving, cheering daughter.

'Amen,' he roared, 'Amen!' – not a submissive, lackadaisical 'so be it', but a resounding and courageous '*Yes!*'

'Yes' to everything.

acknowledgements

I would really need to write another book to thank adequately the many people who helped me with various aspects of this novel; foremost Meryl Jones, Assistant Head of Wandsworth Library and Heritage Service, whose patience, kindness and expertise on library matters provided unfailing support. Thanks are also due to her fellow librarians, Graham Hedges, Selma El Rayah and Marijana Rogers; to the staff at Pimlico Library - Hugh Thomas, Paula Campbell, Steven Parkinson, Layla Palmer and Sally Murphy - and to a host of other people connected with books and libraries: Jan Bild, Neil Simmons, Richard Roberts, Liz Brewster, Penny Markell, Jen Tomkins, Richard Hart, Elaine Andrews, Polly Maclean, and, most especially, to Chris Bennett, Chief Archivist at Croydon Library. I am also most grateful to Joan Thompson, Elspeth Hyams and all other staff at CILIP.

A profound debt of gratitude goes to the library staff at HMP Wandsworth - Oliver Ababio, Javier Delgado and Niamh Fahey - and to members of its Heathfield book club, with a special accolade for Sarah Turvey, of Roehampton University, who runs the club and has been working with prison reading groups since 2001.

Dr Debra Baldwin, advised me on prison matters (displaying truly heroic patience with my queries), and also lent me her PhD thesis on children in care, and thus merits a double citation. And I deeply appreciate Paul Atherton's honesty in sharing with me the story of his own chequered childhood in care - a story with a happy ending, since he is now a film and TV producer. Sue Leifer, Children's Guardian, and Liz Castledine, social worker, also helped me on these aspects of the novel.

On more general matters, thanks are due to John Hughes, Data Protection Manager at Mayday Hospital; to James Stewart, family lawyer at Manches LLP, and his PA, Chrissie Louca; to Andy Curtis, airline pilot, and David Tomlin, cabin steward; to David Wilmot, Customer Services Manager at the London Passport office; to Catriona Young, for additional help on passports; to Keith Walsh, manager of Vauxhall City Farm; to Sam van Rood, author of *Teach Yourself Flirting*; to Don Macallister, photographer; to Jennie Peters, clinical nurse specialist, and to Libby and Stephen Ferguson.

The following also deserve a tribute: Anne and Gemma Pilkington, long-time residents of Croydon; Mary Ann Winterman, author of *Croydon Parks*; Aswin Patel, of Croydon Sports, Parks & Recreation & Community Service, and Peter Holman, horticultural consultant, all of whom provided invaluable information. As did Bill Gingles, with his encyclopaedic mind, and Susie Boyt, whose culinary expertise leaves most average cake-makers at the starting-gate.

For help with the American section of the book, I am indebted to Herb and Ned Hunt; to Marilyn Collins, Beth Baska, Donald and Jean Zatochill, Maxine Howe and Mary Langford.

Jane Tanner and Rachel Besser not only read several of my chapters, but provided information on everything from teen-speak to Internet dating, aided by Jane's husband and children, Steve, Joe and Sophia. Heartfelt thanks to them all.

And last, but very much not least, I'd like to thank the crime-writer, Simon Brett, a truly generous friend, and Dr Robert Brech, frequent flier, mine of information and much-loved brother.